Zero Separation

Also by Philip Donlay

Category Five

Code Black

Zero Separation

A Novel

Philip Donlay

Longboat Key, Florida

FIRST EDITION

This book is a work of fiction. Names, characters, places, and incidents either are the products of the author's imagination or are used fictitiously. Any resemblance to actual events or locales or persons, living or dead, is entirely coincidental.

ISBN: 978-1-60809-068-6

Published in the United States of America by Oceanview Publishing,

Longboat Key, Florida

www.oceanviewpub.com

2 4 6 8 10 9 7 5 3 1

PRINTED IN THE UNITED STATES OF AMERICA

For my agent, Kimberley Cameron

Acknowledgments

This book would not have been possible without the skilled law enforcement professionals around the world whose tireless work and dedication help keep our nation safe. A special thanks goes out to the Federal Bureau of Investigation as well as the Drug Enforcement Administration for all of their valuable assistance.

For their patience, friendship, and insight, I offer a heartfelt thanks to Rebecca Norgaard Peterson, Scott Erickson, Bo Lewis, Emily Burt, Cheryl Bristol, Sheren Frame, Gary Kaelson, Thomas Brandau, Tony Moss, Michael McBryde, Chris Kresge, and Justin Bog. You've played a bigger part in all of this than you'll ever know. For always giving me the unvarnished truth in a way that inevitably makes the stories better, Jonathan Mischkot, Brian and Jen Bellmont, my brother, Chris; my parents, Cliff and Janet; and my son, Patrick. You're an indispensible group of gifted people, thank you for keeping me on course.

A special thanks goes out to Philip Sidell, M.D. and to D. P. Lyle, M.D. for their remarkable medical expertise. Good work, gentleman, I'm most appreciative on many levels. A very special thanks goes to Pamela Sue Martin, who always helps me keep the faith and along the way shows me the world in an entirely different light.

I'd also like to thank dear friends, Pat Frovarp and Gary Shulze, who own Once Upon a Crime, a little bookstore in Minneapolis by which all bookstores should be measured. Thanks for being there.

Finally, to the people who turn words into books. Thank you to my literary agency, Kimberley Cameron & Associates, you're the best. Utmost praise also goes to my publisher, Patricia Gussin, who believed in this project, brought it life, and along the way made it a better book. To everyone at Oceanview Publishing, thank you, there isn't a better team anywhere.

Zero Separation

PROLOGUE

Three miles straight down were the men he'd come to kill. He stood in the open door of the aircraft as the one-hundred-fifty-mile-an-hour slipstream buffeted him, trying to pull him closer to the emptiness that lay beyond. It was a moonless night and there was nothing below him but the darkness of the windswept desert.

Running without lights, the Lockheed C-130 was flying within a very specific set of coordinates over northern Iraq. Temporary markings on the four-engine Hercules read Royal Air Force; the crew wore stolen RAF uniforms and used a valid British call sign. The deception had been months in the making. To the outside world, the aircraft would appear to be flying a routine night-training exercise. Through his headset he heard the pilot tell him they were inside fifteen seconds. Thrill of the hunt. His heart rate accelerated. He could feel it pound in his temples.

When the jump light flashed green, he stepped out of the plane. He arched his back and stretched his arms as he dropped. The wind buffeted his body as he accelerated into a free fall toward the desert floor below. Searching the ground through his night-vision goggles, he finally located the pinprick of light that marked his target. Hurtling earthward, he maneuvered to land far enough away so that no one on the ground would detect his arrival. At the last possible second, he pulled the ripcord and waited for the reassuring jolt that told him his chute had opened. The canopy filled, and as he descended he expertly manipulated the risers until his feet lightly touched the sand. Quickly he worked to shed his harness and then he gathered the folds of his parachute and stuffed the material into a black duffel.

He drew his silenced pistol and started toward his objective. Guided by night-vision goggles, he stayed low, favoring his right hip as he limped his way across the dunes. Inwardly, he cursed the pain from the old injury, but relentlessly pushed himself forward. As he closed in on his target, he flipped up his infrared goggles and waited for his eyes to adapt to the harsh light given off from a powerful lantern. Once his vision had adjusted, he rapidly located all four of the men he'd expected to find. Three were digging a large hole in the sand, and the remaining man was standing above, watching. Quietly, he moved in and positioned himself behind their truck. All four wore body armor, goggles, and each carried a sidearm. He recognized the man watching, he was a friend and compatriot, a deep cover agent who'd worked for months to learn the location of this cache. He also knew the three men digging were former American soldiers, each an exemplary fighter and a highly trained killer. They'd been recruited by a private security firm after their enlistments were up, but their actions tonight marked them as nothing more than mercenaries drawn by greed.

He moved silently alongside the truck and took a quick look inside the bed. He felt a rush of anticipation at being in such close proximity to his prize. Four common cylinders—each was a dirty gray color, four feet in length, a foot in diameter, with a simple valve screwed into the rounded end. They looked like nothing more than the common high-pressure acetylene tanks used by welders. But these cylinders had been modified to carry something besides acetylene, something extraordinarily lethal. The intelligence he'd gathered said there should be two more, for a total of six.

"You're about to have company." The voice sounded in his earpiece. "The second half of tonight's party is coming fast from the south—they're four minutes out."

He acknowledged the warning and exhaled slowly to calm his racing heartbeat. Leading with his pistol, he stepped around the truck and fired at the closest man. Body armor necessitated head shots and the first man dropped instantly, followed by the second. The third managed to draw his weapon before his head snapped backward from a single slug and he collapsed. The last man, the watcher, frantically ripped away his goggles to identify himself.

"Don't shoot! It's me!"

"Relax," he said as he lowered his pistol.

"My God, like some sort of ghost you silently materialize out of nowhere."

"The others are coming," he said. "How much money are they bringing?"

"The price was set at one hundred and fifty thousand U.S. dollars. How close are they?"

"We have time. What of the informant who told you of this place?"

"Dead."

"Will anyone be able to connect him to tonight's events?"

"Doubtful. There are many bodies in Iraq. One more will mean nothing."

"You're right." He raised the pistol and fired twice, the slugs expertly placed for a quick and painless death. His comrade, a confused expression etched on his face, buckled at the knees and fell to the ground.

"Sorry, old friend—but the mission has changed." He holstered his pistol and began to move. According to his internal clock, he had less than ninety seconds until the car arrived. He snatched an M4 assault rifle leaning against the truck, lowered his infrared goggles, and half ran and half limped toward the road. He flung himself against a small sand dune and threw the weapon to his shoulder. A quick check told him the magazine held the full thirty rounds. As the speeding black Mercedes came into range, he squeezed the trigger and sent a stream of bullets into the car, destroying the radiator, exploding both front tires. Using short bursts, he walked the rounds across the windshield until it crumpled inward. He kept firing until the car swerved and flipped, hitting on its side and rolling three times before it came to rest well off the road. Flames erupted from under the wrecked hood as the engine began to burn.

The gun was empty and he tossed it aside. He drew his pistol and limped over to what was left of the Mercedes and surveyed the interior. The two men in the front seat were dead; they'd taken the full brunt of the 5.56-mm rounds. The passenger in the back hadn't been so lucky; he was hurt, but alive, frantically praying aloud for Allah to spare him. He reached through the shattered side window and pulled a metal briefcase free from the clutches of the lone survivor. A quick check found stacks of American one hundred dollar bills. The fire was spreading fast and he was forced to take a step back to escape the heat. He then raised the pistol and with a squeeze of the trigger ended the man's desperate pleadings.

He removed his night-vision optics and replaced them with clear protective goggles; the burning Mercedes would now serve to light the night. He limped to where he'd stashed the duffel containing his parachute, and caught the faint whistle of turbines above the sound of the wind. Seconds later a blinding light erupted as all of the C-130's landing lights were switched on at the last second. The airplane roared over his head so close he felt the rush of turbulence trailing the big four-bladed props as the plane touched down on the road.

The chirp of rubber and the roar of propellers going into reverse pitch announced the arrival of the rest of his unit. The Lockheed C-130's rugged airframe and massive turboprop engines allowed it to spin around in a tight one-hundred-eighty-degree turn and power toward him. He stood on the centerline as the deafening whine from the turbine engines grew louder until the nose of the big transport eased into the orange-yellow light cast from the burning car. The engines remained running and the rear door of the C-130 swung down. He joined the lone figure who exited the plane carrying a satchel. Together they headed to their prize.

The new arrival scanned the bodies, peered into the hole, and then dropped the package he was carrying. "We need to hurry or the American AWACS is going to wonder what we're doing."

"Grab a shovel," he ordered. They quickly finished digging out the two remaining cylinders and carefully lifted them into the back of the truck. As planned, they tossed the satchel of drugs they'd brought with them into the hole and half buried it with sand. The kilo of heroin would be discovered later, along with the bodies.

"Drive the cylinders to the plane and then bring the truck back here." The man with the limp ordered.

As soon as the truck roared off, he methodically searched the men he'd killed. He started with the mercenaries, relieving them of their identification, cell phones, and watches. He took a moment to close his friend's unseeing eyes as he rifled through his clothes and removed his possessions. He felt no remorse. It was unavoidable—the magnitude of this mission demanded a scorched-earth policy. No one with any knowledge of what had taken place here tonight could be left alive.

His hip and leg felt as if they were on fire. He sat heavily in the sand and stretched out his right leg. The pain in his hip was unrelenting and from experience he knew there was only one way to combat the agony—and it was time. From a side pocket he withdrew a small leather kit that held several prefilled hypodermic syringes. He had no time to waste rolling up a sleeve. He pulled the plastic cap off with his mouth then extracted a razor-sharp stiletto from a scabbard in his boot and sliced an opening in the fabric of his fatigues. He jabbed the needle into the flesh of his thigh and hungrily pressed the plunger. Moments later he felt the warm embrace of the morphine.

With the cylinders secured inside the plane, his comrade returned with the truck. He pulled himself to his feet, tested his hip, and limped as fast as he could to the C-130. The man at his side knew better than to offer any sympathy or assistance.

He climbed aboard and threw himself into a seat as the cargo door was closed. He strapped in, pulled off his helmet and goggles, followed by his watch cap and headset. In one practiced motion he unfurled the kaffiya he'd used to protect his face. He smoothed his shock white beard then ran his hands back through his equally white hair. He wasn't an old man; only forty-three years of age, but after the plane crash that ruined his hip and the vertebrae in his back, his hair and beard had turned pure white.

The C-130 roared down the road at full power, lifted off into the night, and flew low and fast. His pain had eased and he leaned his head back against the bulkhead and closed his eyes. As he always did, he mentally replayed each element of the night's operation and analyzed each and every detail. The footprints and tire tracks would soon be obliterated by the shifting windblown sands. All they'd left behind was a collection of dead mercenaries and known criminals. Combined with the heroin and a burned-out, bullet-riddled car, it would look like a drug deal gone bad. He'd executed a perfect misdirection, and it was unlikely anyone would probe further.

He opened his eyes and took in the view of the cylinders now in his possession, and a small smile crept to his lips. It had taken a long time, but part of Saddam Hussein's weapons of mass destruction had finally been recovered and were now his. He understood the destructive power. Inside each canister was a hundred pounds of anthrax spores. Once the spores were dispersed from an airplane upwind of a major city, the world's single deadliest terrorist act in history would be unstoppable.

He envisioned the scenario: The first flu-like symptoms would show up in about twenty-four hours. More than enough time for him and his men to escape, spread out across the globe, and vanish. While he sat back and watched the aftermath on television, hundreds of thousands of people would flood the local hospitals. Antibiotic stockpiles would deplete almost immediately. People would start to die from respiratory shutdown. High fever would give way to shock, then cyanosis as victims turned blue, gasping their last breaths. Within a week, millions would be sick and dying. The sheer numbers of casualties would spark a nationwide panic. Many of the infected would have traveled away from the target city before their symptoms hit, leading a frenzied population to believe that the unseen attacks had occurred in many cities. Rioting would break out and from there the ensuing violence would threaten a complete breakdown of social services. The case fatality rate for inhaled anthrax spores was upwards of 75 percent, so in the end, as many as a million people could die from the contents of one cylinder. He had six. He felt a unique sensation of power as he savored the reality that he alone could annihilate millions of people. He pictured his first target, the gleaming white monuments: the Pentagon, the White House, and the Capitol building—when he was finished they'd all be deserted. He thought back on his training, to the day he'd become a firm believer in the concept that world peace was in fact possible—but a great deal of killing needed to happen first.

CHAPTER ONE

Six months later

"I don't like this," Michael Ross said from the pilot's seat. "We need to do something else."

A flash of lightning briefly lit up the darkened cockpit, and Donovan Nash saw the concern on Michael's face. Dead ahead, rapidly building thunderstorms boiled across the horizon, staccato bursts of cloud-to-ground lightning peppering the earth. Before he could agree with Michael, the Gulfstream sank abruptly.

"Hang on!" Michael shouted the warning as he shoved both throttles all the way to the stops. The Rolls-Royce engines spooled up, their distinctive high-pitched whine filled the cockpit, and the airplane strained against the unseen river of air. Turbulence slammed into the airplane and tossed them up and down in the violent night sky. For a split second Donovan felt the air in the cockpit turn supercharged, the hair on his arms buzzed a brief warning, and then it seemed that a flashbulb went off a foot in front of his face. Blinded, Donovan fought the spots that danced before his eyes and felt the sizzle of adrenaline hit his system. His ears popped from the pressure change. A moment later, he heard the deafening roar of thunder.

Michael banked the Gulfstream hard to the left. "We're out of here. I'm breaking it off to the south! Tell the tower we just took a lightning strike!"

Donovan blinked savagely to clear his vision while the distinct smell of ozone filled the cockpit. Heavy rain pelted the windscreen.

"What's flashing?" Michael asked. "How bad did we get hit?"

"We lost the right generator." Donovan took a quick look at the overhead panel as well as the circuit breaker panel. Cloud-to-cloud discharges bolted across the horizon. The orange-purple glow expanded as it danced upward toward the stratosphere. Tendrils of white-hot lightning arced from the maelstrom and peppered the ground below. The entire western sky lit up with so many individual bursts of lightning that it looked like a solid wall.

"I'm thinking we should break out of this any second." Michael called out as another blistering display of lightning lit up the sky around them.

Donovan found he was holding his breath, mostly out of wonder, but also some trepidation. He'd seen the weather charts before they'd left Washington D.C. A fast-moving front was sweeping down from the northwest, and now it was creating an unyielding line of severe weather marching southward across Florida.

It was just the two of them on this leg. The *Spirit of da Vinci,* one of Eco-Watch's, sixty-million-dollar special-purpose airborne scientific platforms, needed to be in West Palm Beach to begin a series of proving runs for a new camera system. Underneath all the added equipment, the *da Vinci* was essentially a Gulfstream IV corporate jet—minus all the aesthetics. In the rear cabin, among the racks of electronic gear, were modular science stations. The most recently installed was a state-of-the-art, high-resolution imaging system that was slated to begin official flight testing the next morning.

"This is getting uglier by the minute," Michael said as he tightened his harness.

"Forget about landing in West Palm Beach. Once we get out of this, we can figure out where to go." Donovan winced as another burst of lightning lit up the cockpit. Michael was more than his longtime colleague—they were more like brothers. Their deep friendship and considerable flying experience had been honed by over a decade of flying together all over the world. Officially, Donovan was the boss, a detail that Michael frequently ignored, though

Donovan was smart enough to understand that that was one of the ingredients that made everything work. With a camaraderie and understanding that had been forged in hundreds of dangerous situations just like this one, there was no one Donovan trusted more at the controls than Michael.

They were out over the ocean, paralleling the worst of the weather. As they flew toward a small cluster of harmless rain showers that had popped up over the ocean, they clipped the top of the wispy clouds and the airplane buffeted momentarily. Michael couldn't avoid the next one, and the *da Vinci* hit it dead center. The precipitation hissed passed the windows and the Gulfstream reeled from the turbulence, its nearly hundred-foot wingspan flexed up and down in the dark clouds.

They blew through multiple cloud layers. Each sliver of clear air allowed them an all too brief view of the squall line dead ahead. Donovan often thought of this as a three-dimensional chess game played at three hundred miles per hour. They couldn't see the massive anvil tops above them, but he knew the line of thunderstorms blossomed well above fifty thousand feet.

"I saw some lights dead ahead." Michael pointed off the nose as the Gulfstream broke out of the clouds into smoother air. He wordlessly pushed up the throttles, and the *da Vinci* gathered speed immediately.

"We're due east of West Palm Beach. If we can— "

"You smell that?" Michael interrupted and snapped his head toward Donovan.

Donovan turned toward the darkened cabin and tested the air. It only took a moment to confirm what Michael had detected. Smoke.

"We need to get this thing on the ground. Now. Is that an airport out there?" Michael pointed. "See the rotating beacon, just this side of the interstate?"

"That's Boca Raton." Donovan typed KBCT into the flight management system and grabbed the microphone. Donovan watched as the FMS data confirmed that it was the Boca Raton airport. The acrid smell of burning insulation continued to drift up into the cockpit.

"Tell them that's where we're landing." Michael pulled on his oxygen mask and then banked the *da Vinci* and began to slow the speeding jet.

"Tower, this is Eco-Watch zero one," Donovan transmitted. "We've got Boca Raton in sight at twelve o'clock and eight miles. We'd like a straight-in approach for runway two-three."

"Roger, Eco-Watch zero one. You're cleared for a visual approach to Boca Raton. Contact Boca Tower on 118.42. He knows you're coming."

Donovan clicked on a flashlight, turned, and pointed the beam of light into the cabin. The smoke was visible, and as Donovan played the narrow beam around the cabin, he guessed that the smoke was originating from the aft equipment rack.

"Still burning?" Michael said through his mask while concentrating on the fast approaching airport.

"It's not bad, yet. It looks like the lightning fried the new equipment we just had installed. We've still got all our aircraft systems—everything we need to get this thing on the ground is still working." Donovan spun in the frequency for Boca Raton. "We'll deal with it on the ground. Just keep flying. We're almost there."

CHAPTER TWO

Lauren peeked in on Abigail, making sure her two-year-old daughter was tucked in and sleeping peacefully. She adjusted the blanket and then lightly rested her hand on Abigail's forehead, taking in the smooth skin and the perfect smell of baby shampoo.

She quietly left Abigail's room and went back to her own bedroom. She checked that the baby monitor was on, and then collected the paperwork she'd brought home from the office. As a senior meteorological consultant with the Defense Intelligence Agency, the scientific articles were required reading and piled up quickly if she didn't stay current.

Lauren felt her frustration rise, Donovan should have called by now. She operated best with order and discipline in her world and right now, at least as far as her husband went, she had nothing remotely resembling order. He'd been especially distant and distracted before he'd left for Florida. She'd been thinking about it all evening and couldn't shake the feeling that something was wrong. There had been little signs for weeks now until Lauren wasn't even sure when things began to change—only that Donavan was different, or they were both somehow different. Theirs was a relationship trapped in a loop of silent discontent, and she wasn't sure how to identify the issues, let alone break the cycle.

Lauren headed downstairs to make herself a cup of hot tea, but as she passed the closed door to the study, she heard a small beep coming from inside the darkened room. She clicked on the light and went in to investigate. The smoke alarms were fine, they'd been checked recently. The bookshelves held nothing electric, so she moved to the desk just as the beep sounded again. Lauren turned toward the credenza and pushed a key on the laptop computer. The moment the screen blinked to life, she found the problem—a low-battery alert. She located the power cord on the back of the drive and discovered that it was loose. She firmed up the connection and sat down to make sure the battery was going to accept the charge.

It seemed odd that the cord could have worked itself out. In a house with a two-year-old, Abigail was usually the easiest explanation, but she wasn't ever allowed in this room. A row of books lined the wall behind the computer, and as Lauren looked closer, she noticed some dust. In the dust she spotted marks that told her the dictionary had been slid in and out recently.

Curious, Lauren knew that when Donovan needed help spelling something, he defaulted to the computer. There was no way he was going to wrestle with the massive volume to verify a word. She pulled the dictionary out and was surprised when a DVD slid out from between the pages and fell to the floor. Using her thumb and middle finger she picked up and studied the disc. The title, *One Earth,* was printed in bold black letters, followed by the warning that the DVD was an Academy Screener copy, for awards consideration only and not for public viewing.

Lauren knew exactly what she was holding. *One Earth* hadn't been released yet, but somehow Donovan had gotten his hands on a reviewer's copy of the documentary about Meredith Barnes. Over the years there'd been many television shows about the life and untimely death of celebrity conservationist Meredith Barnes, but this was a major Hollywood production and there was early Academy Award buzz for the project.

They'd both known that the movie was being made, and when she'd asked him about it, Donovan hadn't seemed concerned or even acted interested. Despite his history with Meredith. Despite the certainty that he would be depicted poorly in the film. His position was that everything between him and Meredith had happened twenty years ago and that he was happy Meredith's work was still relevant after all this time. End of subject.

She slid the disk into the computer and moved through the prompts until the first images appeared on the screen. A dirt road cut through a lush jungle, the faint sounds of screaming began to grow—there were shouts of alarm and the distant wail of emergency vehicles. The screams began to draw closer and were filled with more immediate urgency. An image began to take shape, a light-colored object surrounded by darkness. Slowly, the screen came into focus to show stark images of Meredith Barnes's murdered body being discovered in a muddy field outside San Jose, Costa Rica. A rapid-fire burst of still pictures ripped across the screen, actual photos from that day. Meredith's sightless eyes, her hair and chalk-white skin matted with blood from the single bullet wound to her forehead.

Lauren watched as the scene faded and was replaced with a young Meredith Barnes, smiling and laughing for the camera. Images showed a warm photo montage of her love for the outdoors as she went through adolescence and then graduated from college. Lauren, as well as most of the world, knew the story. Fresh out of school, Meredith Barnes had traveled the world researching and writing what would become her best-selling book, *One Earth*. Part science, part spiritual expedition, her book, along with her movie-star good looks, thrust her center stage. Her message wasn't just about what was wrong—but how each and every one of us could do something to heal our planet. Hollywood, captivated by Meredith's passion for life, showcased her journey and her message in a motion picture. The world fell in love with her.

After the movie, she produced and hosted a wildly popular television series about the hot-topic issues. Crisscrossing the globe, she and her crew dramatically illustrated how we were harming our planet. She highlighted what needed to be done to stop the damage. She was a frequent guest on late night talk shows. She participated in hot-topic political discussions. She held court at countless environmental rallies, speaking for a voiceless planet and championing a better future. She enlisted powerful allies—Princess Diana, Bono, Elton John, as well as other high profile A-list celebrities to further her causes. The public couldn't get enough—Meredith's fiery temperament coupled with boundless compassion made her a media darling. She influenced politicians and policy makers on a global scale, yet she always came across as warm and genuine.

Meredith's message: peace and conservation, a no-borders philosophy that would serve to save our "one earth" from everything we were doing to destroy it. As Lauren watched and listened, she understood all over again how Meredith had become such a cherished figure in the eyes of the world—and why she was still relevant. Part emissary for the planet, part celebrity, Meredith had touched millions of people. Beautiful and intelligent, powerfully charismatic, using soft-spoken kindness when needed—and her intense passion when calm diplomacy failed.

Lauren fast-forwarded through Meredith's college years then began watching again when she recognized the famous footage of Meredith tearing up a three-million-dollar check written to her foundation by billionaire oilman Robert Huntington. Meredith threw the pieces in his face, poked him in the chest with her index finger, and demanded to know how the heir to the Huntington Oil fortune could sleep at night. She rattled off a dozen ways his multinational company was killing the planet. The narrator of the documentary used the confrontation as evidence of ground zero in a bold conspiracy employed by Robert Huntington and Huntington Oil to murder Meredith Barnes.

The movie continued. Following the fireworks from that first meeting, it explained that Robert sought Meredith out, used her, and manipulated her by proposing a series of initiatives that led Huntington Oil to appear as if they were on the forefront of responsible energy-recovery methods. But the film implied that Huntington had another agenda: he seduced her to get close enough to orchestrate her death. The screen filled with images of the two of them as they traveled the world, their movements tracked by both Hollywood and Wall Street. One shot in particular of Robert and Meredith kissing distressed Lauren to the point that she looked away, as if she were intruding. The narrator continued to reiterate that Huntington was nothing more than a ruthless sociopath. A deeply flawed man who had no problems using a potent combination of charm and his unlimited supply of money in a premeditated, brutal plan to destroy Meredith Barnes and her message.

Lauren watched as the narrator explained that Huntington continued the charade of their relationship, that he exploited their combined influence by arranging an environmental summit in Costa Rica. An unprecedented gathering of political dignitaries and business leaders from all over the world convened to reduce the destruction of the rain forests, to develop alternative energy for emerging economies, and to set controls on commercial fishing as well as ban harvesting of oceanic mammals. By all comparisons to previous attempts, the Costa Rica summit promised to be an epic rally on behalf of our planet, but according to the narrator, Robert Huntington had other plans.

What followed was a series of events Lauren had never heard. The narrator provided details. That despite threats against visiting diplomats and even toward Meredith herself, she and Huntington had left the safety of the host hotel. The trip was unannounced. En route to a rented villa, their limousine was stopped, their driver killed, and Meredith taken at gunpoint. The only living witness to the alleged abduction was Huntington himself, who was beaten badly. Later this was used as evidence of how far he was willing to go to destroy Meredith. A ten-million-dollar ransom demand materialized almost immediately by way of an anonymous letter left at the hotel. The summit evaporated. Weeks of investigations by the police, plus unending posturing by the Costa Rican and American authorities, resulted in nothing except Meredith's death.

Huntington, it was explained, did very little at first. He was a billionaire and yet the ransom demand was initially ignored. It was only later that he started assembling the cash, a delay that pointed to his culpability in Meredith's demise. When he finally had the money, he demanded proof of life; he wanted to speak with Meredith. When the phone call finally came, Robert took the call. It was late at night, and to this day, no one knows what was said. The equipment that should have recorded the conversation was somehow switched off by the police on duty. The next day, Meredith's body was found in a muddy field. She'd been murdered. The backlash was immediate and unyielding. Blamed for everything from refusing to pay for her release to being the actual murderer, Robert Huntington was charged, tried, and sentenced in the court of public opinion. No one was sure what happened to the ten million dollars. Virtually overnight, Robert Huntington became the most hated man in America—if not the world.

Meredith's funeral, attended by a Who's Who of politicians and celebrities, was broadcast around the world. Robert Huntington was notably absent. Instead, a series of photos were published, showing Robert Huntington on an unnamed beach with a young blonde woman. The images fueled the public's unwavering rage toward Robert Huntington—a bitter hate still alive after twenty years.

Family and close friends of Meredith Barnes were interviewed, as well as an array of celebrities and law enforcement experts. All expressed their belief that Meredith had been murdered by Huntington and his oil industry cronies and this verbal condemnation led up to the vivid *New York Times* headline that announced that Robert Huntington was dead. Lauren cringed when the plane crash death of Robert Huntington was celebrated, as if the planet itself had exacted some sort of karma for his atrocities and killed him for what he'd done to Meredith Barnes.

Lauren hit the stop button and was relieved when the screen went black. She hated what she'd seen, and for the moment she didn't know what was real and what was fabricated. This was the first she'd heard of previous threats against Meredith, or the delay in assembling the ransom, or the final phone call, or that there was a question about the ten million dollars. She, of course, knew a much different story, the one that couldn't be told. First and foremost she knew that Robert Huntington hadn't died in a plane crash. She knew he'd been devastated by Meredith's death. She knew that he had eventually orchestrated his own death, that he'd gone to Europe for appearance-altering surgeries. Lauren was one of six people in the world who knew the truth. The reason she knew all of this: the man who used to be Robert Huntington was now Donovan Nash, the man she'd married.

CHAPTER THREE

"Eco-Watch zero one, this is Boca Raton tower. West Palm Beach informed us you've taken a lightning strike. Do you need assistance?"

"Negative." Donovan replied, and then took a quick look over his shoulder into the cabin.

"Still burning?" Michael asked.

"No change."

The Gulfstream touched down smoothly on the main gear. Michael expertly lowered the nose, deployed the thrust reversers, and brought the *da Vinci* to a quick stop. They'd beat the approaching storms, but the squall line was bearing down on Boca Raton as they pulled clear of the runway.

Ground control issued instructions, and Michael swung the *da Vinci* onto the taxiway that would take them to the Executive Ramp. In the distance, Donovan could see Boca Raton Aviation, the hangars and offices brightly lit. They had managed to land ahead of the storm, but one look at the western skyline told them the thunderstorms were only minutes away. Ahead, the doors to a large hangar were open as the line crew pushed a plane into an already packed space.

As the *da Vinci* rolled onto the main ramp, one of the linemen jumped into a golf cart and raced across the tarmac, waving his lighted batons to guide them. They were directed toward a row of larger planes parked well away from both the office and hangar. The planes were dark, the engine covers installed, obviously not scheduled to leave anytime soon. Donovan spotted one empty space situated between a Gulfstream and a Global Express; it was just big enough for the *da Vinci*. He brought the Gulfstream to a rest, shutdown the engines, set the brakes, and turned off the electrical power.

Donovan threw off his harness and raced to the rear of the plane. Using his flashlight in the darkened cabin it was easy to locate the source of the wisps of white smoke: the control module for the new high-resolution camera array they'd just installed. Donovan threw open the door to a cabinet and grabbed a tool pouch. He found the screwdriver, quickly backed out the fasteners, then slid the unit from the rack. He twisted apart the Cannon plug and ran with the smoldering box toward the door.

As he lowered the airstair, the warm humid air poured in from the stiffening breeze. The sudden peal of thunder told him the weather was closer than he'd expected, and he realized how good it felt to be on the ground. He hurried down the stairs past the lineman standing below to set the still-burning component on the ground a safe distance away from the plane.

"What happened to that?" the lineman asked.

"Nothing, it just got a little overheated. It'll be fine."

"Okay, what can I do for you? Do you have passengers?"

"No, it's just the two of us. We're here until at least tomorrow. Is there any way we can get this into a hangar?"

The lineman slid back behind the wheel of his golf cart. "The hangar's already full. At least until the storms move through. Talk to the girl inside; she'll be able to help you with that."

Donovan nodded that he understood, and the lineman whipped a sharp U-turn and sped across the ramp. Heading back up the stairs, Donovan met Michael at the top. "We're on our own for now."

"I checked the back—nothing else is smoking," Michael replied as he hurriedly threw on a windbreaker. "I'm going to go outside and check the exterior for damage while I can."

"Wait, I'm coming with you," Donovan said, "then I'll start making some phone calls."

Donovan grabbed his own jacket, and the two of them trundled down the airstair and stared at the nose of the Gulfstream. It didn't take Michael long to find the pinhole defect in the composite cone that covered the weather radar. A tiny burn mark outlined where the bolt of lightning had struck the airframe.

"That's not bad," Michael ran his fingers over the small indentation. "Maintenance can patch that until we can get a replacement."

Donovan nodded and the two of them walked to the right side of the *da Vinci*. Michael played his flashlight back and forth across the smooth aluminum skin, looking for anything out the ordinary. Then they checked the wing, ducked underneath the airplane, and came up near the tail. The moment his light illuminated the tailcone, the damage became obvious. They could see that the housing for the navigation light was missing and the paint charred. The million or so volts from the lightning surge had raced through the airframe and finally found a spot to exit the aluminum tube and arc back out into the atmosphere.

"Wow, that bolt didn't mess around, did it?" Michael pointed toward the jagged metal where the housing used to be.

Donovan could see the ends of the wires. They looked melted.

"Based on this, we need some maintenance people to give everything a good once-over before we go anywhere."

Donovan felt the first drops of rain hit his face. "I'm going to go back inside the plane and make some phone calls. Once I cancel tomorrow's flight, I'll call Gulfstream and get to work on shuttling some maintenance guys in here first thing."

"Forget tomorrow's flight for a minute." Michael pulled his hood up over his head and shot Donovan a questioning look. "You might want to think about calling Lauren before it gets too late."

"I know." Donovan nodded. "Thanks for listening earlier, I appreciate that."

"You've listened to me complain about Susan over the years. Take my advice and call her, talk to her. Listen to her. Trust me, in my twenty years of experience, war with your wife sucks—women are better at it than we are and usually win."

Donovan allowed a brief smile to flash across his face. Michael did have a point. He climbed the stairs back inside the Gulfstream just as an explosive peal of thunder ripped loose and echoed across the ramp. He winced at each successive report of thunder; each one seeming louder and closer than the one before. As the front pushed closer, the concussive waves from the almost constant thunder resonated deep within his chest. It stirred a primitive response as old as man itself and Donovan felt the flesh on his arms rise in response.

Another flash of lightning lit up the ramp. The fluorescent fixtures illuminating the ramp and distant buildings flickered once, stayed on for another second, and then went out completely, plunging the entire facility into darkness. The only light came from the taxiway and runway lights that were on a backup generator.

Donovan pulled his phone from his pocket and sat down heavily at one of the science stations, switched it on, and waited for it to power up. When he checked to see if he had any messages, his heart sank a little when he realized Lauren hadn't called. His thumb hovered over the button that would ring his house. He hesitated, Michael's advice echoing in his head, and then he pressed it.

"Hello," Lauren answered on the second ring.

"Hi there. I didn't call at a bad time, did I?"

"No, I was just getting ready for bed."

"How's Abigail?"

"She's fine. She went down hours ago. I trust your flight was uneventful."

"Not exactly. We couldn't get into West Palm Beach, so we diverted to Boca Raton."

"I saw the cold front moving through Florida. I'm glad you're safe. Are you going to call it a night?"

"Yeah, we took a lightning strike coming in, so we need to get that looked at before we go anywhere." Donovan was about to tell her more, when through the window, momentarily illuminated by a flash of lightning, a man raced past. An instant later it was dark again, and Donovan was puzzled by what he'd just seen. As the image crystallized in his mind, he decided it must be one of the lineman helping Michael put chocks under the tires to keep the *da Vinci* in place with the coming storms.

"Are you still there?"

"Yeah, sorry, I'm here." Donovan got up out of his seat and peered out into the darkness. Small drops of water dotted the acrylic window making it difficult to see anything clearly. Next to them sat a blue-and-white Gulfstream V. It looked buttoned up, the doors were closed and it was completely dark inside, obviously parked for the evening. Another flash of lightning lit up the ramp. In the millisecond of near daylight, Donovan caught sight of two men toe to toe near the tail of the *da Vinci*. One of them was Michael, and he seemed to be struggling against the other.

"What the—" Donovan spun and hurried toward the door.

"What's going on?" Lauren asked.

"I'm not sure yet. I have to go. I'll call you back!" Donovan pocketed his phone, snatched a black metal flashlight, and took the airstairs three at a time, landing heavily on the wet tarmac. In a crouch, he ducked low under the wing and ran as fast as he could. As he rounded the main landing gear, he searched the darkness, finding only a dark shape lying on the concrete. Donovan recognized the windbreaker and just as quickly caught the unmistakable odor of burnt gunpowder. A second later, someone hit him from behind just below the ear.

The impact dropped him to his knees, and Donovan made a wild swing behind him with his flashlight and connected with something solid. He lunged forward and tried to turn and look at his attacker when another blow connected and he crashed to the ground, his head striking the concrete. The last thing he was aware of before he slipped into the darkness was something warm trickling down the side of his face.

CHAPTER FOUR

Donovan heard the thunder explode and reverberate all around him. Fat raindrops hit his exposed skin. Reality began to seep into his consciousness, his thoughts forming slowly. He knew something horrible had happened before he could actually fix on the events. Another crack of thunder jolted him, and he opened his eyes and blinked against the pouring rain. His eyes darted under the tail of the *da Vinci*. All he could see was a blue windbreaker and short-cropped blond hair—Michael.

He raised himself up on his knees and found his flashlight. He switched it on, the beam cutting through the darkness. Donovan stood and fought off the dizziness that threatened to put him back down. He wavered unsteadily, lurching forward, staggering toward his friend. All the air seemed to leave Donovan's lungs as he knelt. The small puddles of water near Michael's head were stained crimson.

Behind him he heard the sound of running feet splash through the puddles. Donovan turned and found one of the linemen approaching; he was short, a little on the heavy side. He wore a yellow rain suit that covered him head to toe. One look told him this wasn't the man he'd seen from the window of the *da Vinci*.

"What happened?"

"Call 911!" Donovan yelled.

"Oh Jesus." The lineman immediately began talking into his two-way radio.

In the harsh brightness from the flashlight Donovan could see that Michael's skin was slack and colorless and the entire left side of his head was matted with blood. With shaking hands he put two fingers on Michael's neck and found a weak pulse. He remembered the earlier smell of spent gunpowder and imagined the worst. His sense of helplessness added to his fear as the distant warble from emergency sirens ebbed and flowed in the fury of the storm.

The rain fell heavier and the wind began to whip and gust. In the distance, Donovan heard the unmistakable sound of a jet taking off. A distinctive blue-and-white Gulfstream, lights fully ablaze, raced down the runway. Donovan glanced at the empty spot next to the *da Vinci.* The departing Gulfstream was the same one he'd noticed earlier. Plumes of water erupted behind the jet until it lifted off, raised its landing gear, and made a sweeping turn to the east, climbing away into the night.

Beside him, Michael lay bleeding, maybe dying. Donovan cursed his inability to reach his friend in time, and was powerless to do anything but vow retribution. He found growing strength in the declaration, it was something white hot and tangible, and, most importantly, it held his fear at bay.

In the midst of the howling storm, he saw more people running in his direction, a gate being opened. Palm trees danced in a wild frenzy as the wind from the thunderstorms hit full force. Sirens wailed in the night and Donovan imagined they were a part of him—some primal thing inside him that was screaming at the universe and warning all who could hear that he'd make whoever did this pay.

CHAPTER FIVE

Lauren stared at the phone. She expected him to call her back within minutes and when that didn't happen, she finally padded into the kitchen and put some water on to boil. She made her tea and slowly walked back toward the study and the movie. He'd obviously hidden it from her, but she wasn't sure why, or how long he'd had it, or even how he'd gotten it. The fact that he'd kept it from her was disturbing, though Lauren began to wonder if she hadn't stumbled on the root cause of his recent behavior. How damaging had it been for her husband to see Meredith again, hear her voice, and relive her death?

Lauren sat back down in front of the computer, but didn't restart the movie. Already she knew the film was riddled with errors and vindictive half-truths. If there was a conspiracy, Robert wasn't behind it. He'd loved Meredith deeply. Robert had asked Meredith to marry him, and the two were planning a life together when she was killed. They'd decided to wait until after the summit to make the formal announcement.

All those years ago he'd orchestrated his death and left everyone behind. After months of reconstructive surgery in Europe, he'd started his life over as Donovan Nash. The fact that Robert hadn't died was a secret that Lauren had sworn to take to her grave. She wondered what impact this documentary had had on her husband. If she had to guess, he'd had this disk for weeks, about the time he began sleeping poorly, his nights plagued with either bad dreams or outright nightmares. It was if he were being nocturnally consumed by grief or rage—or both. She'd asked him to see a doctor and he'd refused. He took a flight physical every six months to maintain his pilot's license and, according to him, he was fine. But Lauren knew he wasn't, and the end result was that she felt shut out—even more so after what she'd found.

If this documentary was the underlying cause of what was upsetting him, then he wasn't drifting away from her, he was wounded. How could he not be damaged by the power of the images and the memories they invoked. She knew he loved her, that wasn't the problem. Lauren exhaled slowly and was about to restart the movie when the phone rang. She saw it was Donovan and felt a sense of relief as she answered.

"It's me," Donovan said. "Sorry I couldn't call you back until now."

From the tremor in his voice Lauren knew something was wrong. "What happened? What's going on?"

"It's Michael," Donovan's voice wavered. "He's been shot."

"Oh my God." Lauren felt flushed, tears starting to form.

"The police think—" Donovan's words came out haltingly. "We—Michael—may have stumbled into the middle of an airplane theft."

"Someone stole an airplane? Who does that?" Lauren forced herself up out of the chair and made her way back upstairs. Donovan was clearing his throat and she knew he was buying some time, collecting himself. She thought back to their earlier conversation. "When we were talking, you saw something. Did you see what happened?"

"I saw Michael struggling with someone. Before I could get to him, I was hit from behind."

"Are you hurt?"

"I'm fine, the paramedics checked me out."

"Where are you now? Where's Michael?"

"They took him to the Boca Raton Community Hospital. I'm still with the police at the scene. They're telling me I have to go to the station and make a formal statement before I can go to the hospital. It may be a while before I know anything more."

"This is awful. Did they at least catch the people responsible?" Lauren knew her husband's past, his demons, and his tight-knit friendship with Michael were all working against him right now. Her husband's past was littered with the bodies of loved ones who'd died despite his best efforts to save them. His guilt and remorse at the best of times were enough to smother him. It had taken years to rebuild his world, and Michael and his family were the closest friends Donovan had ever had. Lauren had no idea what might happen to her husband if Michael didn't make it—especially if Donovan blamed himself.

"No, they got away. As far as we know, Michael is the only one who saw them."

"Have you talked to either Susan or William?" Lauren asked, her emotions in check for the moment as she allowed her pragmatic side to click into gear, trying to think of everything that needed to be done and then prioritizing each task. She thought of her dear friend Susan, Michael's wife, as well as their two boys, Patrick and Billy. They lived ten minutes away and Lauren wanted to get over there as quickly as she could. They also needed to find William VanGelder, Donovan's mentor and business partner. He needed to be brought into the loop as soon as possible.

"Not yet. We need to get Susan and the boys down here." He paused. "Michael's in bad shape, Lauren. He might not—"

"Honey, calm down and let's do this one step at a time. You need to call Susan now. Tell her I'll be over there as fast as I can, but she's going to want to hear about this from you. I'll call William. He and I can start on the travel arrangements."

"I needed to call you first." She could hear him exhale slowly. "Susan was my next call."

"Hang in there. Talk to Susan—I love you and I'll call you when I know something, you do the same."

"I love you, too," Donovan said.

Lauren hung up and raced upstairs while she speed-dialed William. She felt the urgency of the situation build as it rang.

Opening her closet, she threw an overnight bag on the bed and began pulling clothes out of her dresser when, to her great relief, William finally answered.

"William, it's Lauren. I'm sorry about the hour, but I have bad news." She took a breath and steadied herself. "Donovan just called. Michael's been shot. He's alive, but we don't know anything beyond that."

"Oh, no." William's voice trailed off. "I know they left today. Remind me where they went?"

"They're in Boca Raton, Florida. Donovan is talking to Susan right now, and I'm on my way over there as soon as I'm off the phone with you."

"Okay. I'm assuming we need a chartered jet to carry the six of us?"

"Yes." Lauren always marveled at how intuitive the elder statesman could be. He'd already assumed she and Abigail were going.

"I thought so. How did Donovan sound?"

"Not great. All he alluded to was that he didn't get to Michael in time and that we needed to hurry."

"Oh God, anything but that. How did all of this happen?"

Lauren relayed what little Donovan had passed along to her. Given the circumstances it was no surprise he seemed as concerned about Donovan's state of mind as she was. William had been a part of her husband's life since he was a child. He had become Donovan's guardian after Donovan's parents were killed. The two of them were as close as father and son and William was certainly a calming influence, not only to Donovan, but to her as well.

"Leave the charter to me," William said. "I'll call you back shortly with the details. Let's meet at Susan's. We'll all leave for the airport from there."

"Thank you, William, you're a godsend. We'll be waiting." Lauren instantly felt better now that William was involved. He was one of the most energetic seventy-four-year-olds she'd ever met, and easily one of the most powerful behind-the-scenes men inside the Washington D.C. beltway. If you needed a jet in the middle of the night, William VanGelder was a good person to know.

Once off the phone, she finished packing, then went in and repeated the process with Abigail's things. She dressed, loaded the luggage in her car, and then gently carried her still-sleeping daughter out, fastening her securely into the car seat. During the ten-minute drive, all she could think about was Michael.

As she neared the house, she saw evidence that Donovan had made the call. Inside lights were on, as well as the porch light. Lauren pulled into the driveway, gathered her sleeping daughter in her arms, and hurried up the walk toward the front door. Before she was halfway to the house, the door swung open and Susan appeared, tightly clutching herself. Lauren couldn't help but think Susan somehow looked smaller.

Lauren moved through the open door, went straight to the sofa, and gently laid Abigail on the plush cushions. She turned and hugged Susan. "I'm so sorry," Lauren whispered as Susan sobbed softly, her body shuddering as she wept. Lauren held her friend, thinking of how strong Susan had always been in the past.

"Why?" Susan said. "How could this have happened?"

Lauren fought her own tears as Susan cried. Sitting on a shelf were dozens of pictures, one of a much younger Michael, all blond hair and square jawed. Every bit the good-looking Southern California beach boy, except that he was standing in a flight suit next to a Navy jet. The impish expression on his tanned face hinted at the devilish sense of humor behind his deep-blue eyes.

Susan wiped at her tears, her brown, shoulder-length hair falling across her face. "I don't want to wake the boys yet. I don't know when we're leaving. Donovan said something about a charter, but I don't know anything else. He sounded horrible on the phone. I don't think he's doing much better than I am."

"I know. That's why Abigail and I are going with you. I can help with the boys, that way you can spend as much time with Michael as you want. Plus, I want to be there for Donovan. As upset as he is right now, it won't take him very long to get angry."

Lauren heard her phone ring and was relieved to see it was William calling.

"Lauren, I'm about to get off Interstate 66 in Centerville. There's an airplane being diverted to take us to Florida. We're leaving in an hour."

"I'm at Susan's. We still need to get everyone here up and packed," Lauren said. "Have you talked to Donovan?"

"Yeah. And we need to get down there as fast as we can."

"I understand." Lauren felt her pulse jump at the worrisome tone in William's voice. She ended the call and turned to Susan.

"I should wake them?" Susan asked.

"William will be here in a few minutes. There's a jet on its way, and we'll be airborne in an hour. What can I do to help?"

"Let me go up and talk to Patrick and Billy. When William gets here, let him in and then you can help me get the boys packed."

Susan steadied herself for a moment, and then hurried upstairs. Lauren moved to the sofa and brushed her daughter's reddish-brown curls away from her chubby cheeks. Abigail was a sound sleeper and might not wake up for hours.

Lauren stopped and studied a photo of Michael and Susan's wedding, Michael in his dress whites and Susan beaming, standing next to him. Her eyes wandered to the other images, pictures of their parents and children, nieces and nephews—normal treasures displayed by families. Her own home lacked photographs, the past remaining hidden.

She envied Michael and Susan's marriage. Childhood sweethearts, they'd married young so they didn't have to worry about inadvertently revealing a secret that could cause immediate and severe repercussions. Susan never lay in bed at night reviewing the exact procedures she'd follow to whisk her children into hiding if the truth about her husband were revealed. Lauren craved the simplicity.

Lauren walked from the living room toward the kitchen. On the way, her eyes were drawn to a framed photograph of Michael and Donovan standing in front of the *Spirit of Galileo,* the very first Eco-Watch Gulfstream. They'd decided to christen all Eco-Watch airplanes after notable figures in the world of science. Nearly a decade ago, Donovan had founded Eco-Watch and one of the first people he'd hired was Michael. The two of them were like brothers, and if the worst happened, if Michael didn't make it, Donovan would have lost yet another person close to him. Lauren couldn't help but ask herself how many people her husband could lose and still remain intact.

CHAPTER SIX

Donovan sat in an interview room at the Boca Raton police station. A detective named Turner had driven him from the airport and explained that this was standard procedure. He'd assured him someone would be in shortly before he quietly closed the door.

He hated having to sit in this tiny room, and whatever small reserve of patience he had was dwindling fast. He was on edge, a combination of far too much adrenaline and having been up since early that morning. Images of Michael kept hammering at him, his eyes were gritty, and his clothes were still wet from the rain. The last he'd seen of Michael, he was being loaded into the ambulance. At that point, he was still alive. Soon after that, the crime lab technicians as well as Detective Turner had arrived, and Donovan had answered their questions over and over. He'd given them free reign aboard the *da Vinci* and explained, as did the linecrew, all of the events of the evening.

The paramedics had checked him over. Other than bumps and bruises, he was fine. At some point he was informed that his presence was required at the station to give a full statement. It was another square to fill and he went willingly. He hadn't realized how closed off from everything he was going to feel.

The door opened and Turner held it as a woman breezed into the room. She was strikingly attractive, and tall—he guessed her at nearly five foot ten—and in good shape, long and lean like a distance runner. She had on blue slacks, a white blouse, and a blue blazer. Her blonde hair was pulled back into a ponytail and she wore little makeup. Her credentials hung from a lanyard around her neck, and Donovan saw she was FBI. Turner sat off to the side with his arms folded across his chest. It was obvious to Donovan that Turner was taking a backseat to the proceedings and that the Federal Bureau of Investigation was now firmly in charge.

"I'm FBI Special Agent Montero," she said. "I know you've had a difficult evening, but I need to ask you some questions."

As she sat down opposite him, Donovan was surprised to find she was older than he'd originally thought. At first glance she looked to be around thirty, but on closer inspection he could see the age lines that crept out from her eyes and creased either side of her mouth. He put her at closer to mid to late thirties, though it was hard to tell through the passive expression fixed on her face.

Montero switched on a handheld tape recorder and placed it on the table. "Mr. Nash. Tell me everything that took place since you departed Virginia."

Donovan exhaled, and then began reciting the series of events up to and including when he found Michael and the police and ambulance had arrived at the airport.

"What exactly does Eco-Watch do?" Montero asked.

"Eco-Watch is a private, nonprofit research organization."

"And your title is?"

"Director of Operations," Donovan said, his face bore no trace of the deception. The lie was so ingrained that it had become the truth. Nothing on paper explained his actual position. He was not simply the director of operations. He was the founder of Eco-Watch.

"What does that mean, exactly?"

"I'm the guy the board of directors hired to make the aviation section work. Eco-Watch currently operates two Gulfstream aircraft out of our world headquarters at Dulles airport. There is another division that runs our two ocean-capable research ships and a section that oversees all the land-based research teams we deploy globally. Eco-Watch's mission is to supplement scientific research organizations that have a legitimate need for the assets we can provide."

"I see." Montero glanced at her notes. "Who are you working for at the moment?"

Donovan bristled at all the time being wasted on bureaucratic overlap. He'd given all of this information to the detectives at the scene. "Our current client is the federal government, specifically a joint NOAA and NASA project. We're installing an airborne visible/infrared imaging spectrometer in the *da Vinci*."

"I understand the *da Vinci* is in reference to the name of your airplane?"

"That's correct. Once the spectrometer is up and running, we'll be able to chart and then track small changes in the offshore reef structure as well as the existing shoreline contours."

Montero held up her hand for Donovan to stop. "I don't need to be schooled on the science, Mr. Nash. I get it. It's a big fancy camera. So this team of scientists is planning to depart West Palm Beach in the morning?"

"We were. The plan was to calibrate the camera over the next day or two and then eventually meet up with an Eco-Watch ship currently steaming toward the Turks and Caicos. The overall goal is to make a comprehensive aerial documentation of the existing shorelines and assess the health of the coral infrastructure."

"The weather forced you to divert from West Palm Beach to Boca Raton?"

"That's correct."

"Once you landed, you and Mr. Ross went your separate ways?"

"No. We both surveyed the initial damage from the lightning strike. I went back inside the airplane to make some phone calls. Michael stayed outside to continue his inspection."

"What happened then?"

"I was on the phone when I saw someone run past the airplane."

"And this struck you as odd? Why?"

"It didn't. I assumed it was a lineman coming to help Michael. It was then that I looked out of the window to see if they needed my help. That's when I saw them fighting."

"Describe fighting," Montero said.

"They were chest to chest, locked up like boxers do sometimes."

Montero nodded that she understood. "We know that the assailant had a gun. Why would he engage in hand-to-hand combat?"

"I have no idea, but my guess is he tried to take Michael out quietly, but met with more resistance than he expected. Michael knows how to defend himself."

"Are you referring to his training in the military? To my knowledge, they don't focus on hand-to-hand combat in flight school."

"He grew up in a rough neighborhood. He has street skills."

"How long has he worked for Eco-Watch?"

"I've known him and his family almost ten years. He's one of my closest friends."

"So you have no reason to believe that Mr. Ross was shot for any reason other than being at the wrong place at the wrong time?"

"No, none at all," Donovan replied.

"In your earlier statement, you said you grabbed a flashlight and rushed to aid Mr. Ross."

"That's correct."

"You saw Mr. Ross on the ground and claimed to have smelled the residual effects of a recently fired weapon."

"Yes."

"You were then struck from behind."

"Yes."

"You only saw Mr. Ross and one other person. Is that correct?"

"That's correct."

"Let's back up for a moment. To crew a Gulfstream properly, there are at least two pilots. Throw all the regulations out the window for a moment. Could one pilot get it from point A to point B alone?"

"Sure, I suppose. He'd have to know what he was doing though."

"I think we can assume that whoever did this knew exactly what they were doing. How long do you think you were unconscious?"

"I'm not sure."

"Was the Gulfstream there when you went to help Mr. Ross?"

"Yes."

"You stated earlier that after you regained consciousness you went to Mr. Ross. It was then that you saw the Gulfstream takeoff. My question to you is this: quick and dirty—how long does it take to fire up a Gulfstream, taxi out, and depart?"

"At least ten minutes, I'd say more like fifteen."

"That answers that. Does the name Bristol Technologies mean anything to you?"

"No, should it?"

"They're the company who had their airplane stolen."

Montero's phone rang and she answered it while shutting off the tape recorder. "Yeah, I'm here at Boca PD now. What have you got?" She frowned as she listened.

"You're kidding me, right?" Montero shook her head in dismay. "Then off the top of my head I'd say, eighteen hundred to two thousand miles. If they headed south, they've easily got enough fuel to make it to South America."

Donovan studied her as she continued her conversation. From what he was hearing, she was aviation savvy. He was starting to understand that this woman was smart and inquisitive and no stranger to interrogation.

"Keep me in the loop," she said, and then ended the call. She glanced at Turner then turned her attention toward Donovan. "Okay, that was the team at the airport. We've managed to piece some of this together. You and Mr. Ross touched down at 10:02 p.m. The stolen Gulfstream departed at 10:28 p.m. What does that tell you?"

"I remember seeing the airplane when we arrived, it was dark inside, the covers were installed as if it had been left for the night. What that tells me is that they'd already breached the Gulfstream and our arrival probably interrupted them and forced them to wait. But they couldn't wait too long or they'd be trapped on the ground when the weather hit. So they needed to take out Michael."

"They needed you both out of the picture," Montero said. "Mr. Ross was just the first, and may have been more combative than they anticipated."

"What about security cameras?"

"Nothing, and the communication with the control tower was normal, relaxed, professional."

"I gather they didn't file a flight plan. Any idea where they went?"

"They told the tower they were going to reposition from Boca Raton down to Opa-Locka Airport in Miami. Airplanes do that all the time, and run down the coast, no flight plan needed. When I checked with Miami Center, they said they tracked what they assumed was a small airplane that left Boca Raton and flew out to the eastern edge of their airspace. At some point the transponder was lost or switched off, and the target turned south and flew out of radar range."

"From your phone conversation I gathered you found the Bristol Technologies crew still in Florida?"

"They're present and accounted for at a local hotel. They told us that they'd fueled their Gulfstream when they landed due to an early-morning departure later in the week. The paramedics reported that Mr. Ross had some mild bruising on the knuckles of his right hand. The marks were consistent with someone who'd been in a fistfight. Can you tell me if Mr. Ross had those marks earlier in the evening?"

"No."

"It would seem Mr. Ross managed to get in at least one punch before he went down. He no doubt got a good look at his assailant."

"I overheard the police at the airport say that it was probably drug smugglers. If you would have asked me before tonight what kind of airplanes drug smugglers were interested in, my answer wouldn't be fifty-million-dollar business jets."

"There's been an alarming new trend among drug cartels, and we're starting to see this switch in methodology. A Gulfstream crashed in Mexico; it was loaded with almost four tons of cocaine. Two other Gulfstream jets have been seized prior to flights to West Africa from Venezuela, and we've seen evidence of traffickers using forty-year-old former airliners to fly drugs."

"They used to do that back in the seventies. I remember the stories of farmers in Kansas finding empty, deserted transport airplanes out on remote roads, the shipments long gone."

"Today a DC-8 can be bought for less than three hundred thousand dollars, loaded with tens of millions of dollars worth of cocaine, flown thousands of miles, and discarded in the same manner. Outside of the developed nations, radar is virtually nonexistent and these aircraft can easily move unnoticed. We've also noticed a disturbing trend in the pilots we've apprehended for drug smuggling in the last year or so. They're older, better trained, and have a far higher level of experience than we've seen in the past. A trend that will probably get worse before it gets better. With the sorry condition of the airlines, more and more pilots have been put out of work, or lost pensions. A small percentage of them will use their skills to make a fast buck. Smuggling pays very well. Depending on the trip, pilots could easily make a half million dollars cash."

"How do you know so much about airplanes?" Donovan asked.

"Since nine eleven, the FBI takes a great interest in stolen aircraft." Montero brushed a stray lock of hair back behind her ear. "This isn't my first dance, Mr. Nash."

"So, what do you think happened tonight?"

"In the past, jets were involved in a different caliber of theft than typical drug traffic. As you know, not just any weekend pilot can jump in and fly a jet, so right off the bat we can eliminate almost ninety percent of the licensed pilots in the country. The most recent jet thefts in this country have involved alcohol, disgruntled pilots, and even a few who take off with the company jet to avoid being arrested for other crimes. They change the registration number and then attempt to sell the plane in South America, Central America, or some other offshore location. We usually locate the airplane later when the new owner takes it someplace for maintenance. But this particular theft does raise some eyebrows."

"In what way?"

"It was premeditated. Whoever took the plane was watching the airport. They waited for the perfect set of conditions. It was dark; Boca Raton has no commercial air traffic, so the security is nothing more than a chain-link fence with a little barbed wire along the top. The chaos of the weather made it easy."

"They took an airplane that had been fueled. They'd been watching who fueled and who didn't. Or they had access to that information. Could it have been an inside job, someone who works at Boca Raton Aviation?" Donovan asked as he began to consider the details.

"We're looking at that already," Montero said. "My guess is in a week or so this airplane will be found at a remote airfield in Mexico or the Bahamas—or we'll get a call from a legitimate repair shop somewhere in South America where someone has matched up some serial numbers to a stolen aircraft watch list."

"So this sounds like drug traffickers to you?"

Montero's phone rang again. She glanced briefly at the incoming number and answered. She had a brief exchange with someone and moments later hung up. "Detective Turner, someone from my office is faxing over some information. Could you go find it and bring it to me, please?"

Donovan watched as Turner excused himself. Montero eyed him warily, as if she were sizing him up for the first time. Whatever was going on, this felt more like an interrogation as opposed to a simple statement. What he wanted was to get out of here, but he also wanted to collect as much information as possible, because the moment everyone close to him was safe, he was going after the people who'd done this to Michael.

The door opened and Turner let himself back in and handed a

folder to Montero. The detective took his seat, once again well out of the line of fire—this was clearly Montero's deal.

Donovan waited as Montero skimmed through the paperwork. Over the years, he'd honed his people skills against the best and the brightest big business and politics had to offer. He watched as Montero read the first two pages and set them aside. His carefully altered history should stand up to Montero's investigation, but there was always the threat that a loose piece of thread, no matter how small, could unravel everything if it was pulled hard enough.

As Montero flipped to the next page Donovan saw a brief flash of what could best be described as surprise. Her eyes widened and a sudden rush of color rose up her neck. She looked up from the paper and studied him, then down again. Donovan watched her intently and realized that she wasn't reading, her eyes weren't going left to right: she was thinking, processing—or comparing something. She glanced up one more time, then, as if immensely pleased with herself, slid her chair back. Something had piqued her interest and Donovan couldn't help but feel like the stakes had escalated.

"You know what? I think we're finished here. You can go now, Mr. Nash," Montero said. "I think I have what I need."

Donovan was instantly suspicious of her sudden shift of demeanor. He stood before Montero could slide the papers inside her folder and managed to see what she'd been looking at. The top sheet held six photos—mug shots. At the sight of the photo on the upper-right corner, he was forced to use every ounce of his self-control to remain passive. The photo was of Robert Huntington—the man Donovan used to be. He saw the word "deceased" stamped across the top. Montero closed the folder, snatched the recorder, and their eyes met. She tipped her head slightly and strode from the room.

"I guess that's it, Mr. Nash. We're almost finished." Turner stood. "Wait here while I get someone to type up your statement, and then I'll need you to sign it for me."

Donovan nodded absently and tried to gather his thoughts, put everything into perspective. His heart sank when he remembered the flashlight; it had no doubt been logged into evidence and dusted for prints. They'd run what was probably a partial print and gotten multiple hits. He tried to imagine what Montero was thinking. Surely she'd dismiss Robert Huntington as belonging to the print. How could she possibly think for a moment that a dead man had left a fresh fingerprint at a crime scene?

Since the mug shot had been taken, he'd aged nearly twenty-five years and undergone months of facial reconstructive surgery. He'd changed his name, and possessed not only a complete new identity, but a carefully thought out past as well. With nearly unlimited financial resources at his disposal, it was as perfect as it could be. He'd never seen any reason to bother altering his fingerprints. But once, a long time ago, he'd been arrested and fingerprinted.

As with most memories involving Meredith, he could remember it like it was yesterday. The images never dulled or faded with time. In fact, they seemed to expand and sharpen in his mind. Details he wished he could forget were but a thought away.

It was a Friday afternoon when they raced north out of Los Angeles in his meticulously restored 1961 Ferrari 250 GT. The gleaming red convertible was the latest addition to his car collection, the special roar from the V-12 engine brought a smile to his face each time he pushed the gas pedal. She'd insisted that they both needed to get away and a road trip would be a perfect way to unwind. Once they were out of the city they picked up the Pacific Coast Highway and headed north. Meredith loved the speed and the adventure and egged him on. Donovan could easily picture the scene. They roared down the breathtaking ribbon of highway with the top down, her auburn hair whipping in the wind as she raised her hands into the slipstream and let out a yell of pure joy.

A city limit sign flashed past, and before he could slow down, he was clocked going sixty miles an hour over the speed limit. The police immediately arrested him and threw him in jail. Meredith was a different story; they recognized her and she was treated like visiting royalty. She'd signed autographs while Donovan sat in a cell. It had taken a few hours before she'd been able to secure his release, but the damage had been done.

Whatever joy his memories of Meredith brought him was always short lived. As usual, he paid for his visits with the inevitable countdown toward her murder. Their trip in the Ferrari took place six months before she was murdered. The contrast of her happiness on the wind-whipped Pacific Coast Highway, followed by the image her broken body in a field in Costa Rica, was the price he paid for remembering.

CHAPTER SEVEN

They were the only people in the small intensive care waiting room. Lauren sat between Susan and William, waiting for word about Michael. All three kids were dozing. Susan was a wreck, and conversation ground to a halt as they fell into their own silent worrying.

Lauren turned her cell phone over and over in her hand. She kept touching the display, as if willing Donovan to call.

They'd landed over an hour ago and she'd expected him to be waiting when they'd gotten off the chartered plane. Instead, the police told her that he'd been taken to the station to make a formal statement. William had arranged a limo to whisk them to the hospital, so there had been very little time to ask the police more. Each time she tried to call Donovan, his phone had gone straight to voice mail.

"Excuse me."

Lauren, lost in her thoughts of Donovan, was momentarily startled. She looked up and found a woman standing in the doorway. She was tall, her straight blonde hair tied in a ponytail.

"Can I help you?"

"I'm FBI Special Agent Montero." She flashed her credentials. "I'm looking for Mrs. Susan Ross."

"I'm Mrs. Ross," Susan said, rising to her feet.

"Mrs. Ross, I know this is a difficult time. But I need to ask you some questions."

"Okay," Susan replied.

"In private," Montero added.

"I need to stay here. In case the doctor shows up with news about my husband."

"I understand. Is everyone here with you?" Montero said as she looked around the room.

"Yes," Lauren replied. "We all flew down as soon as we heard what happened."

"Your name, please?" Montero asked.

"I'm Dr. Lauren McKenna."

Montero turned to face William. "And you are?"

"William VanGelder."

Lauren saw Montero's eyes flare momentarily. She wasn't sure exactly why Montero had reacted to William's name, but something had registered. There was another voice behind Montero and two people, both wearing scrubs, came into the waiting room.

"Hello. I'm Dr. Richardson." He waited until he had everyone's attention. "Is everyone here part of the Ross family?"

"Everyone except me, I'm Special Agent Montero, FBI. Do you have news?"

"Yes. Mr. Ross is doing very well. He came through surgery without any major problems. All things considered, he's a lucky man. The bullet was most likely from a small-caliber handgun. Fortunately, the bullet's angle was such that it didn't penetrate his skull; instead, it glanced off, slowed down, and then traveled under the skin and lodged in his neck near the cervical spine. When we got in there to retrieve the bullet, we discovered tissue damage, but no permanent injury. We're watching closely for any further brain swelling, but I think we've seen the worst. He's in the recovery room right now. We're still being cautious and we'll know more in the next twelve to twenty-four hours."

"I'm his wife. When can I see him?" Susan asked, brushing away tears of joy and relief.

"The nurse will be happy to take you now. But I'm afraid the rest of you will have to wait."

"I'll stay here with the boys," Lauren said to Susan. "Take all the time you need."

"Right this way," the nurse said, ushering Susan from the room.

"Doctor, how long do you think it might be until Mr. Ross will be able to give a statement?" Montero asked. "Will he be able to remember the attack?"

"That depends on Mr. Ross," Richardson replied. "In about half of these cases there will be no memory of the actual traumatic event. It can be days or even months before small memories begin to bubble into the conscious mind. There could also be varying degrees of partial amnesia, meaning that the memory loss before the injury could reach back from several hours to several days. We'll know much more when Mr. Ross regains consciousness."

"Thank you," Montero said, and abruptly left the room.

"Doctor, before you go," William said, "when can we take him home?"

"This is a serious injury, and there are still some risks. I'm afraid he'll be with us for several days. I'll be making rounds later today to check on his progress. After that we'll be able to make a further assessment."

"Thank you so much," Lauren said as the doctor excused himself.

"My guess is that FBI agent is headed for Susan," William said. "If you're going to be okay here for a little while, I'm going to go after her. Susan doesn't need to be interrogated right now."

"Go." Lauren nodded in agreement. She sat down on the sofa next to Abigail. Patrick and Billy were sleeping on an adjacent couch. Lauren cradled her child's head in her hands and offered up a silent prayer of thanks that Michael was going to live.

Her cell phone rang and when she saw it was Donovan, she felt both immeasurable relief that he'd finally called, as well as a flash of irritation that it had taken so long.

"Where are you?" Lauren shot up from the sofa and hovered in the doorway so she could talk to Donovan without disturbing the sleeping kids.

"I've been at the police station giving my statement. Have you talked to Susan or William? I'm assuming they've made it to the hospital by now. Do we know anything about Michael?"

"I'm with them here at the hospital. Michael just came out of surgery. The doctor said everything went well and that he should be fine."

"You're here in Florida?"

"I had to come. I couldn't just sit at home and wait."

"I understand."

"What's wrong?" Lauren could hear the tension in his voice.

"I just hadn't expected you to be here in Florida, I had it in my mind you were at home. We may have a problem," Donovan lowered his voice to just above a whisper. "You need to ask William if he kept the chartered jet on standby."

"He stepped out. An FBI agent was here a little bit ago wanting to talk to Susan. William went after her to try and run some interference."

"Special Agent Montero."

"You know her?"

"She's our problem. She may have put some things together. We may need to start thinking about going to visit Stephanie."

Lauren stiffened. Stephanie was William's niece and one of the few who knew the truth about Donovan. There had been many discussions about what they'd do if his identity were going to be made public. The first phase had always been to leave the country and get to Stephanie's flat in London. From London, they'd make their way to a secluded chateau in Switzerland to try and ride out the initial wave of public condemnation. The agreed upon code was: *go visit Stephanie*.

"How could this have happened?" Lauren replied, angry and scared. "What makes you think she could possibly know? Is she someone who knew you from before?"

"They lifted fingerprints. Robert's mug shot was right in front of her. It's just a gut feeling, but I think she suspects."

Lauren had no idea that Robert Huntington had a police record or that Donovan had done nothing to alter his fingerprints. She wondered if that was why the FBI agent had such a curious reaction at meeting William.

"Are you still there?" Donovan asked.

"How soon?" Lauren said with more anger than she intended. Lauren looked across the room at her daughter and felt sick, like all of the dreams she'd held for Abigail had just been put in jeopardy.

"As early as this afternoon," Donovan replied. "I'll be there as fast as I can and we'll talk."

"I'll be here." Lauren ended the call and then thrust the phone into her pocket and went to Abigail. She gathered her daughter in her arms, feeling the need to hold and protect her. Abigail stirred and pursed her lips, then she turned her head to the side and drifted back to sleep. Lauren gently rocked her back and forth. From the moment Donovan had confided his secret, they'd both been resolute about one thing—that at all costs, Abigail would be protected.

Lauren felt an overwhelming sadness, not for herself, or even her daughter, she'd always promised herself that she would do whatever it took for her and Abigail to survive. At this moment she was far more worried about her husband. She couldn't in all honesty convince herself that Donovan would be okay if in the next few hours everything he'd built over the last twenty years dissolved.

CHAPTER EIGHT

In the short cab ride from the police station to the hospital, Donovan saw dozens of trees uprooted, branches strewn everywhere, grim testament to the severity of the storms that had ripped through the area the night before. The Boca Raton Community Hospital was tucked off the main road amongst mature trees and well-manicured grounds. As they wheeled up to the entrance, his cell phone rang. Donovan saw that the call was from Eco-Watch's headquarters in Virginia.

"Hello, Peggy," he answered as he peeled off some bills for the driver and stepped out of the cab.

"What in the hell happened down there last night? Are you okay? I just heard from our liaison at NASA that you cancelled the mission and that Michael is in the hospital?"

"Peggy, slow down. I was going to call you shortly." Donovan backpedaled, he knew he should have called her earlier. Peggy had been with Eco-Watch from the beginning and thought of all the pilots as her children who needed looking after. She was his administrative assistant as well as aircraft dispatcher. Ruthlessly efficient, Donovan couldn't imagine what he'd do without her. He started at the beginning and brought her up to date.

"What can I do?" Peggy asked, satisfied she had the facts.

"I need you to talk to the people at Gulfstream, I want them to send a maintenance team to Boca Raton and inspect the *da Vinci*. I want it airworthy as soon as possible."

"What about a pilot? Randy and Nicolas are still in Alaska with the *Galileo*, you want me to send Kyle down to take Michael's place?"

"Yeah, why don't you. I'll need him at some point. Tell him I'd like him to work with Gulfstream and oversee the maintenance. We'll also need to coordinate with NASA to ensure that the imaging equipment is repaired."

"Anything else?"

"Can you also get us three rooms down here for tonight? Book a room for Lauren and me, we'll need a crib. Then get a suite for William and a suite for Susan and the boys. Maybe a couple of rental cars could be delivered to the hotel."

"I'm on it," Peggy replied. "I'll text you the details when I have them. Tell everyone my thoughts and prayers are with them."

"I will, and thanks." Donovan hung up and walked toward the main entrance, intensely aware that Montero was probably somewhere in the building. He had no idea what the next move was, but he knew without a doubt that it was Montero's, and all he could do was wait and react. Donovan pushed into the air-conditioned lobby and went straight toward the information desk.

"Excuse me. Where can I find Michael Ross?"

She typed into her computer. "He's just been moved from the recovery room to the Secondary Care Unit. Third floor, east wing."

Donovan avoided the small crowd of people waiting at the elevator and opted for the stairs. He took them two at a time until he stepped out onto the highly polished hallway of the third floor. Donovan walked to a nurses' station, which was strategically located at the intersection of three corridors. The enclosure was fairly large, there looked to be work areas for at least five or six people. One section held an array of monitors, full-size color screens that were filled with graphs and numbers. A single nurse positioned in front of the readouts was writing in a chart.

"Excuse me, I'm looking for Michael Ross."

"They just got him settled." She pointed over her shoulder down the hallway to his left. "Room 310."

Donovan walked down the hallway and gently opened the door. Michael was asleep on the narrow bed, his head slightly elevated. His arms were exposed and placed at his side, the sheet was pulled halfway up his chest. Michael's head was wrapped as if he wore a white gauze stocking cap; his usually tanned face seemed drained of color. A bundle of wires snaked out from under the blanket and connected to a stack of machines. Donovan was mildly surprised that Susan or Lauren wasn't in the room, but there was no reason to go look for them. They'd show up soon enough.

Donovan moved closer, his eyes went to the screen displaying his friend's heartbeat; the constantly moving line rose and fell as it streamed across the monitor. He spotted the abrasions on Michael's right hand. Montero had been right. Michael had gotten in at least one good punch before being shot. He pulled a chair closer to the bed and sat, feeling his fatigue.

"I'm sorry I wasn't out there with you." Donovan stared at the monitor, as if his words would suddenly register as a blip on the screen, give him some inkling Michael was aware of him. But pulse, respiration, and blood pressure remained constant. Donovan felt helpless. He had the means at his disposal to make nearly anything happen, but he couldn't fix this, he couldn't buy his way out of this regardless of how he felt. He hated seeing Michael this way, hated being unable to do anything but sit and watch.

"Look, I know you saw who did this. I tried to get to you in time. If I had, maybe the two of us would have made a difference. Maybe he'd be lying here instead of you. I need to know what happened out there last night. What did you see? This thing has gotten real complicated." Donovan couldn't help but think about all the secrets he'd kept from his friends, and how he never wanted to be in put in the position of having to explain all the lies. "It's all my fault, everything happened years ago, but Lauren and Abigail are going to pay the price if things go wrong—hell, we're all going to pay a price. If we knew what you saw, then maybe a certain FBI agent would go away and bother someone else."

Donovan sat for a while and collected his thoughts. Since he met her all those years ago, Meredith was the one he measured the rights and wrongs against. But since he'd met Lauren, the torch had been passed. Lauren now held those scales. Yet, over the last few weeks he couldn't stop thinking about Meredith. Seeing the movie, hearing her voice again, seeing her dead body, everything had welled up inside of him until she somehow seemed very close again.

When Meredith was still alive, he'd always known that being Robert Huntington was at times a burden, a double-edged sword that had ended up owning him in ways he never understood. She'd shown him ways to find a sort of tranquility and freedom, to feel what he'd never discovered for himself. Robert Huntington had enjoyed unbridled privilege, but it wasn't until he met Meredith that he became aware of a different path. As Donovan Nash, he'd continued looking for the elusive contentment that Meredith had shown him, but he'd only drifted even farther away from his goal. All he'd found was a compromise, something he could only describe as a delicate state of negotiated peace, and all of that would vanish in an instant if the world found out Robert Huntington was still alive. The condemnation would be quick and certain. He'd deceived the entire world twenty years ago and lied to everyone he'd met since. It was a risk he'd taken. The price for failure would be the loss of anything he'd built as Donovan Nash.

He pushed himself up out of the chair, unable to sit still any longer. The fact that Montero might be peeling away the layers of his life while he sat doing nothing was pure torture. Thoughts of what would happen if he lost Michael or Lauren or any of his other stabilizing influences began to work away at him, and he was surprised to find himself wanting a drink. He buried that thought; it was only eight o'clock in the morning.

His eyes burned and he could feel the full effects of having gotten so little sleep. He blinked hard at the grit that seemed to be grinding away at his vision. Donovan went to the small bathroom, closed the door behind him, and stood in front of the mirror while the water ran. He winced at his reflection. The lines on his face all seemed to lead straight to his bloodshot eyes. He cupped his hands under the cold water and then pressed his hands to his face as if he could rinse away the exhaustion. He switched from cold to hot water but the fatigue was still irrevocably stamped on his face.

The instant he emerged from the bathroom, Donovan took in all the things that were wrong. The startled expression on the stranger's face, the fact that his scrubs fit poorly, that his shoes were dirty. There was also no lanyard around his neck, no official ID. Donovan's eyes flashed to Michael. The pillow beneath his head had been pulled out and hung in the man's left hand.

Donovan saw the dark shape of a silenced pistol as he started toward the man. In the moment it took the assassin to point the gun toward him, Donovan had covered the distance. Moving fast, he grabbed the assailant's wrist with one hand and used his shoulder to slam him into the wall as hard as he could. Donovan heard the quiet cough of the gun as it went off over his shoulder. Still pinned up against the wall, Donovan kneed the intruder in the midsection.

The man recovered quickly and swung an elbow. Donovan avoided the full force of the blow, but caught part of it off the side of his head. Donovan kept a death grip on the man's wrist and ducked as another wild swing passed over his head. Once again, Donovan slammed his knee upward into the man's stomach, doubling him over, then bent the gunman's wrist backward until he felt it snap and heard the pistol clatter to the floor. The assassin grunted in pain, then swung his leg and took Donovan's feet out from under him.

Donovan tried to break his fall, but he careened backward and crashed hard against the bedside table losing his grip on the intruder. The assassin, holding his broken wrist, kicked Donovan in the stomach. He felt the pain as the air rushed from his lungs. He rolled out of the way away just as a second kick grazed his ribs.

Donovan scrambled to his feet. He turned to rush his attacker and stopped—the barrel of the gun was pointed straight at his forehead. His eyes traveled past the black tube of the barrel and locked onto the man's face. The assassin was breathing heavily, the man's dark eyes flared with a mixture of pain and fury. Donovan knew at that moment he'd lost.

"Federal agent!" Montero yelled from the doorway at the same time she pulled the trigger on her Glock.

Donovan recoiled as the side of the assassin's head dissolved into a red mist that splattered the ceiling and wall. Donovan saw the man's eyes go dead and sightless as he began to collapse. The pistol fell from his hand, his knees buckled, and he crumpled straight down like an imploded building.

Montero kicked away the silenced weapon and then leaned over the body, her Glock poised to fire again.

"Are you all right?" she said to Donovan without looking at him.

The heavy smell of gunpowder filled the room. Behind Montero, two other agents rushed through the doorway. Montero began issuing orders to shut down the hospital. She wanted everyone who tried to leave the premises searched for weapons in case the assassin wasn't alone. Donovan stepped away from the carnage. He went to Michael and searched for any sign that his friend had been injured. A quick inspection found blood spatter on the sheet, but it wasn't Michael's.

Montero holstered her pistol and then dug in the pocket of her blazer. She produced a latex glove and snapped it over her hand. She leaned down and turned the gunman's head to get a good look at his face. She swore under her breath, whipped out her cell phone, and dialed. As she waited for an answer, she raised an eyebrow at Donovan. "Are you still wishing I'd go away and bother someone else?"

CHAPTER NINE

Donovan's ribcage throbbed from where he'd been kicked. The would-be assassin lay in a pool of blood. FBI and hospital personnel were running in and out as they followed Montero's orders to set up a perimeter in the hallway. He glared at Montero as her words began to seep through his fear at having nearly been killed. His fury grew exponentially as it became clear what she'd done. He pushed away from the wall and stood directly in front of her.

"You used the room's intercom system to listen in on me. You knew someone might try this, didn't you?"

Montero hardly made eye contact with him as she surveyed the work being done to move Michael to another room without disturbing the corpse on the floor. "I'm going to need you to get out of my way for now. But don't leave the area."

"You almost got him killed. As far as I'm concerned, we're finished."

Montero straightened and her jaw tightened. "You and I aren't finished, and don't even dream of leaving Florida, let alone this hospital, until I say you can. Now, go wait in the lounge until I have time to talk to you one-on-one."

Donovan stormed out of the room, pushing through the security detail that had cordoned off the hallway. He found an empty waiting area, dug out his cell phone, and dialed.

"William, it's me. Where are you?"

"I'm in the main lobby waiting for an elevator. Lauren just found me and told me you were on your way here."

"Is she still with you?"

"They're moving Michael to a room. Susan took the boys to the cafeteria. Lauren went to find them. We're all going to meet on Michael's floor shortly. Why, what's going on?"

"Someone just tried to kill Michael—and me in the process."

"Are you okay? Is Michael all right? Tell me exactly what happened."

"Everyone's fine. I'll fill you in later. I want to fly everyone out of here as soon as possible. Call Peggy and see what she can do about getting a medevac flight and crew to take Michael home."

"I'll take care of it."

"How much has Lauren been able to tell you about what else is going on?"

"She whispered to me that the three of us needed to talk. What's going on?"

"An FBI agent may have started to put some things together. Is the airplane you flew down here still available? We might need to go visit Stephanie."

"Are you sure? Is this agent a blonde woman named Montero? I met her; she didn't come across as much more than a pushy Fed. How could she possibly know anything?"

"I might be wrong, but a partial fingerprint led her to an old mug shot taken in California. I have a bad feeling this whole thing is about to break wide open. Right now I need to talk to a doctor and find out exactly what Michael needs to make a safe trip home. Then we're out of here, even if I have to buy the whole damned hospital to do it."

"We need to arrange some kind of private security we can trust," William said. "I don't think we should leave Michael unprotected for a second."

"I like that idea. Do you remember that Navy SEAL, Howard Buckley? I met him during Hurricane Helena. He's a good man. I think he'd be the place to start."

"If I remember correctly, he was connected with General Porter from the Joint Chiefs," William said. "I'll have someone in my office track him down. Do you want me to talk to him, or should I have him call you directly?"

"Have him call me." From where he was sitting, Donovan could see more and more cops walking up and down the hallway. "I think it might be a good idea for you to take care of all of our plans before you come up here. The place is crawling with police right now."

"I understand. I'm also going to call someone I know at the Fairfax County Hospital. We'll plan on taking him there," William said. "I'll make the arrangements."

"Thanks." Donovan ended the call, made his way through the growing crowd, and went to the nurses' station.

"Can I help you?" A nurse asked as she looked up.

"I need the neurosurgeon that did the operation on Mr. Ross up here as soon as possible."

She pulled a clipboard closer and ran down the list of names. "I'm not sure if Dr. Richardson is still on call."

"After what just happened, I suggest you find him."

The nurse pursed her lips as she nodded. Without further comment, she reached for a phone. Donovan didn't stay to listen; he suspected the doctor would show up soon enough. He snaked his way through the small army of FBI agents. He avoided the room where the gunman lay dead and instead turned into a room across the hallway. Michael lay in his bed, the only difference from before was the armed FBI agent next to him.

Donovan ignored the agent and went to Michael's side. He studied the monitor, and then his friend's face, looking for the slightest change in Michael's condition.

Montero stuck her head into the room. "If you need any medical attention, go down and get examined in the ER."

Donovan turned at the sound of her voice, his eyes burned with anger. "Where in the hell were you? Where was security? Why didn't you intercept that guy until he was in the room and started shooting?"

"I'm not going to discuss tactics with you."

"Because it was illegal or because it was stupid and irresponsible?"

"It was neither. There was some confusion on the part of hospital security. Simple mistake, really."

"Yeah, I bet. Want to try and explain the intercom? Was it fun listening in on my conversation?"

"It was an accident. Someone must have inadvertently pushed the button. I'm told it happens all the time. Good thing I happened by."

"You're quite the hero. I want to talk to your supervisor. Who's in charge of the FBI here in South Florida?"

"The special agent in charge is Hamilton Burgess," Montero said. "He'll be here any minute."

They both heard a commotion in the hallway, and Donovan stepped out of the door behind Montero just in time to see the collection of people in the hallway part as if they were the Red Sea and Moses had just arrived. Dressed in a dark suit and tie, a short wiry man with narrow, pinched features was walking toward them with purpose. His blond hair was so thin that his face and scalp both burned the same bright red. Donovan thought the man looked like he was about to explode.

Donovan watched with interest as the man pushed past Montero and stepped into the room across the hall.

The man blew out of the room moments later and turned to face Montero, his jaw muscles worked back and forth in what appeared to be a mixture of anger and frustration. He shook his head, and then turned toward Donovan as if seeing him for the first time. "Who are you? Why are you here?"

"I'm Donovan Nash. Who are you?"

"I'm Hamilton Burgess."

"Sir, I was just about to escort Mr. Nash down to the emergency room to be examined," Montero said.

"I'm fine," Donovan said.

"Special Agent Montero," Burgess said, "you're done here.

You've been involved in a shooting. You know the drill. I'm placing you on administrative leave, pending the outcome of the investigation."

Montero lowered her voice. "I recognized the guy in there. He's one of the people who may have been responsible for Alec's death. He's not even supposed to be in the country. Our intelligence sources place him in Venezuela. We need to find out why he's here and why he tried to kill Mr. Ross."

"Please, no more talk." Burgess held up his hand. "You know how this works. The Inspection Division will conduct its investigation. You'll cooperate fully with them. Once you give them your statement, go back to the office, finish the paperwork, then go home. No argument. You'll hear from me when the shooting review board schedules the hearing."

Montero pivoted smartly and walked away, and then she stopped, turned, and said, "Nash is clean. You can let him go."

Donovan turned to Burgess after Montero was gone. "Just for the record, I'm not amused with what's taken place here today. Your agency, your agent, put a man at risk."

"You'll get your chance to make a statement," Burgess replied.

"As soon as we can get clearance from the doctor to move Mr. Ross, we're out of here."

"Feel free to do what you need to do, I can't stop you. Where do you intend to take him?" Burgess asked.

"We're flying him to Washington, D.C."

"Officially, he's a key witness to a felony, but under the circumstances I have no problem with a transfer as long as you agree to cooperate with our Washington office. I'll arrange for someone to follow up and take a statement from Mr. Ross when he's conscious. Can I get your assurances on that point?"

Donovan nodded. "Can you make sure Michael is protected until all of our arrangements are made?"

"It's already done," Burgess replied. "But before you go, I want to tell you that I'm not making apologies for Special Agent

Montero or my department. She's a good agent. I wish I had ten more just like her. You can file whatever complaint you want, but keep in mind what the end result was here today."

Relieved that Burgess didn't try to stop him, Donovan hurried back to the nurses' station. The nurse he'd spoken with earlier assured him that they'd found Dr. Richardson and that he was on his way up. Relieved that he seemed to making some progress, Donovan was standing there when the elevator opened and out stepped Lauren, Susan, and the kids. They all stopped at the sight of the activity in what they fully expected to be a quiet wing of the hospital.

Donovan worked his way in their direction.

"What's going on?" Susan asked, holding her boys close. "They almost wouldn't let us up here."

Lauren held a sleeping Abigail. Donovan hugged Susan and shook the boys' hands. Then he took his daughter from Lauren. Abigail stirred briefly but continued to sleep, and Donovan reveled in how good it felt to hold his little girl. He'd missed her. In fact, it was good to see familiar faces, but he hated the deep concern etched in everyone's eyes.

"Where's William?" Lauren asked.

"I just spoke with him," Donovan replied. "He said he'd meet us back here in a little while."

"Donovan, what's going on?" Susan asked again, her patience quickly evaporating.

"The FBI stopped someone who they think was trying to get to Michael. Nothing happened, Michael's fine." Susan's eyes flew wide then she set her jaw and stepped forward as if getting ready to bolt for her husband's room. "Hold on, they stepped up security for the time being. The good news is the doctor is on the way, and I'm hoping he'll give us the go ahead to take Michael home later today. Once we have the go ahead, we'll put everything into motion."

"Why is the FBI involved in this? Some FBI agent started asking me questions about you and Michael. She kept asking me how long I'd known you and William, and how long you and William had been associates. When William finally showed up, she asked him the same questions. When William asked her why she needed to know, she excused herself. It was strange."

"Don't worry about her—she's just doing her job," Donovan said. He gave the whole episode a dismissive shrug, but inside, his internal alarms were going off. Lauren, too, made the same observation and shot Donovan a momentary look that spoke volumes. Montero was digging, trying to make a connection that stretched back twenty years.

A nurse stuck her head above the counter at the nurses' station. "Mr. Nash, Dr. Richardson just arrived and is in with Mr. Ross."

"Thank you." Donovan gently handed Abigail back to Lauren. "Susan, let's go see what the doctor has to say."

"Boys, I'll be right back." Susan said.

"We want to come," Patrick said.

"Not this time," Susan said. "Donovan and I need to talk to the doctor first. Afterward, you can see your dad."

"We'll be good," Billy pleaded.

"I know you will, sweetie. I'll be right back." Susan followed Donovan's lead.

Once they were halfway down the corridor, Susan put her hand out and stopped him. "Tell me what in the hell happened while we were gone, and I mean everything!"

"I didn't want to say anything in front of the boys. Someone tried to shoot Michael, someone connected to what happened last night."

Her eyes filled with tears of disbelief as what Donovan was telling her registered. "Someone tried to kill him? Here?"

Donovan nodded.

"Oh my God." Her hand flew to her mouth. "Did they catch the guy?"

"Yeah, they got him."

Susan shook her head in anger and disbelief as she hurried to be with her husband. A nurse was waiting at the door to steer them into the room, but not before Susan took a peek into the room across the hall. The body was still there, and Susan stopped abruptly and turned toward Donovan. "Were you with him when it happened?"

"I slowed the guy down long enough for the FBI to arrive. They did the rest."

Donovan eased Susan forward, moving her into her husband's room.

"Doctor," Susan went to Michael's side and placed his hand inside hers, "is my husband okay, can we take him home?"

"As far as I can tell it appears he suffered no ill effects from the earlier incident. But it's far too soon to think about releasing him."

Donovan stepped into the conversation. "Doctor, it's now in Michael's best interest to be transported back to Virginia as soon as possible. His safety, as well as everyone else's, is in jeopardy here. Is he physically able to make the trip?"

"That depends on several factors," Richardson replied. "How would this transport be made?"

"Chartered jet."

"What facility are you transferring him to?"

"A level one trauma center in Virginia—the flight time from here to there would be around two hours," Donovan said, not wanting to divulge any more information than was necessary.

"I'd not recommend it—not for another twenty-four hours. That said, if his safety is in question, it could be done under the correct supervisory care." Richardson rubbed his chin as he thought. "There are a few medevac services around that can facilitate the type of transport he'd need. I'm talking a fully equipped medical transport aircraft staffed with the appropriate personnel."

"We're in the process of making those arrangements," Donovan said. "But before you go, after what happened earlier, I'd like this conversation to stay between us. Let's don't advertise to anyone what we're doing or where we're going."

"I understand." Richardson nodded. "I'll fill out the release and transfer paperwork leaving the destination blank. It'll be at the nurses' station when you're ready to leave."

"Thank you, Doctor," Susan said. "Do you think we can we get Michael somewhere where his boys can see him, without having to be in this particular hallway?"

"Of course. I'm sure there's an empty room in a different corridor," the doctor said. "I'll see to it right away."

Donovan's cell phone sounded. He looked at the caller ID and saw a 212 area code. He stepped toward the window before he answered.

"Donovan Nash."

"Mr. Nash. Howard Buckley here, it's been a while."

"Buck, good to hear from you, thanks for getting back to me so quickly."

"Well, your little group there at Eco-Watch does seem to have some pull. General Porter just called and asked me to give you a ring. He wanted me to render whatever assistance you need. What's up?"

"How much did General Porter tell you?"

"Only that you're flying Michael Ross in from Florida, where I'm told he's been shot."

"Yeah, that was yesterday. Another attempt was made on his life in the hospital today. He's not in great shape, but the doctors said he could be transported. We should land at Dulles airport by late this afternoon. We're taking him to Fairfax County Hospital. I'd feel better if he were being protected by people I know and trust."

"Consider it done," Buck replied. "I'll personally meet you at the Eco-Watch hangar. I'll need an ETA and the tail number of the charter. Plus full access to Eco-Watch as well as the Ross residence."

"I'll make those arrangements. There'll be two aircraft. A dedicated medevac flight with Michael and his family aboard. They're your primary responsibility. There will also be a second chartered aircraft for myself and my family."

"Do you need to be under this protective umbrella as well?"

"Yeah, but Michael and his family are the priority."

"Got it, but it's going to be expensive," Buck added. "The men I have in mind are all former SEALs. I trust them with my life, but the best doesn't come cheap."

"Do whatever needs to be done." Donovan truly liked this man. He was a no-nonsense, results-oriented professional. "Money is no object—whatever it takes."

"I look forward to seeing you again, Mr. Nash. Thanks for thinking of me. I'll be standing by for the information I need."

"You'll either hear from me or my assistant, Peggy, within the hour."

"I'll be ready at this end," Buck said and severed the connection.

"Donovan!" Susan said the moment Donovan pocketed his phone. "What are you thinking? I doubt our health insurance will pick up the tab for chartered planes and private security."

Donovan wrapped his arm around her shoulder to comfort her, secure in the knowledge that a myriad of problems went away if you threw enough money at them. "Don't worry. William does have that kind of money. He told me to do whatever it takes, and that's exactly what we're doing."

CHAPTER TEN

With a police escort leading the way, both the ambulance with Michael and his family and Donovan's limousine with Lauren, Abigail, and William were waved through the airport perimeter gate. Donovan felt relieved when he saw both chartered jets. The preparations had taken longer than Donovan had expected, plus he'd gotten hung up giving his statement to the FBI about the shooting. As angry as he was about what Montero had done, he decided the last thing he needed to do was get into a pissing match with the FBI. He also had no real proof of her eavesdropping, and the end result was she'd saved both his and Michael's lives. With that behind him, he'd rounded everyone up and they'd finally gotten free of the hospital. Once they got Michael loaded aboard the air ambulance, he could start putting some distance between himself and Special Agent Montero.

It seemed like days since he and Michael had landed in Boca Raton, but it hadn't even been twenty-four hours. In a hangar across the ramp Donovan spotted the *Spirit of da Vinci*. Donovan resisted the temptation to go over and inquire about its status. Kyle was on his way down, and he'd get a full report soon enough.

The procession was escorted out to the waiting jets by airport police, and Michael was very carefully transferred aboard the Learjet 60. The medical flight team, which consisted of a doctor and trauma nurse, transferred Michael's electrical leads and IV tubes to the monitoring equipment inside the plane. According to Peggy, this was the most well-equipped, highly recommended medevac service on the East Coast. Michael would be in excellent hands.

Once Michael was stabilized, Susan and the boys said goodbye and were shown their seats in the front of the jet. Donovan waved as the door was closed and he made his way to the Gulfstream that William had reserved for their trip.

Donovan went up the stairs and ducked inside the opulent cabin. He put his hand on the cool marble of the galley countertop. He studied the grain in the highly polished wood and marveled at the difference between this Gulfstream and his own. The Eco-Watch jets, while similar on the outside, were worlds apart inside. This aircraft had the same forty-five-foot cabin, but unlike the Eco-Watch Gulfstream, this jet featured leather seats, deep carpets, and gold-plated fixtures as plush as any boardroom in the world. Lauren and Abigail, with assistance from the flight attendant, were getting situated. He wasn't sure where William had gone.

Donovan pulled out his cell phone. He needed to make one quick phone call before they got underway. Donovan dialed Eco-Watch's direct line, and Peggy picked up on the second ring.

"Peggy, it's me."

"How's Michael doing? Are you about to leave?"

"He's the same. They're taxiing out now. We should be wheels up shortly. I've already texted Buck with the ETA for Michael's flight."

"Buck and I've spoken a number of times in the last hour. He's assured me he's all set."

"Good work. Hey, we also discovered that Michael's keys, wallet, and cell phone are missing. Don't do anything about the phone, or the credit cards, the authorities think maybe someone will be stupid enough to try and use them. I do, however, want us to get all the locks changed at Michael's house. Get the best locksmith you can find and have everything billed to Eco-Watch."

"I'll take care of it."

"One more thing, I need you to contact Captain Pittman on the *Atlantic Titan*. We had the ship and crew blocked out for two weeks to be our eyes on the surface as we flew this latest NASA mission. With *da Vinci* out of service, and the control module for the new high-resolution camera a smoking chunk of metal, we need to reschedule everything. Do you know the *Titan*'s current position?"

"They just checked in with me not twenty minutes ago. The *Atlantic Titan* is currently southeast of Jamaica, heading up through the Windward Passage between Cuba and Haiti. They said they may be delayed by some heavy weather moving in from the northwest."

"That's the line of weather we had here last night. Tell him no hurry. When he can steam north, we'll make a decision. He can think about delaying in Key West or Miami."

"I'll pass along the message. Anything else?"

Donovan spotted William walking briskly out of the passenger lounge, a sheaf of papers rolled up in his hand. "That's all. I've got to go. I'll see you soon." He ended the call, ran down the steps, and met William on the ramp.

"I have a little light reading for us on the trip home." William held up the papers. "An old friend of mine is a senior partner with a Miami Beach law firm. He faxed me a dossier they'd compiled on Montero. At first glance it's fairly detailed."

"Good work," Donovan said. "I talked with Peggy and Buck. They'll be waiting for us at the other end."

"I made a call to the charter company," William said. "This aircraft is being put at our disposal, it'll be on twenty-four standby for a trip to Europe until we tell them otherwise. I called Stephanie. She sends her love and, of course, said you're welcome day or night."

Donovan nodded, thankful that his old friend was on top of things. After they climbed the steps into the waiting airplane, Donovan put his hand on William's right shoulder and gently squeezed, sending an unspoken message of appreciation.

The effects of his sleepless night were dragging him down. Donovan looked forward to trying to catch a nap on the flight home. Abigail, the only member of the entourage who was smiling, sat on Lauren's lap, her face pressed against the inside of the window. She was happily waving goodbye to Florida.

The captain hurried up the stairs and stuck his head into the cabin. "We're all buttoned up and ready to go."

"How's the weather between here and there?" Donovan asked. Like most pilots, he made for a lousy passenger.

"The front that pushed through last night cleared everything out. It's a perfect day to fly."

Donovan settled into a forward-facing seat across from Lauren. Abigail immediately wriggled off her mother's lap and lunged toward Donovan. He lifted her up and placed her on his lap where she could continue to look out of the wide, oval window. He and his daughter had made many trips to the airport together and easily fell into their routine when they were around airplanes.

"Bye, bye." Abigail waved at no one in particular. She puffed up her cheeks and blew the air out of her lips. Donovan smiled at his daughter's antics, mimicking the sound of a jet, though if the truth were told she sounded more like a motorboat. He began pointing at different airplanes and in return Abigail would come up with a sound and wave. Donovan loved these shared moments with Abigail, but he also couldn't help but notice that Lauren wasn't smiling—in fact she'd been quiet most of the afternoon.

Up front, the door swung closed. The flight attendant locked it into place and then introduced herself as Sarah. She instructed everyone to find a seatbelt, and then asked if she could bring them anything before they got underway. Anxious to get airborne, everyone declined.

From thousands of hours flying Gulfstreams, Donovan's practiced ear listened for the subtle clues they were about to start the engines. What he didn't expect to hear was someone pounding on the outside of the airplane.

The flight attendant got up, went to the cockpit, and spoke briefly with the flight crew. She returned to the entryway, shrugged at Donovan, and began to lower the main door. Donovan slid Abigail off his lap and handed her to Lauren.

"What's going on?" Donovan asked as the door opened and began to unfold on its way down.

"Someone wants to talk to us," Sarah replied.

As the door continued its downward arc, Donovan swore under his breath. Special Agent Montero was standing on the tarmac looking up at him.

His anger building, Donovan stomped down the steps and placed himself squarely between Montero and the Gulfstream.

"What do you want?"

Montero remained silent. She simply pulled two folded sheets of paper out the pocket of her blazer and handed them over.

He unfolded the papers. His eyes immediately shot to the grainy, black-and-white photo of the man he used to be. The passive expression of Robert Huntington's mug shot stared back at him. The second page held two photos. One was taken years ago, a picture of Robert Huntington and William VanGelder, just after Meredith was killed. Printed just below was another picture of William and him taken a few years ago at an Eco-Watch function. In a direct comparison, the commonality was there for someone who was looking. He felt his chest deflate as he glanced up at Montero's knowing expression.

"Good, at least we don't have to go through that whole denial thing," Montero said. "You're him."

Donovan felt the blood draining from his face. There was no use acting as if these photos meant nothing. It was time to shift to damage control. "How many people have seen this?"

"So far, just me. You can keep those, I have more."

Donovan fought the impulse to turn away from her and board the jet, to walk away from this woman and the unbridled chaos she was going to unleash.

"What do you want?"

"I want your help," she said. "I need someone with your resources to help me find the people I'm looking for, who are also the people who shot your friend. I'll explain everything later."

"There is no later."

"Get your things," Montero tilted her head to the side. "Because I'm guessing you'd rather I not go to the media?"

"Wait right here." Donovan spun and walked up the stairs where he stopped and quietly asked Sarah to retrieve his suitcase. He wasn't going with them. He knelt on the carpet next to Lauren and kissed her on the lips and transferred the sheets of paper from his hand to hers.

Lauren blinked with surprise and then slumped as she processed the look in his eyes. She unfolded the first page, then the second one.

"I have to stay," he whispered to her. "Don't leave the country just yet. Let me feel this out first. She says she wants my help. Tell the others I'm staying to help with the investigation."

Lauren pursed her lips and nodded that she understood. Abigail, detecting the mood shift in her mother, started to fuss and immediately clung to her.

Donovan leaned down and kissed his daughter and his wife and then turned to William. "Take care of them."

Lauren stroked Abigail's hair and fixed her brilliant green eyes on Donovan. In a hushed but serious voice, she said, "Fix this."

CHAPTER ELEVEN

"Take the battery out of your cell phone," Montero ordered. "I don't want anyone to be able to track us."

Donovan did what he was told. He sat in the passenger seat of Montero's red, 3 Series BMW convertible. She eased into traffic on northbound I-95. She drove fast, but not reckless. Lauren's words echoed in his mind, but he had no clear idea what the fix was.

"You know, I suspected from the moment I saw your mug shot—your former mug shot," Montero said. "Your eyes and your confidence—you reminded me of him. I studied Meredith's case in college, so I know your old face well. Then there's the fact that you're both pilots. When I met Mr. VanGelder at the hospital, I knew for sure. I'll admit it was a pretty surreal moment. In fact I'm still trying to get my head around the fact I'm sitting next to *the* Robert Huntington."

"You'll get over it. Where are we going?" Donovan studied her as she drove. Whatever formalities she'd observed earlier as a federal agent were apparently long gone. He tried to imagine what forces were at work for her to resort to blackmail, and the only reason that came up was the usual one—money.

"I'll get to that in a minute. But first we need to agree on some ground rules. I'm on administrative leave, which means I've officially been hung out to dry. I can't actively pursue any investigation. You and I are hanging out together because you're indebted to me for saving your life."

"But we can both agree in private that this is blackmail?"

"Probably," Montero shrugged. "But don't go all victim on me, it doesn't suit you. We're going after the people who killed my partner and tried to kill you and your friend. I wouldn't have pulled you off that plane if we both didn't have a fully vested interest in what I'm doing. Believe me, when you know the entire story, you'll be a willing participant."

"Keep talking." Donovan noticed that with each lane change, she kept a close eye out for anyone who might be following them.

"The guy I shot today goes by the name Diego Vazquez. He has a brother, Ramone, and they almost always work together. Right now we're going to go have a little chat with a guy named Ricky. He may be able to tell us where Ramone is hanging out. How much cash do you have on you?"

Donovan quickly calculated what was in his wallet, plus what he kept stashed in his briefcase for emergencies. "About three grand."

"That should be enough."

Donovan thought of the detailed report William had on Montero. Right that moment he'd love to see what it contained. It was puzzling that she'd discovered Robert Huntington, a man she claimed to be very familiar with—yet the first order of business was to go shake down someone named Ricky. At least for the moment, it seemed as if Montero was all business again, focused on the case.

Montero took the exit ramp at high speed, expertly downshifted, rolled the stoplight, and gunned the car eastbound. They were on Atlantic Avenue in Delray Beach, but other than that, Donovan had no idea where he was or where they were going. Montero made several turns, her eyes continually shooting to the rearview mirror. Block by block the neighborhood began to get a little more run down.

Montero swung the BMW down a pothole-riddled street and stopped next to a nondescript cinderblock building. The parking lot was a mixture of gravel and puddles. Scattered palm fronds from last night's wind created a minor obstacle course. The BMW was the only car near the building. The lone grimy window had an anemic red neon sign that announced the establishment was open.

"Give me some of your cash." Montero held out her hand. "Make it eight hundred. I've worked with the guy before. He owes me one, so I'm thinking it shouldn't take more than five hundred."

Donovan snapped open his briefcase and retrieved the cash he carried for emergencies. He peeled off the crisp one hundred dollar bills and handed them over.

"Let me do the talking—but keep your eyes open." Montero said as she got out of the car. She folded the bills and stuffed them into her back pocket.

The heavy smell of gun grease tipped him off before his eyes fully adjusted to the relative darkness. The front of the shop was small in comparison to the size of the building. On each side of the room, behind glass cases filled with pistols, were rows of rifles and shotguns. A buzzer attached to the door announced their arrival.

"Be right there," a deep baritone voice called out from beyond a curtain at the back of the display area.

"Ricky, get your skinny little ass out here," Montero said as she closed the door behind them and then flipped the deadbolt to lock them inside.

"Ronnie, is that you? You thinking about my ass?"

"In your dreams, Ricky."

Donovan stood silent as the curtain parted and a lumbering giant of a man appeared. His massive torso looked far too heavy for his stubby legs. His knees looked like they might snap at any moment as they propelled him toward Montero. A sleeveless tee shirt ballooned over his gigantic belly. His shoulders and arms were covered with curly black hair. His head was hairless, except for a goatee that was braided into two greasy strands that nearly reached the folds of his immense fleshy neck. Donovan guessed the guy easily went three hundred fifty pounds, or more. His face lit up when he spotted Montero.

"Ricky, this is my friend Roberto," Montero said.

Donovan bristled at the name. The huge man nodded, grunted once as way of hello, and waddled behind the counter. The glazed look on Ricky's face left no doubt that he was clearly smitten with Montero.

"What can I do for you?" Ricky said, eyeing Montero's chest instead of her face.

"I'm up here, Ricky," Montero said without any trace of anger, as if she were reprimanding a small child for the hundredth time. "I'm looking for two brothers. Ramone and Diego—you know who I'm talking about."

Ricky glanced at Donovan, then back to Montero. He answered with a shrug of his massive shoulders.

"I'll take that as a yes." Montero flashed the stack of hundreds. "Where are they?"

Donovan watched Ricky's eyes savor the cash. Montero referred to Diego in the present tense. If Ricky knew that Diego was lying in the morgue, he didn't show it.

"I ain't seen them in a while," Ricky said.

"Don't mess with me, Ricky. Not today." Montero peeled off the top bill and smacked it down on the table with enough force to make Ricky flinch. "You can make this easy on yourself and pocket a few bucks. Or you can jack me around and see my bad side—your call."

Donovan saw Ricky's eyes narrow. The huge man had just imagined Montero's bad side, and it worried him. Montero slowly took a second bill and gently laid it on the table. Donovan found the contrast interesting. Montero was either smart enough or crazy enough to pull off good cop, bad cop, all by herself.

"I only met Diego once," Ricky's hand worked his braided goatee as if thinking. "Ramone comes in from time to time. He's a 9-mm guy, likes to practice."

Montero slid another bill halfway out of the stack and stopped, waiting for Ricky to continue.

"I don't know where they live or nothin', or even who they work for. They're freelancers. Hired muscle."

Montero let the bill drop. "Who do they run with?"

Ricky looked up at the ceiling as if deep in thought. Montero folded the bills and acted as if she were going to shove the wad back into her pocket.

"Ramone was with this one chick. She strips, maybe she even hooks sometimes. Ramone was always bragging how she was totally hot. The dude was pretty much hung up on her. But that was a while back. I have no idea if she's still around."

"What's her name? What clubs did she work?" Montero asked, as she began to slowly work another bill out from the roll.

"I don't know." Ricky shrugged. "She mostly bounced around between Lauderdale and Miami. You know how that business goes."

"I need a name."

"She's foreign, Russian or Ukrainian, something like that."

"Come on, Ricky, concentrate." Montero slid another bill toward the growing pile.

Ricky gazed upward and snapped his fingers. "Her name is Sasha! Yeah, that's it, Sasha."

Montero let the last bill float to the countertop, and then she shoved the remaining cash into her pocket. "You'd better be right, Ricky."

Ricky shot her a nervous look. An instant later, the money on the table vanished, clenched inside a beefy hand.

Montero's threatening expression vanished, replaced with a warm smile. "I'm glad we understand each other. Now, my friend here needs a throw-down weapon. What have you got?"

"I don't need a gun," Donovan said.

"Yes," Montero said. "You do."

"We each have our gifts. I'll leave the killing to you."

Ricky shrunk from the exchange. The fury that flared in Montero's eyes seemed to fill the room. Donovan stood his ground, realizing that his remark had connected. He waited for her to react, hoping her behavior might tell him something. Instead, much to his surprise, she pressed the remaining bills into his palm, handed him the keys to her car, and walked outside.

CHAPTER TWELVE

Lauren stroked Abigail's hair. The quiet hum of the jet had lulled her daughter into a much-needed nap. The disrupted schedule was taking its toll. Children require structure, their peace of mind dependent on stability and predictability. Lauren put her head back, angry at what had happened to Donovan, uncertain he had the power to change the course of events. She closed her eyes, and one by one, ran through the immediate changes that would shape her life. At Donovan's insistence, for this very reason, she'd kept her maiden name. The media would find out about her and Abigail eventually, but initially, she would be able to move unnoticed.

Stephanie doted on Abigail. If events allowed, they might be able to stay a day or two with Stephanie, and Abigail might view it as a great adventure. In London, there were full sets of forged documents for each of them. They would allow Lauren and Abigail to slip away to Switzerland. Donovan owned a villa not far from Lake Geneva. The Swiss, Donovan maintained, were rather uninterested in outside events, and known for their ability to keep secrets, plus he knew people highly placed in the government who may prove useful.

Lauren thought of everything she'd be forced to leave behind. All of her friends at work, especially her boss and mentor, Calvin Reynolds. She'd known Calvin for years; he'd quietly stepped in after her father had died and subtly filled part of that void in her world. Lauren loved him dearly for his efforts.

She thought of her mother, unable to conceive of what she'd tell her. For the moment at least, her mother was on a cruise in the Mediterranean and wasn't due back for another week. Lauren had known what she was getting into when she'd married Donovan, but that didn't change how threatened and vulnerable she felt at this moment.

"Is she asleep?" William asked, quietly.

Lauren nodded.

William kept his voice down; the flight attendant was up in the cockpit, well out of earshot. "Once we arrive back home, this jet will be on twenty-four-hour standby—just in case."

"Donovan mentioned briefly the security arrangements waiting in Virginia," Lauren said. "Tell me more about this man Howard Buckley."

"He's a former Navy SEAL, and also the nephew of General Porter, who, as you know sits on the Joint Chiefs of Staff. On an Eco-Watch flight during Hurricane Helena, he suffered broken ribs, a collapsed lung, and some damage to his lower vertebrae. He survived, but he's now behind a desk at the Pentagon. Donovan paid for the finest doctors in the world to treat him, but the lower back injuries, while not debilitating, disqualified him from the rigors of SEAL activities. It's a rather sad story, but Buck has never shown a moment's remorse. He's a remarkable young man."

"You think he'll be able to watch over Michael?"

"Our friend Buck, while he's not able to swim twenty miles anymore, is still quite lethal. I, for one, will sleep soundly knowing he's in charge of Michael's safety—and you should as well."

"You know," Lauren said, "we've talked about the logistics, what we'll do if this goes public. I get all that, but what do you think all of this will do to Donovan?"

"I've been around him most of his life. I'm well aware of his demons. I've often wondered how much he's shared with you about his past. Do you mind if I ask how much he's told you about Meredith Barnes?"

"It's odd you should bring her up. Of course we've talked about her, but I never really felt the need to pry. That period of his life is painful for him, I know that. I'm his wife, I'm here, and she's been dead for twenty years; it would be pointless to try and compete with a ghost. In the end, he always maintains that it happened so long ago it doesn't really matter."

"Why is it odd I brought her up?"

"It's not important, forget I said that."

"Really, I want to know. Have the nightmares gotten worse? Is he drinking?"

Lauren didn't answer. Donovan's nightmares had always been there, but now they were as bad as she'd ever seen them. She'd be awakened by his tossing and turning, and then the murmurs would start. Words she could never quite understand. She'd learned to try and wake him before the screams, the thrashing, and the sobs. He'd shiver in a cold sweat afterward—shaken and distant. Lately, he'd been going downstairs, and in the morning she'd find a cocktail glass in the sink. It never occurred to her that perhaps he'd been having more than one drink, or that it might be part of a bigger problem.

"When did his bad dreams start?" Lauren asked.

"Shortly after his parents died," William replied. "He was fourteen."

"He rarely talks about them, but watching your parents drown would give anyone nightmares."

"It was the first tragedy in his life. There, of course, have been others, and I've always believed that our life experiences, both good and bad, are cumulative. As hard as we try to get past certain events, they work on us in ways we can't begin to completely understand."

"Is that what you think is going on with him now?"

"You tell me, I can't believe I'm the only one who's noticed the change in his behavior over the last few months."

"No, you're not the only one." Lauren shook her head. "Tell me what you know about the documentary about Meredith Barnes. I found a copy at the house."

William's shock and disbelief were evident. "He has it? I can't believe he didn't tell me. I declined to be a part of it, and it's not scheduled to be released for months."

"He didn't tell me either. I accidently ran across it. So far I've only seen bits and pieces. It's hard to watch."

"Do you think it's troublesome enough to have an effect on Donovan?"

Lauren nodded and explained what she'd seen and the manner in which it had been shown.

"Those bastards." William shook his head in anger.

"The film talks about some things I never knew about."

"Like what?"

"Were there real threats against Meredith? Did Donovan delay in getting the ransom money together? Did he talk to her just before she was killed?"

William thought for a moment, and then in a reverential voice just barely above a whisper, began. "Yes, there were vague threats. Never anything credible. As far as the money issue, that part was a nightmare. What few people know is how intensely we fought with the bureaucrats from Costa Rica and the United States, who, of course, refused to deal with the kidnappers, calling them terrorists. Against all of the advice from both the State Department and the Central Intelligence Agency, Robert tried to make contact himself, but the authorities did everything they could to block his efforts to pay the ransom. Ten million is a great deal of money and the logistics of getting it together and transporting it to Costa Rica were daunting. Because of the governmental resistance, he was forced to use offshore assets and keep his efforts secret. So, of course, it looked like he did nothing at first. But from the moment the ransom demands were heard, Robert frantically assembled the money."

"The phone call?"

"That's something he's never talked about to me, or anyone else for that matter. He had the money and finally convinced the Costa Rican police to allow him to make contact and set up the exchange. He demanded proof of life, he needed to be positive Meredith was still alive. The call came in the middle of the night. It should have been recorded by the police but wasn't. I don't know what was said, but her body was found early the next morning. The medical examiner said she probably died within an hour of that phone call."

"Why? They were on the verge of getting the money."

"There was speculation that they panicked, that law enforcement was closing in on them. We'll never know why. Robert was devastated. He blamed everyone and refused to cooperate any further with the investigation. It was all so horrible."

Lauren could hear the emotion in William's voice as he spoke. She hadn't expected this to be difficult for him.

"We flew her body home to California and were met with fierce protests. The threats to Robert and acts of violence were round the clock, finally forcing him to leave Monterey. Robert wasn't able to attend her funeral out of fear of reprisal, that someone, maybe even members of her own family, could be hurt due to his presence. To this day, I'm not sure he's ever visited her grave. Then those pictures came out, the ones on the beach with the young woman. Though taken long before he met Meredith, they were portrayed as being recent. He received death threats on an almost daily basis. Huntington Oil was boycotted, bombs were found—it was complete chaos.

"Robert was shattered. I stayed with him as much as I could. He went to live in the old family house on the estate outside Aldie, Virginia. As you know, it was and still is, one of his favorite places. He became a recluse, he drank to shut himself down, hell, we both did. He started taking drugs. There were pills to go to sleep. Different pills to get him through the day. He cut himself off from the outside world and spiraled out of control."

"I had no inkling of any of this."

"Did he ever tell you his boyhood hero was Howard Hughes? Howard was a good friend of Robert's father, back then everyone in the oil business knew Howard. When Robert was just a little boy, Howard would entertain him with stories about his record-setting flights, making movies, building and flying the now famous *Spruce Goose.* Howard actually hated that nickname—instead he referred to it as his 'flying boat.' Robert's passion for flying can easily be traced back to Howard."

"One night we were up late, drinking. I listened as Robert starting talking about Howard, this was long after Howard's bizarre final years and ultimate death, but Robert told me that he understood how easy it would be to completely withdraw from the world. We talked about Howard's tortured life, and Robert promised me he'd never end up like that—he'd kill himself first. I asked him point-blank if he'd thought about ending his life. He was honest, told me he had—and I believed him."

Lauren was horrified; it was as if she were hearing about someone she'd never known. "What did you do?"

"I asked him when he wanted to start? In the weeks it took us to plan the transition, he sobered up. We orchestrated it down to the smallest detail. Robert Huntington died when the plane he was flying crashed into the ocean off the California coast. He parachuted from that plane in the middle of the night. When he landed outside Modesto, California, he became Donovan Nash. I was with him afterward in Europe as he endured the surgeries. It was a difficult time, but to this day, I believe the only part of his past he misses is Meredith."

Lauren nodded—she had to look away. William was teetering on the edge of tears. He'd clearly been close to Meredith, and his obvious pain at the memories threatened to undo her as well. After all this time, she really had no idea how Donovan felt about Meredith's death. Perhaps it was her fault for not pushing harder. Did her husband harbor some kind of deep-seated guilt at having survived the attack when Meredith didn't? Did that explain his years of reckless behavior flying in the Third World? Lauren could rattle off any number of situations where Donovan rushed to the rescue—including saving her life twice. Was he the brave, capable man she'd always thought, or was there a death wish involved, or other mechanism not nearly so healthy that motivated him? Did she really understand her husband at all?

"I hope I haven't said too much. I know it's a lot to absorb," William said.

"It's fine. Thank you." She wished she'd heard this version of history from Donovan. Lauren felt betrayed, like she was left on the periphery of major parts of her husband's life. The pragmatic scientist in her rarely broke down in a puddle of insecurity, but she'd asked herself several relevant questions with no ready answers. She couldn't explain to William that she suddenly felt like one of her husband's carefully constructed compartments, that she felt marginalized in ways that made her feel enormously vulnerable.

William handed her the folder on Special Agent Montero. "You need to read this. It's fairly detailed. I'll be interested in your thoughts."

Lauren looked at the title page and saw the name: Veronica "Ronnie" Montero. "What's the source?"

"It came to us from one of the top law firms in Florida, gathered by a private investigator. I'm told that a criminal defense attorney put this together not long ago in preparation for a trial involving Montero and a rather well-placed drug dealer."

"Did you read it?"

"Not yet, but I did get a quick briefing from my friend at the firm. I'll review it later and maybe initiate an investigation of our own."

She looked at the folder and did her best to clear her mind. Years ago, when she was working on her Ph.D. at MIT, she taught herself how to digest detailed, complex data with her logical left brain, while keeping her right brain in neutral, poised for suggestion and intuition. It was a discipline that had served her well, and right this moment she needed the diversion. The report was less than thirty pages, it would be a quick read. Most importantly, it would provide a focal point for her growing anger.

CHAPTER THIRTEEN

Donovan sped through a yellow light, braked hard, and then made a left onto a residential street. Montero directed another series of turns until they pulled into the driveway of a modest ranch-style house in a nice neighborhood. The door to the double garage slowly receded, and he pulled forward and stopped next to a mountain of cardboard boxes. It was a tight squeeze. Montero got out of the car, hit the button to close the door, then entered the code for her security system. Without saying a word, she went into the house leaving the door open behind her.

Donovan followed. From the garage, a short hallway led into the kitchen, which was almost too neat, as if it were never used. Just past a countertop that served as the eating area was a high-ceilinged great room; a fan turned slowly to keep the air circulating. The décor was modern, simple yet tasteful. Except for books, the room was devoid of personal touches.

"I know what you're thinking." Montero slipped out of her blazer, tossed it on the back of a chair, then tweaked the thermostat. "The answer is yes, I live here. I only moved in a month or so ago. It's still a work in progress. Stay off the landline and don't even think about using your cell phone. I have no idea what the FBI is doing, and I don't want to have to try and explain a bunch of calls I know nothing about."

"Tell them your hostage did it—they'll understand."

"You're funny," Montero called over her shoulder as she disappeared into the back of the house.

Donovan walked to a sliding glass door that led out to the back yard. The lot was small and there was no landscaping, just neglected Bermuda grass. A weathered privacy fence guarded an empty cement patio. He turned his attention back inside and was drawn to the bookcase situated against the wall. It didn't take him long to recognize a familiar title.

He carefully slid the hardcover volume off the shelf and held it reverently in both hands. *One Earth,* by Meredith Barnes. He cracked it open, thumbed to the title page, and read the inscription. It was personalized to Veronica. The soft flowing curves of Meredith's familiar signature seemed to speak to him, as if she was somehow nearby and he could talk to her. He flipped to her picture on the dust jacket. It was a great photo, her eyes radiated her fierce intelligence, but her impish smile, combined with her freckles, softened the image, giving her an almost angelic quality. The slight ocean breeze blew her wild mane of reddish hair just enough to give her the look of the free spirit she most certainly was. He felt the years melt away, like he'd see her soon, and the sensation unnerved him. It had been years since he'd seen this particular picture of her and he couldn't look away. He was pulled in by her eyes, remembering how awestruck he'd been by her. From the day he met her, she'd been a whirling mass of energy and passion, and that was maybe what he missed most. He felt the usual twinge at losing her and the familiar guilt of having failed her and then going on without her.

"She signed it for me," Montero said, standing directly behind him. "I met her at a bookstore when I was still in school. She was my hero. I practically worshiped her. I followed everything she ever did. I religiously watched her television shows. I bet I've read everything ever printed about her—and by default—you. What was she really like? Was she as amazing as she seemed?"

"No, she wasn't as amazing as her public persona—no one is." Donovan did his best to bury his emotions and change the subject. "What was the point of stopping at the gun shop? Some kind of test? And just to double-check, you do know Ricky wasn't telling you everything he knew—right?"

"Of course, which is why he'll be even more terrified next time

I show up. I took you there because I needed to see if you'd cooperate and do what I ask you to do. If you decided to get ugly, Ricky's worthless in a fight, but he keeps a loaded gun close and there are about six cameras in the shop. I'd have plenty of deniability as well as a witness if I had to defend myself against you. You also had a chance to change your mind and bolt. But you didn't do any of those things."

Donovan had guessed as much. She was trying to measure him as well as manipulate him. He also got the impression that she might be a little intimidated by him as well—something to keep in mind.

"I'm still having a hard time believing you're not dead. Do you ever think about her?"

Donovan snapped the book shut, closing off the memories, then slid it back on the shelf. "It was a long time ago," Donovan said. He waited until Montero moved away and sat on the sofa. He then chose the chair opposite her. He couldn't help but notice the holstered pistol still attached to her belt.

"To answer your obvious question, no, I don't usually wear a gun in the house."

"Why are we here? What exactly do you want from me?"

"Right to the point—I like that," Montero replied. "I brought you here for several reasons. It's the one place we can talk freely, and if you try to harm me, I'll shoot you. I understand I've made myself a threat to you. I won't underestimate the gravity of that threat—or what you may try to do about it. After all, I'm more aware than most, that from a certain historical perspective, you've already orchestrated at least one murder in the past."

"I had nothing to do with Meredith's death."

"There are those who would disagree with you. You know as well as I do that most of the world firmly believes you had a hand in killing Meredith Barnes. If it became known that you'd faked your own death, I'm certain the vote would be unanimous. You would be viewed as the billionaire who got away with murder, then gathered up his toys and left. I know what the press did to you back then, and I'm positive that they'd go absolutely bat-shit now."

"Maybe, maybe not." Donovan's world began to wobble on its axis. Montero knew exactly what she was talking about. If nothing else, she represented a microcosm of public opinion.

"All I want from you is your help, so let's cut through the crap. You and I need to reach some sort of common ground. If you had the chance to find the people who murdered Meredith, what would you let stand in your way?"

Donovan inwardly recoiled, it was surreal to be having this conversation, to hear Meredith's name spoken aloud by a stranger, in this context.

"We're alike, you and I," Montero said. "Someone I cared about was murdered, and the people around me believe I had a hand in his death. I need to find out the truth. Then, like you, I desperately want to make those responsible pay for what they did."

"I never hunted down the people who killed Meredith." Donovan didn't bother to add that he'd wanted nothing but vengeance, but he'd been in no condition to do anything about it until it was too late. The private investigators he hired later turned up nothing. "If you remember your history, the Costa Rican police arrested the man they believed was responsible."

"They also killed him. He was a patsy—a sacrificial lamb designed to wrap up the investigation. You never really believed all that shit, did you? In my case, the people who did it escaped, no one was ever arrested or even questioned. They're in the wind."

Donovan saw the pain in her eyes. Her facade was breaking down and the vulnerability he'd seen earlier had returned. It wasn't an act; it was something very real.

"Explain."

If what she'd said was true, he understood all too well the kind of pain and guilt she was feeling. It was something tangible that never left. His own guilt surrounding Meredith was going on twenty years. If he could get her to talk about it, maybe he could find something to use to his advantage.

"You don't really want to hear about my problems. What you should care about is the one common denominator we share. I'm certain that the people who killed Alec, my partner, are the same people who tried to kill Michael Ross—twice."

"What makes you so sure?"

"The man I killed today was somehow involved with the case Alec and I were working on. Your friend is shot and then they send this guy to finish the job. I promise you that's not a coincidence."

"If you say so." Donovan wondered what the proof was, if any, and why Montero was so certain of the connection. Was she trying to sell him on the concept so that he'd be more willing to join forces? Donovan processed her abrupt shift in methodology. The vulnerability of a few moments ago was gone. She'd shut down and then issued him a challenge and made him a promise. He wondered if she was that unstable, or was she shifting tactics to try and manipulate him? He understood that at many levels he was dealing with a dangerous, emotionally charged woman in a great deal of pain—someone who right this moment wasn't unlike himself. The one detail that hadn't escaped his attention was the fact that she didn't seem to want any money beyond what she'd used earlier to bribe Ricky. Or would that come later?

"There's no other explanation. I know I'm right."

"What is it you think you and I can do that the FBI and local police can't? In fact, you know I'm not some sort of field operative. I'm just the opposite. I'm a businessman."

"You're wrong. Your life as Robert Huntington is well documented. You're a calculated thinker, someone who's not afraid to take action or risks. That's exactly what I need. I did a background search of Donovan Nash, though now I'm not at all clear what parts are true and which parts were fabricated."

"That's not important."

"I can only assume you parachuted out of the plane the night you supposedly died. What did you do after your—death? Where did you go?"

"Europe."

"For the surgeries?" Montero leaned forward to study his face. "They did a nice job and you've aged well. It's strange, you're still handsome like him, but at the same time you look very little like you did before, except for the eyes. I can see how you went all these years without anyone recognizing you."

Donovan hated this—found it massively uncomfortable. His past was something he'd buried, gone to extraordinary lengths to get away from, and to have her sift through it uninvited was almost more than he could stand.

"So where do the paths merge? Eco-Watch looks legitimate. It all looked very real, you know—from a law enforcement standpoint. That explains the last ten years. What about the decade before that? Did you really work in Africa and Asia, flying relief flights in support of the World Health Organization and Doctors Without Borders?"

"Yeah, with the help of others. What you discovered about me for the last twenty years is what you were supposed to find. It's real."

"I remember those pictures, airplanes unloading supplies in places no one else would go. Amazing. Then you felt safe enough to come back to the States and start Eco-Watch?"

"I got tired of filling planes with supplies and flying to the latest disaster. I had the idea that perhaps I could use my resources to learn more about the science behind these calamities and try to help people instead of rescue them."

"How very philanthropic of you," Montero said. "So, Eco-Watch is funded by Huntington Oil money. How ironic."

"No irony at all," Donovan replied. "I started Eco-Watch with my own money, but now it's substantially funded by outside entities. I only use my money to fill in the gaps."

"Out of guilt for Meredith's death?"

Donovan leveled a lethal stare at her. A silent warning that she'd crossed a line.

Montero cleared her throat. "The reason I believe you can help me is that back in the day, despite your playboy image, you were a wunderkind in the business world. You were this potent combination of JFK Jr. meets Bill Gates. Looks, money, and intelligence, easily one of the shrewdest CEOs in the country. I mean, who else before or since has had their picture on the cover of business magazines at the same time they were on the cover of Hollywood gossip magazines. Before Meredith, you were always photographed with some A-list movie starlet on your arm."

"Your point being?"

"All I'm saying is you had some serious game back then. That confidence and experience, coupled with what you've done since, makes you a very capable operative."

Donovan said nothing.

"Plus, you have the motivation—like I've said, we're after the same people. You also have a jet and unlimited resources. I am however, without my support system. If we don't move fast, these people will drift away, and we'll never find them."

"I'm not interested." Donovan shrugged without emotion, as if none of what she said meant anything to him. What was important was to test her resolve. "Go to the press. My family and I will be the ones who vanish into the wind. Oh, and before you can sell your story, I'll give the *Washington Post* an exclusive interview. You'll be left here in Florida working for the FBI. Though your continued employment might depend on exactly how the *Washington Post* spins the whole federal agent, blackmail angle."

"Bullshit," Montero said, quietly, unfazed by the threat. "If you didn't care, you'd have blown me off and boarded that jet with your wife and daughter and gone home. You care a great deal, and you'll never convince me otherwise. Most people I interview plead, even demand, that I catch the people responsible for whatever crime has been committed. But the first time we spoke, the one thing that immediately struck me about you was there was nothing on your mind except retribution. You didn't need me to deliver justice. In fact, I was nothing but a conduit for you to start your own investigation. You're not running away. You have every intention of going after these people and you always did."

"Are you finished?"

"I thought you of all people would understand." Montero

seemed to deflate, her voice tailed off to almost a whisper. "All I want from you is your help. I need to find these people—or I will be finished, in every sense of the word. I have to live with myself—look into the eyes of my peers who openly believe I killed Alec—and I may have. Alec is dead and maybe it's my fault. I live with that doubt, that guilt. I don't have the luxury of arranging my own death and taking my millions and running off to Europe to hide."

Donovan studied her. She was right, he did understand. He knew what she was going through; the same survivor's guilt had played itself out far too many times in his own life. As manipulative as she might be, her anguish was real, as was her intent. For the first time since he'd met her, he found a small measure of something—empathy maybe—perhaps even a little respect. His pain spanned decades, Montero's emotional wounds were fresh. It took a distinctive personality not to curl up in the fetal position and beg the gods not to be left behind.

"I do understand," Donovan said, softly, without a trace of hostility. "I can also tell you retribution is a dangerous road to travel. I think I know enough to recognize that you won't be talked out of anything. But can I make a suggestion?"

"Go ahead."

"You shouldn't be the one going on this quest. Trust me when I say you're too emotionally involved. You killed a man this morning. How do you feel about that? How are you going to feel when you try and go to sleep tonight?"

"I don't have a problem with what happened today. Diego was on the list of people tied to Alec's death. This wasn't the first time I've killed someone—or my last. Ramone's next."

Donovan wished he could accurately judge what he was hearing. He wanted to know how much of her attitude was false bravado and how much was her being dead serious.

"It would take me about thirty minutes on the phone to set up something that I think would serve you far better than the path you're on right now. We could establish an offshore numbered account, and I could deposit, say, five million dollars. You'd have the resources to hire your own army of investigators to help you find these guys, plus have enough left over to live on for the rest of your life."

Montero's expression never changed.

"Ten million."

"I want the truth. I want the people who killed Alec to pay. I'm a good agent and I've played by the rules. I bend them once in a while, every cop does, but I've stayed in bounds."

"This is exactly what I'm talking about. Take the money. You're supposed to be grieving your loss, not planning a counterstrike."

"Oh, you are going to throw some of your money around—just not at me. We're going to bribe more people. Then if that doesn't work, we're going to threaten them. Even though I'm on leave, I still have to follow a few rules, but you don't. With your natural arrogance and your bank account, you'll be the perfect partner. Plus, you have a jet. I don't need to hire an army—I already have an Army and an Air Force. I like the name Roberto, don't you? It fits."

Donovan didn't acknowledge her frivolity.

"Just so you know. I sent your dossier to someone I trust. Your secret is safe—unless something happens to me. And quit trying to buy me off. I'm sitting here with the poster boy to prove that money can't buy happiness. How has all that wealth worked out for you so far? Does it keep you warm at night and make the pain go away?"

Donovan felt the sting from Montero's words. She was no doubt flawed in more ways than he could count, but she wasn't greedy, and she didn't come across as a liar. She'd just turned down millions to continue her vendetta. She was, however, reckless and more than a little unbalanced. Donovan knew his job had just gotten far more difficult. He not only needed to go with her on her vigilante mission—he had to keep her from getting herself killed.

CHAPTER FOURTEEN

"Well, what do you think?" William asked the moment Lauren closed the file.

Lauren shuffled the papers and slid them back in the folder, giving herself a moment to fully digest what she'd just read. "To be perfectly honest, I'm not sure. I get that this report is limited, and perhaps more than a little biased. I think you'll understand when you read it for yourself, but at face value, she's overcome a great deal in her life. She's either a role model in dealing with adversity or she's a manipulative bitch with no business carrying a gun. I'm really not sure which."

"Go on," William said, nodding thoughtfully.

"Don't get me wrong, she's certainly intelligent. She's a very capable woman, well trained, but there are issues, some serious psychological tendencies that probably make her dangerous as it pertains to the current situation. I wish Donovan had read this, it might have given him some ammunition going in to try and get the upper hand."

"You're assuming he doesn't already have the upper hand?"

"Donovan will see some of this eventually, but I'm not sure that emotionally he's in the greatest shape right now. It may take him time to recognize this woman for who she is—time he might not have."

"Go on."

"In broad strokes, the part that jumps out at me is that she doesn't hesitate to operate outside the system. More than once she's taken matters into her own hands and dealt with a perceived threat, or at the very least punished someone she felt had wronged her. An example I find particularly troubling is a complaint filed against her that involved the blackmail and assault of an underage girl, a prostitute. The girl vanished soon thereafter and the charges were eventually dropped. Still, that strikes me as someone operating out of bounds, yet, she always seems to avoid the consequences of her actions."

"My friend mentioned that something else happened recently. He told me that Montero is currently in some trouble with the FBI. Perhaps her conduct finally caught up with her?"

"Yeah. The last section references an investigation that somehow went awry. There were several fatalities, including an undercover agent. Montero was directly involved, she was assaulted and hospitalized and there's an ongoing internal investigation. She's been a FBI agent for ten years and she's killed four men in the line of duty. After each instance, she was cleared back to active duty. I know they're highly trained, I get that soldiers do that all the time, but I can't imagine killing someone."

"She's not you," William said. "Do you think Donovan is in physical danger?"

"In the present situation, I don't think her predisposition to violence is really the issue. She's not out to hurt Donovan. My guess is she either wants his help or his money. I'm more concerned with how easily she operates outside the system. That's the biggest problem. The report presents a brief forensic psychological profile, and the expert who put it together felt that Montero could be suffering from several unresolved issues. It's suggested that she has a problem with trust, especially in trusting superiors and maybe even the justice system itself. That's problematic, since she's a part of that system. This woman doesn't play well with others. It goes on to say that she's attractive and she knows it; she uses her looks as a weapon. She feels as if she can get away with anything, which she has done to a point, but she's also impulsive and reckless. The bottom line is that Montero is smart, street savvy, and, above all, highly manipulative. In fact, if you take the report at face value, she defaults to that behavior. That's a lot for anyone, even Donovan, to pick up on in a short period of time."

"In my experience," William said, "it won't take him long to decide the best way to deal with this woman, and then, armed with more skills than most of us, he'll take care of the problem. When I first met Donovan, he wasn't much older than Abigail is now. He's always had to deal with the fact that he's expected to conduct himself at a higher standard because of the Huntington name. After his parents died and he came to live with me, his teenage years were especially difficult, his obstacles significant. He grappled with who he was and who he was supposed to be. The absence of a mother and a father made those questions loom even larger. He acted out, as young men will, and created some problems for himself. My God, was he a handful sometimes; nevertheless, as he matured, he developed and honed this exceptional mental acuity. He found that his considerable intelligence provided him with a rare ability to calculate situations far faster than most. You and I both know how impatient he appears at times. It's because he's already assessed the problem from multiple aspects, decided on the best course of action, and is ready to act. It's a gift few have. When you look at it closer, when was the last time he really screwed up?"

Lauren was once again caught off guard at hearing William speak this way about the man she'd married, and she had no ready response. "What if she's determined to expose him?"

"Then he'll assess the situation and do what's needed."

"We're all living this intricate lie. One mistake and it's going to collapse from the weight of the deception itself."

"Which is why we have to stay focused. We can't afford to make even the slightest offhand comment or innuendo. Do you have any idea how many wealthy people have had their loved ones kidnapped and held for ransom? Besides Meredith Barnes, there's Charles Lindberg, who lost his infant son. Patty Hearst was kidnapped. J. Paul Getty nearly lost his kidnapped son. The fashion designer Calvin Klein had his daughter, Marci, taken, and that's just the short list. There are similar threats issued nearly every day. For Donovan, the mere thought of anything like that happening to you or Abigail is his worst nightmare."

"Worst scenario, how much trouble is he in legally if the world finds out he's alive?"

"Not much, he wasn't a fugitive. Some will cry fraud, try to sue him for one thing or another, but in cases like that deeper pockets usually prevail, which in this case is Donovan. There's nothing that would constitute extraditable crimes. The worst backlash may come from the FAA. They may try and revoke his pilot's license for parachuting out of a perfectly good airplane."

"So, it's just about her? All of this is about Meredith Barnes?"

William pursed his lips and nodded. "Meredith was more than a woman, she was an icon, and still is, more so now that she's gone. The passion behind this issue is what makes it so volatile. We live in a society that worships our heroes and canonizes them until the myth expands far beyond the reality. I saw the media attack him back then and it was brutal. The media today is far more complicated and voracious. It'll be a complete frenzy, and I'm not talking about for a week or two. I'm talking about a lifetime—Abigail's lifetime as well. I promise you, it will never stop. That's what Donovan is trying to avert."

Lauren nodded as she processed the magnitude of William's words and knew in her heart that he was right. She began to feel more than frustration at the present situation, more than her simple anger directed at Montero. Buried in the shifting complexities of their problems, Lauren couldn't ignore a different knot in the pit of her stomach—it was her first stab of real fear.

CHAPTER FIFTEEN

"Tell me about Alec," Donovan asked.

"About five months ago I got an anonymous tip about some Venezuelans setting up shop in South Florida. The source fed us intelligence and it looked credible. These guys were up to something and we wanted to know what it was. The fact that we suspected they were from Venezuela made it even more curious. We wondered if they were organized crime out of Caracas, or if they were into human trafficking, money laundering, or maybe they were terrorists. We assembled a small unit and put these people under surveillance. I was one of the case agents and Alec worked for me."

Montero began to pace slowly back and forth.

"How long had you known him?"

"Alec joined the Miami field office and was then assigned duties out of the West Palm Beach office about ten months ago. That's why Alec volunteered to go undercover. He'd transferred to Florida from Arizona and was a new face in town, so it made sense for him to go under. We put it together quickly, but it was an airtight operation. Miami worked up a background that showed Alec had been court-martialed out of the army for theft, insubordination, and assault. We made him into a real ex-army bad guy. He rented an out-of-the-way little house down in the Florida Keys not far from where the subjects were at the time. Then he hooked up with some of the local bad guys to see what he could learn."

"Were you sleeping with him at this point?" Donovan asked point-blank, if nothing else, to judge her reaction.

"Yes. We were immediately drawn to each other. It was so

strange, he wasn't my type, he was younger, and, God, was he arrogant. I figured he was just another hormone-driven cowboy trying to get me into the sack. Turns out he wasn't like that at all, and it didn't take long for us to become involved. I still don't understand how it happened, but it did."

"What happened then?"

"Alec was doing 'soft' surveillance. A few pictures, notes on the comings and goings of the men involved, very hands off, nothing that should have raised any eyebrows. He did find out that these guys were up to something. They had weapons. They made several reconnaissance trips to local airfields, shook down some locals, but beyond that, nothing. They mostly lay low like they were waiting for something or someone. We were being patient, and then it all went to hell."

Montero's smooth edges began to unravel. Her words were less crisp; she was talking faster. She lowered her head. Her hand covered her mouth as if she could somehow hold her emotions inside her.

"Keep going."

"We'd been apart for nearly three weeks. I hated it as much as he did. Alec finally convinced me that a woman spending the night with him wouldn't raise any eyebrows. I checked a car out of the impound lot and drove to the Keys. Alec and I stayed at his place and made dinner. He showed me the faces of a couple of unfamiliar people he'd photographed. I didn't recognize them, but he e-mailed them to me to run through the system when I went back to the office. After dinner, we had drinks on the deck and talked until the bugs started driving us crazy. We went inside and went to bed."

Montero stopped and took a few quiet breaths to steady herself. A solitary tear raced down her cheek and she brushed it away. "It was later, after we'd gone to sleep, that they stormed the bedroom. It happened so fast neither one of us had a chance to fight back. It was over in a matter of seconds. Whoever they were, they were well trained."

Donovan waited as she drew several deep breaths. There was

nothing about this that was easy for her. He noticed a vein in her neck pounding furiously, and her hands had the slightest of tremors.

"All I have to go on after that are the official reports. Police responded to a report of shots fired at the house the Venezuelans were using at 3:53 a.m. The initial responders discovered four bodies at the scene. Alec was one of them. One survivor was taken to the hospital."

Donovan saw her eyes flood with tears. A muffled sob escaped her throat. She turned away from him, facing the sliding glass door, her shoulders shaking in silent grief.

"You do survive," Donovan said, finally. "You'll never be the same, ever, and despite all of your wishes to the contrary—you will survive. I learned a long time ago that dying is the easy part—it's surviving that's the real trick."

Still facing the window, Montero said. "They found me in one of the bedrooms. I'd been drugged and was unconscious, tied naked to the headboard. The doctor told me there was evidence of intercourse, but then it could have been from earlier in the evening, with Alec. I don't remember anything. I'll never know what happened to us, to me, unless I find the people who were there."

"It sounds to me like someone used the two of you to rid themselves of three drug smugglers."

Montero sniffed and turned around. "That's exactly what happened. We were set up, big time. On the surface, it looked like an FBI agent in search of his kidnapped partner went on a rampage and murdered a houseful of people and was shot and killed in the process. According to ballistics, the bullets that were recovered from all three men's bodies came from Alec's Glock. A single slug hit Alec in the chest and he bled out in minutes. The preliminary assessment was that I was abducted and Alec charged in, guns blazing, and killed everyone in the house."

"Did he?" Donovan asked. "Did he wake up and make a play to get to you?"

"Each of the three men was shot in the head, instantaneous kill shots. In all my time with Alec on the range, I've never seen him do that. We're trained to aim for center mass. They weren't wearing Kevlar so the head shot makes no sense. In my mind someone else was doing the shooting."

"This morning at the hospital, you made a head shot to stop the guy from killing me."

"A body mass shot was out of the question." Montero shrugged. "I had to take out his brain stem or he could have made a reflexive jerk and pulled the trigger on his weapon."

"Maybe Alec was doing the same thing."

Montero nodded. "He didn't kill those men. Alec could shoot, but coming from the army, he was all about automatic shoulder-fired weapons. I spent time with him at the range. To be perfectly honest, he wasn't good enough to enter into a fluid situation and take out three armed men with three perfectly placed head shots. In that situation not many people can do that."

"Who has those skills?" Donovan thought he knew the answer but wanted to hear Montero's response.

"Special Forces guys and spooks. I've seen some CIA types that were scary good with a handgun. To top everything off, we were never able to ID these guys. We ended up with three John Doe's. They had U.S. passports, papers, and credit cards—you name it and it looked real, but everything was a forgery, top-shelf stuff. Each and every paper trail we followed eventually dead ended. It was like chasing ghosts."

"What about Burgess? Did he believe your story?"

"He did, but my actions put his ass on the hot seat in Washington. I broke the rules. Bottom line is that I shouldn't have been there. I set off the chain of events, so Alec is dead because of me."

"You didn't kill Alec," Donovan said as a matter of fact. "What about the informant?"

"We never heard from him again."

"Back up for a second," Donovan said as he rubbed his tired eyes. "So what ties Diego, the guy who tried to kill Michael today at the hospital, to what happened in the Keys?"

"We identified him from some of the pictures Alec shot. He'd been around, so officially he's a person of interest in the investigation. The latest intelligence I saw had both men in either Trinidad or Venezuela. I have no idea why he's involved with the stolen Gulfstream. But I promise you, either this girl, Sasha, or his brother, Ramone, is the key to the puzzle."

"How long ago did all of this happen?" Donovan asked, sorting through all the information.

"Six weeks," Montero said, just before her cell phone rang.

She spun away from Donovan, answered the phone, and then listened. "You're sure? Okay. Thanks, I owe you."

"Who was that?" Donovan asked, sensing the intrusion had interrupted her carefully worded dance of confession and retribution. A look of consternation clouded her face.

"That was a friend of mine. She works Vice down in Dade County. We have a lead on our dancer, Sasha."

"Okay," Donovan said. "So, let's say we find Sasha and through her we discover the whereabouts of Ramone. What then? Do you call in Burgess? Or are you doing this without the rule book?"

"No rules. We find Ramone, he's mine."

If nothing else, Donovan appreciated her direct answer. It was what he'd expected her to say—it was what he'd have said if the positions were reversed. "So we work our way through the bad guys until you find the people who killed Alec. What then, kill them all and call it a day?"

Montero shrugged. "That depends on them, I guess."

"But once they're dealt with, I'm free to go and my secret stays safe?"

"You have my word. But not until it's finished."

She'd said nothing that had dissuaded him from his initial assessment of her. She was a wounded animal. He'd learned a lot in the last couple of hours. That she could be functioning at any effective level so soon after the traumatic events she'd disclosed was hard to comprehend. A month after Meredith had been killed, he'd been a wreck, living on pills and whiskey. He didn't know whether to be totally impressed with how well she was holding it together or terrified that she could bottle up her emotions to the extent that she could orchestrate her revenge. Either way, not only was she completely unpredictable—she was extremely dangerous.

CHAPTER SIXTEEN

Donovan heard the sound of water running as Montero began her shower. He went to the kitchen, poured some whiskey in his glass, then picked up Montero's home phone, and dialed Lauren's cell phone.

"Dr. McKenna."

"It's me. Can you talk? Where are you?"

"Michael's awake. I'm on my way to the hospital."

"How's he doing? Does he remember anything?"

"Susan said he's doing okay. His head hurts. Susan also told me the FBI showed him some pictures, but he didn't recognize anyone. Apparently he doesn't remember much of anything after you two landed."

"Tell him I said hello."

"Why are you whispering?"

"I'm still with Montero," Donovan said. "I don't want her to know I'm on the phone."

"What does that mean?" Lauren asked. "You're not allowed to call your wife?"

"Not when I'm going to talk about her," Donovan took a hard swallow from his glass and grimaced at the burn. "I was hoping you'd read a file today."

"I did. How secure are we?"

"I'm on Montero's landline. I doubt anyone is listening."

"You're at her house?"

"Yeah, this thing might actually be manageable. Based on everything she's told me so far, she's out for vengeance. She lost someone, and there are some connections to what happened to

Michael. We've got a lead and we're going out later to find a few people who may have some answers."

"You're not going to trust this woman, are you? I mean, let's stop and think for a moment what she's really doing here. It's called blackmail. You think running around playing cop makes sense?"

"Did you have time to read her file?" Donovan avoided Lauren's question and waited for her to say something, anything. Briefly, he wondered if she'd hung up on him. He mirrored her silence and waited for a response.

"Her real name is Veronica; she hates that name and goes by Ronnie. She's thirty-six years old, never married, no children. She's an only child, raised in Chicago by her father, who was a United Airlines mechanic. Her mother died in a traffic accident when she was six years old. Her juvenile records are sealed, but there were some early run-ins with the police, typical wild-child behavior, I'd guess. She grew up mostly on her own, spending a great deal of time as a latchkey kid and weekend airport bum with her dad. Most of her early jobs were at a small airport outside Chicago. I guess she got it together, because she went on to graduate from high school as a national merit scholar. She did her undergrad work at Cal State Fullerton and graduated from their criminal justice school at the top of her class."

"What was William's assessment of the person who gave this to him?"

"He seemed to think the source was good, but there is a defense attorney bias at work here."

"Okay, go on."

"She joined the FBI full time shortly after graduation. At one point, she was on a fast track within the FBI, but she was suddenly shipped out, sent back to Quantico for additional training, and then reassigned to South Florida. There were whispers about a sexual harassment issue, one she chose to deal with herself. The file says she may have assaulted a superior officer. There was a similar incident in college, an assistant professor ended up with a broken arm, but no charges were filed. She has an IQ somewhere in the one fortyish range, which makes her Mensa material, *and* she has a temper. Not counting today, she's been involved in four shootings and was cleared for duty after each instance. She's been accused of using excessive force on at least three occasions, but that isn't all that unusual. Criminals love to try and play that card, but who knows? She's an expert marksman and a certified instructor in hand-to-hand combat. Then the report gets a little sketchy, but an agent was killed, and she was placed on restricted duty. Her return to full-duty status is pending the outcome of an internal investigation."

"That's the issue she wants my help with. She lost her partner and may have inadvertently had a hand in it. Overall, what do you think I have to work with here?"

"So, she's fixated on some sort of vendetta?"

"Yes."

"I take it she turned down any thought of financial reward?"

"Yes."

"My guess is she sees you as some sort of kindred spirit. With what she knows, she could view you as a mentor in dealing with what she's going through."

"There are some parallels."

"That should give you some insight into her behavior. You might think about using what you know to manipulate her actions, though I'm not all that sure she's the best candidate for that approach."

"You don't think she can be manipulated?"

"Only that you need to tread lightly, be careful, she's an expert on the subject. I'm no psychologist, but her childhood scenario, coupled with her subsequent actions, point to boundary and accountability issues. She's had several official reprimands for not following procedures. Then there was one other thing that I found worrisome. It was only a footnote with multiple question marks, but it referred to her possible criminal involvement with an underage prostitute."

"In what context?"

"The file only said that the person in question was a fourteen-year-old girl who accused Montero of blackmail and assault, and then the girl disappeared before any kind of formal investigation could be launched."

"Disappeared? As in Montero may have stepped outside the law and dealt with the problem herself?"

"That's how I read it," Lauren said. "In my mind this woman has no real regard for rules."

"She told me she sent my file to someone who has instructions to open it if anything happens to her, which forces me to watch her back."

"This woman is no dummy. This isn't some crazy impulsive maneuver, it was premeditated. Blackmail is illegal and it didn't slow her down for a second. Keep in mind she's an attractive woman who has no problem using her looks to get what she wants. Manipulating others is one of the main weapons in her arsenal. My guess is she's also hypertuned to being manipulated by others, which in my opinion, makes your task more difficult. She's smart, desperate, and, above all, emotionally compromised. You'd do well to remember your Kipling."

It took him a moment, but he finally made the connection. "I'll keep that in mind."

"Please do."

Donovan noticed that the water had quit running. "I need to go. I'll try and call you later tonight or tomorrow."

"Be careful. I mean it. This isn't worth your life," Lauren said.

"If I can't control her, or the situation, I'll bail on the whole thing and meet you in Europe," Donovan said. "Whatever happens we'll be together, okay?"

"Just be careful."

"I will."

Donovan was about to tell Lauren he loved her when he heard Montero's footsteps. He hung up the phone and reached for the bottle of whiskey. When he turned, she was standing there, still wet, one hand holding up her towel, the other a pistol.

"I thought I heard voices."

"That's reassuring," Donovan replied, as he took a drink.

Montero studied Donovan carefully then her eyes darted to the phone. "Who were you talking with?"

"Relax. I called my wife."

Montero used her free hand to tighten her towel. "From here on out, don't make any calls without my direct permission. I'm serious. Don't screw with me again, there's too much at stake."

Donovan stepped close enough to look down on her. Despite the gun, she seemed defenseless wrapped in nothing but a towel. "You bought my help. You didn't buy my soul. Now go put some clothes on."

Montero pursed her lips, her face flushed red. "Be ready to leave here in an hour. And quit drinking, I need you to be sharp."

Donovan watched as Montero padded off to her bedroom. He thought of Lauren's reference to Kipling and decided that his wife may have pretty well summed up Montero. "The female of the species is deadlier than the male."

He dumped out the remainder of his drink as an unsettled feeling came over him. He wondered if the Kipling reference was solely about Montero—or if Lauren had brought it up for other reasons.

CHAPTER SEVENTEEN

Lauren, unhappy about her conversation with Donovan, wheeled her SUV into the Fairfax County Hospital complex and found a parking place not far from the main entrance. She felt completely severed from her husband. It should be the two of them going to see Michael. Instead, he was running around Florida, his phone turned off, with an attractive yet unstable woman who was yanking him around like her own private puppet. When they spoke on the phone, she'd heard the unmistakable sound of ice cubes tinkling in a glass—he was drinking.

It hadn't escaped Lauren that at some levels her husband wasn't all that different from Montero. Both were highly intelligent, they'd each had difficult childhoods and they were also two emotionally scarred, type A personalities, who possessed unique skill sets. Montero carried a gun and a badge—Donovan had private jets and an unlimited bank account. Lauren felt the creeping insecurity that Donovan may have found a measure of commonality, maybe even comfort with a person who was as damaged as he was.

She grabbed her purse, slammed the door, and hurried toward the entrance. It was already pushing nine o'clock, and she wasn't sure when visiting hours ended. She hoped they'd still let her in to see Michael.

As she approached, a man dressed in a suit and carrying a bouquet of flowers came at her from the left. He hurried a few steps, then stopped and smiled widely as he pulled open a door, graciously allowing Lauren to go first. She smiled in return, guessing that he'd come from work, and, like her, was trying to beat the end of visitation hours. She went straight to the information desk. Lauren was given Michael's room number and informed that visiting hours ended at nine thirty. Relieved that she'd made it, Lauren thanked her and followed the directions to the bank of elevators. She only waited a moment before there was an empty elevator going up.

The doors were about to close when the well-dressed young man stepped through. He nodded wordless thanks, and then stood next to her, his hands holding the flower arrangement in front of him.

"What floor?" Lauren said, her fingers poised next to the row of buttons.

"Three, please."

Lauren dropped her hand; it was the button she'd already pushed. "Nice flowers," she said as she admired the arrangement. He smiled again but kept his eyes locked straight ahead as the elevator rose from the first floor, chimed as it passed the second floor. Lauren noticed his hands were shaking and his suit seemed too large for his slight frame.

The elevator chimed once again, and then slowed as they approached three. Without warning, the man slid next to her, and she felt a sharp jab as he pressed something hard into her side. She looked down and saw he held a pistol.

"I will kill you if you don't do exactly what I tell you."

Lauren was stunned. His smile had vanished, replaced by an intensity that sent a shockwave of fear through her body. He was close enough that she could smell him, a mixture of sweat and fresh flowers. He still used the bouquet to hide the pistol from any casual watchers.

"Do you understand me? I will kill you if you scream."

Lauren could only nod as the elevator doors finally parted. She had hoped that there'd be people in the hallway, but the corridor was vacant as they stepped off the elevator. Lauren stopped, not sure where the gunman wanted to take her.

"To the left! Move." He hissed and jabbed her with the gun for emphasis.

Lauren glanced up at the signs on the wall and saw that he was guiding her in the direction of Michael's room. He propelled her forward by pressing the pistol into her left kidney.

"Turn this way," he said, as they reached an intersecting hallway.

Lauren saw a room number as they walked by, it was marked 325. Michael was in room 315, which would be near the end of the corridor. She spotted a vacant chair in the hallway and thought of the security Donovan had arranged. Her knees felt weak—where was Buck? The chair was empty, as was the hallway. The raw fear building in her sent a river of adrenaline into her system. She couldn't get a full breath. Michael and Susan were probably in the room, defenseless. She gathered herself for one desperate effort to stop the attacker. However futile, she decided she wasn't going to die quietly.

Lauren's mind raced. The door to Michael's room was shut and her attacker had his hands full, one held the gun, the other, the flowers. Would he open the door himself, or would he order her to open it? She envisioned both scenarios and decided that would be her signal to do something—anything. She felt as if her nerve endings might explode.

"Stop here," he whispered.

He stepped away from her—his eyes darting between her and the door. "Open it or you're dead."

She felt powerless, he was beyond striking range. She moved toward the door and placed her hand on the cold steel lever. Her last chance would be to slam it in the attacker's face, or his gun hand. Stun him long enough to scream for help.

The door suddenly jerked open from the inside and she was yanked forcefully into the dark room while at the same time a volley of gunshots rang out. Someone had her by the hand and swung her off to the side. She went down hard, slid on the tiled floor, and crashed into the wall. The door slammed shut and a crushing weight fell on top of her.

The explosion seemed to pull all the oxygen from the room, followed by the deafening concussion. Debris peppered her exposed skin and a high-pitched ringing was all that remained as she fought to purchase a breath in the dust-choked air. She felt numb instead of scared, disoriented, as if everything were happening to someone else. The only comfort she found before she blacked out was the fact that she wasn't alone. Whoever had her was still clutching her hand.

CHAPTER EIGHTEEN

"You ready, Roberto?" Montero called out from her bedroom.

Donovan ignored her. He'd showered and had just finished dressing. He wore black slacks, a crisp white shirt, and he hadn't bothered to shave.

He turned and found her standing in the doorway. A short, jet-black wig had transformed her blonde hair. Makeup had altered her already attractive features into what amounted to a different face altogether. Black eye shadow and reddish lipstick gave her face a sultry, dark expression, deceptively sensual. She wore a silky top, her nipples poked against the flimsy material. A black skirt ended mid-thigh and, farther down, her toned legs were wrapped in knee-high black boots. Without thinking, he muttered, "Jesus."

"I'll take that as a compliment."

An invisible trail of perfume hit Donovan as she walked by, something spicy and slightly musky. Donovan stood still until she passed, and then flicked out the bathroom light and followed.

"Where's your phone?" she asked.

"It's with my things in the other bedroom."

"Good. Leave it there."

Donovan slipped on a sport coat and pulled the sleeves of his shirt into position.

"You look nice," Montero said, as she stepped closer and brushed away some imaginary lint from his shoulders. She reached up and fussed with his hair so some of it fell over his forehead.

"Where's your gun?" Donovan asked.

"None of your business," Montero replied and then handed him her keys. "You drive."

Twenty minutes later, with Donovan behind the wheel of the BMW, Montero had directed him turn for turn as they'd traveled south on I-95, past Pompano Beach, until they were in Fort Lauderdale. They got off on Cypress and headed east. He'd watched as she'd carefully kept track of what cars were behind them, issuing abrupt lane changes that would expose a tail. Montero was completely absorbed studying the traffic from the passenger side mirror.

"So, who exactly would be following us?" Donovan asked. "Bad guys, the FBI, or both?"

She shrugged without taking her eyes from the mirror. "Take your pick."

When she was satisfied they weren't being followed, they worked their way back down Commercial Boulevard.

Donovan calculated they'd done nothing but drive in a big circle when she motioned him to pull into the parking lot of a modern, two-story building.

The structure was lit up with garish indirect red and purple spotlights. The driveway arced up to the grand entrance where the front walk wound through tropical landscaping illuminated by a dozen torches. Tucked up near the front door was a neon sign that read: ARENA.

"Skip the valet guys." Montero pointed to an empty space about fifty yards away from the main door. "Park over there, in fact, back the car in so we can make a quick exit if needed."

Donovan did as instructed. Montero pulled down her visor for the mirror and applied one last round of lipstick before she nodded that she was ready. As they walked together toward the entrance, Montero moved closer. She slipped her arm inside Donovan's and pressed herself into him.

"Just remember what I told you. I'll talk. You try and look menacing." Montero squeezed him affectionately, as if completely enraptured by her escort.

Donovan held his fake smile as a tank of a man dressed in a tuxedo and sporting a stub of a ponytail welcomed them to the club. Donovan threw a hundred dollar bill at the girl collecting cover charges and didn't wait for his change. They were handed off to another muscled guy dressed just as stylishly as the first.

"VIP section," Donovan said, and peeled another hundred dollar bill from his roll, pressing it into the guy's hand.

With Montero close, they followed their host into the main room. As they walked together down the narrow carpeted hallway, the music grew louder. Donovan was surprised, the interior was far larger than he'd expected and the décor decidedly upscale. The main room was two stories high with clusters of spotlights aimed at the main stage. Mirrors adorned most of the walls and music poured from dozens of speakers. Above them, a railing stretched around three sides of the room, suggesting a separate, more private area above the noise of the main floor.

They snaked their way through the tables and overstuffed chairs. A dancer, bathed in alternating red-and-white light, performed on the main stage, but Donovan was far more interested in the patrons than the entertainment. The row of seats immediately around the stage seemed to be filled with mostly young men. One group in particular stood out from the rest. Animated gestures and immature catcalls suggested college boys, or perhaps a bachelor party well underway. Other groups of two to four men sat at tables away from the stage. Donovan guessed they were businessmen, still dressed in suits and talking amongst themselves, mostly ignoring the stage. A small bar across the room was crowded with dancers. They, too, were watching the crowd. It struck Donovan as to how a pride of lions might eye a herd of grazing gazelles.

They climbed the stairs and entered the VIP section. Montero selected a table next to the railing for its view of the floor below. The host signaled a waitress who hurried to meet them at their table.

"This'll be fine," Donovan said as the man pulled out a chair for Montero.

"Very well, sir. This is Lindsay, she'll be your server this evening, please let her know if there is anything we can do for you."

Donovan nodded as the man politely backed away, and then he turned his attention to Lindsay. She was young, cute, and radiated cleavage and legs. "Bring us champagne. The best you have."

As Lindsay hurried off, Donovan turned toward Montero. "Do you have any idea what this girl looks like?"

"If she's here, Lindsay will go get her for us." Montero leaned in close. "You do know how to play the rich guy. But then, I guess you already knew that."

Donovan checked out the room. Besides the two of them, there was a female bartender chatting with a white-haired man whose back was turned to him. In a corner booth were two more men with at least three girls curled up close while another danced on the small VIP stage. Donovan watched long enough to verify that all eyes were on the girl. Then he shifted his attention to the scene below. The song ended and the girl who'd been on the main stage was collecting her cash and clothes.

Lindsay arrived with a bottle of Cristal, two glasses, and a bucket of ice. She expertly opened the bottle, carefully poured two glasses, and then twisted the bottle deep into the waiting ice.

"Would you like to start a tab?"

Donovan knew that would require a credit card. Instead, he pulled his roll from his pocket and peeled off several bills and handed them to Lindsay. "Keep the change."

"Can I bring you anything else?"

"There's a girl I'd like to meet. Her name is—" Donovan glanced over at Montero as if he couldn't remember. "Sasha! Yes, Sasha should join us."

"I'm not sure she's here yet. I'll go find out," Lindsay said, and hurried off.

Montero picked up both glasses of champagne and handed one to Donovan. She leaned over and gently tipped her glass to his. "To justice."

"Said the vigilante." Donovan replied. He took a small sip of his champagne and set the glass on the table.

In the crowd below, Donovan spotted Lindsay. She was leading a slender, dark-haired dancer up the stairs. "We might be in business."

"We're going to have to play this kind of fast and loose." Montero grinned. "Let's be nice and see if we can get her to talk."

"If she won't?"

"Then we won't be nearly as nice."

As the two approached, Donovan rolled his chair sideways, away from Montero's. The dancer took her cue. She spun a chair from an adjoining table and pushed it in between Donovan and Montero and sat down. She was wearing a tiny black dress that did very little to cover her body. She crossed her legs, tugged at her hem smartly, and then smiled as she leaned in toward Donovan.

"I'm Sasha." She held out a slender hand. "Your name is?"

Donovan hadn't expected her to be quite so young—or attractive. He caught her Eastern European accent. Her oval face framed large brown eyes that seemed to radiate both innocence and sexuality. She smiled, a knowing expression glimmered on her face, as if she knew her power and wasn't afraid to use it. Donovan caught a sprinkling of glitter on her razor-sharp cheekbones and her suggestive smile accentuated perfect red lips and white teeth. A widow's peak jutted up and split her thick black hair that cascaded down to her shoulders and spilled out onto her flawless white skin.

"I'm Roberto. This is my friend Veronica." Donovan more than enjoyed the angry expression that flashed across Montero's face.

"Hello, Roberto." Sasha smiled, and then turned and greeted Montero. "Nice to meet you."

Donovan flipped several hundred dollar bills onto the table, just out of Sasha's reach, a little incentive for her to stick around.

"Do you come in here often?" Sasha asked as she eyed the money.

"No. This is our first time. Where are you from? I can't quite place the accent. The Ukraine?"

"Very good. Most Americans are very bad with accents. I'm from Kiev. Are you familiar with my country?"

"Yes." Donovan smiled. "I've spent time in Kiev as well as Odessa. I like the Ukraine."

"We're a very friendly people," Sasha purred. "Would you like me to dance for you?"

"Maybe a little later." Donovan stretched out and plucked one of the bills from the table and placed it gently in Sasha's palm. "But, please stay. Would you like something to drink?"

"Champagne is nice."

Donovan caught Lindsay's eye, pointed to his glass, then to Sasha. She nodded and moments later came to the table with another flute and poured champagne for Sasha. Over Lindsay's shoulder, Donovan noticed that a tuxedoed hulk of a man near the end of the bar was looking in their direction and he wore an earpiece, evidence that the club's security staff was wired and communicating. Donovan knew he hadn't been there earlier. Had someone grown suspicious, or was this guy simply making the rounds?

"Where are you from?" Sasha asked.

"Venezuela. I'm here on business."

"How do you know to ask for me?" Sasha held the champagne flute near her lips and leaned over, inviting Donovan to admire her cleavage.

"It seems we have mutual friends." Donovan nodded at Montero. "Veronica can tell you all about it."

"Ramone and Diego Vazquez are both good friends of mine," Montero said, as if they were close. "Ramone told us about you. I thought they might be here tonight."

Donovan studied Sasha's face for any sign that she knew Diego was dead. Sasha immediately removed her hand from Donovan's thigh and cocked her head slightly, as if she were trying to place the name.

"Ramone kept talking about you, told us to be sure and ask for you," Montero said.

"I know Ramone, but I haven't seen him in a long time."

Donovan watched as Sasha's posture shifted subtly, she drew her arms in slightly and tilted her head to allow some of her hair to tumble forward, obscuring her eyes. A sure sign she was either lying—or scared.

"Really?" Montero replied, as if to give the girl time to reconsider.

Sasha shrunk away from Montero, a stricken look flashing across her face. The sultry demeanor vanished, replaced by a frightened young woman. Donovan turned, not at all certain that Montero was the one who had scared Sasha. The only thing that was different was that the white-haired man at the bar had turned sideways. He was well dressed, younger than Donovan had initially thought; his short, silver-white hair and beard were deceptive. Nothing about his demeanor seemed alarming or particularly threatening.

"When was the last time you spoke to Ramone?" Montero pressed. "Or Diego, for that matter?"

"I don't know," Sasha replied as she defiantly swept the hair from her eyes. "I have to go now."

"You're lying!" Montero snapped.

"Leave me alone!" Sasha, visibly upset, started to get to her feet.

Montero yanked Sasha back into her chair. "You know Ramone and you're going to tell me where to find him."

"Let me go!" Sasha cried out, as she twisted her arm, trying in vain to pull free from Montero.

Donovan glanced toward the bouncer. The guy was coming fast. Down on the main floor, he spotted another bouncer hurrying through the crowd toward the stairs. He sat back and wondered how Montero was going to play this.

"I can help you," Montero said, trying to calm Sasha down.

The bouncer reached in and jerked Sasha away from the table. Sasha nearly fell but caught herself and then immediately twisted away and sprinted for the stairs. Donovan lost sight of her as the bouncer squared himself directly in front of him and jabbed a beefy finger into his chest.

"You're out of here, buddy!"

The man had badly misjudged the situation. Montero was already on her feet and threw a lightning fast jab into his fleshy throat. The man grunted as his eyes bugged from their sockets. He fell to his knees, and Montero collapsed him with a knee to his solar plexus.

Donovan kept his eye on the girl. In her rush down the stairs, the panicked dancer shoved aside a customer, and once she reached the main level, she broke into a dead run.

The second bouncer topped the stairs and raced for their table. Montero planted a foot, spun, and in two decisive blows laid him out on the carpet as well.

"Where'd she go?" Montero asked, as she straightened her skirt and snatched her purse from the table.

Donovan pointed below. Sasha was already near the main stage, pushing her way through the crowd.

"I see her," Montero shouted. "Get the car, I'm going after her. There's an outside door on that side of the building. Meet me there."

They hit the main floor running. The place was filling up and Donovan ducked behind a group of new arrivals as two more bouncers moved through the crowd in his direction. Donovan moved quickly and pushed through the main doors only to be met outside by the large tuxedoed man. Never breaking stride, Donovan hit him full in the chest with his shoulder and shoved him to the side. Caught off guard, the security guard toppled backward over a small fence into the dense landscaping. As Donovan ran, he dug in his pocket for the keys to Montero's BMW.

He cranked the engine to life, threw the gearshift into first gear, and gunned the car toward the side of the building. In his mirror he saw a man in a suit burst from the front door and stop; in his hand was a pistol. Donovan spun the BMW around the corner, and was immediately forced to slam on his brakes as a silver Lexus sedan wheeled right in front of him. Farther down the lot, running toward a distant row of parked cars, was Sasha.

Montero exploded out the side door. Sasha turned, startled, and as she did, she stumbled when one of her platform shoes came off. Sasha stopped, her shoe lying on the pavement behind her. Headlights off, the Lexus never slowed and drove straight for her. Sasha was defenseless, still looking over her shoulder at Montero and so she never saw the Lexus coming. The force of the impact snapped her backward over the hood and slammed her hard into the windshield. She never made a sound as she bounced skyward, cartwheeling lifelessly in the air. When she hit the pavement, she rolled to a bloody stop at Montero's feet. Donovan was horrified. He could tell from the unnatural way her torso was cocked that Sasha was dead—her spine no doubt broken on impact.

Montero sprinted toward the BMW and was about to climb in when a pair of hands grabbed her from behind. Donovan saw her elbows fly at her assailant, freeing her from his grasp. She spun and let loose a furious kick that ended solidly in the man's groin. His determination evaporated, and in a gurgle he toppled face first to the pavement and curled up into a ball.

"Go!" Montero threw herself into the passenger seat, slamming the door shut.

Donovan jammed the gearshift into reverse and backed up. In the headlights, he could clearly see Sasha's face. Her eyes were open, staring out at eternity.

When he had enough room to maneuver, Donovan threw the car into first gear and ripped around both Sasha and the man curled up on the pavement. The speedometer was winding through sixty as he roared out of the parking lot trailing smoke from the tortured tires. Donovan yanked the wheel, straightened the car, and accelerated into the night.

CHAPTER NINETEEN

Lauren felt like she was being crushed, she shook her head from side to side, and started to panic and flail in the darkness. As the weight on her chest lifted, her breathing came in ragged gasps. She felt a hand go behind her back and ease her up to a sitting position. She coughed and choked at the dust-filled air. A hand went beneath her knees, and she was swept up from the floor.

She managed to open her eyes despite the tears streaming down her cheeks. Her rescuer was a man she didn't recognize, he mouthed some words she couldn't hear, the ringing in her ears the only sound that reached her. She was whisked through what was left of the blown-out door into the decimated hallway. When Lauren blinked away the tears, she saw that the walls were streaked black, with severed wires and pipes hanging down from missing ceiling panels. Debris littered the floor, as well as blood and body parts. She pressed her face into the stranger's shoulder until she felt herself being set down. Other hands steadied her on a gurney as they wheeled her into a brightly lit cubicle. She opened her eyes and found the faces of other people. They were working on her, but she had no ability to focus, everything seemed abstract, yet she felt immense joy at still being alive. In the disjointed kaleidoscope of activity surrounding her, Lauren became aware of the throbbing pain that raged between her temples. Gradually, sounds began to register, though at first they seemed as if they were spoken down a long tube.

A man in blue scrubs breezed into the room. "Dr. McKenna. I'm Dr. Phillips. Can you hear me? How do you feel?"

"Confused. My head hurts and my ears are ringing."

Lauren lay quietly as the doctor glanced at the clipboard. He flipped through the pages and then he set it aside and used his stethoscope to listen to her heart.

"What time is it? How long was I out?" Lauren asked.

"Only a minute or two. You blacked out, it's sort of nature's way of shutting down and rebooting your nervous system." The doctor took a small penlight out of his front pocket and clicked it on. "Keep your eyes on the light."

Lauren did as she was instructed, then he had her move each limb and joint, running her through a full range of motion tests with only minor pain. "Can you sit up?" The doctor peered into both her ears until he seemed satisfied.

"All things considered, I think you'll be fine. You're lucky your friend did what he did, I'm afraid he got the worst of it."

"What friend? What happened to Michael and Susan? Please tell me what happened."

"I understand Howard Buckley is the man who saved your life. I'll let him give you the details. Your other friends are fine—they were nowhere near the explosion."

Lauren felt immeasurable relief at the news, but she was even more confused. What exactly had transpired in Michael's room?

The doctor took out his pen and jotted furiously on the chart. "I imagine you'll be a little sore in the morning, take some Tylenol or Motrin before you go to bed tonight. The ringing in your ears should subside completely in a few days, but if it doesn't, I'd recommend a visit to an ear, nose, and throat specialist. You seem to be in fine shape otherwise."

"I have a young daughter at home. I need to get out of here." Lauren swung her legs off the table and cringed a little at a pain in her lower back.

"Stay here. Someone will be in shortly. I'm releasing you medically, but I understand the FBI needs you to stay put until they can speak with you."

As soon as he opened the curtain to leave, she saw William and another man standing just beyond. William stopped the doctor and the three men exchanged a few words. The stranger's hair was cut so short as to be almost nonexistent, his handsome face held startling blue eyes. He seemed as if he were carved from granite. He wasn't overbuilt, but looked solid. Underneath the easy smile and handsome face, Lauren could detect the deadly undercurrent that told her he was good at what he did. Beneath his lightweight jacket, Lauren spotted the butt of a pistol. Lauren couldn't hear what was being said, but she could see blood on the legs of his trousers.

The two shook hands with the doctor and then moved to her side and smiled warmly.

William put a hand on her shoulder. "Lauren, this is Howard Buckley."

"Dr. McKenna. My friends call me Buck. How are you feeling?"

"I'm alive. The doctor said I have you to thank for that," Lauren replied. Her ears were still ringing but her hearing was improving. "What happened? Where's Michael? That man—a bomb?"

"I apologize for that," Buck said. "We didn't pick up on the intruder until he'd already joined you in the elevator. To be honest, I didn't know you were coming to the hospital until you arrived and asked for Mr. Ross's room. We'd set up a decoy room number in a section of the hospital that was being remodeled. It's not scheduled to open until next week. We were monitoring the entire situation using video surveillance cameras and we quickly identified that the man was armed, and that he appeared to have a detonator in his hand. The explosives may have been in the base of the plant itself."

Lauren listened to what Buck was telling her. They'd known she was in trouble from the moment she stepped into the elevator.

"How did you know it was me? We've never met."

"Before you landed at Dulles, I prepared a dossier of every person who knew Mr. Ross was in Virginia. I recognized you the minute you arrived."

She silently thanked Donovan for the trust he'd placed in this man.

"I raced to the empty room and waited. Both of his hands were full, so I knew you'd be the one opening the door. I was the one that yanked you into the room." Buck shrugged as if it were an everyday thing. "Sorry about all the brute force, but I needed you clear so I could eliminate the intruder while he was still in the hallway."

"I remember gunshots—they came from you?" Lauren recalled how close they seemed.

Buck nodded. "Trust me, the bomber never got off a single shot."

"How come I'm not hurt and you are?" Lauren asked.

"I wore Kevlar body armor and did my best to cover you up. I got nicked a little bit, it's nothing really, a few scratches. Most of the concussion wave was deflected by the room's heavy door and thick walls. The kinetic energy went upward through the ceiling tiles and down the hallway instead."

"Who was he?" Lauren asked.

"We're not sure," William replied. "The FBI is on the way. Once they secure the scene, they'll run the security tapes through their databases."

"FBI?"

"Yeah," Buck said. "An attempt on the life of a federal agent, in this case you as a DIA analyst, makes this an automatic FBI investigation. It's standard procedure. I spoke with a Mr. Calvin Reynolds at the Defense Intelligence Agency—he's particularly upset about what happened. He said to tell you he's on his way."

Lauren nodded. Of course, Calvin would be on his way. "What about my daughter? I need to get home."

"She's safe," Buck said. "The police should already have your house secured."

"Oh God." Lauren laid her head back on the pillow and stared at the ceiling. A million things started running through her mind and none of them were good. There were police officers in her home and what must be one terrified babysitter. She knew enough about how the FBI worked to know that it was going to be a long night. What if she needed to get Abigail and leave the country? How could she possibly escape?

CHAPTER TWENTY

"Damn it! We need to turn around," Montero said, furiously searching the streets and parking lots around them. "If he went this way we would've caught up with him by now."

Donovan downshifted, checked his mirror, and then swung a hard U-turn. He punched the gas as they sped off in the opposite direction.

"I can't believe it." Montero punched at the air as they drove. "We had her. She was sitting right there with us and we let her get away."

They came to an intersection, and Donovan stopped at the red light. His eyes swept every car that moved past, hoping they could catch a break and spot the Lexus.

"We did lose her, right? She was dead?" Montero asked, quietly. "I mean, as fast as that car was going—the way she hit."

"Yeah, she was gone." Donovan glanced at Montero, trying to judge if she was being somber out of respect for Sasha, or remorseful because she couldn't interrogate her. Donovan looked beyond Montero down a side street to the parking lot of a Walgreens. People had gathered. He could see that it wasn't a casual group. Arms were waving and people were running back and forth.

"What's going on over there?" Donovan asked.

Montero snapped her head around and found what he was looking at. "Get us over there."

Donovan was in the wrong lane for the turn, so while the light was still red, he made a hard right from the inside lane. He ignored the blaring of horns as he accelerated toward the parking lot.

"It's the Lexus!" Montero instantly had her pistol up and

ready. "It looks like someone's down in the middle of those people. Pull up over there and stop. You take the group and see if you can find out what happened." Montero slid out of the car holding her weapon low along her right leg, trying to hide the fact she was armed. "I'm going to check out the Lexus."

Donovan approached the cluster of onlookers. There were no more than a dozen people, mostly customers from the store, but a woman in a blue smock looked to be an employee. As he drew closer, he saw they were standing five or six feet back from a body sprawled on the pavement. A man was face down on the asphalt, the back of his head was a bloody mess, and he was half laying on a white bag from the store.

Everyone seemed to be talking at once. One part of the group was speaking rapidly in Spanish, the other, English. As he listened, they mostly repeated the same thing. That it was a tragedy. That no one heard or saw anything. Where were the police when you needed them? Why was it taking so long for an ambulance to arrive?

Donovan backed away from the crowd and moved toward the Lexus. He looked down the curb line and spotted two shiny metal objects—spent shell casings.

"Montero, check this out." Donovan pointed to his discovery.

"The victim came out of Walgreens and was killed for his car. Sasha's killer is long gone, and now we have no idea what he's driving."

The front of the Lexus was dented where the car had hit the girl. Donovan stepped around to the rear of the car when he heard the pop of the trunk release.

Montero stepped beside him, her pistol up and ready. She carefully lifted the lid and Donovan could see the oddly contorted body. Donovan turned away and glared at Montero. This was the third corpse he'd seen in the last twelve hours.

Montero leaned in for a closer look. "It's Diego's brother, Ramone. Someone is cleaning house."

"Police! Drop the weapon, hands behind your head!"

Donovan froze. He watched as Montero carefully raised her hands, holding her gun by two fingers. "I'm a federal agent," she said, without turning around.

Donovan was so caught up in watching Montero surrender, that he was completely unprepared as someone came up from behind him and forcefully drove him down to the pavement. Shouts filled the night and Donovan felt his hands being drawn up behind him, followed by the cold bite of handcuffs as they encircled his wrists.

CHAPTER TWENTY-ONE

"You're free to go," the nurse said as she slid the curtain open.

Lauren looked up at Buck and William. "Okay, get me out of here. I want to go see Michael before the FBI arrives."

Buck held out a hand, but Lauren waved it off. She sat up and closed her eyes against a spike of pain that shot out from her temples and radiated throughout her head. She fought off the worst of it, and lowered herself off the table until her feet touched the floor. Lauren stood for a moment, testing her legs to make sure all of her appendages were working correctly. Her head continued to pound inside her skull, but it wouldn't keep her from walking.

Lauren followed William's lead as they rode the elevator up one floor and walked to a doorway marked ICU. William pushed through first and held the door open for her. Lauren saw a man positioned outside one of the cubicles, a radio up to his mouth. He was short and wiry with longish hair and a beard. There was an intricate snake tattoo running the length of his left arm. The stranger nodded as they approached.

"Dr. McKenna," Buck said, "This is my friend Andy. Andy, Dr. McKenna."

"Hello, can I go in?" Lauren asked, realizing that she probably only had a few minutes to spend with Michael before Calvin, as well as the FBI, descended on her.

"Of course."

Lauren found Susan sitting in a chair next to the bed, she and Michael holding hands. Michael looked up and smiled. His lopsided grin brought an almost boyish look to his face, and she wanted nothing more than to give him a big hug. Instead, she leaned in and carefully kissed him on the cheek. She pulled away and felt the tears well up in her eyes.

"It's good to see you too." Michael's smile waned and his voice wasn't much more than a croak.

"I can't tell you how happy I am that you're awake."

"Dr. McKenna," Andy stuck his head into the room. "Calvin Reynolds is on his way up here. The FBI is about ten minutes out."

"Thanks, Andy," Lauren replied.

"Calvin's here? The FBI is on their way?" Michael offered up a puzzled expression, first at Lauren, then Susan. "Who in the hell is Andy?"

Lauren heard a gentle tap behind her. She turned as the door opened, and in walked Calvin Reynolds. Nearing sixty, Calvin was tall and thin, almost birdlike. His thinning hair was combed straight back and perfectly in place despite just getting off a helicopter. He was wearing a suit and tie, as well as his trademark suspenders. Lauren guessed he'd been at DIA headquarters putting in yet another sixteen-hour day. His position as a senior deputy director made great demands on both him and his staff. She'd known Calvin since her days at MIT. Lauren didn't need to make any introductions. Everyone in the room already knew each other.

"I wish you'd stay out of trouble," Calvin whispered as he hugged Lauren. He and William shook hands. "Nice to see you again. Thanks for watching out for Lauren."

Calvin moved to Michael and Susan. "How are you two doing?"

Lauren felt herself smile. Calvin loved an entrance and he was good at it. His warmth and charm lit up the room.

"We're much better now," Susan replied.

"I wish I'd have been briefed earlier." Calvin shot Lauren a look of disapproval. "But I wasn't aware of any of this until I was told a bomb went off."

"A bomb?" Michael said.

"Michael is a little behind on current events," Lauren said. "If it's all right with you, I thought you and I could talk in here and bring everyone up to speed at the same time."

"No one is going to rest until we know what's going on," Susan squeezed her husband's hand. "I'm not sure I know everything that's happened at this point."

"I'm sorry," Calvin shook his head. "I need to speak with Lauren privately. At the moment, I'm only authorized to talk to people that report directly to me. Once the FBI has clearance from the doctors, they'll be in to debrief Michael."

"Michael, do you remember anything about the man or men who shot you?" Lauren asked.

"Everyone's already asked me that. Sorry, I don't remember anything," Michael said.

"You managed to hit one of them with your right hand." Lauren pointed to the marks on Michael's knuckles.

"So I've been told." Michael flexed his hand. "I guess I didn't win."

"Lauren, you're with me." Calvin said. "Good to see everyone. Sorry it isn't under better circumstances. Michael, I'm glad you're okay, but I need to remind everyone to sit tight until the FBI arrives."

"I'll come back in when I'm finished." Lauren said as she turned to go. "I promise."

"Lauren," Michael's voice was just barely above a whisper, "where's Donovan?"

"I'll explain it all later." Lauren followed Calvin out of the room, past Andy, and down the corridor. Escorted by two DIA agents whom Lauren had never seen before, they were guided through a conference room to a private office where they took a seat on a sofa that lined one wall.

"This has become a far bigger issue than it was an hour ago." Calvin took off his glasses and cleaned them with his handkerchief, holding them up to light to check his work. "Due to your position within the DIA and the security clearances you hold, the FBI, as well as myself, were immediately called in to investigate."

"Why? I wasn't the target."

"Really?" Calvin pulled a transparent evidence bag from his

inside jacket pocket." This was found in the hallway where the bomb went off."

Lauren saw it was a charred portion of a photo. Only the top section had survived the explosion, but as she looked closer, she was taken aback to find that the two people in the picture were herself and Susan.

"Do you have any idea when or where this was taken?"

"This was taken early this morning when we arrived in Boca Raton."

"That's what William said," Calvin replied. "This suggests the bomber waited in the parking lot for one of you to show up and lead them to Michael. It was very premeditated. Where Michael was being taken, while not a state secret, wasn't widely advertised."

"These people are nothing more than drug smugglers who think Michael can ID them. Right? Florida drug people called Virginia drug people and tried to get to him."

"Drug smugglers don't do what this guy did," Calvin said. "Before he died, he cried out 'God is great,' in Arabic, and then blew himself up."

CHAPTER TWENTY-TWO

Despite Montero's furious protests, both she and Donovan were handcuffed and placed in the back of an unmarked squad car. More and more official cars arrived as well as an ambulance. Someone strung crime-scene tape over a wide area, and once it was determined that the man on the ground was beyond human help, a blanket was placed over his body.

Donovan noticed there were three distinct groups gathering at the scene. There were uniformed police, plainclothes officials, and then there were the civilians. Each wanted a good look at him and Montero. Inside the car, muffled bursts of walkie-talkie transmissions were all they could hear.

"God, I hate this!" Montero said for the fourth time.

To his surprise, Donovan saw someone he recognized. Walking toward the car was a very unhappy-looking Hamilton Burgess —Montero's boss.

"Oh shit," Montero said under her breath. "This is not good."

Burgess was on his phone, pacing the perimeter, stopping at times to angrily glare at them both. Moments later, one of the uniforms came over and opened the car door. They were released from the handcuffs and ordered to stay put. Montero started in by demanding the cop return her badge and gun. Donovan leaned against the squad car, rubbed his wrists, and watched.

Burgess ended his phone call, inhaled deeply, and then blew out his breath as if trying to calm himself.

"Walk with me." When they were safely out of earshot of anyone else, Burgess stopped and faced Montero.

"I can explain, sir."

Burgess raised his hand to stop her from speaking. In a voice not much more than a harsh whisper he began, "You have no idea how much trouble you're in this time. I told you to go home. What part of go home did you not understand?"

"I can—"

"Don't say a word," Burgess hissed.

Montero nodded, but she didn't avert her eyes.

"Did it occur to either one of you that you might not be the only ones out playing cop tonight? Did you bother to consider that maybe we were bright enough to have dug up some information without you?" Burgess ran his hands over the stubble of whiskers on his face. "While you were out playing dress-up, trying to do God knows what—there was, in fact, a joint ATF/Broward County Crime Commission task force doing the same thing. Which forces me to admit to the locals, and my superiors, that I either have a rogue agent and her boy-toy out in the field screwing up an official investigation—or that I assigned an agent on administrative leave to invite a civilian to go undercover. How do you think I feel about those options?"

"Mr. Nash and I were simply out for the evening." Montero shrugged. "We accidentally found ourselves in the middle of something I felt should be investigated."

"You beat the crap out of two bouncers, Veronica. Then, as if that wasn't bad enough, you assaulted an undercover detective."

"Which one was the detective?" Montero asked as if not overly concerned.

"He was the guy in the parking lot of the Arena. He tried to keep the two of you from leaving the scene of a hit-and-run felony."

"He grabbed me from behind," Montero said with a shrug. "By allowing me to kick his ass, he maintained his cover very well, sir. He should be commended."

"Nash," Burgess asked, "what's your part in all of this?"

"I invited Ms. Montero out for a drink, to thank her for saving my life earlier today."

"So you brought her to a strip joint? Yeah, I'm buying that. From what I saw earlier, you couldn't wait to get out of Florida."

"Sir, did anyone run the plates on the Lexus?" Montero asked, clearly wanting to forgo any more ass chewing.

"Yeah, they belong to a Volkswagen Jetta registered in Jacksonville. The Lexus was reported stolen three days ago in Miami," Burgess said. "There aren't any cameras on this part of the parking lot and no witnesses. The guy over there doesn't have a wallet or a cell phone. He paid cash inside, so it's going to take a little while to sort all this out. There have been some other developments this evening, and I'm told that the NSB now has full jurisdiction. I've been ordered to hand over the entire investigation to them."

"That's crazy!" Montera roller her eyes. "The National Security Branch doesn't come in on what happened to us tonight. Hell, this case wouldn't get them out of bed unless— "

"I'll get to that in a minute. But first, here's how this little stunt of yours is going to go down. I'd recommend that you stick to your story exactly as you explained it to me. The NSB and specifically the Counterterrorism Task Force won't buy it any more than I do, but I doubt they're going to spend much time with the two of you."

"Yes, sir," Montero replied.

"Mr. Nash, you volunteered to accompany Special Agent Montero out for a drink to thank her for saving your life?" Burgess asked. "Can I count on that?"

"Sure," Donovan replied.

"Why is Washington involved all the sudden?" Montero asked. "What's changed?"

"Earlier this evening a man detonated a bomb in the Fairfax County Hospital where Mr. Ross was taken."

It took a moment for the words to register through Donovan's fatigue. "What did you just say?"

"Slow down, Mr. Nash," Burgess said. "I've been trying to reach you, but your cell phone is turned off. The attempt to kill

Mr. Ross was unsuccessful. The information I have is that the bomber was intercepted and taken out. Your wife was also involved in the attempt, but I understand she's fine."

"Someone give me a phone." Donovan demanded.

"You can call her in a minute. There are some other details you'll want to know before you call," Burgess said. "According to a Navy SEAL, the last words the assassin said before he detonated the bomb were, 'God is great,' which immediately earmarks him as a possible terrorist. The FBI and a multiagency joint task force are preparing recommendations for the president. The question is how best to respond to a missing Gulfstream we now believe is in the hands of terrorists. The NSB is now the lead office in the investigation. We've been ordered to cooperate but to stand down into a support role, so—"

"Stop it!" Donovan cut Burgess off midsentence. "You two can stand here and discuss all the interagency bullshit you want. But right now, someone better give me a goddamn phone!"

CHAPTER TWENTY-THREE

Lauren was drained. For the last hour she'd sat with two FBI agents and gone over and over what had happened. She'd described the bomber's appearance, his actions, what he'd said, and the slight accent when he spoke. Despite her nearly photographic detail of the events, she knew it amounted to very little useful information, and the FBI had finally excused themselves.

"We're free to go," Calvin stuck his head into the room. "I have your things, and there's a vehicle standing by to escort you home."

Lauren dug her cell phone out of her purse and was relieved that she hadn't missed any calls. Earlier, she'd phoned the babysitter and found out that, yes, the cops were there, and, no, Aimee wasn't going to leave until Lauren came home. Lauren was touched by the girl's dedication.

As she stood, she groaned from battered muscles that had gone stiff sitting in the chair. "How small is this escort? I'd rather not arrive home by motorcade."

"They're being cautious," Calvin said. "I, for one, am happy with the security arrangements. The FBI demanded that they take over Michael's security as well as Susan's and the boys'. I approved Buck and his men to go with you, with twenty-four-seven backup from the DIA. Buck is fully vested in this mission. I'm confident you'll be safe. Now, is there anything else I can do for you?"

Lauren didn't have a way to explain that there was another threat looming on the horizon, one she couldn't talk about. Being guarded around the clock would make it next to impossible for her and Abigail to leave for Europe at a moment's notice. Even if she did go, what was waiting there, another bomb, a bullet? Every time she analyzed her situation, examined each set of facts, she kept coming up with one result. She was trapped.

"Are you okay?" Calvin asked.

"I'm fine." Lauren shook her head as if to collect her thoughts. "I want to see Michael again, and then we'll go."

"This way." Calvin held the door open for her.

"Do we know anything more than we did an hour ago?" Lauren asked.

"No, but this thing has everyone's full attention. Until these people are found and the stolen Gulfstream recovered, everyone in Washington is going to be a little edgy."

"What does Langley think?" Lauren said, her voice dropping to a whisper as she tested Calvin for any information he might have from the CIA.

"They're alarmed. But since the Gulfstream was immediately flown out of the country, they think the principal threat is outside our borders. In their opinion, the Gulfstream will be used in some kind of attack against our assets in Central or South America. The security at our foreign bases and embassies is at the highest level, as well as the airspace surrounding Guantanamo Bay and the Panama Canal. I tend to agree with them. The best and the brightest are focused on this problem. In the meantime, why don't you go home and get some sleep. You've had an extremely difficult twenty-four hours."

"I will, right after I look in on Michael," Lauren said, as the cell phone in her purse began to ring. The number came up as unknown.

"Dr. Lauren McKenna."

"It's me," Donovan said. "I just heard what happened. Are you all right? Where's Abigail?"

Lauren could tell from her husband's tone, along with the rush of words, he was concerned and frightened. She stopped walking and leaned against the wall. "I'm fine. Abigail is at home sleeping—she's surrounded by a houseful of police. I'm still at the hospital with Calvin."

"Calvin's there? How's Michael? Where's Buck?"

"Slow down." Lauren was surprised at how wound up he sounded. She immediately wondered what was happening in Florida. "I just finished talking to the FBI and I'm on my way to Michael's room. Buck is probably there with Susan. He saved my life tonight."

"I heard. I'm so sorry I wasn't there with you. I'm sorry I'm not with you now."

"I'm fine. Abigail is fine. So, you think you'll be home in a few days then?" Lauren said, needing Donovan to understand that she wasn't free to talk.

"Calvin's standing right there, isn't he?"

"Yes, I understand," Lauren continued her charade, hating every second of her deception. "Call me later if you can. I should be home in an hour or so."

"Gotcha," Donovan said. "Love you."

"Talk to you soon." Lauren said, hanging up and shoving the phone back into her purse before turning to Calvin.

"Is he coming back?" Calvin asked.

"He wasn't exactly sure." Lauren couldn't miss the questioning look on Calvin's face. He seemed to have more questions, but thought better of asking. Thankfully, they walked in silence to Michael's room. As they rounded the corner, they found Buck positioned outside. She noticed his legs were bandaged.

"Michael's still awake," Buck said. "I think he's waiting for you."

"I can't thank you enough for everything you're doing."

"I let you fall in harm's way, and I'm sincerely sorry for that."

"Nonsense, you saved me." Lauren patted Buck affectionately on the arm. "Calvin said something about you coming with me when I leave."

"Yes," Buck replied. "The FBI has the hospital wrapped up tight, as well as the Ross residence, which frees Andy and me to accompany you back to your house."

"I hope you'll be able to get some rest."

"Not likely, but thank you for the thought."

Lauren quietly let herself into Michael's room and gently closed the door, leaving both Buck and Calvin behind. The only light on in the room was a small reading lamp. Susan was curled up in her chair, fast asleep, but still holding Michael's hand. Michael smiled as Lauren came into the room.

"Hey there," Michael whispered. "They just gave me a pill to make me sleep, so if I drift off, that's why."

"How are you feeling?"

"They've got me on so many painkillers, it's hard to know exactly how I feel."

"I just talked to Donovan," Lauren sat down on the edge of the bed next to Michael. "He wishes he were here."

"Exactly where is he?"

"He's in Florida helping the FBI with the investigation."

"I know I'm still pretty out of it, but I'm not buying that. He's up to something else, isn't he?"

"Like what?" Lauren tried to keep her face emotionless. Despite the drugs, Michael was smart and intuitive.

"You tell me," Michael said. "The Donovan I know would be here with you if he could. In fact, he'd be the first one to tell the Feds to shove it, and he'd move heaven and earth to get to you and Abigail."

"It's complicated." Lauren was touched at Michael's assessment of Donovan. "He's angry."

"I'm sure he is. I'm angry too," Michael said. "But if someone tried to hurt my family, I'd be standing over them twenty-four-seven. So would he. I just don't get it."

Lauren knew Michael was dead-on with his assessment of Donovan. If Montero hadn't intervened, Donovan would be standing in this very room. "I think he took this harder than anyone would have guessed. He wants the people who did this to pay dearly."

"Oh, believe me, I know how he gets. He wants to kick ass and take names. But if I'm not there to back him up, he gets into trouble. Tell him to be careful."

"He'll be fine." Lauren said the words, but they felt hollow. She was relieved that this conversation was nearly finished. Michael was about to succumb to the drugs.

"Tell him—I'm worried—come home." Michael's eyelids closed and he was asleep.

"I'm worried too." Lauren whispered to herself.

CHAPTER TWENTY-FOUR

They weren't hiding from anyone anymore so the moment Donovan walked into Montero's guest room he turned on his phone. Burgess had ordered her to go home and stay. When he came out of the bedroom, Montero was in the kitchen. Her wig was gone and she was barefoot, dressed in sweatpants and a tee shirt. She was about to pour herself a drink when she froze and cocked her head, listening. Moments later Donovan heard a noise that sounded as if someone was walking on the front sidewalk and then there was nothing but silence.

Montero killed the kitchen light and whispered to Donovan. "Someone's out there. Whatever you do, don't open the door until you hear my voice." She didn't wait for an answer. Glock in hand, she hurried to the sliding glass door and quietly slipped out into the darkness.

Donovan could feel his heart pound in his chest as he crept in the darkness to the front door and listened. It suddenly seemed foolish to have made the assumption that these people were only trying to eliminate Michael.

"FBI! Don't move! Keep your hands where I can see them!" Donovan could hear her clearly through the front door.

"Open the door!"

Donovan twisted the deadbolt and pulled the door open. Standing on the step was a man dressed in a suit. His hands were locked behind his head and Montero prodded him forward into the living room and ordered him to kneel. She kicked the door closed behind her, and keeping the gun trained on the intruder, turned on a lamp. Then she told Donovan to frisk him.

"You must be Mr. Nash?" the stranger said. "I'll warn you that I am armed. A holster under my left arm. Inside my right-hand jacket pocket, you'll find my identification."

Donovan said nothing as he slid the stranger's pistol from its holster. He found the wallet and patted the man down further but found nothing else beyond his cell phone.

"Who is he?" Montero asked.

"His name is Aaron Keller. He's with the Israeli Consulate." Donovan showed the ID to Montero, who snatched it from his hand.

"Special Agent Montero, may I put my hands down now? It's important that we talk."

"Why are you lurking outside my house at midnight?"

"I was about to knock on the door when you came up behind me. I guess I shouldn't be surprised by your aggressiveness."

Donovan studied the man closer. Medium height, dark hair cut short, he looked to be in his mid-forties. The man was in shape, he was wearing a suit and tie, yet there was no evidence of perspiration despite the South Florida heat and humidity.

"I'm not here on official business," Keller said. "I'd just like to talk to you both."

Montero handed him his credentials and phone.

"Stand up," Montero said. "You can have your weapon when you leave."

Keller turned to face Montero. "Thank you. I see someone was about to pour drinks. Please, don't let me interrupt, and might I join you?"

"Israeli Consulate, huh?" Montero eyed him with caution. "How does a Mossad agent know us both by name?"

It made sense, Donovan thought to himself. An Israeli diplomat that carried a pistol may very well be Mossad, which was Israel's equivalent to the CIA.

"Please, can we sit? This meeting is off the record—it never happened. Can we all agree on that?"

Both Donovan and Montero nodded their consent.

"I have a great deal of respect for you, Special Agent Montero. It's my job to be familiar with law enforcement entities that may be working cases that overlap our own interests. You're a talented investigator, which is the reason I'm here."

"How do you know him?" Montero gestured toward Donovan.

"I've been brought up to date on events at a certain gentleman's club this evening. After which I made it a point to learn about your new partner. Mr. Nash is, of course, not law enforcement—but a man with a vendetta. I can appreciate that."

Montero gestured for Keller to have a seat. She went into the kitchen and poured three glasses of whiskey, neat. Donovan took one and she handed the other to Keller. Montero kept her gun close and set her glass down untouched.

"Why do you care what happened tonight?" Donovan asked.

"The same reason you do. Sasha."

"Why?" Montero said without hesitation.

"It's late," Keller said, taking a sip of his Scotch. "Let's not play these games. We'd be naive to ignore the problem we all face. After events tonight in Fairfax, Virginia, as well as here in Florida, all the evidence points toward an Islamic fundamentalist group with a stolen Gulfstream jet. It's very simple. I need to know who has it and what they have planned."

"Every federal agency in the country is tasked with that mission," Montero said. "I'll warn you, I'm not real comfortable talking to member of a foreign intelligence service about an ongoing investigation."

"You're not officially involved in this or any investigation. We're just having a friendly drink. After everything that went down tonight, it's no big secret you've been working this case on your own, and at this point I'm not sure what you do or don't know, but I believe you're correct in linking the events of the last twenty-four hours to what happened to you and Alec in the Florida Keys."

"What do you know about Alec?" Montero jerked as if Keller had struck a raw nerve.

"I know you were set up."

"It doesn't take a genius to figure that out."

"I believe the deception goes far deeper than anyone realized. The men Alec had under surveillance may not have been Venezuelan," Keller said. "That was what your informant wanted you to believe."

"What do you know about my informant?"

"Same as you." Keller shrugged. "Absolutely nothing."

"So who do you think they were?"

"We both know they were well funded, had impeccable documents, and their trail vanished completely. It's my guess they were professionals of unknown origin, perhaps even mercenaries. In fact, until tonight I was fully convinced that you were on the right trail with this being drug-related activity. But after the bomber in Fairfax, I'm not certain of anything. We uncovered some new information about Diego and Ramone. They aren't from Venezuela. They're from Trinidad, a small island nation off the coast of South America with a significant Muslim population. Diego, Ramone, and Sasha were the last direct links to the people who stole this jet, and now they're all dead. What did Sasha tell you before she was killed? Ms. Montero, I'd like to know everything you've learned since the Gulfstream was stolen last night."

"Sasha spooked and ran. We didn't learn a thing."

"That's unfortunate. Did either one of you catch even a glimpse of the man driving the Lexus?"

Both Donovan and Montero shook their heads.

"I understand." Keller calmly pulled out his phone, pressed several buttons, and then handed it to Montero. "Have you seen this man?"

Montero ran her hands back through her hair, pulling it behind her ears, looked, and shook her head. "I don't recognize him." She passed the phone to Donovan.

There was a color image of a man; the angle was down and to the side, revealing no remarkable features except that the man's hair and beard were almost pure white.

Donovan was careful not to betray his recognition. The photo was the guy he'd seen earlier tonight at the club, the one sitting at the upstairs bar. Donovan shook his head.

"Are you positive?" Keller sat up straight, his fatigue seemed to multiply. He set down his drink and rose to his feet. "I thank you both for your time."

"Since we're working together, you won't mind sharing this picture." Montero slid Keller's phone from Donovan's hand, pushed several buttons, and forwarded the image to her own phone. When she finished, she handed it back to Keller, who looked less than amused.

Keller tossed a simple white business card on the table. "My being here tonight is off the record, so I trust you'll not share this visit with anyone else. It was intended as nothing more than a professional warning for both of you to be very careful. You can reach me at that number if you remember anything else. May I please have my gun?"

Donovan handed over the man's pistol. "I have one more question. Why would Mossad be so concerned about a stolen Gulfstream? We're a long way from Israel."

"It's a small world and it's not always the direct threat that concerns us as much as the far-reaching implications. Good night, Agent Montero, Mr. Nash, and good hunting."

Donovan closed the door and waited as Keller's footsteps receded into the night.

Montero put her finger to her lips to silence Donovan and then went to where Keller had been sitting. An exhaustive search turned up nothing. Montero finally grabbed her untouched drink and downed most of it and then settled into the sofa. "I don't see a bug, but I'm convinced that he's completely full of shit. He was here fishing. I'm not sure anything he told us tonight was true."

"I saw that guy tonight in the bar," Donovan said.

"Who? Keller?"

"No, the guy in the photo."

Montero's eyes grew wide. "And you didn't say anything?"

"The only reason Keller was here was to find out if we'd seen that guy. Everything else was camouflage. We're not even sure exactly who Keller is—he flashed some credentials, but who knows? I wasn't about to give him what he came for without knowing what was going on."

"Good call. Where was this guy? I don't remember him. What was he doing?"

"He was standing at the bar. He had his back to us most of the time. I didn't think much about him until Sasha got agitated. It momentarily crossed my mind that maybe she'd reacted to seeing him. He may have been the one who scared her, not us."

"Think about the timeline. Did you see him leave? Is it possible he could have beaten you to the parking lot?"

"I didn't see him leave, but he could have slipped out while we were tied up with the bouncers. If that's the case he could've easily made it to the parking lot before I did. We need to ID this guy. He could have been the one driving the Lexus."

"I don't know how we can." Montero shook her head in frustration. "I can't explain where the image came from. If I tell Burgess we took it in the bar, he'll want to know why we didn't say something earlier. The FBI would go ballistic if someone caught wind of the fact that I'd talked to a Mossad agent."

"Okay, forward the photo to my phone." Donovan said. "I'll find out who he is."

"How?"

"Let's just call it Washington connections."

"Give me your number," Montero said as she picked up her phone, going into the kitchen to pour herself another measure of whiskey. Moments later she told him it was sent.

Donovan checked the image, and then finished his Scotch. He relished the warmth of the liquor as it began to soften the razor-sharp edge he'd been riding all night.

"I have to get some sleep." Montero yawned. "You should too."

"I will. What time in the morning?"

"Let's sleep in and then figure out what's next." Montero collected her drink and she padded back to her bedroom and closed the door.

Donovan refilled his glass before heading to the guest room. He guessed Lauren was home with Abigail by now and that both were safe. He hated what this was doing to his family. He thought of what Lauren had told him earlier about the police being at his house. More than anything he wished he could hold his daughter and tell her that everything was going to be fine. Courtesy of Calvin and the DIA, there was a secure landline at his house, and he hoped that Lauren would be free to talk. He let himself into the guest bedroom, quietly closed the door, sat on the bed, and downed the remainder of his whiskey. He was stalling and he knew it. He couldn't imagine what Lauren had been through tonight, and he had no real idea what to expect or what was causing his sudden uneasiness.

CHAPTER TWENTY-FIVE

Lauren heard the soft chime of her phone announcing a text message from Donovan. She opened it, but there was no text, only the image of a man. A quick look confirmed she had no idea who he was, only that he had startling white hair for such youngish facial features. *What in the hell was she supposed to do with this?* she wondered and set the phone aside.

She was too wired to sleep. Buck and Andy were somewhere close, and they'd told her to go about her normal activities. The only deviation from normal: insistence that she close all the drapes and avoid standing near a window. That, and the armed men lurking inside her home. How could that not feel like an intrusion? From the study, she heard her work line begin to ring, and as she headed that way she knew it had to be Donovan calling.

"Hello," Lauren said.

"It's me," Donovan said softly. "I didn't wake you, did I?"

"No, I just walked in. Where are you?"

"At Montero's. Can you talk? How's Abigail?"

"She was asleep when I got home. The babysitter said she's fine. I can talk for a little bit, but it's still chaotic here."

"You doing okay?"

"I've been better. I spent most of the evening being interrogated by the FBI, the house is now under armed guard, and I have a massive headache that won't go away. Other than that, I'm fine. Hang on, let me close the door." Lauren quietly shut the door and went back to the desk. She saw the book where Donovan had hid the movie and felt her displeasure flare again. "Okay, I'm here."

"Who's there with you?"

"Buck and one of his friends, a guy named Andy. The Fairfax County Police are parked outside the house as well as making regular patrols through the neighborhood. Calvin has the Defense Intelligence Agency on round-the-clock support. Whatever that means. The FBI has taken over the protection detail for Michael and Susan."

"It'll all be over soon. How's Michael doing?"

"He's Michael. He asked me where you were. Even pumped full of drugs, he knows something's wrong."

"It'll be okay."

"You know what? I've had a really crummy night and the last thing I need to hear right now is a bunch of empty platitudes. Earlier, at the hospital, a minute or two either way and everything might not have been okay." Lauren felt her anger rise and she practically dared Donovan to lock horns with her.

"You're right. I'm sorry."

"Why did you text me this picture?" Lauren ignored his frail apology. "Who is this guy?"

"It's a long story, we think this guy might be involved, but we don't know who he is. An Israeli diplomat named Aaron Keller gave us the photo. Can you run both men and see what turns up?"

"Why can't you get the FBI to do it for you? It would probably be a whole lot faster."

"I'm afraid they'd leave us out of the loop."

"All right, I'll see what I can do."

"As far as the situation here, we're in better shape now than we were a few hours ago. The investigation is in full gear. It's gotten everyone's attention, and I think the FBI will turn up something soon."

"Not according to Buck."

"Why? What does Buck think?"

"I overheard him talking to someone with the FBI. He thinks that somehow we've become a target, that some jihadist group has leveled a fatwa against us and that it's far from over. What happens if I have to jump on a plane to Europe? We won't have any protection at all from the people who are trying to kill us."

"If we have to go, we'll take the security with us. It was how we were going to have to start living anyway."

"God, I really hate this. I can't go to the grocery store, let alone sneak off to Europe."

"If you think it sucks living in an armed camp for a few days, imagine being Mrs. Robert Huntington. It'll be armed guards twenty-four-seven."

"I don't want to be Mrs. Robert Huntington, but most of all I don't want to be a widow."

"Nothing's going to happen as long as Montero's with me—she's not a threat as long as I'm here. She's been sidelined by her superiors, and if I can keep her in check until the case is solved, then my part of the bargain will have been met."

"I don't know why you're applying simple business principles to a volatile, emotionally impaired woman. You don't have a single assurance that she's going to do what she tells you. How can you trust that she won't string this out indefinitely? Why should she ever let you go? She has her own personal billionaire on a string. I'm not seeing an endgame here that turns out well at all—for anyone."

"I'm not on a string, and despite what we know about her from the file, I think her behavioral issues are manageable. I feel I can trust her."

"Oh, perfect. I'm so glad you can trust the woman who's blackmailing you. I'm sure Montero's been grilling you about your past. Why wouldn't she, you're an icon. Does she know about the documentary? It must be great to hang out with someone you can trust." Lauren hated that she'd said the words, but somewhere down deep she knew she needed to confront him about what she knew and how much it had hurt her.

"I was going to tell you about the film. I just wasn't sure how to explain certain things."

"I'm your wife, I don't expect you to have every negative emotion quantified and catalogued before you bring it up to me. In fact, I'd prefer you bring me the unvarnished truth, and we'll work on the problem together."

"I'm sorry. I don't operate that way."

"Give me one good reason why not," Lauren said with more bite than she intended.

"Meredith thought very much the same way you do, and my unfiltered actions got her killed. If you watched the movie, my guess is you have three questions about Costa Rica. The threats, the delay in my getting the money, and the phone call."

"I already know about the threats and the money. William explained the delay and he told me the threats weren't anything specific."

"William doesn't know everything," Donovan said, his voice almost a whisper. "There was one threat that came straight to Meredith. We came back from a meeting to find an envelope placed on the bed in our hotel suite. Inside was a letter written by some political extremist that basically threatened to kill Meredith. She shrugged it off and said that security at the conference was perfectly adequate. I was furious that some crazy man knew what room we were in and I let my fear get the better of me. Without thinking it through, I convinced her to leave the hotel and get to the villa we'd rented, thinking we'd return when we had beefed up security. I didn't really think it through, and as soon as we abandoned the security of the conference, she was taken. I'd reacted emotionally. Took a manageable situation and turned it into the scenario that got Meredith killed."

"You tried to protect her."

"What I did was get her killed. She's dead because of me, plain and simple. I can't change what happened. I can't bring her back. I can't change places with her. All I can do is never forget her and with that comes not forgetting what I did to her. With every molecule of my being, I want to keep something like that from happening to you or Abigail. I may appear impulsive at times, but I can assure you that I process everything, and that will never change—ever."

Lauren felt stung. His fury, guilt, and shame possessed an energy she'd never known him to have—and he'd unleashed it at her, as if his revelation came with a measure of punishment. Then she felt her resentment rise. He'd made her feel like she'd crossed some sort of line, but in her mind this was his mess, issues he'd never dealt with, and most certainly wasn't her doing. She decided that as long as he was talking, she'd ask him the one question still on her mind. "What was said when you talked to her that night?"

"That's private."

Fully rebuffed, Lauren felt the last of her patience dissolve into anger. "Fine. You and Montero do what you need to do. I'm exhausted. We'll talk later." Lauren slammed the phone down and found that her hands were shaking. She felt the tears come and did nothing to try and stop them. She lowered her head, pressed her hands over her face, and began to sob.

CHAPTER TWENTY-SIX

Distant screams filled the morning sky. The sun hadn't yet cleared the trees, but already the air shimmered in the heat. As always, everything started from far away and drew closer. What at first sounded like only a few scattered people's cries of alarm, quickly grew to dozens, then hundreds. Donovan felt his growing panic and fought the muddy field, each step forward a monumental effort. Turning back wasn't an option. In the distance, he could see her lying motionless, pale skin and auburn hair. His terror grew and he pushed harder, heart thudding furiously in his chest as the screaming around him grew in intensity. The voices of a thousand people were now wailing and sobbing. The field resembled an amphitheatre and Donovan clawed his way closer to her body. Lurching forward, pulling himself with his hands, he kicked furiously with his legs to cover the last few yards. Tens of thousands of tortured voices shrieked at him from every direction.

With a hand darkened by the soil, he gently touched her shoulder so he could see her face. Her skin was cold and lifeless; her green eyes stared past him. The single bullet that had neatly perforated her forehead told him she was beyond help—but it wasn't Meredith—it was Lauren. The thousands upon thousands of voices went silent at the same moment and the only scream was his.

"Donovan! Wake up! It's just a dream."

Arms wrapped him up and he fought the restraints until the images in his head faded and then dissolved. In the darkness he slumped, spent from exertion, and he felt hot tears roll down his face. His breathing was shallow and rapid. His heart pounded and he felt sticky and flushed. He couldn't remember where he was—only the paralyzing fear that Lauren was gone.

"You're safe," Montero said as she clicked on the bedside lamp.

Donovan brought his hands up to his face to ward off the light. He struggled in the purgatory between the nightmare and reality.

"Take long, steady breaths."

Donovan let the pieces began to arrange themselves in his head. He was in Florida. Montero's house—she had her arms around him. He opened his eyes to find a genuinely concerned expression on her face. Donovan spotted her Glock on the nightstand and understood that his night terror must have alarmed her.

"You were yelling—calling her name."

"Whose name?"

"Meredith's. I'm sorry if I've dredged up old wounds."

"You didn't dredge them up. They're always there."

"Is it always the same dream?" Montero asked. "I have the same one over and over. In mine I keep trying to wake Alec up to tell him we're in danger and I can't—he never wakes up."

"Yeah. Something like that." Donovan didn't want to share his dreams with her, or anyone else for that matter. He gradually became aware of the fact that Montero's hand was still on his shoulder. Sitting on the bed next to him, her proximity made him feel uncomfortable. "What time is it?"

"It's a little after five."

"I'll never get back to sleep. I think I'm going to hit the shower and get dressed."

"I'll make coffee." Montero stood up and grabbed her Glock. She hesitated for a moment and then left the room, gently closing the door behind her.

Donovan threw off the damp sheets, swung his legs off the bed, and rested his head in his hands for a moment. He recalled his conversation with Lauren. It was a miracle he'd even gotten to sleep at all last night. He needed to talk to her, but he also needed time to process a response. The fact that she'd found and watched the documentary about Meredith was bad enough, but he'd hidden it from her. He was eventually going to tell her. He just hadn't been prepared for how hard it had hit him. Until he could get through watching it unfazed and intact, he hadn't wanted to share it with her. All of that sounded rational, but now she'd discovered his deception. She was angry, and he didn't blame her. What he hadn't been prepared for was the intensity of her anger. Last night she was hurt, tired, and scared, and he was an easy target. After all, he was at fault. She'd said last night she didn't want to be Mrs. Robert Huntington. Right now he wondered if she was all that thrilled about being Mrs. Donovan Nash.

"You better get in here and see this!" Montero shouted from the living room.

Donovan threw on his pants and shirt just as his cell phone began to ring. He didn't recognize the number, but he snatched it from the table and ran to join Montero.

She was standing in front of the television, the remote still pointed at the set.

"CNN has learned from the FAA that a search is now underway for an overdue airliner. Pan Avia Flight 17, flying from São Paulo, Brazil, to Washington Dulles is listed as missing."

Donovan answered the phone. "This is Nash."

"Mr. Nash. It's Captain Ryan Pittman onboard the *Atlantic Titan*. I'm sorry if I woke you."

"Ryan, I was already up. What's going on?"

"We have a situation. About an hour ago we encountered a fairly large debris field coupled with a fuel slick on the water. We've discovered bodies as well. At this point we've recovered enough wreckage to determine that it's from an airplane."

"Are you certain? Any idea whose airplane it is? I'm watching a CNN report about an overdue Pan Avia flight. Do you think that's what we're dealing with?"

"Too soon to tell."

"Bodies?"

"Fifteen, so far. Judging by the amount of kerosene floating in the ocean, my guess is it's something big."

"How long until you have some assistance?"

"We've notified the Coast Guard and they should have a cutter here by midday. The British Navy has a destroyer steaming our way, as does the U.S. Navy, but they won't be here until sometime late tomorrow or the next day. Right now we've been asked by the Jamaican authorities to secure the site and recover as much debris as we can until more help arrives. I've already deployed all of our underwater acoustic and sonar assets to try and pinpoint the wreckage."

Donovan turned to Montero and mouthed that he'd be right back. He went to the bathroom and closed the door and lowered his voice. "Ryan, I need a favor."

"Sure, name it."

"If you're in contact with the Navy or the Coast Guard, ask them to route a request to the FBI field office in West Palm Beach. Tell them my presence is required immediately onboard the *Atlantic Titan*. The guy you need to talk to is Hamilton Burgess. Don't mention to him we've spoken, only that you're trying to find me."

"You got it." Ryan replied.

"Where exactly are you?" Donovan asked. "And what's the closest airport that will handle the Gulfstream?"

"We're a hundred thirty-five miles east of Kingston, Jamaica."

"I'll call when I have more details. Plan on having the helicopter meet me in Kingston."

"Will do," Pittman replied and severed the connection.

Donovan ignored the sad state of his reflection in the mirror. He could feel the effects of the liquor he'd consumed the night before and the gritty hollow feeling of not enough sleep. He waited until the water turned ice cold and leaned in and splashed as much as he could stand on his face. The jolt would have to get him through until he could pound down some coffee and properly shower. When he emerged from the bedroom, he found that Montero was on the phone. Donovan moved past her and began loading the coffeemaker.

When Montero finished her phone conversation, Donovan was surprised to find that she looked deflated, both frustration as well as resignation showing in her eyes.

"What's wrong?"

"That was Burgess." Montero said. "I have to meet with the shooting review board this morning at nine sharp. It's routine, but it would be helpful to know what the one eyewitness said in his statement."

"The truth, that you saved my life."

"You didn't mention the intercom mix-up?"

"There was really no proof and it didn't seem relevant."

"Thank you for that." Montero seemed relieved. "Burgess also informed me that there's an Eco-Watch ship on the scene of what everyone now thinks is the site of the Pan Avia airliner crash. It seems your presence has been requested aboard your ship. I talked Burgess into thinking it's a good idea for me to stick with you—for your protection. I think he's relieved I'll be out of South Florida. So it sounds like we're going out to your ship."

"I just heard about all of this myself. We need to get to Kingston, Jamaica as quickly as we can," Donovan said without any trace of the pleasure he felt at maneuvering Montero out of South Florida into an environment of his making.

"And Nash," Montero added. "The moment we get any kind of lead on the guy with the white beard and hair, we're on it. I don't care where we are when it happens. Do I make myself clear?"

CHAPTER TWENTY-SEVEN

Donovan climbed the *da Vinci* to 37,000 feet, relieved to finally be leaving Florida behind. The rarified air was intensely clear, as if the entire atmosphere had been scrubbed clean by the cold front. Kyle Mathews was seated in the right seat acting as first officer. Kyle had been with Eco-Watch for almost two years and was steadily working his way up to captain. He was in his early thirties, born in the Midwest, down to earth and easygoing. Donovan enjoyed flying with the young man and was impressed with how he'd overseen the maintenance performed on the *da Vinci*.

Montero was seated in the jump seat, which placed her between and slightly behind the pilots. Donovan and Kyle quickly drifted into the easy conversation of professional pilots at work, which, by design, excluded Montero from most of the conversation.

Donovan scanned the instrument panel, then shifted his view out the side window. From seven miles up he could see the green vegetation and stark white beaches of the Bahamas. Under the gin-clear water were the muted contours of miles and miles of submerged sand dunes, shaped and reshaped by the ceaseless storms and tides of the Atlantic.

Kyle opened a high-altitude aeronautical chart and smoothed it out on his lap. Using a pencil he marked an *X* between Jamaica and Haiti. From a file, he pulled a sheaf of paper and began organizing.

"What do you have there?" Donovan asked.

"We all saw the latest televised reports of the Pan Avia crash before we left Boca Raton, and I'm trying to fill in some of the blanks. The news outlets want it to sound all mysterious, comparing this accident with that Air France A330 that went down years ago over the Atlantic Ocean. But I don't think that's the case."

Donovan nodded his silent agreement. The Boeing 767 was a proven design that had been flying for decades. Nothing in its history resembled the Air France crash, which was eventually ruled as being caused by a multiple onboard flight computer failure coupled with probable pilot error causing the airliner to plunge into the ocean in stormy weather.

"The only aspect of the Pan Avia flight that was out of the ordinary was the significant course change to avoid weather," Kyle explained. "Instead of flying the normal track over the Windward Islands, it deviated west to get on the backside of the front. Given the conditions, I say it was a good call."

"Is this the same weather that you dealt with coming into Florida?" Montero asked Donovan.

"Yeah, same cold front, it just moved offshore."

"The fact that the crew deviated this far to the west, toward Jamaica, speaks to the core intensity of the thunderstorms." Kyle said. "San Juan reported radar tops nearing fifty thousand feet at several places along the line. According to the reports from the ship and the Eco-Watch crew on-scene, the wreckage is spread over a large area which points toward an in-flight breakup. But the large volume of raw, unburned jet fuel in the ocean tells me that there wasn't a large-scale explosion."

"Go on," Donovan urged. Kyle had obviously been giving this some thought.

Kyle extracted a stack of papers from the file. "I printed out the archived images from the DMSP F16 satellite. It starts with a multispectral image that combines both infrared and visual aspects. This goes back twenty-four hours and each subsequent page marks a fifteen-minute interval."

Donovan took the papers from Kyle and flipped through them. The sharp line of thunderstorms tracked quickly across the Caribbean until the frontal system ran out of energy and fell apart as it passed the Virgin Islands.

"I had to extrapolate some data based on available winds aloft and projected speed of the airliner, but here's a higher-resolution satellite image of the area where the 767 went down at approximately the time the crash would have occurred." Kyle handed the sheet to Montero.

"That's amazing," Montero said. "Where did you get this stuff?"

"What do you mean? We're Eco-Watch; this is what we do." Kyle shrugged. "We have access to nearly all of the weather collection agencies in the world."

Donovan studied the visible infrared image. Its nighttime dark-blue hues seemingly otherworldly, but it clearly showed the gap in the storms the 767 captain had elected to fly through. A yellow outline depicted the islands of Cuba, Jamaica, Haiti, and the Dominican Republic. Donovan agreed with their decision—the estimated flight path looked relatively clear. He'd have made the same choice. Any pilot would have.

"What's this one?" Montero took the next sheet from Kyle.

"This is microwave imagery that gives real-time rainfall amounts. On either side of the 767, the precipitation rate is roughly one inch per hour. That tells me the closest thunderstorms to the doomed airplane were relatively tame—certainly not the towering super cell it would take to destroy an airliner."

"At some point, well before they encountered the actual thunderstorms, the Pan Avia crew would have seen the bright discharges of lightning marking the storms. They also would have seen the gap on their weather radar," Donovan said. "We've penetrated similar storms with no ill effects other than turbulence."

"They probably had a conversation with air traffic control and the decision was made to turn through the hole. Despite what the media has been reporting, I doubt that whatever brought down the Pan Avia flight had anything to do with the weather—which tells me that whatever happened took place quick enough to keep the crew from sending a distress call. The airplane broke up at altitude. In my mind it has to be from a bomb or some other outside source."

"Who else has this information?" Montero replied. "I mean, how fast does the National Transportation Safety Board come to the same conclusion you have?"

"I'm sure they already have—it's not proprietary information," Kyle explained. "Before the NTSB is finished, they'll have raised every salvageable piece of the airliner from the ocean floor and painstakingly reconstructed the airframe. Only then will they offer even a preliminary report as to the cause of the accident."

"I need to get up." Donovan released his harness. "I want to check on some of the equipment in back. Yell if you need me."

"Will do," Kyle replied.

Donovan slipped past Montero into the privacy of the empty cabin. He slowly walked to the back of the plane, looking, listening, and testing the air for the distinct odor made by an electrical fire. Satisfied that everything appeared normal, he sat down at one of the science stations and opened a small compartment that housed a laptop computer. He flipped open the screen and waited. He'd debated using the satellite phone to call Lauren, but a light would illuminate in the cockpit, and Montero might notice and come back and start asking questions. Instead, he'd decided that a short note to Lauren via e-mail might work better.

He clicked his way through the icons until he secured the uplink and then quickly rifled through his in-box. Mostly things that could wait, though there were several he forwarded to Peggy to handle. As he worked down the list, he saw a message from Lauren. Closer inspection revealed it had been forwarded to her from someone at the DIA, no doubt the information he'd asked her for last night. He took it as a good sign that she wasn't so angry that she wasn't communicating with him. Though when he opened the mail, he discovered she'd written nothing, only sent the attachment. He registered the obvious omission and began to read.

Subject: Nathan David Strauss. b. 1969–

Facial-recognition search identified the individual in question as Nathan David Strauss, former senior opera-

tive with the Israeli Defense Forces. Strauss served with the IDF Special Missions Unit—severely injured in an airplane crash. Deactivated and retired. Divorced, no dependents. Confirmed heavy drug user due to severe hip injuries. Whereabouts unknown. Thought to be living near Haifa or possibly deceased.

"Why is Keller trying to find this guy?" Donovan said out loud. "He's one of their own."

Subject: Aaron Benjamin Keller. b. 1968–

Aaron Benjamin Keller is currently diplomatic attaché at large, assigned as a special envoy to the Israeli ambassador in Washington D.C. Current duties include multiple liaison duties between Mossad and pertinent antiterrorist task forces of the United States government. Holds full diplomatic immunity. All other information classified above this clearance level.

Donovan scrolled down and found what looked like a passport photo of Keller. He was legitimate. He printed everything out and then opened a fresh page to write Lauren back.

When he'd finished typing, he gave it a quick read through and was satisfied. He sent the message and then logged out. He looked out the window, enjoying the moment of solitude. When he glanced back up the aisle, he saw that Montero had turned in the jump seat, watching him. He motioned her to join him.

"Are you okay?" she asked.

"Yeah. Why?"

"You seem preoccupied. You're not suffering any aftereffects from last night, are you?"

He had no idea what Montero meant. Was she referring to being handcuffed and thrown in the back of a police car? The three dead bodies? Or the nightmare she'd witnessed? Did she have some inkling how much he hated going out to sea? Could she sense that? He exhaled heavily. The last thing he needed was Montero thinking they'd shared a moment or that she had some sort of insight into his soul.

"I'm fine. How did the review go?"

"It was routine. The statement that you gave, that you were about to be killed when I shot the gunman, made it all pretty perfunctory."

He handed her the report Lauren had sent. "I got this a few minutes ago."

"What the hell?" Montero said as she finished reading. "Keller is full of shit. He knows exactly who Strauss is."

"What we do know for sure is that Keller was playing us. I think Strauss is on the run and Keller can't find him. The question is: what is Strauss doing and what's his connection to all of this?"

"I have no idea," Montero replied. "Is Strauss a Mossad agent hunting bad guys? Or has he gone solo? Either way, I want to talk to him. Whatever game Keller is playing tells me that Strauss knows more than we do. If we don't find Strauss before Keller does, then I doubt anyone will have a chance to interrogate him. Keller will deport him or eliminate him before he can be any kind of an embarrassment to Israel."

"We need to leak this information to the FBI," Donovan said. "They'll find Strauss."

"We can't. They'll trace it back to you and me and we'll both be screwed. The only option we have is to find Strauss before Keller does."

CHAPTER TWENTY-EIGHT

Donovan banked the *da Vinci* over the last of the lush hills and settled onto final approach to Kingston International Airport. He touched down smoothly and then taxied clear of the active runway and fell in behind a battered yellow truck with a weathered FOLLOW ME sign bolted to the roof.

Kyle busied himself with the checklists as they were led past the main terminal to the east side of the Kingston airport. As they rounded the edge of the cargo terminal, Donovan spotted a row of private airplanes. There were two other Gulfstreams, as well as an older Challenger and some smaller airplanes, a Westwind and a Cessna Citation. There was also a Falcon 900, and Donovan noted the tail number as being Brazilian. He surmised it was probably connected in some way with Pan Avia Airlines.

Off to the side, sitting on a separate concrete pad was the Eco-Watch's Bell 407 helicopter. It sported the same blue-and-gold paint scheme as did the *da Vinci*. Along the slender tail, the words ECO-WATCH were clearly visible. Standing next to the helicopter, hands on hips, was Eric Mitchell, pilot aboard the *Atlantic Titan*.

The FOLLOW ME truck sped up and swung in a wide arc to show Donovan where to park. The handler jumped out of the truck and positioned himself on the tarmac. He raised red batons, flipping them smartly as he guided Donovan into a spot that placed the *da Vinci* in perfect alignment with the rest of the corporate airplanes. Satisfied, the handler crossed the batons signaling Donovan to stop. Kyle quickly ran through the process of shutting down the airplane while Donovan moved past Montero and opened the door. The heat and humidity hit him immediately. There wasn't much of a breeze and the thick air felt like he'd just stepped into a sauna. Within seconds his clothes begin to cling to his skin. A large man, who introduced himself as Javier, welcomed them to Jamaica.

"Javier," Donovan shook the man's hand, "I'm not sure how long we're going to be here, it might be a day or two."

"Captain," Javier smiled, "you are welcome to stay as long as you want. I have a driver standing by to take you into Kingston once we're finished here."

"Actually, it'll just be my copilot who is going to stay in town." Donovan had already discussed the logistics with Kyle. Since living space aboard the ship was limited, it would be best if he remained onshore. "Ms. Montero and I will be leaving on the Eco-Watch helicopter."

Javier promised to return shortly with paperwork. Beyond a perimeter fence Donovan spotted a cluster of vehicles sporting tall antennas that could only belong to the media. He cursed under his breath, lowered his head, and went back into the cabin. He knew all too well that a dozen high-powered lenses would be focused on the ramp. The images would be broadcast around the world. Though it was already widely reported that Eco-Watch was involved in the salvage process, any thought of he himself being photographed made him uncomfortable.

With the *da Vinci* secured, Kyle left for Kingston. Donovan took a long look at the airplane, locked the main door, and walked toward the helicopter, careful to position Montero between himself and the media vans. For the most part, Donovan disliked helicopters. They were loud, slow, and vibrated more than anything operating properly should. As he neared the machine, he reluctantly twirled his index finger for Eric to start it up.

Minutes after liftoff, they'd coasted out and were heading toward the *Atlantic Titan*. Donovan hated the water more than he disliked helicopters. Attached to the landing skids of the 407 were emergency floats that, if needed, could be instantly inflated. Donovan found no solace in the technical side of the equation, and couldn't imagine that a helicopter made much of a boat.

When he was just a boy, he'd nearly drowned in the Pacific Ocean. Since that day, he'd done everything he could to keep the ocean at arm's length. He could never shake the feeling that given half a chance, the ocean would try and finish the job. As the helicopter raced past the beach out over the open water, Donovan felt his stomach churn, his hands clenched into sweaty fists, his entire body tightened, and he was forced to close his eyes to blot out the vast blue ocean. Montero and the threat she represented was the only earthly reason he'd purposely get on a helicopter and fly out to a ship. Donovan wore headphones due to the noise, but he switched off his interphone to tune Montero out, and lowered his head as if asleep. His eyes remained closed, a defense mechanism against everything going on around him. If he couldn't see or hear his surroundings, then he could control his apprehension at being such an easy target for what he knew was a vengeful sea.

Donovan withdrew into himself and focused on his breathing. He thought of Lauren and Abigail and wished he were home with them. He remained fixed on each precious detail of what it meant to be a husband and father, and how much he missed Abigail. Being a father had changed him, made him a better man. Abigail had introduced him to unconditional love and schooled him daily. She was Daddy's little girl and they both knew it. He thought of the lengths he'd go to protect them, which were infinite—including going to sea.

A hand shook his leg and Donovan opened his eyes. Montero was looking at him, speaking into her microphone, but Donovan had no idea what she was saying. He found the knob and turned up the volume on his headset.

"We're almost to the ship," Montero repeated.

Donovan leaned to his left so he could see out the front of the helicopter. The *Atlantic Titan* was far from sleek, but she more than made up for it with her functionality. At 285 feet in length, with a beam of 55 feet, she stood tall and proud in the water. Her helicopter pad was set forward of the bridge, which cleared the stern for the heavy lift cranes used to deploy the deep submersibles. Her true beauty lay within; she could cruise for nearly a month carrying a total of twenty officers and crew, as well as up to thirty scientists who enjoyed over four thousand square feet of laboratory space. She was easily one of the most well-equipped research ships afloat and her hull bore the same blue-and-gold paint as the Eco-Watch aircraft.

Eric approached the *Atlantic Titan* at a ninety-degree angle and slowed gradually as he neared the forward superstructure. Michael had handpicked Eric from a small group of former navy helicopter pilots. Michael had maintained that living on a ship was a special skill, and if they didn't hire an ex-navy pilot, they'd have turnover problems. Michael had been right. Eric had been with them for years, and was very good at what he did.

Donovan's muscles tensed as Eric swung abeam and brought the helicopter into a hover. With thousands of hours logged in airplanes, Donovan fought the unnatural sensation of flying without actually moving. As they descended, Eric matched the ship's forward speed with a perfect sideways nudge and gradually closed the distance. On the pad, a deckhand issued precise hand signals to assist Eric in touching down in the exact center of the circle. Eric made it look easy as the skids nestled onto the platform and he let the engine fall to idle.

The second the all-clear signal was given, Donovan opened the door and stepped out onto the deck. The first thing that caught his attention was the smell of raw kerosene. The second was the unsettling motion of the ship gently rolling beneath his feet.

From a hatchway, Donovan heard someone call his name. He looked and found Captain Pittman striding in his direction. Pittman was in his early fifties, fit and trim, and still moved with the determination of the college running back he once was. Eco-Watch Marine was run out of the Norfolk, Virginia, office but the two men had met many times. Donovan smiled at the captain and they shook hands in earnest. Donovan, in turn, introduced Montero before the three of them moved inside to escape the noise from the helicopter.

"That's better," Captain Pittman said as he turned down the volume on his handheld radio. "Eric is refueling and going back out."

"Where are we in the search for the black boxes?" Donovan asked.

"Let's head up to the bridge. We've got everything plotted on the charts."

Donovan fell in behind Pittman and Montero as the three of them wound through the ship's superstructure, climbing up several stairwells until they emerged on the bridge. As expected, everything was organized and professional. Donovan and Montero were introduced to the chief mate as well as two other crewmen. Pittman motioned them toward a chart table. Donovan found a handrail and then took in his surroundings. They were standing at least four stories above the water, and he couldn't help but be impressed by the nearly three-hundred-sixty-degree view. Forward, he could see that the helicopter had lifted off from the pad and was speeding away from the ship. Aft, the deck was busy with crew as well as science staff. Several cables were stretched from the ship and vanished into the ocean off the stern.

"We deployed the *Atlantic Titan*'s acoustic equipment and have located the pinging from the flight data recorder and the cockpit voice recorder. Once we had a rough idea of where the wreckage might be, we dropped the side-scan sonar array and have a rudimentary picture of the debris field on the ocean floor, or at least part of it." Pittman pointed to a spot on the chart. "We're here, and the debris field is outlined in red. Each yellow mark is where we've found floating debris."

"What are the other colors for?" Montero asked.

"The black marks are where we found bodies. The orange notations are body parts."

"What's next?" Donovan said.

"We're preparing ROMEO to go down and give us a look at the sonar findings. Once we all concur on a deployment point, we'll send him down."

"Who's ROMEO?" Montero asked.

"It's an acronym for our Remotely Operated Marine Exploration and Observation system," Pittman said. "We're near the Morant Trough, the depths in this part of the ocean range anywhere from three to five thousand feet. It's an inhospitable world down there, far too deep for divers, but with ROMEO we have an array of lights and sensors with both video and still cameras. It's also equipped with powerful manipulator arms that can be fitted with different tools. ROMEO's state-of-the-art technology will allow us to get a close-up look at whatever wreckage we find."

"How soon will that happen?" Donovan asked.

"For that I'm going to turn you over to Dr. Crawford. She's our expert."

Donovan turned to find Dr. Mary Crawford standing behind him. She was a mere wisp of a woman who didn't top five feet and probably weighed less than ninety pounds, but she was pure energy. In her late fifties now, she'd made a considerable name for herself in the field of marine biology. She'd grown up in London and her scientific résumé was expansive, as was her politics. Donovan loved her relentless attacks on the fishing industry and the worldwide pressure she continued to bring to bear on the few rogue states who still hunted whales. It was one of the many reasons he and Eco-Watch had heavily recruited her years ago. He and Mary went way back, and, in a small way, Dr. Crawford reminded him a little bit of Meredith.

"Hello, Mr. Nash." Mary smiled.

Donovan leaned down and gave her a hug. "It's so good to see you."

"It's good to see you, too. I trust you have pictures of your daughter."

"Of course," Donovan turned to Montero. "Mary, I'd like to introduce FBI Special Agent Montero. She's watching over us on this one."

"Nice to meet you," Mary shook Montero's hand. "We can use all the help we can find. Before we get all bogged down with science, let me show you to your quarters, and then we'll go on a brief tour of the ship. The rest of crew would like a chance to meet you both before dinner."

Donovan smiled, allowing Dr. Crawford and Montero to lead the way while he lagged behind out of sight and tried to get a full breath. There was a distinctive smell that he associated with ships that made him uncomfortable. A tour and meet-and-greet sounded like a nightmare, as did food. He was acutely aware of his racing pulse and the nervous perspiration collecting down his spine. He questioned his own sanity for coming up with this plan. He tried to focus on the most important aspect of being on this ship. The fact remained, that no matter how difficult this was, at least while they were on board, no one would be trying to kill them.

CHAPTER TWENTY-NINE

Lauren was busy loading the dishwasher after dinner. Trying to help, Abigail held a paper towel in her small fist and trundled across the floor to hand it to her mother.

When Lauren turned, her elbow caught a drinking glass and knocked it off the counter. It shattered on contact with the tile floor, shards of glass skittering in every direction. When Lauren yelled for Abigail to stand still, the little girl scrunched up her face, her lower lip jutting out, a sign that she was about to cry.

Lauren bent down, picked up her daughter, trying to prevent her daughter's tears. "It's okay, honey. That wasn't your fault, Mommy has butterfingers." Abigail's pink lips turned upward into the promise of a smile as the fear left her eyes.

"Down, get down!" Andy, gun drawn, charged into the kitchen. He raced to where Lauren stood holding Abigail and thrust his body between them and the window, forcing them both down below the level of the kitchen counters. He yelled into his radio for others to clear the area surrounding the rear of the house.

Abigail's shrieks knifed through Lauren as she pulled her frightened child close. Lauren felt her own tears push to the surface as tiny arms clutched her neck in a panic.

"Stop it!" Lauren yelled. "Get off of us. All I did was break a glass!"

"Stay down!"

"No! Listen to me! I broke a glass. There's nothing happening!"

Andy rose up and carefully examined the window, pulling back the curtains, cautiously looking for the bullet hole he'd imagined.

"Stand down. All units stand down. " Andy holstered his gun, and offered his hand to help her to her feet. "I'm sorry, Dr. McKenna. We're just doing our job."

Lauren ignored his assistance as well as his apology. She said nothing out of fear of what might come out of her mouth. Instead, she spun and carried her screaming daughter upstairs.

In Abigail's room, Lauren gently rocked her daughter until she quieted down. Lauren had tried to explain that the men downstairs were their friends and that they weren't going to hurt them. Lauren allowed her daughter to drift off to sleep. She'd pay for it later, but she thought a nap would help Abigail separate herself from the trauma of being pinned to the floor by an armed man. Instead of putting her into her bed, Lauren kept rocking back and forth. She didn't want to leave the room; she didn't want to face the reality of soldiers living under her roof. It took a while, but she managed to calm herself. Then she began to think rationally, and as she always did, she began to organize each and every thing she needed to do. First thing was to get everyone out of her house. She wasn't going to have Abigail traumatized by armed strangers.

A small, nearly inaudible knock came from the door. Lauren ignored it, not wanting to get up or even call out to whoever was there and disturb Abigail. It could only be Buck or Andy, and she most certainly didn't want to talk either one of them right now.

The knock sounded again, this time slightly louder, followed by the door opening gently. Buck stuck his head in the room. "Dr. McKenna, can I have a minute?"

Lauren nodded reluctantly, and Buck's expression seemed to soften. He hesitated, waiting until they made eye contact.

"What do you want?" she whispered.

"I'm sorry about what just happened." Buck spoke quietly. "We've been concerned about the wooded area behind the house, which is why we wanted you to keep all the curtains closed. So when Andy heard glass shattering he rushed in, expecting the worse, and reacted exactly as he should have."

"Is that all you came to say? You certainly don't need my blessing or forgiveness."

"I've been around long enough to know that war is oftentimes hardest on those left waiting at home."

"This isn't a war." Lauren said the words far louder than she'd intended.

"Tell that to the guys with guns trying to kill you." Buck waited for a response, but got none. "Permission to speak freely?"

"Sure, why not?" Lauren braced herself for what she was sure was some sort of military pep talk.

"How long since you've had any quality sleep?"

Lauren blinked in surprise. The question was direct, but heartfelt.

"Prolonged stress is a warrior's biggest enemy," Buck said. "I know quite a bit about you from your work at the DIA, as well as the intel I've gathered in the last twenty-four hours. You're an exceptionally bright and talented woman, and, given the situation, you're holding up pretty well—on the outside. But the cracks are starting to show. I'm not your commanding officer, but if I were, I'd order you to stand down and get some sleep. Take a pill, close your eyes, and trust the rest of us to do our jobs."

Lauren honestly couldn't remember when she'd had more than a quick catnap—it seemed like days.

"I've known grown men who'd still be in shock after what happened last night at the hospital. But we all have limits."

"Can I ask you a question?"

"Of course."

"Do you think these people will go after my husband?"

"Yes, ma'am," Buck said without hesitation. "And to be honest, I'm not entirely clear on his current mission or why he felt compelled to stay in Florida."

"He's assisting the FBI."

"I know that's the story, but it doesn't make any sense. After last night, every level of federal law enforcement is on the trail of these people, and while your husband is clever and resourceful, I sincerely doubt he can do more than the government at this point."

Lauren shrugged, but inside, alarms were going off.

"I also have no idea why there's a chartered jet on twenty-four-hour standby to take you and Abigail to London. I can promise you the FBI is wondering the same thing."

Lauren tried to hide her shock at how quickly this conversation had become dangerous. Buck was thorough, and he'd put a few things together that she couldn't readily explain. "William arranged the plane in case he thought we should leave."

"My job is to protect the people in this house. I was hired by your husband to do just that—and I will. But I can't shake the feeling that there's another threat I'm not aware of."

"Another threat?"

"Is your husband being blackmailed?"

Lauren felt the blood drain from face and her mouth dropped open. "I... I can't imagine."

"To be honest, I can't either," Buck said. "He doesn't fit the profile of the usual blackmail target. He's not rich. He's not gambling, or in debt beyond what you owe on your house. He works for a nonprofit organization—it doesn't fit. I've looked at this from a hundred different angles and I can't figure it out. If anyone in the family was a candidate for blackmail, it would be you. With your security clearance at the DIA, you could possibly be a target. Is that what's happening? Say the word and I can help you."

"I'm not being blackmailed, and if I were, there are strict protocols in place at the DIA to deal with external threats." Lauren felt the weight in her chest let up just enough for her to take a breath. Buck had done some digging into their shared financial history and found what he was supposed to find. All he was doing now was fishing.

"I do know that his behavior isn't making sense, and I'm paid to worry about the unknown, especially when it involves your safety."

"It's none of those things," Lauren lowered her head as if she were preparing some monumental admission. She had to give Buck something to chew on or he was going to keep chipping away at the façade until it crumbled. She took a deep breath. "My husband and I are having marital problems. It's why he's not here. Everything's up in the air right now. We haven't really told anyone, so I ask you to please not say a word."

"I'm sorry to hear that." Buck nodded and tried to give her an understanding smile. "I promise it won't leave this room."

"I appreciate that." Lauren reached out and affectionately squeezed Buck's hand. "I really do."

"Dr. McKenna, please try and get some sleep tonight. If you'd like, I can get you something to take, nothing too strong, but you'll rest."

"I'll let you know," Lauren whispered as he let himself out.

Lauren thought about what she'd just said to Buck. She'd purposely lied to him. As she rocked back and forth, she wondered about the other lies, the lies she'd told to Michael, Susan, even Calvin. They would all come to an abrupt halt if Montero leaked what she knew. The other reality was that the fabrications would never stop—they would pile up until something gave way, and the entire charade would implode.

She got up and gently placed Abigail in her crib. She grabbed the baby monitor and went down the steps into the study. The more she thought about what she'd told Buck the more she thought about Meredith. There was something in that DVD that had been bothering her, something her subconscious had been grinding on and now she thought she knew what it was. Relieved she didn't run into Buck or Andy, she closed the door, sat at the desk, and clicked on the computer.

Out of habit she logged on to check her e-mail and found one from Donovan, she opened it and began to read.

Dear Lauren—

With everything that's happened over the last twenty-four hours, the phone hasn't really been the best way for us to talk. I'm in the back of the da Vinci headed to Kingston in what I hope is one of the last legs of this journey. Under the banner of overseeing the salvage of the crashed Pan Avia flight, I've taken Montero off the front lines and stranded her at sea. I've gotten a feel for the situation, and from experience I don't think she can sustain her rage much longer. When her bubble bursts, I think I'll be able to help her move on—hopefully without any repercussions for us.

If this were any other situation, I would be there with you, I know I have much to explain. I hid some things from you because my past has come back to haunt me in ways I didn't think were possible, and for that I'm sorry. I wasn't sure how to explain certain things to you when I couldn't readily explain them to myself. As for our conversation last night, all I can say is I'm sorry.

If I don't think I can fix this current problem, I'll come home and we'll face the future together and deal with whatever comes. Give Abigail a hug from me, and I'll talk to you soon.

Love,

Donovan

Lauren knew about the plane crash and knew what Donovan was trying to do, but it felt open ended—as did everything right now. She read the letter again and then deleted it. She retrieved the DVD from the book where her husband had hidden it and slipped the disk into the computer, positioning the screen so that if Buck or Andy came in they wouldn't see what she was watching.

The main menu materialized and Lauren clicked on the icon that would give her the individual chapter segments. She knew exactly what she wanted to see, it had been troubling her since she'd seen it the first time, and she quickly found the place. The movie played for a moment and then she gently touched the pause button. She inched it along frame by frame and then stopped on the precise image she was after. It was a close-up of Meredith and Robert.

Lauren's hand shot to cover her mouth, as if she needed to stifle a scream. Her eyes were drawn to Meredith, her face turned upward toward Robert's. Lauren advanced the scene several more frames and then froze it. Robert's face filled the screen. Though twenty years had passed and surgeries had altered his facial structure, his eyes were unchanged. Lauren sat back and studied the image. She flashed back on moments in her marriage, not wanting to accept what she was seeing. She wallowed along in self-imposed denial until a definite sense of clarity finally overwhelmed her. She hadn't imagined it and she couldn't ignore it—the truth was right in front of her. Lauren couldn't stand it anymore and she mashed the button to eject the disk and in that split second before the screen went dark, Meredith and Robert moved together and kissed. Lauren closed her eyes. She felt hollow, gutted, and knew for sure that her world had just shifted on its axis.

CHAPTER THIRTY

Donovan had survived the evening. He'd met everyone, thanking each and every one of them for the difficult job they were doing. He'd finally left Montero in the mess hall and escaped into the aft storeroom, where the recovered debris was being stored. He'd been around wrecked airplanes before, but not so soon after the accident and never on this magnitude. A Boeing 767 was a large airplane, piloted by highly trained and skilled individuals, yet they were unable to stop the process that brought this airplane down. Donovan always felt a tragic bond with fallen aviators, especially with those he considered his peers. He, too, flew day in and day out in high-performance jet aircraft, and he couldn't help but wonder if he were put in the same situation would he have fared any better than the now silent crew of the 767.

Donovan slowly made his way amongst the recovered debris. Meticulously affixed to each object was a tag that offered latitude and longitude, plus a time stamp of when it was recovered. Smaller pieces were bagged so the NTSB would be able to identify the seemingly random parts and use the information to construct a detailed map of what ended up where. He examined several of the transparent bags and was saddened to find a cluster of personal effects. A purse, a shoe, a soaked boarding pass, all giving sad testament to the people who were aboard the airliner when it crashed.

The human remains were below in the infirmary. The Jamaican Coast Guard was scheduled to receive the bodies tomorrow and deliver them to a makeshift morgue in Kingston for autopsy.

Many sections of the twisted metal were coated with zinc chromate, a yellowish-green anticorrosive agent that easily identified them as internal parts of the aircraft. Bare aluminum marked surface skin. The largest piece in the room was about the size of a mangled canoe, its aluminum edges jagged and scratched from the crash. He ran his hand over the once smooth surface and felt the aberrations and the gouges in the metal.

He spent time studying each of the larger pieces and tried to picture what part of a 767 he was looking at, but couldn't. The only reason any of it had floated was from rubber or foam sections that had created a modest amount of buoyancy, or a sealed section had trapped an air pocket. When he pictured an intact Boeing 767 and then compared it to the amount of wreckage before him, he was beset by the enormity of the recovery job that lay ahead.

"Mr. Nash, there you are. I've been looking for you." Mary announced with an air of excitement in her voice. "ROMEO is approaching the debris field, and I thought someone with your aviation expertise should sit in on this."

"Thanks, Mary." Donovan said, as he fell in step behind her. They wound through the maze of gangways, and he held open a watertight hatch for Mary to pass through, then ducked and went through himself. They went down a passageway and through another hatch until Donovan found himself in a room that resembled a home theatre. At the front of the space was a wall full of screens. Situated below the monitors were computer keyboards as well as an assortment of controls and smaller screens. Off to the side was a stack of electrical components and computer hard drives, small green lights glowing in the semidarkness. Technicians were positioned at strategic stations around the largest work area, and Donovan knew they were the ones guiding ROMEO. Rising up at a gentle slope were six rows of large padded chairs—the observation section. In the second row sat Montero.

Donovan took a seat next to her.

"We're almost there," a technician reported. "Sonar is showing what looks like a significant amount of metal on the bottom. It's fairly scattered, but the echoes concur with our earlier estimation of where the tail section may have come to a rest. The signal strength from the locator beacon inside both the cockpit voice recorder and flight data recorder confirms our data."

In the background, Donovan could pick out a faint pinging sound, ROMEO's relay of the directional beacon.

Montero leaned over and whispered, "I didn't know the black boxes had homing beacons."

Donovan nodded. "Immersion in water automatically triggers the beacon. They are designed to operate for thirty days before their battery runs out."

"We're fifty feet from the bottom," the technician reported, careful to speak into a microphone as all operations were recorded. "Total depth is almost forty-seven hundred feet, and I'm bringing the lights up to step one."

Donovan watched as the largest of the screens flickered to life. At first, all he could see was what looked like snowflakes, tiny organisms that threatened to block the view, but seconds later he began to make out the subtle contours of an unremarkable ocean floor. Smooth brown mud stretched out in every direction and vanished into the darkness.

"The first object should be visible shortly," one of the technicians said.

"Very good." Mary nodded. "Maneuver slowly."

Donovan leaned forward as he started to see a vague shape materialize in the murky haze of the deep.

"I think we've got something here," Mary said. "Roll video."

Donovan knew there would be a video record made of everything they saw. There were also several still cameras that could be used for photographing specific objects of interest. As ROMEO silently approached the object, Donovan was the first in the room to understand what they were seeing.

"It looks to me like we're seeing a section of the fuselage. It's upside down, the top of the plane is partially submerged in the sediment."

"You have a good eye, Mr. Nash." Mary made a note on her clipboard.

"Can you maneuver us all the way around it?" Donovan asked. "I'd like to get a closer look at where this section separated."

"Slowly, we don't want to raise a cloud of silt from the sea floor," Mary said to her team.

As ROMEO was guided in a slow circle, Donovan could finally see where the smooth aluminum gave way to the harsh tearing of the metal. Insulation, fragments from seat cushions as well as wire bundles were strewn everywhere. They could now peer into the interior of the airliner itself. ROMEO's bright lights cast harsh shadows into what was once part of the cabin. Donovan braced himself for the sight of bodies. Most would have been sucked out when the fuselage ruptured or thrown clear when the wreckage hit the sea, but there was always the chance that some unfortunate souls would have ridden the wreckage all the way to the ocean floor. Initial inspection showed the small section devoid of passengers.

"The masks have dropped," Montero said, pointing to the tangle of plastic tubing and yellow face masks floating inside.

"They could have dropped from the impact with the water. Even a hard landing can pop them out sometimes," Donovan replied, his attention focused on where the metal had separated. The amount of force required to rip the metal apart had been enormous.

"Mr. Nash," Mary asked, "can you positively identify the aircraft or airline from what we're looking at here?"

"No," Donovan replied. The room was quiet as ROMEO made a slow three-hundred-and-sixty-degree circle. The image told of a massive impact.

"If everyone is finished here, we'll move to the next location." Mary looked around the room and everyone agreed.

"How long?" Donovan asked.

"Just a few minutes," Mary said, glancing at a screen. "This next debris field is larger, or at least appeared that way on the sonar returns."

The steady one-ping-per-second beacon sounded in everyone's

ears as ROMEO motored along the ocean floor toward the next contact.

"Object is dead ahead, fifteen meters," the technician called out. "I'm switching on the video cameras."

As before, the object came into view as though it were shrouded in a dense, snowy fog.

"What is it?" Montero said.

"Can you pan upward?" Donovan asked, as he too tried to make sense out of what he was seeing on the screen. He couldn't find a point of reference to determine what it was they'd found. Slowly, the perspective shifted, but it wasn't until Donovan spotted the distinct shape of an airfoil that he understood.

"According to the directional microphone we're getting close to the black boxes," Mary said.

"It's what's left of the tail," Donovan announced. "That smooth surface is the vertical stabilizer. Below that, partly sunk in the mud, is the section of the fuselage where the horizontal stabilizer is attached. You can just start to make out the gray-and-red stripes of Pan Avia Airlines and there's the registration number, PR-GFT."

"Okay, good work, people. We have positive verification that this is indeed the Pan Avia Boeing 767. Now, let's do a three-hundred-sixty-degree survey and figure out the best way to get at the black boxes."

"Can ROMEO cut through the metal and reach them?" Montero asked.

"Doubtful," Mary replied. "We'll, of course, have to confer with both the NTSB and Boeing, but my best guess is we'll end up raising this entire section to the surface."

A phone next to Mary rang and she answered immediately. "Yes, Captain. I understand. They're both right here. I'll pass the message along to her."

"What's going on?" Donovan asked.

"Captain Pittman just received an urgent message for Special Agent Montero from a Mr. Hamilton Burgess at the FBI," Mary replied. "He's requested a video conference. The two of you need to go to the computer lab."

"Follow me," Donovan said.

They went down the passageway, up two flights, and into a long, narrow room lined with computer workstations. At the end of the space was a glassed-off room with a large flat screen on one wall.

"Right in there," the computer tech said as the two of them drew closer.

Donovan trailed Montero and walked into the room and was greeting by a life-sized image of Montero's boss. He didn't look happy, but then Donovan didn't think he'd ever seen the man when he didn't have a scowl on his face.

"Mr. Nash, I invited you to this meeting since it pertains to you as well as Special Agent Montero." Burgess cleared his throat. "Earlier today we were called to a crime scene. Ricky Lee Vaughn, one of your confidential informants, was killed in his gun shop. We know from the time stamp on the security footage that he was killed last night at 8:25 p.m."

"Ricky," Montero said. She lowered her head for a moment before she looked up at Burgess. "You have whoever did this on video?"

"Seems Vaughn was kind of a computer nut and the whole place was wired. There's no audio, but I have some video to show you." Burgess nodded to someone off camera. "Watch this and then we'll talk."

The image jumped from color to black-and-white, and Donovan realized he was looking at the inside of the gun shop he and Montero had been in yesterday afternoon. Ricky was behind the counter when a customer wearing a baseball cap, the visor pulled low, entered the front door. Despite being slightly pixelated, Donovan instantly recognized Nathan Strauss. With no wasted motion, Strauss drew his weapon and pointed it at Ricky's forehead. Words were exchanged, and Ricky reluctantly removed the pistol from a holster on his hip and placed it on the countertop and raised his hands in the air. Strauss motioned for Ricky to lead the way into the back room.

The picture jumped as the feed from a different camera came into view. Ricky was seated at a laptop and Strauss was standing behind him. The gun was pressed into the folds of Ricky's neck. The camera was mounted high enough that over Ricky's shoulder Donovan could see the computer screen. It looked like Ricky was fast-forwarding through recorded video of some kind, maybe searching for something. Ricky clicked the mouse and the image froze, then he backed it up slowly until two people were shown coming into the gun shop. Donovan didn't need audio to know what was being said. He'd been there—Montero was doing the talking while laying down one hundred dollar bills.

Ricky turned and said something to Strauss. Then Donovan saw the carnage that had been exacted on Ricky. Momentarily confused, Donovan's eyes darted to the time stamp; thirty minutes had elapsed since Strauss had walked into the shop. Ricky's bloody and swollen face told of a half hour of savage violence at the hands of Strauss. The silent, one-sided conversation went on for another sixty seconds and then without flourish Strauss pulled the trigger. Ricky's blood splattered on the computer screen and the big man toppled sideways out of his chair and collapsed to the floor. Strauss turned and glanced up briefly for the first time, though his features were still mostly obscured by his cap and beard. He studied the camera installation momentarily, reached for the connections, and then the screen went black.

"Care to elaborate?" Burgess asked as his face once again materialized. We edited out the beating, but I can tell you that the assailant knew what he was doing. According to our experts, he's been trained by professionals."

"I gather he walked off with Ricky's hard drive. How is it we have these images?" Montero asked.

"All of Vaughn's security feeds were sent to the hard drive that was stolen, but the stream was also sent in real-time to an off-site server. The local police located the security firm that did the work and they surrendered the files."

"Did anyone figure out what Ricky said at the end?" Montero asked.

"He gave the gunman two names, Sasha and Roberto. Mr. Nash, I gather that Roberto is the name you use when you're out playing cop?"

Donovan said nothing and waited for Burgess to continue.

"We know who Sasha is; she was killed within hours of this murder. What I don't understand is why the gunman didn't ask what your name was, Special Agent Montero."

"I don't have the slightest idea," Montero said. "Maybe Ricky told him when his back was turned to the camera."

"Possible," Burgess nodded. "I don't happen to think so. I think you're holding out on me, Veronica. The only way I even heard about this debacle was the local cops recognized you on the tape and called me. Do either of you know who this killer is and why he was interested in the two of you?"

Donovan knew that Montero wasn't going to give up Strauss's name. She wanted the guy all to herself.

"I've never seen the guy," Montero said. "I take it you didn't get anything when you ran him through facial recognition?"

"We're still working on it, but preliminary reports are we don't have enough to go on."

"Is there any footage of the parking lot? Was this guy driving a Lexus?" Montero asked. "He finds out about Sasha, kills Ricky, and thinks he's removed all the evidence by taking Ricky's computer."

"No camera coverage of the parking lot. Police are going door to door in the area. But so far no witnesses have been found."

"Sir, might I suggest I be brought back to Florida to assist in finding the man who killed my informant. I have other sources that I might be able to lean on. Maybe we can use my presence to draw this son of a bitch out from hiding."

"Officially, you're still on administrative leave, but for the moment I'd rather have you back here even if it is behind a desk. Mr. Nash, I've been entrusted with your safety. Do you feel like you're secure on your ship or shall I make some other security arrangements?"

"I'll be fine," Donovan replied.

"Veronica, make the necessary travel plans and let me know the minute you're back home. Good luck out there, Mr. Nash." Burgess drew a finger across his throat and the picture went black.

Donovan turned to Montero. "Strauss isn't after us. He saw us at the club after he killed Ricky and did nothing."

"I know that, and you know that, but Burgess doesn't know anything. There's still a chance we can find Strauss before anyone else. That's all I need. Pack your stuff. We're out of here."

"What are you thinking?" Donovan snapped. "You heard your boss. You won't be able to do anything from your office."

"That's why I have you. We'll let Burgess believe you're still out here on this ship, when, in fact, you'll be my eyes and ears on the street. I'll be plugged into the investigation again, that's the only way we're going to be able to find Strauss before anyone else does. Now, how soon before we can be airborne?"

CHAPTER THIRTY-ONE

Despite being strong-armed by Montero, Donovan was thrilled to be off the ship. After telling the crew of the *Atlantic Titan* that Montero urgently needed to return to West Palm Beach, they were in the helicopter, flying back to Kingston. He and Montero had been in such a scramble to depart the ship that he hadn't had time to call Lauren. As soon as they were airborne in the *da Vinci*, he'd try to reach her.

Montero had once again elected to ride up front with Eric. Donovan switched on a small overhead reading lamp and pulled out the flight plan that had been faxed to him just as they were leaving the ship. He studied the route, which would take them north over Jamaica, across one of the designated corridors over Cuba, then up the eastern seaboard into West Palm Beach where they'd land and clear customs. The weather in Florida was nearly perfect, mid-seventies with clear skies and light winds out of the west. When he switched off the light, he discovered the glow from Kingston low on the horizon and silently urged Eric to fly faster.

"I just radioed the handler," Eric reported. "He's aware of your departure and wants to know if you need fuel."

"Yeah, have the truck meet us." Donovan replied. "But you get your fuel first."

"I'm good," Eric replied. "I topped off onboard ship. If you don't mind, I'll drop you two and head straight back."

"By all means, and I appreciate the last-minute lift."

Eric descended toward the same open area where he'd landed earlier in the day. Donovan surveyed the airport and discovered that the news trucks were gone. Good, their late-night departure would go unnoticed and unreported.

The skids touched firmly and Donovan stepped onto solid ground. He breathed a small sigh of relief. It was a little cooler than earlier, but the humidity was still oppressive. He pulled their bags out and secured the door. Montero joined him and they both ducked under the rotor blades and moved to a safe distance. The rotor wash buffeted them as the helicopter clawed at the air, lifted off, and headed east.

Donovan heard the low growl of a diesel engine in the distance and he saw the fuel truck headed toward them, its gears grinding as it rumbled across the tarmac. Once they fueled, all they needed was for Kyle to arrive and they could get underway.

Donovan ducked under the nose and set their bags on the ground. He fished in his pants pocket for his keys and thumbed the correct key just as the fuel truck swung into position.

"Tell him I'll have an exact amount for him in a second," Donovan called out to Montero. "Once he's hooked up, he can start pumping."

Donovan turned his attention back to the door of the Gulfstream and hesitated. It was unlocked. He tried to remember if he'd just unlocked it before he spoke to Montero. He shrugged it off, it was such an automatic action. He must have done it without thinking.

Once the door was unlatched, he pulled it over-center and allowed it to swing out and extend all the way down to the ground. He grabbed their bags and took the steps two at a time up into the cabin. He reached into the cockpit and switched on the valves that would allow the fueling to begin. Halfway to the back of the plane, he stopped—he sensed them before he saw them. He dropped the bags just as someone drove a fist into his stomach. He doubled over and something solid hit him on the back of the neck and he went down on his hands and knees. A kick to his ribs flipped him over and Donovan landed on his back, straining to draw a breath.

"Don't make a sound or you will die."

Donovan was stunned into silence. He felt the cold circle of steel as a gun barrel was pressed against his forehead. He couldn't see the face of the man who'd spoken, but in the dim light he could see a finger on the trigger.

"Take care of the woman quickly and quietly," the man said to his accomplice.

Donovan heard Montero call out to him as she came up the steps. The next thing he heard was Montero giving out a surprised groan, then the sound of a body hitting the floor.

"Get up," the man said to Donovan.

Donovan winced as he did what he was told. He felt the gun leave his head, followed by the distinct pressure of the barrel pressed against the small of his back.

"How much fuel is onboard?"

"Four thousand pounds."

"I want you to stand in the doorway. When the man fueling the airplane comes, I want you to tell him to pump six thousand liters. After he's finished, you sign the ticket, smile, thank him, and wave goodbye. If you fail to do this, then not only will he die, but she will as well."

Donovan was prodded forward. Montero had been dragged down the aisle and tossed on the floor near one of the science stations. He let the rough hands jostle him into position at the top of the stairs. As predicted, the lineman appeared at the foot of the stairs. Donovan called down that he wanted six thousand liters.

"Very good. Now we'll stand here and wait for him to bring the paperwork."

Donovan turned his head slightly; there was just enough light coming in the door to catch a glimpse of the man standing behind him. The white hair and beard made it easy—it was Nathan Strauss.

"I'm not going to fly you off this island," Donovan said, trying to get some kind of read on the situation—trying to stave off his fear at what he knew about the man holding a gun to his spine.

"Don't talk. I don't need you to fly me anywhere. I only need you to stand here and wait for the lineman to come back with the ticket."

Donovan could hear the pump on the fuel truck slow and then finally disengage. The lineman appeared on the tarmac at the foot of the steps. Donovan motioned him up, but blocked him from entering the cabin. He signed the receipt, smiled, and waved—exactly as ordered. Moments later the engine growled, gears ground together, and the truck pulled away from the *da Vinci*.

With his back to Strauss, Donovan never heard the sound of the arm swinging. All that registered was the momentary shock of being slammed in the back of his head. His knees buckled and he put out an arm to break his fall, but his world dissolved into darkness before he ever hit the floor.

CHAPTER THIRTY-TWO

Lauren opened her eyes with a start, confused, not sure what had woken her. She listened to the baby monitor, but it remained silent. She threw on her robe and went into Abigail's room and checked on her daughter anyway.

From downstairs, she heard the faint murmur of voices. Halfway down the steps she smelled the strong aroma of coffee. Lauren was about to round the corner when Buck began talking and she stopped to listen.

"She needs to sleep. You've seen her, she'll go until she collapses, and it's only going to get worse from here."

"Keep your voice down."

Lauren wasn't sure who was with Buck, but she held her ground, wanting to hear more.

"This makes no sense!" Buck began. "Years ago, the first time I met Nash we were headed out on a rescue mission into Hurricane Helena. In an unguarded moment he admitted to me that once upon a time something happened to him out in the ocean. It traumatized him. He's a pilot, not a sailor, and he's certainly not a salvage expert. From where I sit, he had no reason to be out on a ship while his friends and family are under siege. Perhaps there's an explanation as to why he was out there, but I don't know what it is."

Lauren heard a cell phone ring and William's familiar voice answered the call. She was shocked that William was here and had no idea why he would be taking calls at this time of night. She rounded the corner into the kitchen and found Buck at the table. William was on the phone, though the moment she made eye contact with him, he told whoever it was he'd call them back.

"What's going on?" Lauren asked. The expression on both men's faces spoke volumes, but no one said a word. William's eyes were red rimmed and swollen.

"I came as soon as I heard." William said quietly. "It's the *da Vinci*. We just received word the plane is missing. "

Lauren heard the words, but couldn't immediately grasp their enormity.

"Calvin Reynolds called," William continued, his voice ragged and measured, as he struggled to maintain control. "We don't know much at this point, but it seems Donovan had flown to Kingston, Jamaica. Did you know anything about this?"

Lauren could only nod that she had, he'd mentioned it in the e-mail she'd read earlier.

"Donovan told Captain Pittman they needed to leave and fly back to Florida on urgent FBI business. They were taken by helicopter from the ship to the airport in Kingston. The *da Vinci* had taken off and was climbing out when they radioed a Mayday. They reported an emergency and they were returning to the airport. That's the last communication anyone heard."

Lauren was silent, no sound escaped her, and she felt as if she were being squeezed to death. She felt an overwhelming desire to run to where Abigail was sleeping and hold her daughter—to protect her—tell her everything was going to be okay, but she couldn't move. William helped her into a chair then knelt down next to her. Tears spilled from her eyes and she sat motionless—the words too painful to accept.

"Is there anything you can tell us about why he was headed back to Florida?"

Lauren shook her head.

"I think we need to agree that we don't know anything for sure at this point," William said as he lowered his head. "We're not clear on why he and an FBI agent were leaving in the middle of the night to fly back to Florida."

Lauren hadn't thought to ask if Montero was onboard the *da Vinci*. If she was, then according to Donovan, the clock was counting down. Whoever she'd sent the dossier to would be obligated to open it and reveal the contents. Nothing she could do now would stop that process.

"Do Michael and Susan know?" Lauren tested her voice, trying to grasp all of the elements of the coming storm.

"Not yet." William shook his head. "I thought we'd wait until we know something more concrete."

"I need to understand. What did they say—before?" Lauren said, slowly, terrified she'd spin out of control. The rational, deductive side of her needed to hear the facts, as bad as they might be, even as the emotional devastation threatened to sweep her away.

William nodded, a determined look formed on his face, but no words came, only silent tears. It took him a moment to collect himself before he could speak. "According to Calvin, the helicopter that flew Donovan and Ms. Montero to Kingston was airborne, headed back to the ship when Eric, the *Atlantic Titan* helicopter pilot, heard the distress calls from the *da Vinci*. He immediately returned to the airport and began flying a search pattern to locate the airplane. We've been told that the emergency was declared shortly after takeoff, as they were climbing out to the northwest of the Kingston airport. The airport radar facility was shut down for maintenance, so authorities had no exact location for the *da Vinci*. Based on how long they'd been airborne, it's estimated they were no more than twenty-five miles from the field."

"What was the emergency? I've heard the words Mayday, emergency, distress call, but no one has said what the emergency itself was." Lauren felt the bite of her anger beginning to rise. She glared at Buck. "Pilots don't just say Mayday. They tell the people on the ground what the hell is happening to them—right?"

"They reported a fire," William said quietly, his voice breaking.

"What kind? What was burning?"

"Electrical," William said. "In the cockpit."

Lauren caved in and lowered her head. She couldn't avoid the image of her husband being burned alive while he tried to fly the airplane. "We have to leave for Jamaica as soon as possible." She squeezed her eyes shut as the images assaulted her and her control began to unravel. Sobs rose in her chest and threatened to unravel her completely.

"A black sedan just arrived," Andy reported. "Deputy Director Calvin Reynolds."

"I copy," Buck said. "Send him in the front."

Lauren stood and wiped at the tears in her eyes, then turned as she heard Calvin's footsteps on the hardwood floor.

"I got here as fast as I could." Calvin went directly to Lauren and they held each other tightly.

Lauren basked in the voice of the man she'd long ago adopted as her mentor and father figure. They stood together for a very long time, neither one speaking.

"I promise we're doing everything we can." Calvin said, finally. "We've been friends for a long time. You know you can trust me, right? Will you do something for me—for yourself?"

"What?" Lauren replied.

"Buck told me earlier that he felt like you were on the verge of exhaustion, and I believe him. We've all been worried about you. I know how you get sometimes and I know you've been running on nothing but fumes for days. I put in a call to Dr. Rhodes. He called in a prescription, something to help you sleep."

Lauren shook her head defiantly. "No."

"You can't do anything more right now. It's a waiting game and nothing will likely happen for hours. You don't want to go to Kingston and sit in a hotel room or ride around in a search helicopter. You're with people who care. Abigail is well taken care of—you need to look after yourself."

"I can't sleep. I need to be awake when—" Lauren stopped. She'd almost said *when Donovan calls.* She wished there were some fragment of hope in the uncertainty surrounding her, but she couldn't find one. If she could only reach out and grasp one single molecule of anything but despair, she would—but she'd seen the look on William's face. He knew. If Donovan had gotten the plane down safely, they'd have heard. She had another thought that caused her stomach to lurch. What if Donovan had gone down in the ocean? It would be the cruelest stroke of fate for him to die in the water. For his sake, she hoped he'd died from the smoke, not the flames, and that he never saw the ocean coming at all.

The last fragments of her control melted away—the harder she tried to hold on, the more it slipped away. Donovan's secret would come out in a day or two, and the public would be outraged that he hadn't died years ago and would at the same time applaud his death. Her thoughts, her plans, everything she needed to keep going collapsed. Her rational, scientific approach to dealing with problems was gone and all that remained was unbelievable loss combined with sadness and rage.

She stopped and sagged, as if she'd hit a wall. Lauren put her hands over her face as her body shook. Calvin held her to keep her from sinking to the floor. Sobs wracked her body and she couldn't get a breath. She had so many questions, there seemed as if there were things she should try to say, but her mouth wouldn't form the words, it was as if some essential element for communication had been disconnected. She tried to find her voice, but she had nothing. A rush of images raced through her mind—each more terrible than the one before.

CHAPTER THIRTY-THREE

Donovan gradually became aware of a droning sound. It wasn't constant; the noise rose and fell without warning. The back of his skull pounded, the slightest movement ended with searing pain. His ears popped, and he tried to bring his hands to his head but found they were securely fastened behind his back, and his feet were bound tightly together at the ankles. He opened his eyes and blinked against the pain, trying to understand where he was and what was happening around him. The sound finally registered; it was the hum of jet engines. He made out some of the shapes surrounding him. He was in an airplane, more precisely, on the floor in the back of *his* airplane. He began to feel the sensations of flight, the motion of the *da Vinci* matched the surges of the engines. Whoever was flying was maneuvering as if getting ready to land.

The main gear hit hard and the brakes were applied heavily. The vibrations from the sudden deceleration acted like a hammer beating the back of his head. The thrust reversers howled in protest and the airplane rocked back and forth as it slowed. Just as fast as it had happened, it was over. The *da Vinci* was taxiing.

Donovan twisted upward to look toward the window. Wherever they'd landed, it was pitch-black outside. He felt the airplane pivot sharply, power up, and then come to an abrupt stop. Moments later, the engines were shut down and everything went silent. His mouth was dry and his tongue felt swollen. His head throbbed each time he moved, and he felt like he might throw up.

Donovan heard the main cabin door open, and the beam of a flashlight bounced around the interior of the plane. He heard the snap of a plastic tie wrap being cut and he was dragged roughly out of the plane and unceremoniously dumped on the ground. Several minutes later Montero was tossed onto the dirt next to him. In the instant that a beam of light played across her, he could see that her hands and feet were bound and she was still unconscious.

He rolled onto his other side to look at the *da Vinci*. Inside there was a steady light. Someone had set up a powerful lantern and it created just enough ambient light for Donovan to take in some of his surroundings. The *da Vinci* was sitting on thick steel plates to keep it from settling in the dirt. Above his plane, steel cables were fastened to the tops of nearby trees and supported a series of nets. Leaf-covered branches and palm fronds were woven throughout the webbing to create a realistic camouflaged canopy. There was absolutely no chance that the Gulfstream would be spotted by either a satellite or a low-flying plane. Just beyond the perimeter he spotted a fuel truck.

Donovan heard the baggage door open from the inside. A bundle was rolled out of the opening and hit the ground with a thud. It took him a moment to understand that it was a body—Kyle. Donovan felt both sickened and enraged. Donovan closed his eyes and tried to control his anger. He rolled over and inched himself closer to Montero.

"Veronica," he said as loud as he dared. "Wake up. I need you to open your eyes. Veronica. Look at me! Tell me how badly you're hurt."

"Don't call me that." Montero squeezed her eyes shut and swallowed. "My head is killing me."

Donovan, closer now, could whisper. "I think we've been drugged. Push through it and tell me if you can you move your hands at all?"

"Drugged? Where are we? What happened?"

"We've been kidnapped and flown somewhere. It's Strauss."

Montero blinked heavily and looked around. Donovan followed her eyes as she surveyed the *da Vinci*, the netting, and the men inside. He saw her crestfallen expression the moment she spotted Kyle's body.

"How many of them are there?"

"It's dark, but I think there're only two."

Montero lowered her head. "Here they come."

Rough hands gripped Donovan by the ankles and he was dragged down a pathway. He was forced to close his eyes as dust flew into his face. He guessed he'd been dragged about fifty feet when his legs were released. He opened his eyes and discovered he was lying on the dirt floor of a tent. Overhead, a bare lightbulb provided the only light, and the tent was crawling with hundreds of insects. The space smelled of canvas, sweat, and raw earth.

They dragged Montero in as well, and the man knelt down and looped together several plastic tie wraps, which he slipped around Montero's wrists and then through the restraints that held Donovan. He threaded the last restraint through the others and pulled it taut around the center tent pole. The instant the man left, Montero twisted and turned, testing her bonds, but they held firm.

"What in the hell happened in Kingston?" Montero asked.

"Strauss was waiting inside the *da Vinci*. He took us both out before we knew what was happening."

"He killed Kyle. Why leave us alive?"

"He wants to know what we know," Donovan replied. "When we're of no use to him, he'll kill us."

The canvas flap on the tent was thrown back and a solitary man walked in and stopped as if surveying his property. For the first time, Donovan could clearly see their captor. Nathan Strauss was no more than five foot ten, lean and wiry. He walked with a distinctive limp, his vivid blue eyes generated no discernable warmth, and his entire face was framed by a shock of white hair with a matching beard. Strauss looked much older than his forty-three years, but there was no mistaking the air of lethality that surrounded the man.

Strauss limped to the table and picked up a glass, blew into it to remove any dust, and poured himself some water from a plastic gallon jug. He swung a chair out from under a nearby table and sat down, a wince passing over his face as he eased his full weight into the chair.

"By the look of you both, you've recovered from the drugs. It's a mix of Ativan and morphine. It makes for compliant passengers. You'll be groggy at first, a little nauseous, but it wears off quickly enough." He pulled a wallet out his pocket and began to examine the contents. "Mr. Nash. I need some questions answered and it's completely up to you how we do this—with or without pain. If you choose pain, it will end with one of you dying."

"Go to hell," Montero snapped.

Strauss shot to his feet, toppling the chair, and straddled Montero's chest. He cupped her chin in the palm of his hand, and pulled her face within inches of his own, then slid a slender knife from its scabbard, made sure she saw the glistening blade, and then touched the steel against the soft flesh of her neck.

"Special Agent Montero, I let you live the last time we met."

Montero's eyes grew wide then narrowed into slits, her face a portrait of pure hatred. "*You* killed Alec."

"I did, in fact, kill him, as well as the others, so you understand what I'm capable of. Don't think for a moment that I won't kill you."

"You sick bastard! Is this how you get off?" Montero said defiantly, ignoring the knife at her throat. "Assaulting women who are tied up and can't fight back?"

"You weren't assaulted. No one touched you that night. I only needed to give everyone the impression you'd been kidnapped and violated. It added an essential bit of credibility to the situation."

Montero used every muscle in her body to fight her restraints, trying to buck the man off of her. "You piece of shit!"

The man swung from the shoulder and slapped her hard across the face. The impact popped and echoed through the tent. Donovan saw the fury in Montero's eyes cloud over in pain.

"Screw you!" Blood trickled from Montero's split lip. "Did you regret not being able to slap Sasha around before you killed her?"

Nathan pressed his hand firmly over Montero's mouth and nose, cutting off her oxygen, and then turned toward Donovan. "What has the investigation into the theft of the Gulfstream from Boca Raton uncovered so far? Tell me the truth, or I'll start cutting her up in front of you."

Donovan didn't doubt for a moment that unless he was honest, Montero would die. She was suffocating, starting to writhe helplessly under Nathan's iron grip.

"The authorities think that an Islamic terrorist group took the plane. The bomber you used in Virginia was very convincing."

Nathan removed his hand from Montero's face and wiped the blood and saliva from his hand across her blouse. She lay spent, gasping for air. "Have the black boxes from the Pan Avia flight been recovered?"

"No," Donovan replied. "We located them, but they're buried deep in the wreckage. It'll be days, if not weeks, before they're analyzed."

"Do you know who I am?"

"All I've heard is a name." Despite Montero's eyes pleading with him to lie, he decided this wasn't worth her life. "You're Nathan Strauss."

"Who told you?" Strauss swung himself off of Montero and got to his feet then secured the knife. He stared at Donovan. "Keep talking."

"Someone from the Israeli Embassy."

"Really?" Nathan said with an amused grin. "Was it my old friend Aaron Keller?"

Montero was still breathing hard. "You were him. The informant—I recognize your voice. You set us up."

"Yes, I was your anonymous informant. The men I tipped you off about weren't Venezuelan drug smugglers. They were Keller's hunting party, a Mossad-sponsored hit squad looking for me. I discovered their presence and brought you and Alec in to take care of them. I arranged it to appear as if the FBI had eliminated them. You gave me the perfect opportunity to rid myself of these people, and it forced Keller to back off."

"They were Mossad agents—sent to stop you?" Montero asked.

"Not Mossad, a contract wetwork team Keller dug up somewhere. He's always so concerned with maintaining his deniability."

"Why didn't you kill me that night?"

"As I explained, a terrorized woman seemed to sell the story even better than a dead one. I only delayed the inevitable. Right now everyone thinks both of you have been in a plane crash and are most likely dead."

"How did you know we were in Kingston?" Montero asked.

"Thanks to live coverage from CNN most of the world knew of your arrival. I was only after your airplane. Collecting the two of you was just luck on my part. I was about to steal your Gulfstream when your copilot showed up. Everyone is looking for you, but by this time all they're really trying to find is the wreckage of your plane—about eight hundred miles from where we're sitting."

"You ambushed Kyle. You had Michael's keys." Donovan saw it all now, though he was way too late to do anything about it. "Why did you shoot my friend in Boca Raton, but not me?"

"Simple logic—he'd seen me—you hadn't." Strauss replied. "A little sloppy, but I was in a big hurry that night. The weather was moving in fast, and we needed to leave."

"Where's the airplane you took from Boca Raton?" Donovan asked. "Where are we?"

"None of that is important. If you were to somehow escape, believe me, you wouldn't last a day out there in the jungle and most certainly not the night."

Strauss picked a wrench off the table and limped to the back of the tent to a stack of battered acetylene tanks. There were three of them, each about four feet long, resting on their sides. Nathan spun the valve fitting counterclockwise until it came free. He snapped on latex gloves and coaxed a small amount of white powder into his palm. He carefully threaded the valve back in place and went to where Montero lay and brushed part of the powder onto her face. She shook her head back and forth in vain before she finally inhaled the substance, coughing. Strauss knelt over Donovan and repeated the process.

Donovan held his breath as long as he could, but in the end he had no choice but to inhale the powder.

Nathan peeled off his gloves, stood up, an expression of pain flashed across his face and his hand shot to his right hip. He went toward the door and stopped just short of leaving. "In case you're unclear, that was anthrax. Each one of those tanks holds roughly fifty kilograms, part of Saddam Hussein's weapons of mass destruction that you Americans could never seem to find. I've had a vaccination, but I'm guessing by the expression on your faces you haven't. As of this moment, you're both as good as dead."

Strauss limped heavily out of the tent and for the first time since he'd met her, Donovan found genuine panic in Montero's eyes.

"Oh, shit!" Montero's eyes darted around furiously. "I can't believe we're going to die like this."

"Save your energy. It's not going to kill you," Donovan said.

Montero's head jerked toward him and her eyes bore holes in him. "What in the hell do you mean? You don't think it's anthrax?"

"Strauss is not the type who bluffs. My wife explained anthrax to me once. She said that the spores need time to multiply before any of the symptoms appear. Sometimes it takes days. If you and I are treated quickly, say within twenty-four hours, we probably won't die from the bacteria. Much beyond that though, we'll be past the point of curing."

"You're telling me you think we're going to die from something else?"

"I doubt anthrax will be the cause of our deaths. That'll take up to a week. Strauss has got something else planned. The anthrax was just to terrorize us. Don't give him the satisfaction."

"He's responsible for it all." Montero closed her eyes. "He was the one who stole the Bristol Technologies Gulfstream. What's he doing? What's his endgame? Why did he steal another Gulfstream? What happened to the one that he took from Boca Raton? If I hadn't forced you to fly to Florida, we wouldn't be here, and Kyle would still be alive. I've done nothing but play into Strauss's hands."

"It's not your fault. Strauss killed Alec, Sasha, Ricky, and Kyle. You didn't cause anyone's death. He did."

"I wish it was that simple."

"Strauss pulled the trigger. Focus on that. Don't underestimate this guy. He's former Israeli Defense Force and he's been planning this for months, maybe years. He uses people and then he eliminates them, and so far he hasn't made a single mistake. He's smart and he intends to get away with whatever it is he's doing."

"He steals jets and has a cache of anthrax," Montero said. "Is he smuggling this stuff into the United States or is he moving it from the States to buyers in other parts of the world?"

"I have no idea." Donovan had done the math and knew Strauss had enough anthrax to kill millions. As Montero once again closed her eyes, his thoughts drifted to Lauren. By now, she'd know his plane was missing. Did she think he was dead? Of course, she would. The way Strauss had explained it, no one would have any reason to believe otherwise. He and the *da Vinci* were gone. With Montero presumed dead as well, the news about Robert Huntington would soon be released to the media. Lauren was about to face all of his past coming at her—and she was going to face it alone. In the process of trying to protect her and Abigail, he'd failed them both on nearly every level imaginable—just as he'd failed Meredith.

CHAPTER THIRTY-FOUR

Lauren heard footsteps in the hallway outside her bedroom followed by someone softly knocking. She knew it was Buck and didn't want him to see what she was doing. She had no way to explain why she was packing two large suitcases. She went to the door and cracked it open less than an inch.

"Mr. VanGelder just returned," Buck said. "Shall I show him up here?"

"Please, if you don't mind," Lauren replied. William had stayed last night, even after Calvin had finally convinced her to take something to help her sleep. William left word that he needed to return home for an hour or so and would be back as soon as possible.

Buck hesitated for a moment, like he was going to say something else, but instead turned and walked away.

Lauren quietly closed the door, knowing that she'd never get used to bodyguards. Donovan's words echoed in her head, *"If we have to go, we'll take the security with us. It was how we were going to have to start living anyway."* She felt a stab of resentment as she thought to herself. *No, it's how I'm going to have to live.*

Abigail was lying on the bed watching cartoons. Lauren had brought up the picture-in-a-picture feature on the television, and when she walked past the screen, she'd see the CNN coverage. Each time she passed, she held her breath, bracing herself for the sight of Robert Huntington—the signal that her life had irrevocably changed.

Her daughter clutched Shadow, the largest of her stuffed dogs.

Did Abigail feel like she needed a dog, even if it was stuffed, to protect her? Lauren didn't know what to tell her. When the time was right, she'd try to explain to her that Daddy was gone. Lauren fought another wave of tears and focused on the task at hand—packing as if she would never return.

The moment the news about Robert Huntington broke, Lauren would contact Michael and Susan. After all the years they'd spent with him, they deserved to hear the details from her. It was one of many conversations she dreaded. Another knock on the door told her William had arrived.

"Grandpa's here," Lauren called to Abigail as she opened the door. William hugged her before reaching to scoop up Abigail as she slid down off the bed and rushed toward him.

"How's my favorite little girl?" William kissed Abigail on the cheek and got a fierce hug in return. He walked over and plopped her on the bed amidst Abigail's playful shrieks and giggles. She grabbed Shadow and rolled out of William's reach.

"I just came from the hospital," William said. "I broke the news to Michael and Susan."

"How'd they take it?"

"Susan fell apart, and Michael tried to be strong for her, but he was having trouble keeping it together. They're coming home later today. I told them that maybe you needed some space right now and that we'd see them tomorrow. I hope you don't mind."

"Thank you." Lauren knew the minute she saw them she'd lose whatever tenuous emotional control she'd found.

"Stephanie was hell-bent on catching a flight over, but I convinced her we'd see her in a few days and to stay put for now. The State Department reached your mother. Her cruise ship was off the coast of Greece. She's being met at their next port and escorted home."

Lauren nodded, trying to convey her gratitude with her eyes.

William handed Lauren a soft-sided briefcase. "I brought you some things Donovan wanted me to keep safe. Most of it's self-explanatory, but there's some paperwork in there we should talk about."

William began to talk to Abigail as Lauren walked around the bed to the sitting area, unzipped the case, and found four large envelopes. Each had a name printed on the outside: Donovan, Lauren, Abigail, the fourth, marked Cash. She easily recognized Donovan's crisp block lettering. She pulled out the one with her name and opened it up to find three U.S. passports with three corresponding sets of ID: driver's licenses, credit cards, insurance and pharmacy cards. Closer inspection showed a different name and address for each identity. A cursory glance into the other envelopes told her the addresses all corresponded with what she'd found in her own packet. The fourth envelope held neatly wrapped bundles of cash. Dollars, euros, and British pounds. Lauren thumbed through the bills and counted roughly one hundred thousand dollars. This was only the first part of their escape kit—she knew another stash of documents and cash were waiting in London. She had no idea when he'd done all of this, but in typical Donovan fashion, he'd been thorough.

The last item in the case was a folder. Inside was a slender legal document. As she removed it, William extricated himself from Abigail, taking the seat across from her.

"It's Donovan's will," William said gently. "I hope you don't think it's callous of me, but I thought we should go over this now, take advantage of the calm before the storm. Are you up for this?"

"I guess." Lauren nodded. "You're right. We should do this now, before—"

"It's fairly simple and straightforward. Donovan left the bulk of everything to you and Abigail. His wealth is invested in a labyrinth of trusts and foundations, there's partial ownership in companies all over the world, as well as real estate, precious gems, art, and, of course, he still holds shares of Huntington Oil. Total assets are roughly twenty-eight billion dollars. Money will never be a problem for the two of you."

Lauren heard William say the words and she scanned the typed list in front of her, each line breaking down the entities that held Donovan's fortune. She'd always understood on one level that there was money, but to actually see it written down was surreal. There were at least two dozen global companies she recognized. Several airlines, car and aerospace manufacturers, industrial conglomerates, and both software and hardware giants were listed with a numerical value next to each entity. The numbers were huge—almost too large to grasp. The life they led in Virginia was upper-middle class at best. The money was just another part of the secret they didn't talk about. She closed the folder and shoved it, along with the false papers and cash back into the case. Everything she'd just learned felt like yet another facet of her husband's life that she'd really never been invited to share.

"What's wrong?" William asked.

"Nothing." Lauren stood, suddenly wanting to do anything else rather than deal with the enormity of what she'd just learned. The words *Special Report* glared at her from the television and she wordlessly swept the remote control off the edge of the bed and switched the picture to CNN.

"Mommy!" Abigail cried out as her cartoon vanished.

> We bring you this CNN exclusive special report from Miami, Florida. We have confirmation from Dade County law enforcement that a hostage crisis has developed aboard a Holiday Cruise Ship. Details are still unclear, but at least one gunman, believed to be related to his hostages, has barricaded himself on board—

Lauren switched the channel back to Abigail's cartoons. The report was about someone else's life falling apart. She let the remote slip from her hand, and hurried to the bathroom where she leaned over the toilet and threw up. She kept heaving long after her stomach was empty.

She overheard William reassure Abigail that everything was alright, that Mommy just had an upset tummy. He let himself into the bathroom and ran water in the sink. He handed her a warm washcloth and then sat on the edge of the tub.

The washcloth felt good as she pressed it to her face. She sat unmoving, waiting for the slightest hint that her body wasn't finished. For the moment at least, her stomach seemed quiet. William took the washcloth and handed her a towel.

"Thank you," Lauren whispered, her voice raw.

"I know it's a lot to absorb," William said. "When he was Robert, he had no illusions about how money changed people's perceptions of him. He was determined not to have that happen again. He never wanted the financial side of his existence to be a burden, or to impact you in any negative way, so he elected to keep it separate."

"Yeah, he was good at that," Lauren said. "I can't stop wondering, what if he's not dead? He did it once—could he have done it again? Is there any chance he's left us all behind?"

"He'd never leave the two of you," William said without hesitation. "Believe me, I've processed this from every angle and it just doesn't work. If he were going to erase Donovan Nash, then he'd have to deal with Kyle as well as Agent Montero. I can't see how that could happen. I'm afraid this is real."

"What if Montero and Kyle died in the plane crash, but Donovan didn't. Would he take the opportunity to vanish before the truth about Robert Huntington made the headlines?"

"No," William shook his head emphatically. "I can't see him doing anything like that, and I don't believe you do either."

"Right now, I'm not all sure what he is, or isn't, capable of." Lauren looked up at William and felt as if he were complicit in all of Donovan's lies. Everything came rushing to the surface. "William, I'm his wife, and he hid everything from me. His past that we could never talk about, the nightmares he wouldn't share. I watched a movie he couldn't tell me about that centered on a woman he never stopped loving. I saw it, William, the look in his eyes he had for her. I went back and watched it again. I can promise you he gave Meredith a look he's never given me."

"I don't believe that for a second. It had to be the effects of seeing him before the surgeries."

"It was in his eyes, and they're the same. I feel like a fool for never allowing myself to believe that Meredith was a threat. I've been so pragmatic all this time. From the moment I learned the truth about Donovan's past, it seemed pointless to compete with a woman who had been dead for nearly two decades—but now I know without a doubt that I've been wrong. I've never felt so humiliated. Meredith was the love of his life and Donovan has never gotten over her. Why did he marry me when it's so obvious I was never more than the runner-up?"

CHAPTER THIRTY-FIVE

Donovan and Montero took turns trying to sleep. They'd given up trying to get free. Even if they did work themselves loose, the only place they could escape to was into the jungle, where, as Strauss had promised, they'd probably die before they reached help. Donovan guessed it was now late afternoon or early evening. Strauss had removed both of their wristwatches—a basic tenet—keep the prisoners off balance and confused. On and off, Donovan heard noises, the sounds of wood being cut with a handsaw, as well as nails being driven. There was also the banging of hammers on metal—activities not typically associated with airplanes. At one point, both Strauss and the other man came into the tent and one by one carried out all three of the tanks. It was later that Donovan heard the unmistakable sound of the truck pumping fuel into the *da Vinci*. By how long it took, either the pump was slow, or they were going to fly a very long time.

The heat of the day was draining, the humidity oppressive. He was hungry and thirsty. He thought of Meredith, how she'd been held for weeks. Had she been immobilized like this, her hands and feet tied? He'd have gladly traded places and died for her. When had she known with certainty that she was going to die? Had she blamed him? She should have. He'd always believed that the blame was all his.

He thought of that final phone call in Costa Rica, the last time he'd heard her voice. As always, remembering was like a twisting knife in his chest. He'd been asleep when her kidnappers had called. He assured them he had the money, but he demanded to hear her voice, to know for sure she was still alive. When they put her on, all she said was not to pay them. Don't give them the money because she was already a dead woman. The last thing he heard was Meredith calling out that she loved him. The call terminated—but she'd been right, they'd never intended to keep her alive. Meredith knew it, and Donovan's guilt would never abate.

The last time he'd spoken to Lauren, he'd promised her everything would be fine. Now, in her mind, he was dead. He hated himself for what he'd done—the things about his past that he'd hidden from her. He'd justified it under an altruistic banner. He'd wanted to protect her, but all he'd really done was alienate her.

"Are you awake?" Montero whispered.

"Yeah."

"I can't stop thinking about why Strauss asked about the Pan Avia black boxes."

Donovan closed off his thoughts of Meredith and Lauren. "What did you say?"

"The black boxes from the Pan Avia flight. Why did Strauss ask about them?"

"Maybe his plans don't call for an armada of naval vessels anchored in the Caribbean Ocean."

"Armada or not, he's not getting anywhere near the U.S. in a stolen Gulfstream. I can't figure this thing out. We know Strauss is from Israel and he hired two thugs from Trinidad, Diego and Ramone, who may or may not be Muslim. Then when he wanted to kill Michael Ross in Virginia, he made it look like the work of a jihadist suicide bomber. How does any of this make sense?"

"I don't think you can look at this with traditional borders in mind. Strauss is nothing more than a mercenary, an arms dealer who happens to be ex-Israeli Defense Forces. I think he's simply hired himself out to the highest bidder, and he'll use any means possible to remain undetected."

"You're saying he sold anthrax to Islamic terrorists and is helping smuggle it into the United States?" Montero asked. "I'm having a hard time buying that an Israeli would do that."

"He's a psychopath, what's hard to believe?"

"I think he's working toward some greater end than getting rich."

"Like what?"

"It's like any crime, you have to look for the motive. If it's not money, then it's either love, or he's covering up a bigger crime."

"That doesn't make him any less of a psychopath."

"Who gains if there's an anthrax attack on one of our major cities?" Montero asked. "Say Washington D.C. or New York. Or even Miami or Atlanta? What happens on a global political scale?"

"I don't know if anyone gains, but the knee-jerk reaction would be to blame any number of Middle Eastern terrorist groups."

"We have the jihadist who bombed the hospital. That's where the evidence leads. Strauss is making that part easy. He's dangled the Islamic extremist carrot for all to see."

"Strauss loves deception." Donovan said, a picture starting to form in his mind. "What if he's manipulating this entire operation to appear as if, say, Iran, or some other Middle Eastern group is behind the attack?"

"You think he's planning this anthrax attack himself, hoping to point the blame at the Middle East? Do you think Strauss and Keller are in this together? Do you think Israel would really manipulate events to try and trigger a war between the United States and say, Iran?"

"I doubt Keller or Mossad or Israel is behind this. Strauss played you and Alec to kill the team that Keller had sent to eliminate him. The way I see it is Strauss is working alone and Keller is looking for him. Keller wants Strauss dead."

"We all want Strauss dead," Montero replied.

"It sounds like they're building something out there. I also heard them fuel the plane which makes me think that they plan on departing soon."

Montero started to say something but stopped.

"What is it?" Donovan asked.

"It's just—I'm taken aback that you're not the monster I always thought you were."

"Really? Well, you're still the one I thought *you* were."

"I probably deserve that. I've been wrong about you. I've always read about you in terms of being the playboy billionaire who killed Meredith Barnes. I worshiped her and you were easy to hate. If it means anything, I'm sorry."

"I do have a question for you. In your personnel file there's mention of assault and blackmail charges. The person who made the accusations then disappeared. You already know about revenge, don't you? Strauss isn't the first person to cross you that you've fixed a vendetta on, is he?"

"What file?"

"You don't think my people sat around and did nothing while you blackmailed me, do you? A young girl accused you of assault and then she vanished. What did you do?"

"Screw you, that's none of your business."

"How does it feel to have someone dig around in your life and take everything at face value?"

"I don't have to explain anything to you."

"I want to know about Veronica Montero's version of revenge. You've always handled your own payback. The professor when you were in college, the superior officer in the FBI. They crossed a line, and you took care of the situation personally. That took some guts. But all of a sudden I'm hearing more remorse than rage. You better not be giving up."

"You're telling me you're not afraid right now?" Montero said. "Tough guy Robert Huntington or Donovan Nash or whoever you are, isn't afraid?"

"Of course I'm scared, who wouldn't be. What I'm trying to tell you is that we need to work together because it's going to take both of us to stop these guys."

Donovan watched as Montero clenched her jaw and glared at him. Keeping her agitated and on the verge of violence was his best weapon and it also gave him something to focus on, to cope with his own fear.

"Her name was Tanya, she was a runaway," Montero said. "A

fourteen-year-old girl pimped out by her boyfriend, a guy I'd wanted to bust for a long time. When she showed up at a shelter I'm familiar with, they contacted me. I tried to use her to get to him, except she was being coached by her boyfriend the whole time. She made the assault allegations and then tried to blackmail me as a way to slow down my investigation against her boyfriend. One night I grabbed her off the street and took her down to the county morgue. We'd just put another underage hooker in the cooler, a friend of hers. The girl had been murdered by a violent methhead who was good with a straight razor. That night I convinced Tanya to go back to Denver. She signed a statement that exonerated me of any wrongdoing. Then I contacted her older brother and I personally put her on a flight home. Word on the street grew that I'd made the girl vanish. I leaned on the boyfriend and he finally left town. He set up shop in Jacksonville and he was finally busted. He's at the state prison in Raiford, Florida, doing at least five years on a ten-year sentence. I didn't take the law into my hands, I used the law and everything else I had at my disposal. I hated that guy and what he did to those girls."

"What about the others?"

"You mean the professor and the instructor? Both were jerks who tried to use their positions of authority to pressure me to have sex with them. As you said, they were dealt with."

"You're very unusual in that regard." Donovan chose his words carefully. "Why do you resort to action when most other people either run away or cower in fear?"

"It's none of your business."

"What happened to you?"

"Leave it alone."

"Did someone close to you betray you, hurt you?"

"I said leave it alone."

"We're probably going to die—what difference does it make?"

"Stop it!"

"I need to know what keeps you angry. What makes you the one to dispense justice?" Donovan waited for her reply, but she remained silent. He cautioned himself not to push her too hard. He needed her and was about to apologize when she began to talk.

"My mother was killed by a drunk driver," Montero said quietly, but the words were filled with anguish. "The bastard walked on a technicality and never served a day in prison. I was just a kid. I couldn't believe he wasn't punished—the system had failed me. He drank himself to death before I was old enough to finish what the system failed to do. I know what you're thinking—and you're right. I'm part of that same system. On my watch, I owe it to the families of the victims to make sure that doesn't happen to them. Those who would harm me personally are a different story. They're dealt with immediately. I handle it myself so I don't have to worry about the system failing. I have a badge and a gun. Hell, the entire law enforcement community is only a radio call away. Three words: officer needs assistance, and everyone races to the scene, guns drawn. This is different. No one is looking for us. We have nothing."

"We have each other and we have to work together to stop Strauss. We need to be ready to do anything to stop him, which means we need to stay focused. You need to maintain your rage for what he did to you and Alec."

"You're saying we stop him no matter what, even if we have to die in the process?"

"If that's what it takes. Yes." Donovan then asked the question that would impact Lauren and Abigail. "How long before everything about me is made public?"

"If my contact doesn't hear from me by tomorrow morning, he'll read the contents of the packet. He'll call a friend of mine who works for the Associated Press. After that, it won't be long before someone holds a press conference to tell the world what I uncovered."

"If someone holds a press conference in Miami, I'm pretty sure the attention of the world will be focused elsewhere. The uproar about me won't last long once people start dying. The media will have something far bigger to talk about—like a large-scale anthrax attack."

CHAPTER THIRTY-SIX

As each minute crawled by, Lauren felt even more fragmented. Abigail had been bathed and was asleep, but Lauren continued to rock her daughter, unwilling to face the world that waited outside the nursery. Over the course of the evening, she'd run the full range of emotions. From betrayal to self-pity, to anger that Donovan was dead, to the impossible hope that he was somehow still alive. She knew that the story would break soon and she'd be forced to run. Part of her was hoping it would happen so she could finally begin to deal with the new reality of her life. She felt caught in a vicious cycle that played over and over in her mind, each element of her personal disaster more overwhelming than the one before. She placed her daughter into her bed and quietly walked out of Abigail's bedroom. She was momentarily startled to find Buck standing in the hallway.

"I was just about to knock. Can we talk?" Buck said.

"Sure." Lauren blinked back her momentary surprise. "What's on your mind?"

"I can't find any easy way to say this, so I'll come right to the point. Earlier, you were reluctant to open your bedroom door, but I saw the reflection in the mirror, you were filling suitcases. May I ask why you're packing? And please don't try and tell me you're going to Jamaica. From what I saw you were packing like you were going to be gone a long time."

Buck had caught her, and there was no lie that was going to deflect his curiosity. "The walls of this house are closing in on me and it's only going to get worse. At some point Abigail and I are going to Europe."

"Who's going to protect you over there?"

"I was hoping you'd take the job," Lauren said just as Andy's voice crackled over Buck's radio.

"Buck, we've got a limousine with blacked-out windows and diplomatic plates headed our way."

Buck reached for his pistol. "I need you to go back into Abigail's room and lock the door."

Lauren felt the tears began to well up in her eyes. "It's someone coming to notify me they found Donovan, isn't it? The State Department."

"I think we'd hear it from William. We'll both wait here until we know for sure." Buck said to Lauren then clicked his microphone. "Andy, I'm upstairs with Dr. McKenna and Abigail. Check it out and report back."

"Roger," Andy replied. "They just pulled up in front."

Lauren wrapped her arms around herself and leaned against the wall for support.

"The passenger is Aaron Keller. He's got credentials that identify him as a diplomat assigned to the Israeli Embassy here in Washington. He says he needs to speak with Dr. McKenna."

"Do you know him?" Buck asked Lauren.

"I've never met him, or even heard of him, until day before yesterday. Donovan asked me to check him out."

"Did he check out?"

"Most of it was classified, I didn't look very deep, just verified who he was and what position he held. According to the DIA database, he's Mossad."

"Andy, we're coming downstairs," Buck said. "How many men does this guy have with him?"

"He has a driver and a bodyguard. I checked; the FBI confirms he's legitimate. He insists he needs to speak to Dr. McKenna alone."

"That's not happening," Buck said. "Frisk him for weapons and then bring him to the front door—alone."

Lauren dabbed at her eyes with a tissue. "I can't imagine what Mossad wants with me."

"Have you ever worked with them before?" Buck led the way down the stairs.

"There have been several joint assignments over the past few years. But names were never revealed."

"I don't want you alone with this guy," Buck said as they approached the front door. "I want to be in the room to listen to what this guy has to say."

Lauren nodded.

Buck pulled the door open and invited Keller into the house. Outside, the Fairfax police closed ranks and blocked the limousine's exit.

"Dr. McKenna. Please pardon the intrusion. My name is Aaron Keller. I'm with the Israeli Embassy."

Lauren studied the man. Medium to slight build, he was dressed in an expensive suit and he appeared to be in his mid to late forties with short brown hair and brown eyes. He stood relaxed and took in his environment. Despite a polished demeanor and a casual smile, Lauren sensed the same kind of understated superiority that Buck possessed.

"Mr. Keller, this is Mr. Buckley. He's in charge of my security. Can I offer you something to drink?"

"That's very kind of you, Dr. McKenna, but I'm afraid I can't stay very long. Is there someplace where we can talk in private?"

"Let's go into the living room, but I must insist that my head of security join us."

"Of course, I understand," Keller replied. "In light of recent events, I'm thankful for your time."

Lauren led them into the living room where she switched on two lamps and sat down. Buck waited as Keller settled into the sofa across from Lauren before he too took a chair.

"What can I do for you, Mr. Keller?" Lauren said.

"First, I want to say how sorry I am about your loss. Your husband seemed like an exceptional man."

"Thank you. When did you meet my husband?"

"Two nights ago in Florida," Keller replied. "But then you

knew that because he sent you a photo of a man and no doubt asked you to check me out as well. I'm here as a courtesy, Dr. McKenna, but I need to know what else was discussed that evening."

"Nothing of consequence. He'd been consulting with the FBI and then he was called away after the crash of the Pan Avia 767. I e-mailed him what little information I'd gathered."

"You identified the man in the photo?"

"Yes. Nathan Strauss—he's one of yours."

"Not exactly." Keller put his fingertips together and brought them to his chin. "Mr. Strauss is a person of interest to my government, but we've been unable to locate him. I was hoping to enlist your help in narrowing that search."

Lauren didn't for a second miss the fact that something had just gone off kilter. "If you want to locate a fellow Mossad officer, I'm sure the FBI would gladly assist."

"Nathan Strauss is certainly not Mossad," Keller replied. "At this point I don't know for sure if Mr. Strauss is involved in any of the recent events in Florida or here in Virginia, so I'm sure you can understand my reluctance to call in the FBI when there may be nothing amiss."

"I'm certainly not a professional diplomat, but what I see is a Mossad agent trying to track down one of his own while maintaining enough distance to maintain plausible deniability."

"Well said, Dr. McKenna." Keller gave her a respectful nod. "There are, of course, diplomatic considerations in this matter, but first and foremost I'm trying to uncover the scope of Nathan Strauss's actions, if there are any. It is, however, a matter that directly impacts you and your daughter's safety."

"Is that a threat?" Buck said, breaking his silence.

"I'm not the threat, but if it's Nathan Strauss we're dealing with, then he's most certainly a threat, one that you'll stand very little chance of stopping."

"I can't help you," Lauren replied. "I shouldn't even be talking with you right now. I can't work with any member of a foreign government without the approval of my supervisor at the DIA."

"Dr. McKenna, I believe there's a distinct possibility that Nathan Strauss and the death of your husband are linked. Your husband thought strongly enough about this threat that he teamed up with FBI Special Agent Montero to try and stop Strauss. I believe those actions were unsuccessful and may have resulted in their deaths. Nathan Strauss is as deadly as they come, and I need to find him."

"What is it you think I can do?" Lauren replied.

"I have a theory, but I need access to the distress calls sent from the Eco-Watch plane. I have reason to believe that Strauss may have stolen the plane from Kingston. He would have then sent the distress calls to give the impression of a crash and then flown the airplane somewhere else. It's why there hasn't been any wreckage located."

"Why would Strauss be in the cockpit of an Eco-Watch Gulfstream?" Lauren's mind was reeling with the sudden implications. "Wait, are you trying to tell me that my husband has been kidnapped? Do you think he might still be alive?"

Keller held up his palms. "Please, Dr. McKenna. I know what I've said comes as a shock. I'm very sorry. It's not my intention to offer up any false hope. In fact, I very much doubt that your husband, his first officer, or Special Agent Montero are still alive. If it's Strauss, he has no reason to keep hostages. He's trained to kill anyone who may be able to identify him. My theory is that Strauss stole the Gulfstream and kidnapped all aboard to cover his tracks."

"What's the potential threat if Strauss has the Gulfstream?" Buck asked. "What can he do with it?"

"Anything he wants," Keller replied. "Strauss was a Special Missions pilot within the Israeli Defense Force. For almost two decades he was involved in clandestine missions in a wide variety of aircraft, including the Gulfstream. Hands down, he's one of the most skillful pilots Israel has ever produced. If he has a Gulfstream, it's because it's the airplane he needs for his mission."

"Is this something that Strauss has done before?" Buck asked. "Steal a plane and fake a crash?"

"All I can say is that the tactic, in theory, works," Keller replied.

"Did he steal the Gulfstream from Boca Raton?" Lauren asked. "Is he the one who shot Michael Ross?"

"It's possible, though again, I have no proof."

"You seem well informed," Lauren said. "So you should know that actual Air Traffic Control tapes are never released to the public, transcripts perhaps, but not the actual tapes."

"You and I are not the public."

"What is it you hope to prove?" Buck said.

"I have a voice imprint of Nathan Strauss. I believe if we compare it to the actual distress call, we'll find a match."

"Then what?" Buck asked.

"Then we have him positively linked to activity that requires the immediate action of both our governments. For obvious political reasons I would like to confirm this before I sound the alarm."

"He's working without the knowledge of your government? Why? What went wrong?" Lauren asked. The possibility Donovan had been murdered made it difficult for her to collect her thoughts.

"Strauss was injured and forced to retire. I'll admit that perhaps my government didn't do enough to follow up on him. There is no forgiveness for our shortsightedness. Strauss suffered from injuries that virtually destroyed his right hip and damaged his lower vertebrae. It's a miracle he isn't confined to a wheelchair. In retrospect, it's thought that he also suffered from post-traumatic stress disorder. At some point, Strauss may have had a full psychotic break, possibly aided by the enormous amounts of narcotics he was forced to take to combat his chronic pain. We lost track of him, as well as three other pilots from his former unit, men who would follow him without question. Each of them is extremely dangerous."

"But the man who tried to kill Michael Ross and Dr. McKenna here in Virginia has been identified by the FBI as part of a jihadist group trained in Yemen," Buck said. "How does that fit with a psychotic Israeli soldier?"

"Former soldier," Keller corrected. "I'm not at liberty to discuss specific recent events, but there is a remote possibility that Strauss may have acquired the means to manipulate certain deep-cover terrorist networks."

"He's not working alone, is he? Someone's helping him," Lauren snapped. "Strauss has sources inside your government, which is why you need to find Strauss and then uncover his handlers."

"This is a potentially devastating dilemma, which is why I need your help, Dr. McKenna. I came here for two reasons. I need to compare those voiceprints without setting off international alarms, and I'm also here to offer you immediate round-the-clock protection to counter any threat that may exist."

Buck started to talk, but Lauren silenced him with a quick look and a raised hand. "Mr. Keller, I've heard enough. You've got a big problem floating around out there, and I strongly suggest you take this to the FBI. Play the Nathan Strauss crazy card, maintain your deniability, but you need to find him without my help."

"I understand." Keller stood and smoothed his suit. He reached into his pocket and held out a business card to Lauren. "Dr. McKenna, I can't thank you enough for your time. I wish you the best. I hope I'm wrong and that your safety isn't in jeopardy."

Lauren took the card and immediately felt something attached to the back. A quick glance told her it was a small jump drive. Keller had strategically positioned it to be invisible to Buck. When she looked in Keller's eyes, she caught a glimpse of what she could only describe as a final plea for her help.

Lauren slid the card and jump drive into her pocket and let Buck show Keller to the door.

"Are you okay?" Buck said as he returned to the living room.

"I don't really know," Lauren replied. "That was so strange. I don't know what to think."

"From my standpoint, this situation just got ten times worse. It's one thing to have some jihadists trying to kill you, and it's quite another to have a former Israeli Defense Forces team who wants you dead. You might be right about getting out of here and finding a safe house. Right this moment you're far too easy to find."

"I can't process all of this right now." Lauren rubbed her temples.

"I'm going to brief Andy—I think we need to bring in some more people and widen the perimeter."

"Wait." Lauren reached out and clutched Buck's arm. "Is this beyond what we can do? I mean, I don't want you or anyone else to get hurt because of me."

"Don't worry." Buck shook his head. "All that's happened is we have a better idea who our enemy is, and we might need to ramp up security. You're safe, and I'll continue to keep you and Abigail safe. Please believe that."

"I do." Lauren tried to smile, but she knew her effort fell short. She wondered how much death he'd been surrounded by as a SEAL. He seemed to know when to talk and when to act. Lauren was thankful and appreciative for his presence.

As Buck went out the front door, Lauren went to the study where she ripped the jump drive free from the card and slid it into the USB port. She discovered two files. One was an audio file labeled "Nathan Strauss"; the second was a JPEG simply titled "Strauss." She double-clicked the JPEG.

A slideshow started and she watched as one by one, still images filled the screen. Underneath were short descriptions. The first few were black-and-white photos taken inside a living room. There were four bodies; the caption explained the victims were three professional assassins and one FBI agent. It was suspected they were all killed by Nathan Strauss.

The next photos were taken at another crime scene after the victim had been removed. The caption revealed that the blood was Michael's and the outline was where Donovan had found him. Lauren felt her stomach lurch at the starkness of the image. The next picture was from the hospital in Florida—a man lying on the floor of a hospital corridor, half of his head appeared to be gone. It was the man sent to kill Michael, the one that Montero had stopped.

The next series of shots were of Donovan and Montero. They were talking to an overweight man in what appeared to be a gun shop. Montero was throwing bills on the counter. The scene that came up next looked like a back room where the same overweight man sat at a computer. Lauren covered her mouth as Nathan Strauss pointed a gun and fired. The overweight man's brains splattered onto the screen. The next image was a close up of the computer monitor. Lauren forced herself to look beyond the carnage until she understood what she was seeing. It was Donovan and Montero—earlier footage from when they were in the shop. Strauss had been looking for this, and when he found it, he'd killed the man. The pictures that followed were in vivid color. A dead girl lying in a parking lot. Another body in a different parking lot followed by a man stuffed into the trunk of a car. The slideshow ended. Keller wasn't being subtle. He wanted her to believe that Strauss had killed them all, as well as Kyle, Montero, and Donovan.

Lauren pondered her options, and decided that as persuasive as Keller was, she wasn't going to help him. It was his responsibility to be proactive—not hers. If Strauss was involved then the world could deal with him without her involvement. She yanked the jump drive out of the computer and jammed it into her pocket, suddenly very tired of her surroundings, exhausted by the ever-changing complexities of her current situation. Everything around her in this house spoke of her life with Donovan. He was dead, and when it was revealed that Donovan Nash was in reality Robert Huntington, Donovan's existence would evaporate and cease to exist. This home would simply be a house. She'd married a ghost, a mirage, and now there was no reason to stay. Why fight the inevitable? The life she'd had was over. When she finished packing, she and Abigail would get on the chartered plane and be gone by tomorrow morning.

CHAPTER THIRTY-SEVEN

The tent flap was thrown open and Strauss, wielding a knife, went straight to Montero. He quickly sliced the restraints holding her to the tent pole and yanked her to her feet by her wrists. Then he hit her in the stomach with a savage blow that dropped her to her knees. He moved behind her, cut her ankle restraints, and pulled her to her feet by her hair.

"Need any help?" Strauss's sidekick stood in the doorway, a pistol in his hand. "She's quite the hellcat when she's awake."

"I dare you to come closer and say that," Montero spat.

"I've got this, Rafael," Strauss said. "Make sure all the charges are set. I don't want anything left of this place after we leave."

"They're ready." Rafael leered at Montero. "I'm just saying we might have time for some fun. Last time we met her we were in a bit of a rush."

Montero tried to leverage Nathan's feet out from under him, but her leg kick found only air.

Strauss pressed the blade of his knife hard against her throat and whispered, "If you fight, I'll give you to him. He'll hurt you before he's finished, and you'll suffer enormously all the way to D.C."

Montero's struggles ended, but hatred burned in her eyes. Strauss shoved her from the tent.

The flap on the tent hadn't fully closed. Donovan twisted against his restraints and was rewarded with his first view of the outside world. The setting sun cast long shadows, but it was still light out. Through the trees, he could see the back half of the *da Vinci* under the camouflaged netting. The baggage door was open, and on the ground next to the Gulfstream sat a worktable and a toolbox. He spotted two orange boxes on the table—the *da Vinci's* cockpit voice recorder and the flight data recorder. Nathan had removed them so no taped evidence would be on board when it was found. Donovan had no idea what modifications had been made to his jet, but the thought of what Nathan had planned seemed all the more real at the sight. He'd also told Montero that Washington D.C. was the target.

They were getting ready to leave. Charges had been set to obliterate the camp. True to form, Strauss was following his scorched-earth policy, leaving nothing in his wake that would trace back to him. He thought of Meredith, she'd been alone as well. Had she known the bullet was coming? Had she been afraid? Donovan had no problem admitting that he didn't want to die—that he felt the fear. He'd left so much undone, so many loose ends that would forever be neglected. With everything he knew about being the survivor, the guilt that never ended, how had he managed to leave Lauren and Abigail with so many unanswered questions?

It didn't take long. Donovan offered no resistance when Strauss came for him. Once his ankle restraints were cut, he found his balance to be precarious after having been prone for so long. Strauss propelled him forward by pushing the barrel of a gun into his spine.

Once outside the tent, beyond the *da Vinci,* Donovan could see what passed for a runway. The jungle gave way to a narrow ribbon of compressed oil and dirt. He recognized it for what it was—an old oil company service road. It was once a common practice. Oil was mixed with and compacted with the soil to harden the surface of the road. The method also cut down on the dust and kept the jungle from encroaching on the road.

"It's a little more than a mile long and not much wider than the wheelbase of a Gulfstream," Strauss said, as if reading the expression on Donovan's face. "Just long enough to get a Gulfstream in and out."

Rafael came bounding down the air stairs of the Gulfstream. "I've got her on board. I just need a syringe."

Strauss handed Rafael a small leather pouch, and then ordered Donovan to walk down a narrow path.

"I'm guessing this place was once used by drug smugglers," Donovan said.

"It was a long time ago. It was abandoned when I found it. But it was drug smugglers who inspired me. They've been penetrating American airspace with impunity for decades, and your government has been unable to do much about it. It only seemed logical to borrow their techniques—and add a few of my own."

"You're not just smuggling the anthrax, are you? You're going to disperse it over Washington."

"It's of no concern to you."

"Why? You're not a terrorist," Donovan said, but he still couldn't get any kind of read from Strauss. The Israeli was intelligent and methodical, as well as a blank slate. Was he a soldier so well trained that his focus was single-minded, or was he a cold-blooded sociopath?

"It doesn't matter who I am. Only that the blame is placed on Islamic extremists who would love to commit such an act if they had the ability."

Donovan was prodded forward until he spotted the latrine. It was nothing more than a three-sided canvas enclosure around a crude seat. He could hear the buzzing insects as he neared and recoiled from the stench.

Nathan gave Donovan a shove with the gun. "Relieve yourself. We have a long flight, and I won't have you soil yourself aboard the airplane. Try and run and you will die here."

Donovan complied.

Afterward, Donovan was shoved back in the direction of the camp. Nathan forced him up the stairs into the Gulfstream. He spotted Montero lying on the floor. She'd been secured with tie wraps to a steel leg that supported one of the science stations. A thread of bloody saliva ran from her mouth to the front of her blouse. Rafael finished injecting the contents of a syringe and then slid the needle from her vein. He turned toward Donovan and looked him up and down as if calculating his weight, then picked up a bottle of clear liquid, turned it upside down, and began drawing down the fluid for the next injection.

It was the close proximity he'd been waiting for. Donovan planted a foot and threw his elbow behind him to a point in space where he thought Strauss's head would be. His effort found nothing but empty space, and he nearly lost his balance. Before he could gather himself, Strauss hit him hard in the solar plexus, and Donovan dropped to his knees, gasping for a breath that wouldn't come. Battered, he wanted to get up and fight, but couldn't, so he tried to twist away in an effort to buy more time. Strauss leaned in and hit Donovan savagely in the face, and any further resistance was eliminated.

Strauss whipped out fresh tie wraps and secured Donovan to the science station across the aisle from Montero. Rafael handed him the syringe, and Strauss found a vein, slipped the needle in, and depressed the plunger. Within seconds, Donovan felt the narcotic heat begin to spread through his body. Had they lost their opportunity to stop Strauss? His pain and fear evaporated and his eyelids grew heavy. He felt as if his body weighed only a few ounces—that he could simply float away if he wanted. The darkness pulled at him and he tried to resist, but couldn't. His last drug-laden thought was wondering if he would wake up—or had Strauss just killed him?

CHAPTER THIRTY-EIGHT

Donovan's first sensation was the vaguely metallic taste of blood inside his mouth. He was cold and he fought the urge to vomit. His stomach heaved and he began to gasp in and out, trying not to be sick. Tears trickled from his eyes and when he blinked them away, he found it was dark, though enough light was coming from somewhere that he could make out formless shapes. He was lying on his side. Across from him was Montero.

He tried to reach for her with arms that wouldn't move. Donovan tried to put everything together, but his thoughts drifted in and out, unfocused, unmanageable. A bolt of pain knifed behind each temple as he slowly turned his head. If he moved cautiously, the nausea was less pronounced. He recalled disjointed thoughts of dying and closed his eyes and took one deep breath after another, focusing on the reality that he was still alive.

He turned until he was looking down the carpeted aisle at a cockpit. There he found the dim light cast by the instruments as well as Strauss and Rafael. He pulled against his restraints and found the familiar sharpness of the plastic tie wraps used on his wrists and ankles. Working behind his back in the near darkness, Donovan traced each plastic strand with his fingers until he understood that each wrist was encircled by its own tie wrap. It felt like a third strap looped his hands together as well as encircled the metal leg of a science station.

All of the science stations in the *da Vinci* were modular. They could be adjusted to suit the requirements of a given mission. The leg was bolted to a track in the floor, but underneath the edge of the table was a removable pin that would separate the leg from the table. If he could remove the pin, he'd be free.

Donovan gathered his legs underneath him and coiled himself into a squatting position. A wave of nausea enveloped him and he swayed and fell to the side. He closed his eyes and swallowed hard, trying not to be sick.

Long minutes passed before he felt like another try. Donovan positioned his legs and once again tried to slide his hands up the leg of the table. Breathing hard against the exertion, a sheen of sweat broke out on his face. He balanced himself, positioning his weight over his feet and tried to picture which way the pin faced. With his hands secured behind him this was going to be difficult. Satisfied that he wouldn't fall this time, he slowly thrust upward with his legs and was relieved when his hands slid upward along the smooth metal of the table leg. His knees and thighs screamed in protest as his fingers touched the pin. Forced into a semicrouch, as if stopping in the middle of a deep-knee bend, Donovan fumbled behind his back for the button on the quick-release pin. He found it and had to twist himself slightly to one side for more leverage. The hard plastic from the tie wrap dug painfully into his wrists. He teetered momentarily before his knees gave out and he slid back down the leg to the floor. He gasped at the pain in his shoulders and legs, frustrated by his failure.

Donovan fought to get his breathing under control and steeled himself for another attempt; his legs wouldn't allow him many more tries. Once again, he grimaced and raised himself up from the floor. He found the pin and managed to push the button and pull. The pin came halfway out and Donovan jiggled it back and forth until it finally popped free from the housing and the leg tilted off to the side, away from the table.

Donovan raised himself the last three inches and pulled his wrists up and over the top then lurched sideways leaning against the side of the fuselage. His knees and thighs burned from the exertion while pinpricks of pain from the circulation returning to his hands were intense enough to make him wince. With his wrists still secured behind him, Donovan turned until he could see out the window.

Above the *da Vinci's* wingtip stretched the wing of another airplane and its size dwarfed the Gulfstream. It was so unexpected that Donovan momentarily grappled with the implications and then everything Strauss was doing made perfect sense. Strauss had intercepted and joined up with a commercial airliner, an Airbus. Perched far out on the tip of the airliner's wing, beyond the flap tracks and engine, a single strobe light flashed in a completely dark sky. Being this close to an airliner while flying seemed surreal, but as Donovan watched closely, he could see the gentle movements Strauss was making to keep the *da Vinci* positioned perfectly underneath the other plane. If anyone were watching on radar, all they would see was the solitary target belonging to the Airbus. Both the Gulfstream and the anthrax were headed toward Washington, D.C., completely undetected. No one would know they were there until it was far too late to do anything to stop the murder of millions.

Donovan now understood why Strauss had asked about the Pan Avia black boxes. Strauss had needed to know that what he had planned hadn't been discovered. They must have tried this before with the Bristol Technologies Gulfstream—and failed. The 767 was brought down in a midair collision. The featureless world outside told him they were either out over the ocean or above a thick cloud layer, but in reality they could be anywhere. Donovan had no idea how long he'd been unconscious or, more importantly, how much time he had to try and stop Strauss.

Donovan peeled himself away from the window, replaced the leg of the table, and then slowly stood upright, careful not to make any sudden moves. He stepped softly, not wanting to make a sound. The rhythmic flashes from the airliner's strobe light allowed him to briefly make out the shapes close to him. Across the aisle, Montero lay motionless. With his bound ankles limiting his mobility,

Donovan inched past her and slowly worked his way toward the rear of the *da Vinci.*

It seemed to take forever, but he finally reached the very back of the cabin. Donovan kept looking toward the cockpit to make sure his movements were as yet undiscovered. He stopped in front of a narrow equipment locker, turned, and rested his back against the metal door. He carefully felt around until his fingers found the smooth steel indentation that marked the door latch. Working quickly, he managed to get two fingers under the lever and lift with just enough pressure to silently unlatch the door.

Working from memory, Donovan searched the third shelf from the bottom until he touched the soft-sided bag. He unzipped it and felt each tool until he found the one he wanted. It took him a moment to maneuver the edge of the plastic restraints into the opening of the wire snips, but the moment he did he squeezed and felt the plastic snap apart. He brought his tortured hands into his lap and massaged his wrists. He cut the remainder of the tie wraps from his wrists and ankles and then pocketed the cutters. Donovan searched the tool bag and found a screwdriver, a set of hex wrenches, a small penlight, an assortment of small box end wrenches, and a roll of electrical tape. The kit was designed for electrical work not mechanical jobs, but at least the screwdriver could be used as a weapon. The roar from the engines was louder back here, and he could easily hear the small corrections Strauss was making to hold formation with the Airbus. It gave Donovan hope that they were far too busy up front flying to turn around and notice that he'd gotten free.

Donovan slipped into the lavatory and gently closed the door. He clicked on the penlight, faced the mirror, and gently examined the right side of his face. The cut above his eye had stopped bleeding, the swelling felt like a golf ball parked under his skin. He opened the door to the baggage compartment and swept the small beam inside the confined space.

The three anthrax-filled cylinders were strapped onto a makeshift wooden rack, their openings positioned toward the floor. Once the valves on the tanks were opened, the deadly toxin would pour out through a funnel that led to a manifold. It was simple, all Nathan had to do was depressurize the airplane, release the baggage compartment door, and open the valves. Judging by the shape and position of the manifold, the airflow would suck the anthrax out into the slipstream and death would begin to rain down on those below. It was straightforward enough to work perfectly.

Donovan switched off his light, and stood impatiently in the darkness until his eyes readjusted. With the screwdriver at the ready, he opened the lavatory door, prepared to lunge at anyone standing there. To his great relief the aisle was empty.

He crept forward and knelt down next to Montero. He reached around and clipped the bonds on her hands and feet and then gently placed her arms at her side. Donovan brushed the hair from her face, placed two fingers on her neck until he found a steady pulse. He bent down until his mouth was almost touching her ear.

"Wake up," he whispered. He shook her shoulder. "Veronica, wake up."

She groaned.

"I need you to open your eyes. Can you do that? Open them and look at me." Donovan couldn't tell if he'd reached her. Her eyelids fluttered and then squeezed together tightly. "Don't talk, just listen. It's me. Don't make any noise at all. We have to be quiet."

Her hand went to her forehead, searching for the source of her pain, and then she curled up and wrapped her arms around her midsection.

"You'll feel nauseous for a little bit," Donovan whispered. "It's from the drugs they gave us. It'll pass."

"Where are we?" Montero said as she opened her eyes.

"Other than being in the back of the *da Vinci*, I don't really know."

Montero looked at her hands, held them in front of her face. "I'm free?"

"Yeah," Donovan replied. "Now we have to figure out how to deal with them."

"What do you mean?" Montero pushed him away and then grimaced from the pain. "In a minute I'm going to the cockpit and I'm going to kill them both. I can promise you that Nathan Strauss isn't going to survive this. When I'm finished, you come up and fly the plane."

"Look out the window."

Montero eyed him suspiciously then inched up until she was even with the Plexiglas. Donovan waited until the sight fully registered. She turned toward him, eyes wide open and unblinking.

"It's another airplane," Montero said. "We're underneath another goddamned airplane!"

"If we make a move on the cockpit right now, we'd probably cause a collision."

"How did they—how can it —I mean it's the middle of the night! How can they see what they're doing?"

"This airplane is equipped with an enhanced vision system. It's basically an infrared camera that feeds the picture to a dedicated display for the pilot. Just like any night-vision device, Strauss has a monochromatic view of everything in front of the *da Vinci*. It turns night into day, and while what he did is difficult, he's a good pilot. The EVS just makes it easier."

"The Bristol Technologies airplane," Montero cocked her head to the side as she pieced it together. "This is what they were doing, right? A brand-new Gulfstream like theirs would have the same EVS thing, wouldn't it? Only they collided with the Pan Avia flight."

"That's my guess." Donovan nodded. "Remember how the Pan Avia crew was shooting that gap in the line of thunderstorms? Sudden turbulence could have easily caused the two planes to make contact."

"What do we do? We have to stop Strauss."

"We have some time before we resort to storming the cockpit," Donovan replied.

"So we sit here and wait? Wait for what? I'm not real big on this cloak-and-dagger crap," Montero whispered. "I say we make some noise and draw one of those guys back here. I'll kill him and then we go forward and kill the other one. Again, you come up and land the plane. End of problem."

"They're not stupid, and they're armed. There's no place for us to take cover. We'd be sitting targets back here if one of them decided to start shooting. I promise we'll reserve the right to charge the cockpit, but only as a last-ditch effort. In the meantime, let's try and contact the outside world. Maybe we can find someone to help us."

"Help us?" Montero hissed. "Who could possibly help us?"

"If we could make contact with the crew of the airliner, maybe they could provide some distance between the planes before we rushed Strauss. If we do it now, everyone dies."

"Isn't there a phone back here?" Montero said, searching in the near darkness, as if trying to remember where it was.

"We can't risk it. A light comes on in the cockpit when it's in use. Strauss would see it immediately. But the computer uplink doesn't have a light. That could work."

"To do what exactly? Send an e-mail, blog about our situation? That seems a little low impact. It's the middle of the night. Who in the hell would you even send it to? We have to kill Strauss!"

"Rushing the cockpit is suicide—that's our last resort. I've been to the baggage compartment. I saw the anthrax tanks. There's no way they can release the toxin without depressurizing the airplane, opening the baggage door as well as the tanks. One of them has to physically go back and make that happen. We'll make our move then. I promise."

Montero closed her eyes, took a deep breath, and nodded.

Donovan moved across the aisle and quietly slid the laptop out of its cushioned slot. He motioned for Montero to crawl over to where he sat.

"Wait a second." Montero placed her hand on his wrist. "If you switch that thing on, it might put out enough light for them to notice."

Donovan handed her the computer and the screwdriver. He stood and snatched a blanket from one of the compartments.

"Okay." Montero tested the weight of the screwdriver in her hand. "You type, I'll stand guard."

Donovan slid the blanket over his head and switched on the computer. Despite the cold air, his hands were damp as he immediately muted the sound and then waited as the screen lit up and started to cycle through its start-up routines. When the screen blinked to life, Donovan's eyes shot to the clock. It read 3:52 a.m. He tried to imagine any reason the clock could be wrong—but there wasn't. They'd been unconscious for hours, which meant they were far closer to D.C. than he'd guessed.

As fast as he could, he clicked through the prompts and typed in his password. He had to wait for the next screen to appear and when it finally did, he pulled down the e-mail page, thought for a moment, and then typed the heading:

From Donovan: URGENT! In the body of the e-mail he simply wrote: *Reply immediately—need help. Nash.*

He opened his address book and quickly clicked on the people whom he thought might be in a position to help. Then he sent the message. If this didn't work, then he and Montero's options would quickly dwindle down to two distinct possibilities. They'd either die from a bullet—or in a midair collision with an airliner.

CHAPTER THIRTY-NINE

Lauren glanced at the clock; it was a little after three in the morning. She felt both physically and emotionally battered. She'd been in bed for hours but hadn't slept. All of the packing was finished, but her mind wouldn't shut down. Her thoughts kept running through an entire range of possibilities, wondering what would happen next—news about Donovan's crash, or breaking reports about Robert Huntington. What happened first would dictate her actions. She was packed—poised to run, but now she was having second thoughts. If the Robert Huntington news broke first, she processed how each person in their mutual world would handle the news.

Michael and Susan would be the most difficult. Donovan's deception had spanned all the years of their friendship. He worked with Michael, had traveled with him, they'd faced death together. As with any high-stress job, a level of trust must exist for the partnership to succeed. When Michael found out the depth of Donovan's betrayal, Lauren imagined he'd be furious.

There was Calvin, she didn't even want to think about him—he'd not only be livid that she'd been complicit in what amounted to an epic lie—he'd be disappointed that she hadn't trusted him. The list of disappointed, hurt people seemed to stretch forever.

Exasperated, Lauren gave up on sleep and threw off her covers. She slipped into blue jeans and a tee shirt. She grabbed her phone and then, as always, she made a quick trip to check on Abigail before she headed downstairs.

In the darkness she made her way into the study. Out of habit, she clicked on the television and muted the volume. By now every set in the house was tuned to CNN. As a commercial ended and the hour's top stories began, Lauren stood in the middle of the room and waited. Long moments passed as they previewed the upcoming news stories, she felt a small reprieve when Robert Huntington wasn't mentioned, but then she doubted the news would break in the middle of the night. Whoever had the information would probably wait for maximum impact.

On a nearby table sat her and Donovan's wedding picture. She tried to remember every perfect detail of that day, but all she could think about were the words: *till death do you part*. Lauren walked to the table and turned the frame face down. Still clutching her phone, she sat down on the oversized leather sofa, brought her knees up, and curled herself into a ball as if she could somehow make herself a smaller target for all that was about to come. She'd never felt so lost and alone. The tears came quickly, followed by wracking sobs that tore through her entire body. Her sorrow was so overwhelming she had no idea how she was going to make it through the next hour—let alone the rest of her life.

A tiny red light on her phone began blinking. She immediately thought the worst. If someone were trying to reach her at four in the morning the news couldn't be good, but it was only an e-mail. She opened the screen and as she read the contents a shock ran the entire length of her body.

> *From: Donovan. URGENT! Reply immediately—need help. Nash.*

Lauren tried to imagine how this was possible. What if this was just some sort of a weird delay? She prayed that wasn't the truth, and through tear-flooded eyes she typed her reply.

> *Is this really you? I need proof.*

The tears rolled down her face as she waited. Her frayed nerves felt as if they were ready to collapse. Could this be some cruel joke? Had someone hacked Donovan's e-mail account? The light flashed again.

Yes, it's me. You were right about Kipling. Have been kidnapped and now I'm in the back of the da Vinci—we're shadowing an airliner. D.C. anthrax attack imminent. Need help. Donovan.

Lauren had her proof. Donovan was using the computer in the back of the *da Vinci* and he was in trouble. She quickly created a reply.

What can I do?

Find us. I don't know where we are or what airline. We're flying underneath an Airbus A330 coming from the Caribbean. Estimate 150 kilograms of anthrax aboard set to be dispersed.

Typing quickly, Lauren pictured the situation.

I'll find you. Are you able to reach cockpit?

Yes, but any action will cause collision. Somehow need separation from Airbus.

Give me five minutes and I'll have some answers.

Lauren changed functions on her phone and called a number from her directory. A groggy-sounding Michael picked up on the fourth ring.

"Michael, it's Lauren. I need your help."

"Lauren? What the—"

"Donovan's alive and he's in trouble. He just e-mailed me from the back of the *da Vinci.*"

"What?" Michael replied. "He's where?"

"He's been kidnapped. He said the *da Vinci* is flying underneath an airliner, an Airbus A330. There's anthrax aboard the Gulfstream and D.C. is the target."

"Oh God. How far out are they?" Michael said, sounding fully alert.

"I'll know after I make my next phone call."

"I'm on my way over. Tell your protective detail I'm coming. I don't want to get shot."

"Will do." Lauren severed the connection. Adrenaline was flying through her body as she wiped away the last of her tears, opened the door, and yelled for Buck.

Moments later he appeared. "What's happening?"

"I just got an e-mail from Donovan. He's alive."

"Are you sure it's him—someone might be trying to draw you out in the open."

"I'm positive it's him. He's in the back of the *da Vinci* and it's headed this way. Whoever is flying is planning to release anthrax on D.C."

"That's crazy—no unidentified airplane will get within fifty miles of D.C."

"Donovan says they're flying underneath an airliner. If he storms the cockpit, he's afraid there will be a collision, which means they're flying with virtually zero separation to look like one target on anyone's radar."

"I'm calling the Pentagon." Buck stepped away and pulled out his cell phone.

"No! Buck, can we wait before we make that call? We both have a pretty good idea what their response will be. If you call the Pentagon, they'll scramble fighters and shoot them down—no questions asked. Am I right?"

"We have credible intelligence about a biological attack." Buck's fingers hovered above the keypad. "What would you have me do?"

"Donovan told me he could reach the cockpit, but it would probably cause a collision. Same result. Mission accomplished. Let's try and find a way to save all those lives." Lauren snatched the secure phone from its cradle and punched in an unlisted number.

"Who are you calling?"

"The DIA. I already called Michael, he's on his way over. Can you get him in here as fast as possible?" As she waited she could hardly draw a full breath. There was no time to fully absorb what was happening. All she could do was react to the situation and do it quickly. Donovan was still alive, but if she failed, then she'd have lost him all over again.

"Ops desk, Fletcher speaking."

"Regan, this is Dr. Lauren McKenna. I need a favor."

"Dr. McKenna, of course. What can I do for you? Is everything okay?"

"I'll explain later, but I need you to pull up the FAA data stream and tell me how many A330s there are inbound to the D.C. area from the south, say South America or the Caribbean."

"Uh, yeah, sure. Hang on a sec," Regan replied. "Okay, that was easy. There's only one. Liberty Airways Flight 401, en route from São Paulo to Dulles."

"Can you give me a position for that flight?"

"Let me pull up the NORAD screen. Here we are. Flight 401 is just about to cross overhead Norfolk, Virginia. They'll be on the ground in about half an hour."

"Thank you, Regan. Do you happen to know exactly where Liberty Airways Operations is?"

"Yes," Regan replied. "Concourse B."

"I thought so. Thanks again, and I'll see you later."

"What did you find out?" Buck asked.

"That we have to get to Dulles Airport as fast as possible."

"Michael Ross just pulled up," Andy transmitted to Buck over the radio.

"We're coming out," Buck replied. "Abigail is your responsibility."

"Roger that."

Buck threw a jacket on, covering his holstered weapon, and turned to Lauren.

"Do you have your DIA credentials?"

Lauren grabbed them from the desk drawer. Buck held the front door open for her just as Michael came up the stairs. He was dressed in jeans, loafers, and a dark blue sweatshirt with Eco-Watch printed in gold letters across the front. She could tell that he was in pain; he winced at each impact his foot had with the ground. She hugged him and quickly explained what she knew as the three of them piled into Buck's SUV.

Buck fired up the throaty V-8, it was a Pentagon vehicle and he lit up the red-and-blue flashers embedded in the grille. He backed out of the driveway, then slammed it into gear and burned rubber as he accelerated down the street.

"Did you find him?" Michael asked.

"Liberty Airways Flight 401, en route from São Paulo, Brazil, to Dulles International," Lauren said then hesitated. "They're over Norfolk, Virginia. Which is why we need to get to Liberty Operations."

"Oh no," Michael said under his breath as he quickly did the math. "That puts them less than thirty minutes out."

"I've got to make a phone call," Buck said. "We can't ignore this threat."

"Who are you calling?" Lauren was torn between what she knew was right and how she felt. If Buck sent up the alarm, the Air Force would scramble their fighters, intercept Donovan, and fire on the *da Vinci*. The protocols had been in place since nine-eleven. Everyone who died would simply be chalked up as an acceptable loss, collateral damage in the war on terror.

"General Porter made it possible for me to take this assignment," Buck said. "I'm going to report directly to him."

Lauren looked at her watch. "Are there fighters already airborne or will they have to scramble from their base?"

"That's classified," Buck replied.

"I probably have a higher security clearance than you do. What I'm trying to ask is: will they have time to intercept the Airbus before it reaches Washington D.C.?"

"Yeah, there's time." Buck said. "Can I at least tell General Porter we're working on a plan to get control of the Gulfstream? Would I be lying if I told him that?"

"No, you wouldn't be lying," Lauren replied.

"What is our plan?"

"We have to get to Operations," Lauren said. "Concourse B.

Donovan said he needs some separation from the Airbus, and then he can storm the cockpit and get control of the airplane."

Lauren's phone flashed that she'd received another message. "It's from Donovan." She read the message out loud.

> *This is not the first attempt. We think the Bristol Technologies airplane collided with the Pan Avia 767. The anthrax is from prewar Iraq. The terrorist is Israeli. Nathan Strauss.*

"Oh Jesus," Buck whispered.

"Who's Nathan Strauss?" Michael asked.

"He's the man who shot you." Lauren turned to Buck. "If we can get to Liberty Operations, I think we can communicate directly with the crew aboard the Airbus—without Strauss knowing. Donovan can maintain his element of surprise."

"She's right," Michael said. "This Strauss guy is without a doubt monitoring each and every frequency that the Airbus crew is given. With the equipment in the *da Vinci*, they can monitor VHF, UHF, as well as HF frequencies. Our only advantage is they don't think anyone knows they're there."

"How can we do that then?" Buck asked. "You already pointed out that the terrorists could be monitoring all of the frequencies."

"They can't monitor everything," Michael said. "There are dedicated data links that can communicate directly with the Airbus. Once we're inside Liberty Operations, we could send what amounted to a text message, via satellite, to any of their airliners, anywhere in the world. Not only that, the crew could send a message back to Operations the same way. We need that secure data link."

"I'm sending Donovan a message telling him what we're doing," Lauren said.

"I've got to make my call," Buck said. "Tell Donovan he's going to have company shortly. If I can convince General Porter not to shoot, they may get at least one chance to get control of the airplane."

"Tell Porter that if they launch a missile, the pressure wave from the explosion will undoubtedly disperse some part of the anthrax into the atmosphere," Lauren said. "Donovan told me he thinks there's at least a hundred fifty kilograms of anthrax aboard, that's roughly three hundred pounds."

"Is that a lot?" Michael asked. "I mean, how bad is this?"

"It's apocalyptic," Lauren replied. "I worked on a project to calculate biological and nuclear fallout models factoring varying atmospheric conditions. We calculated models for this very scenario. There won't be enough antibiotics stockpiled to cure more than a fraction of the victims. The rest of the people are going to die a horrible death. If they release the full hundred fifty kilograms of anthrax aloft, on a clear, calm night like tonight, the fatalities could reach over a million, maybe even as many as five million. This is why you need to tell General Porter not to shoot them down. If even three percent of the anthrax is dispersed into the atmosphere, the death toll could easily reach into the tens of thousands."

"I'll tell him," Buck said.

Lauren sent her message to Donovan. She took a moment to examine the cloudless night sky. She imagined dozens of armed fighters roaring off into the sky to intercept her husband, their afterburners shattering the predawn calm. She had no idea how much time Donovan had before the Air Force started shooting. She knew enough to understand that after 9/11, the official position of the military was to shoot first, ask questions later. She hoped Buck was persuasive. She looked at her watch—she and Michael now had less than twenty minutes to find a solution or Donovan was going to die.

CHAPTER FORTY

Donovan opened the e-mail:

> *I'm with Michael. We're on our way to Liberty Airways Ops. Will forward plan when we arrive on site. Buck forced to call military—company soon. Hoping you'll get one chance to storm cockpit before fighters intervene.*

Donovan typed a quick reply, and then turned toward Montero. "Okay, Lauren found us. They're on their way to Liberty Airways Operations. She also says that we're going to have company real soon."

"What do you mean by company?"

"Air Force fighters."

"Oh, perfect. Who's with her, and exactly what is it you think they can do?"

"My wife is an analyst at the Defense Intelligence Agency. She's got some serious resources. Michael Ross is with her and he knows airplanes, and Buck is the guy you want around when you need some doors opened. I trust all of them with my life."

"Buck?"

"He's a former Navy SEAL. I met him several years ago on a joint mission. He's one of the smartest, most capable men I've ever met."

"You don't do anything half-assed, do you? Did you tell anyone on the ground that we've been infected with anthrax?"

Donovan shook his head. "I think we gave them enough to worry about. It isn't spread person to person, so it's not like we're going to pass it to anyone else."

"Do you think if we make it down in one piece, we'll still have time to get treated?"

"I don't know."

"I hate sitting here and waiting. Alec died without being able to fight back, and I don't want to go that way. I'm serious. We need to get this over with before those fighters arrive."

"Let me pose a theoretical question," Donovan said as he watched Montero continually turn the screwdriver over and over in her hand, her eyes fixed on the cockpit. "If we rushed the cockpit, how fast could we take them both out? I mean, if we took them by surprise, could we neutralize them both where they sat?"

"I've been thinking about that very thing," Montero said in a hushed tone. "There's only room for one of us to get within striking distance in such a confined space. What you're asking is: do I think I could kill them both without Strauss flinching and causing us to collide with the other plane?"

"You're the one with the screwdriver."

"Realistically, I doubt it. I could probably take out Rafael, but by then I'd have lost the element of surprise. There's going to be a fight with Strauss, which leaves no one flying the plane. If I took Strauss out first, then I have a fight on my hands with Rafael. Again, there'd be no one flying the plane. I don't see any way to make it crisp and clean."

"We need to take Rafael out first and then do something to get Strauss to let go of the controls, just for a few seconds. I'll reach around you and get us clear of the Airbus. After that, I'll help you with Strauss."

"Strauss is going to be a handful. There's no room up there to apply any leverage."

"Rafael's getting up!" Donovan caught the unmistakable movement in the cockpit and whispered the alarm. Montero immediately slid across the aisle, and Donovan snapped the computer shut, threw the blanket over it, and slid it as far under the table as he could. He stretched his arms behind him, and draped his wrists around the table leg and lowered his head as if still unconscious.

Across the aisle he saw that Montero had done the same thing. Donovan half closed his eyes and waited.

Cloaked in the shadows under the table, he watched as Rafael rummaged around the galley. He opened a drawer, took out a bottle of water, unscrewed the cap, and took a long pull. Donovan risked eye contact with Montero and shook his head as if to say that this wasn't the scenario they needed. She shifted slightly onto her side, the screwdriver visible in her hand.

Donovan shook his head once again—imploring Montero to sit tight. If she bolted, Rafael would see her coming before she reached him. A slight tremor ran through the Gulfstream, followed by the rolling bounce of some light turbulence. Rafael turned his back to the cabin and put out a hand to steady himself.

Montero got up on her knees and gathered her feet under her like a sprinter. Donovan stretched across the aisle and just as she sprang forward, his fingers clutched her belt. She launched herself, but instead of going forward, she went down on the carpet. Donovan pulled her into him, terrified that Rafael would sense what was going on behind him and turn around.

She fought momentarily, but Donovan held her tightly while he kept his eyes on Rafael. Long moments passed before the Israeli finally took his water and slipped back into the cockpit.

"He's gone." Donovan could feel her trembling in the darkness.

"Don't ever grab me again!" Montero's voice wavered with unchecked anger. "You should have let me take him. He was relaxed and didn't give us more than a cursory glance!"

"He would have seen you coming."

"Yeah, but he wouldn't have been able to do anything about it!" Montero hissed. "Look, I don't have your faith in the others. If we don't do something now, then someone else will make a decision, and we'll both die for nothing sitting on our hands."

"You'll get your chance," Donovan whispered. "If we die, it won't be for nothing. His plan is to kill millions, and it's not going to happen. We've stopped Strauss—he just doesn't know it yet. But we can't afford to make a single mistake."

"What's happening?" Montero steadied herself and looked around.

"It feels like we're turning." Donovan quickly looked out the window and made sure the Airbus was still above them, the strobe light confirmed that they were. He reached under the blanket and retrieved the computer from under the blanket.

"Is it starting?"

"It's part of the normal arrival into Dulles," Donovan said, having flown this route a hundred times. "The south arrival gate takes us over Norfolk, then a turn to the west toward Richmond, then straight north into Dulles."

"If we wait any longer, some fighter pilot is going to fire a missile and eliminate all of our options. Ask them how much time we have." Montero nodded toward the computer. "We need to know if they've bought us a reprieve from the fighters. If they haven't, I say we make our move."

Donovan started typing when he saw the red *X* on the connection icon. His eyes shot to the signal strength indicator and lowered his head. "We lost the link."

"Reboot it or something."

Donovan tried to reconnect, but there was no signal to be found. "I don't think it's the computer. That last turn may have put the Airbus between us and the satellite, so it's blocking the signal."

"We're cut off from the outside? Do you have any idea what their plan might be?"

"No, and without the satellite link, we're not going to know until it happens."

"We're on our own then?" Montero asked.

"Yeah." Donovan locked eyes with Montero. "It won't be long now. Get ready."

CHAPTER FORTY-ONE

Tires squealing in protest, Buck accelerated the SUV around the ramp that led from Highway 50 onto Route 28. Lauren was pinned against the door as they whipped around the cloverleaf and then shot north on the major thoroughfare. Traffic was light, and Lauren watched as the speedometer hit one hundred twenty.

Buck disconnected the call. "General Porter says the fighters will shoot when the airliner reaches the thirty-mile no-fly zone around the White House. No exceptions."

"We're running out of time," Lauren said. "How do you think we should handle this when we get to the terminal?"

"You're the DIA agent," Michael said. "Throw your credentials around and get us inside."

"Whoa." Buck let up off the accelerator.

Lauren looked up to find that the windshield had misted over. "What happened?" Visibility had gone to nearly zero, causing Buck to hit the brakes.

Wiper blades swept back and forth, clearing the windshield. Once Buck could see, he put the accelerator to the floor. "The guy in front of us blew through a puddle of water."

"That's it!" Michael sat bolt upright in his seat. "That's how we do it!"

"Do what?" Lauren turned and could see the inspiration etched on Michaels's face.

"We get the Airbus to dump fuel. Airliners dump fuel in an emergency, right? It's how they reduce their weight so they can come back and land. The fuel vaporizes as it leaves the tank and creates a mist, almost like a contrail. What it should do is force these guys out of position long enough for Donovan to storm the cockpit. The guys flying the *da Vinci* will never see it coming."

Buck handed his cell phone to Lauren. "The last number I dialed was General Porter. He needs to hear about this."

"I have another idea." Lauren reached into her pocket and pulled out a business card. "Guys, I've always heard that there's one airline in the world that has the best security. Is that true?"

"El Al," Michael replied. "Everyone in the aviation business knows that. Do you have connections within Israel's national airline?"

"I hope you know what you're doing," Buck said.

Lauren entered the number and waited—each precious second ticking off in her head. A man answered the phone. Lauren recognized his voice.

"Mr. Keller, this is Lauren McKenna. I need you to listen carefully. Nathan Strauss is about to make a biological attack on Washington D.C. He's in a Gulfstream jet shadowing a Liberty Airways commercial airliner. Liberty Airways Operations is in the B Concourse at Dulles Airport. I need access. Yes or no, can you help me?"

"How soon?" Keller asked without hesitation.

"Ten minutes."

"I'll call you back in five."

Lauren looked at the screen and found that Keller had disconnected the call.

"Call Porter," Buck urged. "He needs to know what we're trying to do."

Lauren took Buck's phone, and as the call went through, she slipped into the mind-set she used at work to deal with the military.

"General Porter here."

"General, this is Dr. Lauren McKenna, Defense Intelligence Agency. I'm with your nephew, we're headed to Dulles Airport and we need your help."

"I'm listening, Dr. McKenna."

"Sir, we now have credible intelligence that the anthrax aboard the Eco-Watch Gulfstream is from Saddam's prewar stockpile."

"You've got my attention. Go on."

"My team and I have devised a way to take control of the Gulfstream and keep the anthrax from being released. General, if you shoot down the Gulfstream, you run the risk of releasing some, if not all, of the anthrax. Tonight, with the light breeze out of the west, you'll easily expose all of the population centers downwind, which adds up to millions of people. Our plan can perhaps preserve the evidence as well as possibly capture the terrorists, but we could use your help in opening a few doors."

"I'm sorry, Dr. McKenna. The FBI as well as Homeland Security is running this show, not me."

Lauren took a carefully measured breath. "Get us past security at Dulles, and we'll do the rest."

"Dr. McKenna," General Porter continued, "if you think about the situation, you'll find there aren't really any options here. We have protocols—"

Lauren heard her own phone ring. "General Porter. If you fire on those planes, you'll not only kill the passengers and crew, but the fallout from the anthrax will kill thousands more. That's on you."

"Dr. McKenna, I won't—"

She cut Porter off midsentence and answered her phone.

"Yes or no?" she said to Keller.

"West side of the B Concourse. A man will be waiting for you at door seventeen. His name is David."

Lauren ended the call and turned to Buck. "North side of B Concourse—door seventeen. Keller says someone named David will be waiting for us."

"Who in the hell is Keller?" Michael asked.

"A Mossad agent we met last night."

Buck swung around a taxicab as if it were standing still. "We can either breach the fence, or we go through the terminal. I say breach the fence and apologize later."

"How about we go through the gate at the Eco-Watch hangar,

drive across the perimeter of the airport, and get to Concourse B without committing major felonies," Michael offered.

"The gate at Eco-Watch," Lauren replied. "Going through the terminal puts us at the mercy of the TSA. I think we all know that's not a solution to anything."

"Send a message to Donovan," Michael said. "Tell him to be ready. We're going to get the Airbus to dump fuel."

Lauren nodded. She could feel the tips of her fingers buzzing from the adrenaline and her heart was pounding feverishly in her chest. When she looked up, Buck was roaring down a frontage road toward Eco-Watch. To the side of the hangar was the gate that led to the ramp.

"Pull up to the left side. I've got my key card." Michael lowered a rear window, swiped his card, and punched in a code. Moments later the gate sprang to life and began to trundle open.

The instant the gate permitted, Buck slammed down on the accelerator and they powered across the open tarmac, lights flashing, leaving Eco-Watch far behind. The tires squealed as he turned and joined up with a vehicle service road and raced toward the distant terminal.

Lauren kept looking at her watch. Buck slowed as they became visible to the control tower. He crossed part of the open tarmac and swung parallel to Concourse B.

"That's door twenty," Lauren pointed. "Straight ahead. Seventeen, I can see it!"

Lauren threw off her seatbelt and was opening the door before Buck slammed to a complete stop. As the three of them ran toward the door, it opened from the inside.

"You must be David." Lauren said as she slipped her DIA credentials out of her pocket and clipped them to her belt.

The man nodded, and then put his finger to his lips so they'd remain quiet. He whisked them through a series of hallways and open entryways beneath the passenger concourse until they came to a steel door marked "Liberty Airways Operations." David swiped his badge once and a resounding click resonated down the quiet hallway.

Inside, David waved at a man across the room who motioned them toward a door at the far side of the room.

"David, who are you?" Lauren asked.

"I'm with Shin Bet, Israel Security Agency. Liberty Airways code shares with the Israeli airline, El Al. I oversee security for connecting passengers, I'm usually here early, which is why Mr. Keller was able to find me."

"We need to hurry."

David led them down a hallway to a door that he quickly swiped with a card and punched in a code. He silently shook hands with a man waiting on the other side, then introduced him to the small group. "This is Trent Foster, senior man in charge at Liberty Airways."

"Trent, thank you." Lauren said as they were ushered directly to a medium-sized room that held a computer workstation that filled half the office. One person was seated at the keyboard.

Lauren saw that Trent was sweating, his cherubic face flushed red.

"Did David tell you why we're here?" Lauren asked.

Trent nodded.

Three large LCD monitors glowed in front of the single individual seated at the computer. One monitor displayed the national radar picture and the screen next to it was all text. The last one had the familiar coastlines and borders of the Eastern seaboard depicted on the screen. Scattered across the map were small, green airplane symbols.

"This is Kirk, senior dispatcher on duty," Trent explained "We maintain a separate work area away from the rank and file to deal with emergencies. We can do anything from here."

Kirk turned and looked up at Lauren, his fingers never leaving his keyboard.

Buck's phone rang and he looked at the caller ID. "It's General Porter. I'm going to talk to him."

Lauren leaned over Kirk's shoulder. "Which one is Flight 401?"

"That's him," Kirk used a pencil to point to the solitary target.

"General Porter says nothing has changed. Neither one of those jets is going to be allowed within the thirty-mile no-fly zone," Buck said. "He also says the fighters are in position and have confirmed the presence of the Gulfstream."

"Damn it!" Lauren turned back to Kirk. "Exactly where is the thirty-mile arc? How close are they?"

"See this line that cuts just north of Fredericksburg? That's the boundary."

"How long until 401 reaches that point?" Lauren asked.

"At their current speed, three minutes from now."

"Kirk," Michael began, "we need you to send a secure data link message to the crew aboard Flight 401. Tell them they're in the middle of a Homeland Security red alert. They are to say nothing on the open frequencies and await further instructions from you and you only."

"They're the only ones that will see the message—right?" Lauren added.

"Yeah. It's totally protected. Only the crew on 401 will see this," Trent said. "Though shouldn't we tell them more than that?"

"Let's get their attention first," Michael said. "We'll work our way up from there."

"Michael," Lauren warned, "the clock is ticking."

"Send the message," Michael said.

Lauren watched as Kirk typed out exactly what Michael had instructed. She placed her hand reassuringly on his shoulder.

"Message sent," Kirk confirmed, as he exhaled a sigh of relief.

"Anything from Donovan?" Michael asked. He and Lauren exchanged worried glances then they both looked up at the big clock on the wall.

Lauren looked at her phone. "Nothing."

"Something just came in from 401." Kirk began typing. "They're asking for the action code."

"What's that?" Lauren said as she turned toward Trent.

"It's a code to prevent unknown persons from implementing nonstandard instructions to flight crews."

"Send it!" David urged.

"It's Hotel, Sierra, Delta, Eight, Seven," Trent said.

"Give them the code, and then I want you to explain to them that there's a Gulfstream IV flying in close formation with them." Michael leaned closer to Kirk. "They need to create some separation by dumping fuel."

Kirk began typing.

"Michael, we're down to two minutes!" Lauren felt like screaming at everyone to hurry.

Michael turned to Trent. "Where exactly are the fuel dump nozzles on an A330?"

"There are two of them, one on the trailing edge of each wing. They're positioned just outboard of the engines."

"Good." Michael closed his eyes and squinted against a sudden wave of pain. "How much time do we have left?"

"Ninety seconds," Buck said, cupping his phone with one hand. "The Air Force is asking for some definitive sign that Donovan has control of the airplane—if it happens."

"Like a code word?" Lauren said.

"What's your daughter's middle name?" Buck asked. "The Pentagon is real nervous about being able to confirm who's actually flying the Gulfstream."

"She has two actually. Elizabeth, Sarah." Lauren turned toward Kirk. "Have we received a reply from Donovan yet?"

Lauren looked at her phone. Nothing. She shook her head.

"I've got a reply from Flight 401," Kirk said without looking away from his screen. "They say they've confirmed the code and are standing by to dump fuel."

"Do it! We're out of time! He knows we wouldn't desert him," Lauren said. "He knows we're here. He'll be waiting for something. He'll figure it out faster than the terrorists do."

"Tell them to dump," Michael said. "They need to give it a good, solid, thirty seconds. If it hasn't worked by then, it's not going to."

Lauren moved beside Michael and grasped his hand. She was tempted to ask him what he thought Donovan's chances were, but she remained silent. This was all they had, and in a matter of minutes everything was going to happen even if Donovan's chances were zero. As Lauren waited, she discovered she was terrified on a level she didn't know existed.

CHAPTER FORTY-TWO

Donovan felt the blood thumping from his chest to his head. His breathing was shallow and rapid. On the horizon, peeking through the clouds, he could see the glow of Washington D.C. Coming up below them was Fredericksburg, Virginia, the White House no-fly zone began there. He knew they had to go soon. He studied the wing that loomed large ahead and above the *da Vinci*. His eyes were drawn to the steady flash of the strobe light that seemed to hover in space. An instant later, the strobe light vanished. Donovan looked closer, not sure what had happened. In the near darkness out the window, he saw the opaque vapor trail streaming back from a nozzle in the wing. The *da Vinci* shuddered beneath their feet.

"Go!" Donovan whispered in a rush. In a haze of misting jet fuel, the *da Vinci* again rocked hard. Donovan felt the negative g-force as Strauss instinctively dove away from the airliner.

Montero reached the cockpit, and with one quick jab, ran the length of the screwdriver deep into Rafael's ear straight into his brain. The man was dead before his chin hit his chest. Montero pulled out the shaft, swung to her left and drove the screwdriver deep into Strauss's thigh and threw three quick elbow jabs into his face. As anticipated, Strauss's hands flew off the controls to the wound in his leg and then up to try to protect himself from Montero's blows.

Donovan went to the right, reached over Montero, past Rafael's corpse, and pushed the controls down violently, forcing the *da Vinci* away from the Airbus. Strauss and Montero were struggling, arms flailing, and Strauss pulled back on the controls. Donovan felt the Gulfstream rocket upward. Out the windshield, Donovan spotted the A330, just above them—fuel still billowing from each wing. Donovan strained against the g's and grabbed the controls. The Airbus filled the windshield and he had no choice but to haul farther back on the control column and force the *da Vinci* nearly vertical. A second later, the Airbus flashed past as they narrowly missed the tail and flew back through the plume of jet fuel. The Gulfstream shuddered violently as it cut through the Airbus's powerful slipstream. They were running out of airspeed. Using all the strength he had, he forced the controls to the right and allowed the nose to drop while trying to roll the *da Vinci's* wings level.

In the near-darkness, Donovan saw that Montero had lost her footing, and Strauss had somehow gotten his right arm around her neck. He pulled her into him, tying her up like a boxer, only he was trying to choke off her air. Rafael's lifeless body had slid sideways and obstructed Donovan's ability to fly the plane. He shoved him aside with his shoulder and fought to level the wings as the *da Vinci* nosed down into a steep dive.

Strauss let out a cry as he pulled the screwdriver out from his thigh, and in one fluid motion he raised it above his head to stab Montero's exposed back. Donovan released the controls and put his hand out to deflect the blow only to watch in horror as the blade of the screwdriver punched cleanly through his palm, jutting out of the back of his hand. The blade stopped inches from Montero's spine.

Donovan didn't feel any pain as he locked eyes with Strauss, but in that one moment, he saw the look of an enraged animal—one that was fighting for its life. Donovan made a fist and as hard as he could hit Strauss below the eye. Strauss had no way to protect himself and the next blow hit the same spot, and the next crushed the bridge of Strauss's nose. Donovan took three more swings before he stopped. Strauss had gone slack, blood coursed from his nose down the front of his shirt.

"Montero! Don't move!" Donovan yelled between clenched teeth. His left arm was tangled up with Strauss, the screwdriver still sticking through his hand. He used his good hand to reach out and try to steady the pilotless Gulfstream. "Watch my left hand. I need you to pivot slowly to the right."

"Oh my God," Montero, disentangling herself, stared at the screwdriver impaled in his hand.

Donovan focused on gaining control of the *da Vinci*. The airplane had been descending, but he'd gotten the airplane to climb once again. The Airbus was nowhere to be seen as Donovan awkwardly leveled the wings and brought the Gulfstream back to straight and level. Moving quickly, he turned on every outside light the *da Vinci* possessed, hoping the fighters would take it as a sign that he was in control.

Montero reached up without warning and in one fluid motion pulled the screwdriver free from his hand. His knees nearly buckled, and for a split second, he felt like he might black out. He fought off the first wave of pain, then made a fist and drew the injured hand to his chest. Donovan used his good hand to engage the autopilot then dialed the emergency frequency on the VHF radio. He picked up the microphone and broadcast in the blind.

"Mayday, Mayday! This is Eco-Watch zero one on 121.5. Aircraft in the vicinity please acknowledge."

"Eco-Watch zero one, this is Viper Leader. Confirm you have UHF capability?"

"Affirmative."

"Please switch to tactical on 381.3."

Donovan switched from VHF to UHF. Using the military frequency would make it less likely for someone to monitor the transmissions. "Eco-Watch 01 is up."

"Please identify yourself."

"This is Donovan Nash, and I'm with FBI Special Agent Montero."

"For verification, what is your daughter's middle name?"

"She has two," Donovan replied. "Elizabeth, Sarah."

"Nice job, Captain Nash. Give us your aircraft status."

"Stand by."

"What do you need me to do?" Montero asked as she gingerly

touched the side of her face then used the back of her hand to wipe away the small trace of blood she found there.

"Can you get Strauss out of the seat so I can fly? Unbuckle his harness. But don't let him fall forward on the controls."

Montero released the straps while she held Strauss. She dug in her heels and used muscle and leverage to drag the deadweight out of the seat into the aisle. The moment Strauss was clear, Donovan jumped into the empty pilot's seat.

He did a quick inventory. They were headed northwest at twenty-two thousand feet. Donovan exhaled and momentarily closed his eyes while he thought for a second about what to say on an open frequency. "Viper Leader, the airplane is flyable, one casualty, one person in custody."

"Fuel status?"

"Five thousand pounds remaining," Donovan replied. "Also, be aware that hazardous cargo is contained, but both myself and Agent Montero have been exposed."

"I copy," Viper Leader replied, calmly. "How long since your exposure?"

"Twenty-four hours. Maybe longer."

Behind him, Donovan heard the beginning of what sounded like a low groan coming from one of the engines. His eyes went straight to the instrument panel. The left engine was overheating, the core temperature climbing steadily. Donovan brought the thrust lever all the way to idle, but nothing good happened. The engine grew hotter and obvious vibrations began to resonate through the controls. The engine started to surge, the rpm going up and down regardless of what Donovan did with the throttle. With a flick of his wrist, he did the only thing he could do and shut down the engine. He quickly secured the associated fuel pumps and generator and then set up the proper descent angle to keep the airspeed where he wanted.

"I'm down to one engine," Donovan reported to the fighters.

"Was it a precautionary shutdown?" Viper Leader replied. "Or do you have a problem?"

"Precautionary, I don't think jet fuel being sucked into the inlet did it any good." Donovan studied his remaining engine and after several long moments decided for now his problems had stabilized.

"Eco-Watch zero one, whenever you're ready I need you to turn right to a one-two-zero degree heading. We'll be escorting you to the Naval Air Station at Patuxent River. Altitude is at your discretion, there is no traffic between you and the airport. I know you're busy, but when you get a chance, do you have the coordinates for your point of origin and any information about where the airplane was ultimately going to land?"

"Hang on," Donovan replied.

With the airplane stabilized, he could finally take in all the information on his displays. The destination that Strauss had programmed was a familiar four-letter code: KHEF.

"Viper Leader. The destination entered into the FMS is Manassas, Virginia."

"Roger. And your origin?"

Donovan pushed a series of buttons on the FMS. He was holding his damaged hand as still as he could, but it throbbed and ached all the way up to his elbow. He worked one handed and ran through different screens on the FMS until he found the latitude and longitude where the flight had originated. Blood traced down his arm and dripped onto his trousers as he retrieved the microphone. "I have the coordinates. Are you ready to copy?"

"Go ahead."

As Donovan read off the data, he pictured the point on the globe that the numbers represented. They'd been in Venezuela. He wondered how long it would take for U.S. forces to arrive at the primitive airfield there.

"Thanks, Captain Nash. We'll pass along the information."

"Be advised, they set explosive charges before we departed."

"Roger. We'll pass that along as well. Are you ready to make a turn back to the east?"

"We're still trying to get squared away up here. I need to make a wide turn out to the west and lose some altitude before I come back around toward Patuxent River. That'll give me some time to get situated."

"No problem, Captain. Whatever you need."

Montero slipped up beside him and put her hand on his shoulder. She held up the first-aid kit. "Give me your hand."

Donovan had been holding his wounded fist firmly against his chest to try and staunch the bleeding. As soon as he extended his arm to Montero, it began to drip fresh blood.

"Hold still." She began to clean the wound and, once she'd finished, she applied an antibiotic cream and then put pressure on the wound with a gauze compress. "Did I hear something about Manassas? Where are we landing?"

"Strauss was going to land at Manassas. We're being escorted by the Air Force to the Naval Air Station at Patuxent River." Donovan turned and gave her a quick nod. "Nice job with those two."

"What in the hell happened?" Montero said. "What was that cloud?"

"It caught me off guard, too. Someone came up with the idea of getting the Airbus to dump gas. It was a cloud of jet fuel that made everything work."

"Thanks for the assist," Montero said. "I knew Strauss was going to be a problem."

"Is he alive?" Donovan asked.

"Yes."

"I didn't think he was going to survive."

"I was back there holding a gun to his head, but I couldn't shoot him, not when he was unconscious. Then the political magnitude of this thing hit me—it's staggering. As much as I'd love to end his miserable little life, I can't ignore the bigger picture. We won. He'll suffer—never see the light of day again—maybe that's enough."

"What did you do with him?"

"I found his duffel bag in the front closet. There were more of those tie wraps in there, as well as my gun and badge. I did stop his leg from bleeding; can't have him dying on me before he and I can—chat."

Montero examined Donovan's hand, then began wrapping an elastic bandage tightly around his palm.

"How's that?" she asked when she was finished. "Can you fly?"

"It's good, thanks."

She leaned in and put her arms around his shoulders and gently kissed him.

Donovan was caught off guard and, as she pulled away, a little more than surprised by this sudden show of affection. "What was that for?"

"Saving my life." Montero gestured toward Rafael. "You want me to drag this guy out of here?"

Donovan looked past Montero where Rafael's chin rested on his chest; a single rivulet of blood ran from his ear down his neck.

"Don't bother. We'll be on the ground in a few minutes."

CHAPTER FORTY-THREE

"There's a message from Flight 401." Kirk said in the deathly quiet room. "It says: The fuel dump worked. Trailing airplane has separated and is being escorted by fighters. It's using the call sign Eco-Watch zero one. There's a Captain Nash in control."

Cheers and fist pumps erupted from both Kirk and Trent. David glanced at the clock, the look on his face left no doubt that it had been close. Lauren felt Michael sag, his energy completely spent. She, too, was exhausted. It seemed abstract, almost incomprehensible that her husband was still alive, but she felt like she needed to hold his face in her hands before she could allow herself to believe everything that had transpired. She thanked David, Trent, and Kirk, and then hugged Michael and whispered, "Thank you for being there for us."

"This was all you." Michael hugged her in return, and then he turned toward Buck. "Where are they taking him?"

"The Naval Air Station at Patuxent River," Buck said, his phone pressed to his ear.

"Are you still talking with General Porter?" Lauren asked. "What's the fastest way for us to get to Pax River?"

"General Porter says we'll all be debriefed later. He also says we've got two medevac choppers with a hazmat team being launched from Andrews Air Force Base to take Mr. Nash and Agent Montero straight to Walter Reed Hospital to treat them for anthrax exposure. He'll dispatch another one to pick us up."

"What did you just say?" Lauren's eyes grew wide. "They've been exposed?"

"According to information passed along from the fighter pilots, they were both exposed nearly twenty-four hours ago."

"That's not good," Lauren said. "What else did my husband tell the fighter pilots?"

"From what little he's been able to pass along, we now know that they were being held in Venezuela," Buck relayed. "The destination Strauss plugged into the airplane's flight management system was the airport at Manassas. FBI as well as local police assets have been sent to cordon off the entire area."

Her phone rang. She glanced down and saw that it was William. She motioned to Buck that she was going outside the office to take the call. He nodded as she stepped into the relatively quiet hallway.

"Hello," she said.

"What's happening? Where are you?" William asked. "I just got a call from the State Department telling me that a Gulfstream carrying anthrax was inbound to D.C. The president has evacuated the White House and the military has gone to DEFCON 2."

"It's over. The Gulfstream is the *da Vinci*. Donovan is still alive." Lauren realized her hands were shaking. "It's a long story. He just now regained control of the airplane and is being escorted by fighters to the naval facility at Pax River. He's going to land shortly."

"I don't know what to say." She heard William's sigh of relief. "I'm stunned. That's wonderful news."

"We still have some problems. He and Montero have both been exposed to anthrax. They're going to medevac them directly from Pax River to Walter Reed."

"What does that mean?" William asked.

"It means we could still lose him."

"Worst scenario, how long would they have?"

"No more than a few days," Lauren replied.

"Okay, one step at a time. Let's plan to meet at Walter Reed. I'm on my way now. Call me if there are any changes."

Lauren ended the call with William and leaned against the wall. She felt her control slipping away and the thought of going back into that room with all of those people seemed incomprehensible.

She retraced the route they'd taken earlier, walked down the carpeted hallway, and pushed through both steel doors leaving Operations behind. She began to run as she wound through the concrete passageway until she burst out into the night air. Her chest heaved and tears clouded her eyes. That Donovan was alive was almost too much for her to process. That, and the fact that he could still die from anthrax. She wasn't equipped to deal with enormous emotional swings that ripped at her psyche—it had only been forty-five minutes since she'd gotten his e-mail. She couldn't find the elation she should be experiencing, only a deeper level of worry and fear.

A Liberty Airways Airbus taxied into view and was guided up to a jetway near where Lauren was standing. From the number of airport security vehicles that surrounded the airliner, Lauren knew that this was the A330 whose unflinching crew had saved them all. The noise was deafening and she took refuge in Buck's SUV and scanned the sky to the south of the airport. She doubted the *da Vinci* was close enough to see, but she wondered if she could, would it make any of this feel more real?

A bright light above the horizon caught her attention—followed by a large orange flash and a trail of fire as something began a descent. Lauren could only watch in curious silence as the flames seem to grow brighter and then winked out.

Off to her left, she saw two Liberty Airways ramp guys on a belt loader stop and point toward the convoy of emergency vehicles beginning to roll past. She felt for the ignition and was surprised to find the keys there. She cranked the engine, threw the SUV in gear, wheeled up within easy earshot of the radio-equipped ramp workers, and powered down her window.

"What's happening?" She called out.

"All we've heard is that some inbound airplane has declared an emergency—they've rolled the equipment."

"Any idea who it is?" She couldn't believe how fast her heart was beating as more firefighting vehicles thundered past.

"They said it's a private jet," the guy replied. "They're based here. It's Eco-Watch."

CHAPTER FORTY-FOUR

Donovan heard a deep rumble from the back of the plane. A muffled thump rocked the entire Gulfstream, followed by the low whine of grinding metal. It was the unmistakable sounds of a jet engine tearing itself apart from the inside. Two distinct explosions followed and Donovan felt the shudders run through the length of the airframe.

"Eco-Watch zero one, this is Viper Leader. You've got some significant flames and debris coming out of your right engine."

"Viper Leader. Uh, standby."

The engine temperature was shooting through nine hundred degrees centigrade. Power was dropping off dramatically. There was nothing Donovan could do as the entire core of the engine disintegrated. Combustion failed, and within seconds, red lights began to flash, the engine fire-warning bell sounded, and the now powerless *da Vinci* started down.

Donovan silenced the fire-warning bell. He shut down the fuel supply to the burning engine and waited a moment to see if the fire would go out by itself. It was still burning when he pushed a button that sent the first rush of retardant into the engine. He breathed a momentary sigh of relief as the red light went out.

"What in the hell is happening?" Montero said as she rushed up behind him.

"Engine fire. I had to shut it down. We're going to crash land. Go back and strap yourself in tight! Use one of the aft-facing seats."

"Are we going to make it to an airport?" Montero asked.

"I don't know yet. Now go!"

"Eco-Watch zero one, this is Viper Leader. Say your intentions?"

"We're going down," Donovan radioed to the fighter pilot. "What's the closest airport?"

"Dulles is due north nineteen miles."

"I'm turning now."

Donovan gently banked the airplane—he pegged the airspeed at exactly two hundred knots. In the distance he could see the airport. His eyes darted back and forth from the altimeter to the runways, which looked impossibly far away.

"Eco-Watch zero one, this is Viper Leader. Confirm you have the field in sight. Tower has cleared you to land on runway one left. You're fourteen miles from touchdown. All of the emergency equipment is rolling. Tower advises the surface wind is three one zero degrees at ten knots."

"Airport in sight," Donovan said. Dulles had three parallel runways. One left, one center, and one right. It made sense they wanted him to use the left one, it was the farthest from the terminal building. Out the side window, silhouetted by the lights on the ground, Donovan found the sleek dark shape of one of the F-16s. There were at least two to a flight, the other one was probably directly behind him with a missile locked onto what was left of his heat signature.

Donovan once again eyed the distance and altitude to the airport and came to the realization that he was losing this battle. They weren't going to make it. He systematically scanned the immediate horizon to find a field big enough to crash land the *da Vinci,* but everything was either buildings or trees. Highway 50 was a few miles off his nose, but it was a divided four lane road with light poles and a median that ran down the middle. The Gulfstream was too big—he'd never make it down safely.

Donovan glanced behind him and saw that the F-16 that moments ago had been flying next to him was gone. Where was he?

In one last effort, Donovan reached up with his good hand to the overhead panel and began pushing buttons. The right engine had exploded and was worthless, but he'd shut down the left one before it had self-destructed. He was down to three hundred feet. In the back of his mind he made the solemn decision that if it came down to it—if this didn't work—he'd simply pick an empty lot and nose the *da Vinci* straight in. One big smoking hole would help contain the anthrax and hopefully keep the body count to three. Ahead and to his left he spotted Stone Middle School. Just to the east was a strip mall with a Safeway at one end. The parking lot was virtually empty at this hour. He decided if it came to it, everything would end there.

Donovan did everything from memory—no time for a checklist. It was either going to work or it wasn't.

Two hundred feet above the ground the parking lot loomed large in the windshield. Donovan lifted the throttle up over the gate and fuel poured into the combustion chamber. Snapping igniters instantly lit the mixture. The temperature climbed dangerously, but Donovan didn't care how hot it got, as long as it started producing thrust.

Donovan picked up the microphone and made one last transmission and hoped it was enough. "Viper Leader, I've got a relight on my left engine."

The massive fan blade at the front of the engine began to spin faster, causing the internal blades to develop more speed. The *da Vinci* shuddered and vibrated as the damaged engine soared from idle to maximum thrust. The Safeway parking lot passed beneath him, and Donovan was able to coax the Gulfstream away from the ground and get the *da Vinci* to climb before the engine thrust peaked, stayed there for several seconds, and then dropped off to idle.

Donovan had no control over the engine—his throttle lever was worthless. Each time the engine spooled up near its upper limits, the temperature climbed well past the design limits. Donovan used each surge of thrust to climb the *da Vinci* away from the ground, and then as the thrust ebbed, the Gulfstream began settling toward the ground.

Off to the side, he caught sight of the F-16 silhouette. His escort had moved back into position. Donovan struggled to react to the variables in engine thrust. He used the speed brakes to keep from going too fast and then slammed them closed when the engine dropped off to idle thrust. Once again he spotted the airport, it was close, and he felt a small flicker of hope that he'd make it to a runway.

He was fighting the controls; his instruments told him he was losing hydraulic pressure. The fire warning bell went off and more red lights began flashing on the panel. Despite his efforts the airplane drifted sideways; he couldn't control the direction. Another explosion rocked the *da Vinci.* The tortured engine, like its twin, had finally reached its limits and come apart violently.

Donovan fired the last remaining charge of fire retardant into the engine. Nothing happened and the red light glowed brightly on the panel. He ignored it and measured his distance to the field. Dead ahead the rescue vehicles were lined up on either side of runway one left, but he was too low. There was no way he was going to land on that runway. It was going to be a miracle if he made it to *any* of the runways. The nose swung farther to the right and kept drifting. No amount of rudder was making any difference. The *da Vinci* was pointed at a row of buildings that housed all of Dulles Airport's cargo operations. He was going too fast—he lowered twenty degrees of flaps and with the last of his hydraulic pressure used it to lower the landing gear. The *da Vinci* blew over the airport perimeter in a steep right turn, the runway momentarily flashed underneath him and the emergency vehicles that lined each side of the runway were left behind in seconds.

The fire was still raging inside the engine, and he was eating up ground at an alarming rate—the cargo buildings were coming fast. At a hundred sixty knots, he leveled the wings and raised the nose to flare. The Gulfstream hit the ground hard, tried to bounce, and then settled. The *da Vinci* weaved as both tires on the right main gear blew apart and shredded. Shards of cast-off rubber peppered the airframe and ripped into the aluminum belly rupturing the fuel tanks. Donovan knew exactly what was happening but was helpless as the *da Vinci* plowed through the infield grass. The nose gear collapsed in a crush of twisted metal, and the front of the airplane slammed into the sod. Both main gear struts snapped off cleanly from the stress, and the airplane skidded sideways on its belly throwing up great chunks of dirt and debris. As the *da Vinci* reached the empty cargo ramp, it slid onto the concrete in a shower of sparks that ignited the jet fuel spewing from its wings. The flames marked a path where the *da Vinci* crossed the ramp, hit the edge of a building, plowed through a chain-link fence, and sheared off the left wing before finally dissipating the last of its energy.

The nose of the creaking, hissing wreck pushed through the fence and came to rest in a parking lot, the fuselage wedged between two buildings.

Donovan sat, stunned at the realization that the *da Vinci* had stopped. Off to his left, a ribbon of fire trailed across the pavement toward him. Overhead the deafening roar of two fighter jets raced past.

Propelled by the fear of fire, Donovan rolled out of the seat and dropped to the floor. His legs felt rubbery and his head pounded. The emergency lights were on and in the dim light he saw that Montero had strapped herself in like he'd told her—she was facing away from him but moving. In the rear of the plane Strauss was curled up on the floor, injured. But as Donovan drew closer, he was shocked to see that Strauss wasn't reeling in pain but reaching down to free a stiletto from his boot. Two furious slashes later, Strauss was free of the plastic restraints, pivoting to face Montero who was still strapped into her seat. Donovan saw that her Glock was lying at his feet. She must have dropped it during the crash.

Strauss launched himself at the same time Donovan reached down for the gun. Montero put up her arms in self-defense, but she was no match for Strauss who plunged the blade into her chest.

Donovan leveled the pistol and squeezed the trigger. The gun bucked in his hand and the round flew high. Strauss ducked, and then pulled the handle to release the emergency exit. Donovan fired again and the bullet hit the headliner just above Strauss's head. The Israeli dove headfirst out the opening and tumbled out onto the wing. By the time Donovan reached the window, Strauss was nowhere to be seen.

Donovan couldn't tell if Montero was breathing or not. A breeze brought the heavy smell of burning jet fuel into the cabin, and he knew they had to get out in a hurry.

He supported her with his good arm and eased her out of the emergency exit and stood on the wing. A nearly empty parking lot was all he could see on this side of the wreck. Behind him, cut off by the wreckage and the fire, he could hear the sirens and throaty engines of the rescue vehicles. He stepped off the wing onto the ground, and with Montero's limp body in his arms, ran from the burning airplane. He spotted flashing emergency lights across the parking lot. He recognized a Dulles Police Force squad car, but just as quickly, he saw the police car speeding away from them instead of toward them. He knew almost everyone on the force. Not a single one of them would race away from a crash.

Donovan carried Montero a safe distance and laid her down on a patch of grass beneath a streetlight. He gently brushed her hair out of her eyes and put two fingers on her neck until he found a pulse. He turned. The *da Vinci* lay forlornly on the asphalt, like some crippled bird splayed on the pavement. The left side of the plane was now fully ablaze—cutting him off from the rescue vehicles' ramp side.

Heavy footfalls told him someone was coming up fast behind him. Donovan spun, the Glock instantly in his hand as he leveled the weapon at the approaching figure. The startled man wearing white coveralls stopped in his tracks and raised his hands in immediate surrender.

"Don't shoot, man, I'm only trying to help."

He lowered the weapon and motioned the man closer. "She's a

federal agent, stay with her. Try and slow down the bleeding if you can. People will be here shortly."

"What in the hell happened? I heard the crash. Is everyone out of the plane?"

"Everyone's out. Keep pressure on her wound." Donovan gathered himself to his feet and began to move away.

"Where are you going?" The man knelt next to Montero and did as he was told.

The parking lot held a smattering of cars, but Donovan knew they'd all be locked. Then, in the distance, he spotted a yellow neon sign and began to run.

CHAPTER FORTY-FIVE

Lauren watched with absolute helplessness as the set of lights had descended out of sight. It appeared again and climbed above the distant tree line. As the airplane drew closer, she could see it was trailing a long plume of fire and headed straight for her. Moments later she could make out the size and shape of the airplane. It was the *da Vinci.*

The Gulfstream banked dangerously as it turned ninety degrees to the runway, descended, and abruptly slammed down hard on the infield grass. The airplane shed parts and threw up huge clumps of turf as it skidded toward a set of buildings. Skidding on its belly, it reached the apron and a shower of sparks erupted as the metal met concrete. The *da Vinci* veered away from a solid brick wall, collapsed a fence and finally came to a halt, wedged nose to tail between two buildings. She could see flames immediately erupt around the plane and it felt as though every nerve fiber in her body screamed in agony. Donovan was inside the burning plane and there was nothing she could do but watch and wait for the explosion that would surely follow.

The emergency vehicles had been caught off guard. They were still across the airport, but closing fast. She pleaded with them to hurry as the fire trucks roared past her and set up a perimeter near the burning Gulfstream. Once they'd barreled past, she slammed the SUV in gear and shot off across the ramp in pursuit.

Lauren watched as thick foam was spewed from first one truck and then more converged on the crash site. The foam instantly covered and suffocated the fire. Foam as well as water was sprayed onto the jet fuel pooling under the airplane in a bid to dilute the volatile fluid. Figures in silver firefighting suits began slowly lumbering toward the Gulfstream.

Legs shaking, Lauren stepped out of the SUV. An ambulance was parked close enough for her to hear the static-filled radio reports pouring in from the men on the scene. Overhead, two military helicopters came in low from the east. They swung around smartly and landed a safe distance away on an empty taxiway. Their rotors remained spinning.

"We have a male victim in the cockpit," came the first radio broadcast. "We're bringing him out now."

Lauren felt sick as she stepped closer to the ambulance and its radio. She needed to hear everything that was happening. A figure was passed through the emergency over-wing exit and she instantly knew it wasn't Donovan. The man was too short to be her husband, which made him one of the terrorists. Lauren waited for more information. She knew there were four people on board. She only needed two of them to be alive—Montero and Donovan.

"We just arrived on the east side," came another radio burst. "We found a woman in the parking lot. She's alive but in bad shape. Can we get one of those choppers to come around on this side? We need to fly her out of here. Now!"

Behind her, one of the Black Hawks immediately throttled up its engines. The rotors changed pitch and the helicopter lifted abruptly off the ground, hovered momentarily, and then climbed into the air. As it flew overhead Lauren caught a flash of the interior and the hazmat-suited paramedics seated inside. The helicopter skirted the wrecked Gulfstream, cleared the buildings, pivoted sharply, and then settled out of view on the other side.

"That's it," a voice reported. "It appears the cargo is secure. It's sealed in three steel cylinders. The interior of the airplane and the perimeter has been secured. There isn't anyone else aboard. We've got a single witness that says he heard what sounded like gunshots after the crash. A man carried the woman clear of the plane, and then fled the scene. He was armed with a pistol."

Lauren staggered back toward the SUV. Her mind was racing

to decipher events that made no sense. Donovan *and* Strauss were missing. Montero had been carried clear of the burning plane. It had to be Donovan who did that—Strauss wouldn't have bothered. If Donovan left the scene, it was because he was chasing Strauss. Out of pure frustration and anger, Lauren kicked the side of the SUV. Why would her husband go after Strauss alone when the one thing he needed most was medical attention?

She assembled the facts in her head and then pictured the aeronautical map of the area she'd seen in Liberty Operations. As if imagining a chess game, she finally understood what had happened. Then she saw the next series of moves before they were being made and it all made sense. Lauren swore under her breath, turned, and climbed into the SUV. She slammed the door and backed away from the chaos. She couldn't explain her suspicions to anyone else. The only reason Donovan wouldn't send up an alarm would be if Strauss could use it to his advantage. Lauren deduced that Strauss was somehow in a position to monitor police frequencies, so an all points bulletin would be useless. Donovan had figured out where Strauss was headed and gone after him.

Lauren focused on each detail that had taken place in the last hour until she too had a good idea where Strauss might be headed. Her phone began to ring. First it was Michael, then Buck, who she knew was no doubt infuriated by her disappearance. All the SEAL knew was that the women he was hired to protect and Nathan Strauss were both missing. She ignored the calls, stepped on the gas, and drove away from the crash scene.

CHAPTER FORTY-SIX

Donovan reached the Hertz rental car property and jumped full stride onto the chain-link fence. He used his momentum to boost himself to the top. His bandaged hand protecting his palm from the barbed wire, he dropped to the other side. He stayed low and sprinted toward what looked like the return lane. The cars were lined up three abreast, but no one was around. Donovan opened the door to a slate-gray Chevy Trailblazer and, as he had expected, found the keys in the ignition. He slid behind the wheel, cranked the engine, and then pulled out of the queue and drove unnoticed off the lot. Once free of Hertz, he gunned the Trailblazer toward the north airport exit.

In his rearview mirror he watched as the emergency vehicles began to arrive at what was left of the *da Vinci*. Every cop car in the area was headed toward the *da Vinci*, except the one he'd seen earlier—the one he was sure Strauss was driving. It had to be him, Donovan thought, which meant that Strauss was also listening to a police radio and was once again armed. If Strauss heard anything on the radio about him driving a police vehicle, it would be a simple matter for him to pull over some unsuspecting motorist and hijack another car, most likely killing that person in the process. It was the same maneuver he'd pulled in Florida after killing Sasha.

Donovan roared onto the Dulles Greenway and shot through the E-Z Pass lane and swung into the left lane. As he hit ninety, he found nothing in his rearview mirror but the night. Strauss was nothing if not a consummate planner. Donovan had seen it in the way he flew, the way he'd stolen two Gulfstreams—the way he'd used Montero. Strauss was going to land the *da Vinci* at Manassas, so he obviously had an escape already planned from there, which was now compromised. Donovan was positive that Strauss would have another exit strategy planned for himself—his emergency backup plan.

The Chevy's speedometer climbed past one hundred miles per hour as Donovan searched the road ahead for the blue-and-white squad car. Donovan knew most of the men and women on the Dulles police force and had for years. For Strauss to have escaped as quickly as he did, Donovan could only assume the worst. He'd probably killed the officer in the cruiser who'd responded to the crash. Donovan eyed Montero's Glock that he'd set on the passenger's seat. He'd already fired three times. He had no idea how many bullets remained. He wished she were here now. This was her game, not his.

The cough started deep in his chest and caught him by surprise. He put his fist to his mouth and rode through the spasms until his sternum hurt and his eyes watered. In the distance, just above the trees, he saw the flash of a green light followed by a white one—the rotating beacon that marked the Leesburg airport. Donovan braked hard and pulled to the shoulder. He swung the Trailblazer off into the grass, through a ditch, and up onto the frontage road that led to the airport. The shortcut shaved precious minutes and he floored the Chevy toward the airport entrance.

Leesburg, like many satellite airports, didn't have enough traffic to warrant a control tower. It would be exactly the setup Strauss would want. Donovan killed his headlights and drove toward the parking lot of Landmark Aviation, the primary operator at the airport. As he'd expected, everything looked closed.

Donovan powered down the window to listen. Just beyond a chain-link fence sat twenty or thirty small airplanes, mostly single-engine propeller types. The only sound Donovan heard was the gentle crunch of the Chevy's tires on the pavement. Across the parking lot, away from the building, Donovan spotted the police cruiser.

Donovan eased to a stop. He picked up the gun and used the

butt to smash the overhead dome light—no use giving Strauss a lighted target.

He slid out of the car, staying as low as he could as he ran. Besides the distant sounds from the main road, all he heard was the ticking of the Chevy's engine and the pulsing noise from the summer insects. Leading with the Glock, he went to the passenger's side of the cruiser. In the seat, slumped sideways in a bloody uniform, was a Dulles police officer. Donovan recognized the dead man as Bobby Henderson, a veteran of the force. He tried the door and found it was locked, as was the door on the driver's side. There was no one else in the vehicle.

Staying in the shadows, Donovan snuck to the chain-link fence where he waited, looked, and listened. He was about to climb over when the sound of a rattling chain drifted in the wind, catching his attention. He scrambled over the fence and dropped to the other side. Donovan ran to the first row of planes and found they were tied to the ground by chains, not rope. All of the airplanes were secured by chains, and somewhere across the six acres of aircraft, the sound he'd heard was Strauss untying an airplane so he could escape.

Donovan kept his ears tuned for any sound that would steer him closer. He stayed low, and quickly went from one plane to another, searching each row in the darkness. He knelt by the tail of a plane as his breath caught in his throat. He buried his face in his hands, but there wasn't anything more he could do. Like before, the cough erupted from deep in his lungs, ripping at his chest and shattering the silence.

Three quick gunshots rang out. The first two slugs punched holes in the metal next to him, but the third bullet slammed into his left shoulder and knocked him backward against the fuselage of the small plane. Donovan rolled away as two more shots sounded in the night. He struggled to his feet and ran. He wanted to return fire, but he hadn't seen a muzzle flash so he had no idea where Strauss was hiding.

Donovan had used the labyrinth of airplanes and tie-downs to separate himself from Strauss. He felt weak, sick to his stomach, and collapsed to the pavement. His shoulder burned and when he touched it, he could feel the sticky warmth of blood. The hollow feeling and chills told him he was in danger of going into shock. The cough that had given him away was probably from the anthrax exposure. He'd gambled everything in his effort to catch Strauss, and he may have paid for his efforts with his life.

The sound of an airplane starter shattered the calm. The engine chugged once, twice, and then caught as it roared to life. Donovan forced himself to his feet; by the sound of the airplane, Strauss was at least a hundred yards away.

Donovan began to run in the opposite direction—toward the parking lot. Each footfall resonated painfully up through his legs to his shoulder. He pushed himself harder as he heard Strauss rev the airplane's engine. Donovan looked back at the ramp and caught the tail of a Cessna as it rolled forward out of its parking spot. Now he knew where Strauss was. The pain in his shoulder snapped his head frontward and his hand shot to his collarbone and the wetness there. An overhead light let him see that the left shoulder of his shirt was saturated with blood.

As he neared the fence, he gathered speed and leaped, using the right side of his body to take the initial impact. He cried out in pain as he slammed into the chain-link barrier. He used his good hand to clutch the top rail and pull hard while his feet found purchase against the fence. With his legs kicking, he rolled over the top and dropped to the grass below, the pain reverberating through his entire body. He stumbled the last few yards to the Chevy, making sure the gun was still tucked into his belt.

The Trailblazer cranked immediately and Donovan threw it into reverse, backed up, mashed the brakes, threw it into drive, and slammed the accelerator to the floor. The SUV shot forward, jumped the curb, and plowed through the fence. Donovan could hear part of the chain-link fence dragging beneath the car and in his rearview mirror he found a shower of sparks.

He raced across the ramp and tried to spot Strauss. He roared down the rows of neatly secured airplanes. As he neared the end, he braked heavily and then burst free of the airplanes and out onto the taxiway that paralleled Leesburg's single runway. Off to his right, nearing the far end of the runway, was the Cessna. Donovan swore as he spun the wheel and floored it once again—Strauss was farther away than he'd have guessed.

As the Chevy hit eighty, whatever was dragging underneath snapped free, and the SUV surged forward as he quickly roared through one hundred miles per hour. The Cessna was pointed away from him, still moving down the taxiway. In the dark, running without lights, Donovan hoped he had at least a small element of surprise. He watched as Strauss abruptly turned the Cessna and swung out onto the runway. Startled, Donovan understood that Strauss wasn't going to taxi all the way to the end of the runway. He didn't need the full length. He was going to start his takeoff from there. Strauss kept the airplane moving as he began his takeoff roll. Donovan kept the accelerator pressed firmly to the floor.

The Cessna leaped forward as Strauss added full power. Donovan dismissed thoughts of using the Glock, made one final decision, then gripped the steering wheel and slammed on the brakes. In a matter of seconds it would be too late to do anything to stop Strauss. The SUV slowed dramatically, and Donovan wheeled the SUV ninety degrees to the left until he was pointed at the runway. He floored the Chevy. Now there was nothing between him and the approaching Cessna except a narrow strip of grass.

Coming from right to left, the speeding Cessna hurtled closer. The spinning prop sliced through the air at twenty-four hundred rpm. The Chevy bucked over the grass until it found the edge of the runway. Everything seemed to slip into slow motion as Donovan realized he'd judged it perfectly. The last thing he saw through the windshield was the image of Strauss, a shocked expression frozen on his face as the Trailblazer ripped into the Cessna just behind the passenger compartment.

Donovan sought refuge below the line of the dashboard and closed his eyes as the windshield imploded and the sound of tearing metal and a roaring aircraft engine filled his ears. The detonation of the airbag was like a gunshot as the solid frame of the Chevy sliced through the thin aluminum skin of the Cessna and burst through to the other side of the runway. The Chevy lurched sideways and Donovan grabbed the steering wheel just as the vehicle skidded off the pavement onto the grass. He slammed on the brakes, brought the Chevy under control, and rode it across the rough ground until the Trailblazer slid to a stop on the wet grass.

Over his shoulder, Donovan watched the wreckage of the Cessna careen down the runway. The wings had ripped free and the tail was a shredded mess. Donovan had caught the Cessna exactly where he'd aimed, where the fuselage was thinnest. He'd punched straight through and not gotten tangled up with the wreckage. Surprisingly, there was no fire.

Donovan found the Glock, opened the driver's side door and staggered uneasily toward the Cessna. He had to stop for a fit of coughing, but he finally made it to what was left of the cockpit. In the growing light from the coming sunrise he spotted Strauss, still strapped into the pilot's seat. The door of the Cessna, as well as most of the metal on that side of the plane, was stripped away. Donovan could hear the muted law enforcement transmissions from a walkie-talkie somewhere inside the wrecked cockpit.

Strauss's eyes were closed and at first Donovan thought he was dead—until he blinked and groaned as if he were just regaining consciousness. Donovan raised his gun and leveled it at Strauss as he moved closer to locate the radio. Before Donovan could react, a flash of steel whipped across his right wrist and the Glock dropped harmlessly to the ground. Donovan twisted away from Strauss, but not before the Israeli's stiletto flashed again, this time leaving a deep gash in the flesh of his right thigh. Donovan staggered backward out of range and discovered that his wrist was squirting blood. He clamped his hand around the pulsating wound and dropped to his knees.

He waited for Strauss to come at him again. His knife was poised, ready to strike, but he didn't move. His lower torso was twisted at an odd angle and his right knee was bent in the wrong direction. Strauss hadn't come after him because he couldn't, he could only glare at him, his eyes filled with a killer's thirst for violence. Donovan spotted the Glock. It was lying on the ground between himself and Strauss.

"Give it up, Nash. You're bleeding to death."

"You're the only one dying here tonight," Donovan said as he struggled forward on his knees. "Montero's still alive and so am I."

"You're lying. She's dead."

Donovan inched toward the Glock. If he wanted to pick up the gun, he needed to hurry. He'd have to reach in with his left hand, the one Strauss had run a screwdriver through, which meant releasing the pressure on his severed right wrist, which meant more blood loss.

"You're going to bleed out before you can do anything to me." Strauss said. "I might not get away—but I'll outlive you."

At the taunts, Donovan felt his rage surge through his battered body and override everything. He let go of his damaged wrist and reached out for the pistol. Strauss swung wildly with the knife but Donovan stayed below the murderous arc. Severed artery pumping out blood, his fingers touched the barrel. He managed to lock them around the steel and pull the pistol toward him. He rolled away, and immediately pressed his spurting wrist tight against his chest to try and staunch the flow of blood. He raised himself up and aimed the gun. Donovan was rewarded by the expression of resignation and defeat on Strauss's face.

His vision became blurry and Donovan lost focus. He swayed backward, losing his balance. He tried to squeeze the trigger, but nothing happened. He didn't possess the strength. He was about to tumble backward when someone steadied him from behind.

"I've got you," Lauren said as she eased her husband to the ground and clamped a hand around Donovan's open artery. "Stay with me. Can you get up? My cell phone's dead."

"Plane... police radio," Donovan said his voice not much more than a whisper. "Strauss... knife."

Lauren slid the Glock from Donovan's hand, raised it with both hands and fired three rounds straight into Strauss's chest. The Israeli's head slumped forward and the stiletto tumbled harmlessly to the ground.

"Stay with me, Donovan," Lauren said as she dropped the gun to the ground. "I need you to stay awake. Can you use your good hand on your wrist while I find the radio?"

Donovan let her guide his hand over the wound, and he pressed with what little strength he had while she retrieved the radio. She returned and resumed the pressure.

"All units, all units," Lauren transmitted in the blind. "Leesburg airport, shots fired, officer down, need immediate helicopter medevac."

Donovan looked from Strauss's body, then up at his wife, profoundly sorry he hadn't been able to pull the trigger and that Lauren had been forced to finish the job. He wanted to tell her —apologize.

"How did you know where I—" Donovan's mouth felt dry, he was cold, and wanted to close his eyes.

"Don't talk." Lauren held him tightly as she stroked his face.

Moments later the night air was filled with the sounds of sirens. Donovan heard the beating rotor of an approaching helicopter. It was coming fast, and within minutes he and Lauren were bathed in a harsh white light from the hovering chopper. Soldiers secured the scene and EMT personnel forced Lauren to move away. Donovan tried to reach for her, but he felt his clothes being cut apart and bandages pressed over his wounds. IVs were inserted and he felt a stretcher slide underneath him. His eyes were closed, but he could feel the paramedics lift him up and hurry across the open field toward the waiting helicopter. He heard his wife ask them how long it would take to fly to Walter Reed. He heard doors slide shut and rotors begin to accelerate, and then there was nothing.

CHAPTER FORTY-SEVEN

"Dr. McKenna, would you please answer the question?"

Lauren looked across the table at high-level members of the FBI and three Department of Justice lawyers. Everyone was button-down proper except her—she was still wearing clothes stained with her husband's blood. Next to her sat Calvin and two DIA lawyers. The meeting was taking place in a conference room at Walter Reed Hospital with the promise that she'd be excused when her husband was moved from recovery and settled into his own room.

The moment they'd landed, he'd been whisked into the operating room and had endured four and a half hours of surgery. She'd seen him briefly afterward as the doctor met with her and explained what had been done. The sliced artery in his wrist had been repaired. The blade hadn't gone very deep, so the damage was mainly to the artery and not to major nerves and tendons. His leg was sutured and would heal fine. The gunshot wound to his shoulder had nicked his clavicle and they'd had to find and remove all of the bone fragments. The wound to his hand was trickier, but the specialist they'd brought in had felt as if Donovan would recover full use of his hand and fingers, though he would need extensive physical therapy to regain strength and motor skills. He was being administered massive doses of intravenous antibiotics to combat the anthrax exposure, along with an experimental treatment that promised to reverse any footholds the bacteria had already gained. The doctor had warned her that they'd done everything that could be done for now. If they stopped the spread of the anthrax, Donovan would survive, though a full recovery from all of his injuries would probably take months.

"Dr. McKenna, again, would you please answer the question?"

Lauren looked at the man who'd spoken. FBI Deputy Director Norman Graham was a thickset man with deep-set eyes and no neck. Lauren thought he had the smallest hands she'd ever seen on an adult.

"Yes, I initiated a phone call to Mr. Aaron Keller that allowed me access to Liberty Airlines Operations."

"How long have you been working for Mossad?"

"I don't work for any foreign intelligence service."

"How long have you known Aaron Keller?"

"Less than twenty-four hours."

"Why did you call him?"

"He seemed motivated to help."

"Which is why you hung up on General Porter?"

"Are we here to discuss my phone manners?"

"You elected to seek help from a Mossad agent rather than a member of the Joint Chiefs? A man, I might add, who convinced the president to issue you and your friends complete immunity in this matter?"

"I guess he didn't have a problem with my phone manners—or my tactics. I believe the president's intention was to spare my friends and me hours of needless interrogation."

"Dr. McKenna, exactly when did you elect to join in the manhunt for Nathan Strauss?"

"When it became clear that my husband and Strauss were both missing from the crash site."

"So, with all of your years of tactical field work, you felt compelled to give chase, unarmed, and alone, without asking for backup?"

"Norman," Calvin said, quietly, "lose the sarcasm or this meeting is over."

"I've got this," Lauren said, putting her hand on Calvin's arm as she turned back to Graham. "Exactly where was I supposed to find this backup?"

Graham ignored Lauren's jab at the absence of agents on the

scene. "When did you ascertain that Nathan Strauss was alive, and that Leesburg airport was his destination?"

"Almost immediately," Lauren replied. "It was an obvious deduction."

"Yet you didn't tell anyone?"

"If my husband elected to give chase and not sound the alarm, there had to be a good reason. The only one I could think of was that Nathan Strauss must have a police radio or a scanner or some other way to monitor law enforcement transmissions. Once I figured that out, the rest was simple."

"Do indulge us."

"My husband should have sought immediate medical treatment. Instead, he made the decision to give chase. He must have thought he was in a unique position to stop the fugitive. He did this, I remind you, after he carried FBI Special Agent Montero to safety."

"We're not questioning Mr. Nash's decisions or his bravery," Graham replied. "Now, back to the Leesburg airport question. How did you know?"

"Immediately after the crash, I was on the west side of the buildings, as were most all of the fire rescue elements. I couldn't see what was happening on the east side—no one could. In fact it took considerable time for any official vehicles to reach the east side due to the way the Gulfstream came to rest between the two buildings. From the accounts of the first witness on the scene, I reconstructed the sequence of events following the crash. Because my husband had taken the time to carry Special Agent Montero clear of the burning plane, it seemed likely that Strauss had a head start. My husband wasn't actually following the suspect, but had instead figured out Strauss's likely destination. If he could do it, I surmised I should be able to as well."

"The Leesburg airport." Graham nodded as he said the words.

"We already knew that the Manassas airport was Strauss's initial choice. It only made sense that Strauss choose another satellite airport as an alternate to try and make his escape via airplane. It was how he operated."

"What did you discover upon your arrival at Leesburg?"

"I found a Dulles Airport Police car with the body of an officer locked inside. I also found a large section of fence that had been knocked down, presumably by a vehicle. It was then that I heard the sound of an airplane beginning to take off—followed by the sound of a crash."

"What did you do then?"

"I drove through the hole in the fence and headed for the runway."

"Dr. McKenna," Graham held up his stubby hands as if Lauren had missed the obvious, "I'm deeply troubled by the fact that at no time did you attempt to contact the FBI. With your knowledge of government protocols, you know that the FBI is the lead agency for domestic terrorism."

Lauren stared directly at Graham. "Let me make this a little clearer for you. My cell phone battery died from talking with a great number of people. By the time I arrived at the Leesburg airport, there were no FBI agents within earshot—so, no, I did not ask for your assistance. I would have liked that option, but at that point, I believe your nearest agent was either at the Dulles or Manassas airport, not exactly where I needed them."

Everyone in the room glanced at Graham to gauge his response at her caustic response.

"There was a radio in the SUV you were driving," Graham shot back.

"I believe I've stated my concerns about radio traffic and the possibility of Strauss being able to monitor them," Lauren said. "May I continue?"

"Please do," Graham replied.

"On the runway I came upon the debris from a crashed airplane. In the headlights, I found a destroyed Cessna and in the distance was a damaged vehicle. It was then that I saw my husband."

"Go on." Graham said.

"I was worried about the risk of fire from the Cessna, so I parked my vehicle about fifty yards or so and ran to him. I was able to reach him as he collapsed from his injuries."

"Gentleman," Calvin interrupted, "we're all aware of the physical damage suffered by Mr. Nash. I suggest for Dr. McKenna's sake we skip these details and try and wrap this up."

"There's a process involved here," Graham said to Calvin. "We'll stay the course. Dr. McKenna, what was your husband doing just before he collapsed?"

"He was pointing a gun at Nathan Strauss."

"Do you feel it was your husband's intention to fire the weapon, or had he decided that apprehending Nathan Strauss would be more prudent?"

"I have no way to answer that question," Lauren replied. "Though I sincerely doubt apprehension was on his mind. When I reached him, he was close to bleeding to death. Taking prisoners would have been a bit problematic at that point. The last words my husband said to me were to warn me that Strauss had a knife and that there was a police radio in the wrecked Cessna. I could hear the transmissions, and I assumed my husband was trying to reach the radio and call for help."

"So you made the decision to kill a man, even though his back was broken and he posed no real threat to you."

"Strauss held a knife and my husband was dying from what looked like knife wounds. I'm not a medical doctor, but I say he was a serious threat." Lauren felt her patience dwindle to nothing and her temper flared. "Let's get one thing straight here. The threat this man posed was monumental. I killed a man that over the course of three days had shot two of my friends, one fatally. He tried to blow me up, and then kidnapped my husband as well as an FBI agent. Let's not forget the deaths of all the people on the Pan Avia flight and of course the impending anthrax attack he was very close to completing. The man was nothing if not lethal."

"The question on the table isn't whether Nathan Strauss was

a criminal. He clearly was. The bigger question is: did you kill him under orders from Aaron Keller?"

"That's the most absurd statement I've ever heard." Calvin shot to his feet. "We're finished here!"

"Answer the question!" Graham fired back, his eyes fixed on Lauren. "The last thing the Israelis would have wanted was one of their own to be put on trial for terrorism."

"A prisoner might have been a nice trophy for you, but don't blame that failure on me." Lauren did her best to hold her anger in check. "I think the bigger question here is the fact that the FBI, how did you phrase it? The obvious lead agency in domestic terrorist matters did virtually nothing to prevent the largest threat this country has ever faced."

"Dr. McKenna," Graham hissed, "you're out of order."

"You can go to hell!" Lauren snapped. "How dare you even insinuate that I murdered a man on orders from Aaron Keller or anyone else for that matter. I think you're scrambling to save your ass by pointing fingers at me. It won't work."

"I think we should all take a break," Calvin said.

"We're not taking a break until Deputy Director Graham apologizes for his implication." Lauren's anger had boiled over. She stabbed her fingers into the table for emphasis. "You've got ten seconds, Mr. Graham. Then you can stop trying to figure out how to best spin this story. I'll do it for you. I'll walk out of here and call a press conference to explain how a Mossad agent, a civilian pilot, and a suburban mother did more to stop an anthrax attack on the nation's capital than the entire Federal Bureau of Investigation."

The room went silent as Lauren and Graham glared at each other.

"Five seconds. And do I need to remind you that I have full immunity?"

Graham blinked and then cleared his throat. "Dr. McKenna, I apologize if my comments seemed insensitive. My intent here is to examine all of the options that may or may not have come into play in this matter."

Calvin took of his glasses and used them to gesture toward Graham. "Norman, one more remark like that and this meeting will be over. I've known Dr. McKenna since she was finishing her doctorate. I personally recruited her straight out of MIT. Her service and patriotism is beyond reproach."

"Mr. Graham, I accept your apology. I can't tell you how much I wish someone else had been there to pull that trigger, or even be able to make the decision not to. I wish that an army of FBI agents had ridden in to my rescue, and that you could stand on a podium somewhere and decorate your own, but I was the only one there. I made the call and I killed Strauss. All I wanted was to get to that radio to try and save my husband's life."

"Excuse me," one of the FBI attorneys seated next to Graham said, "Dr. McKenna's comments a few minutes ago about putting the correct spin on today's events are interesting. I believe if we look hard enough, we might have a ready-made solution to this matter. Nathan Strauss died from multiple gunshot wounds fired from FBI Special Agent Veronica Montero's weapon. But the shots were fired by another federal agent, one who works for the Defense Intelligence Agency. In the interest of national security we would not name Dr. McKenna. We could then set plans into motion to present FBI Agent Montero as the undercover agent who was actually on board the Gulfstream. We could focus attention on the fact that even though she was injured, she made the difference in this matter. Then, of course, we'd try and not make any mention of Mossad, a civilian pilot, or a suburban mother."

"That's an interesting angle. Dr. McKenna, would that be agreeable?" Graham asked. "And would you sign a nondisclosure statement to that effect?"

"If it's done with the approval of Calvin Reynolds and DIA council present," Lauren replied. "I'd also like to minimize the impact of this ordeal on my family. If there is a way to downplay my husband's involvement, I would be extremely grateful."

"His name is already out there as being kidnapped along with Agent Montero. But we'll see what we can do." Graham turned to his people. "Draw it up fast. I want to send a statement to the White House as soon as possible."

"One more condition," Lauren said. "I'd like to be free to open a dialogue with Mr. Keller and personally express my thanks without any further insinuations about my patriotism."

Graham eyed Lauren and then Calvin and finally nodded his approval.

Someone in the hallway knocked briefly and then cracked the door. "Dr. McKenna? Your husband is in his room now. You can come with me."

"Dr. McKenna." Graham got his feet. "Thank you."

Lauren left the room without looking back.

"Is there any news about Ms. Montero, the FBI agent?" Lauren asked the nurse as they waited at the elevator.

"All I've heard is she's out of surgery and in intensive care. She's in critical condition and we won't know anything for a while yet."

Even if Montero survived, Lauren had no idea what the time frame was for the full disclosure of her husband's secret. For all she knew, it could be happening at this very moment. She could only hope that news of Montero's survival would somehow stop the process.

They walked the rest of the way in silence until Lauren was shown into her husband's room. His face was pale and slack—it looked as if most of the life had been sucked out of him, but he was alive, and that's all Lauren cared about right now. Seated on one side of the room were William and Michael. She hugged them both.

"How are you?" Michael asked.

Lauren looked down at her blood-stained clothes, "I'm fine. Tired."

"We won't stay long," William said. "Michael just finished his statement and he needs to rest, so I'm going to take him home."

"How was it?" Lauren asked. "Did they come down on you pretty hard?"

"You know, the one question I couldn't answer is why you ran off. You left poor Buck all alone and went looking for a known killer? I knew that question was coming and as hard as I thought, I didn't have a ready answer."

"I know he's upset with me. He should be. I just didn't have time to wait for either one of you." Lauren didn't look forward to her coming conversation with Buck.

"Buck will get over it," William replied. "You did what you thought was needed. And you were right. Donovan might not have made it if you hadn't done everything exactly as you did."

"Were you here when they brought him in?" Lauren glanced at her husband. "Did they tell you anything?"

"No, only that the doctor would be in later," Michael replied. "And before I forget, Abigail is at our house. Susan insisted, so take all the time here you need."

"Well, we should get going," William said and gave Lauren a knowing look that said she might not have much time before things started happening.

"Call if you need anything," Michael said. "You're also free to stay at the house. We know you'll be spending a lot of time up here and we're more than happy to watch Abigail."

"Thank you," Lauren said, touched that her friends were there for her.

After they'd left, Lauren went to Donovan. She leaned over and touched his face, tears clouding her eyes as she pulled out a chair and sat next to him and tried to sort through her emotions. She was exhausted, yet she felt supercharged, the adrenaline still pushing her forward. The sight of Donovan brought out a strange mixture of relief and resentment. If he'd simply stayed put after surviving the crash, she wouldn't be dealing with all of these conflicting issues that she couldn't yet fully comprehend.

She'd killed a man today. Picked up a gun and pulled the trigger without a moment of hesitation. Beyond the factual elements of the act, she felt nothing. No remorse, no relief, nothing. As if she'd sealed off the horror so it couldn't touch her. Yet it sat deep inside like an emotional fault line, threatening to shift at any moment and cause a vast upheaval.

In the corner of the room was a television. She turned it on and immediately tuned it to CNN. She muted the volume and switched on the closed captioning. Lauren watched as aerial videotape footage of the *da Vinci* was shown. She read that the anthrax had finally been removed and transported to a safe location. She knew that today's news could have been so very different; the first attempt had gone wrong, but if it hadn't, the anthrax attack would have been a very real thing. Lauren shivered at the thought of her and Abigail, as well as everyone else downwind, being infected. The screen shifted to footage of the crashed Cessna. Lauren felt sick to her stomach when she realized that her husband had been in both airplane crashes.

Lauren thought of Strauss, and then Montero. For the first time she felt a small glimmer of kinship with the woman she'd grown to despise. Lauren had condemned Montero for killing in the line of duty, but that had all changed in the instant that Lauren had pulled the trigger and shot Strauss. Montero had lost someone she loved, and all she wanted was the truth. The last few days had been a nightmare of losing Donovan and not knowing what had happened. What would Lauren have done if she'd been in Montero's place? What if the last few days had stretched into weeks—what level would Lauren have gone to seek the answers? Montero had resorted to blackmail. Lauren had committed murder. Montero's actions didn't seem quite so appalling.

Lauren heard a gentle knock at the door and she looked to find an older, clean-shaven black man peeking into the room. "Excuse me," He said, his voice barely above a whisper. "I was told I might find Mr. Donovan Nash in here."

"I'm his wife." Lauren stood and motioned him to come in the room. He was tall and thin, and his suit looked expensive. She didn't think this gentleman was on staff—but he had to have some sort of major pull to get past the security that had sealed off the entire floor. "May I help you?"

"Hello, Mrs. Nash." The man stepped quietly into the room. "I apologize for the intrusion in what must be a very difficult time. My name is Thomas Milford."

Lauren was struck by the man's presence. He had the warmest eyes she thought she'd ever seen. In his left hand he held a weathered leather briefcase; in the other was a bouquet of flowers. His gentle eyes and voice made Lauren feel at ease.

"I brought these for Mr. Nash."

"Thank you." Lauren took the offered flowers, set them on a table, then turned back to face the stranger. "What can I do for you, Mr. Milford?"

"Please, call me Thomas. I'm Ms. Montero's attorney."

Lauren felt her defenses go up. Why was Montero's lawyer here? What did he want with Donovan—unless he knew about her husband's past and was making a play of his own before he went public.

"May we sit?" Milford asked.

"I'm fine. Have you checked on her, Ms. Montero? Is she going to be all right?"

"I just came from there. They told me it would be a while before we knew anything for certain." Milford continued smiling, despite Lauren's cool response. "I came to see you because of very specific instructions Ms. Montero gave me."

"Go on."

"Allow me to back up a moment while I explain. Ms. Montero sent me an envelope not long ago, with instructions to open it if I didn't hear from her at specific intervals. She told me she was going on an important assignment and that the envelope contained information that needed to be addressed in the event of her death."

Lauren began to shake and she suddenly didn't trust her own voice.

"Are you okay, Mrs. Nash?"

"Please—just get on with it."

"Yes, ma'am. When Ronnie called me early this morning, she

instructed me to not open what she'd given me—instead to hand it personally to either her or Mr. or Mrs. Donovan Nash." Milford reached into his briefcase and handed over an envelope. "If it was important enough for her to take the time to call me from the back of that plane, well then, I felt compelled to bring it as fast as I could."

Lauren took the envelope, turned it over, and found a wax seal still firmly in place. She looked up at the attorney and tried to speak, but couldn't.

"I think you should sit down, Mrs. Nash."

Lauren nodded and absently gestured toward the other chair—the chair she hadn't offered him earlier. "I don't understand. She called you from the plane?"

"Yes, ma'am. She was fine when I spoke to her, so it was before she was injured." Milford lowered his head as he spoke. "I flew up here as fast as I could. I'm her attorney, but I'm also a friend. She's a very special woman, and it was a brave thing she did for her country."

Lauren felt the warm rush of tears flood her eyes, tears of relief and joy. She made no effort to stop them. Somehow Montero had done what she'd promised. Lauren pressed the envelope to her chest and found Milford's warm eyes with her own. She'd been wrong. Until only a few moments ago, she'd chosen to focus on the parts of Montero that had threatened her.

Lauren dabbed at her tears. "Please, tell me something about her, what's your favorite part of knowing Agent Montero?"

He smiled as he thought. "I can promise you she isn't an easy person to get to know. She's as tough as they come—has to be, I guess, to do everything she does. A woman in a man's world and all that, but what I love most about her is seeing her on Saturdays. Not many people know she volunteers at a shelter. It was set up for women at risk—Ronnie helps raise a lot of the money for the place. I got involved when she asked me to come down and talk to some of the women. I give them legal advice, but mostly I just listen. But my joy comes from seeing that other side of Ronnie. It's amazing how so many of them look up to her, even though she's a cop. I know she had her own problems growing up, but she pulled through and is giving back. She's making a difference with some of those kids, both on and off the job. I guess that's the part I like most, Mrs. Nash, seeing the other side of Ronnie."

"Thank you, Mr. Milford," Lauren said. "Thank you for sharing that story about—Ronnie. It's nice to know a little about her, beyond her role in the FBI. And thank you for bringing the envelope to my husband. I know he'll be pleased by your efforts."

"Well, Mrs. Nash, I won't intrude any longer. It was a pleasure to meet you, and I hope Mr. Nash makes a speedy recovery."

After he'd left, her thoughts were broken by a woman's photo on the television. It was Special Agent Veronica Montero's service photo. It hadn't taken Graham long to feed part of the story to the media. In silence, Lauren read the caption; Montero had been catapulted to the forefront as the hero who stopped the terrorist attack on D.C. The brave FBI agent was the new poster child on the war against terror. It struck Lauren that there had been no mention yet of the terrorists' nationality, only that they had ties to the Middle East. Lauren wished she could hear the dialogue going on between Tel Aviv and the White House.

Just as William had promised, Donovan had judged the situation and done what it took to counter the threat. Lauren sat and idly fingered the sealed envelope, still amazed that Montero had done what she'd promised and let her husband go.

Donovan stirred, his eyes fluttered open, and he blinked heavily, unsure of his surroundings.

Lauren was instantly at his side. "Hey there. How do you feel?"

"Where am I?" Donovan said—his voice sounded thick and dry.

"Walter Reed Hospital."

"Thirsty."

Lauren gently guided the straw to his swollen lips and he took in some of the cold water from the cup she held.

He sipped slowly, his eyes opening and closing. He finally

stopped drinking and took in his surroundings. "Are you okay? Where's Abigail?"

"I'm fine. Abigail is with Susan."

Donovan looked up at the television where Montero's picture was once again on the screen. He turned to Lauren. "Did she make it?"

"She's still alive," Lauren squeezed his hand. "Her lawyer just left. At some point she used the phone in the back of the *da Vinci* and made the call. It's over."

"I think she found what she was looking for." Donovan tried to move, winced, and then laid still. "I'm sorry. I'm sorry you had to kill him."

"It's over. Don't worry about it."

"I'm sorry for a great many things."

Lauren looked away, not sure what she should say.

"Everything's my fault."

"Look, this isn't the time or the place. We'll talk later. You just rest."

"I want to talk now. The drugs are wearing off, and I'm going to need some painkillers in a minute, and I need to tell you everything."

"Please don't. It'll wait."

"No, it won't. It's all I thought about the entire time I was being held. How wrong I've been."

"Don't force this now. You just concentrate on getting better."

"I have to tell you." Donovan reached with his good hand out and wrapped his fingers around hers.

"I only want to know one thing." Lauren asked the one question that burned in her mind, everything else could wait. "The threat was over. Why'd you go after Strauss? He wouldn't have gotten far."

"I did it for Michael and Kyle. I did it for Montero and all of people Strauss had killed. For all he knew, he'd killed me as well. I've never felt that much rage. It was as if I had no choice. Whatever it took, I wanted him dead."

Lauren's eyes welled up with tears and they trickled down her cheek, one silently dropped onto Donovan's hand then rolled off. Lauren slid her hand from his.

Donovan reached out and tried to find her hand again, but she stepped away.

"You did have a choice, and you went after Strauss. You could have died, but you went anyway, without a single thought about Abigail or me. I've always put you first, but that's not what I get in return—and I don't think I ever really have. You lost Meredith, and I'm sorry you've had to endure that, but why did you marry me? It's so clear to me now that I'm your second choice—I'm the runner-up."

Donovan was speechless as she gathered her things and headed toward the door. She hesitated for a moment and turned toward him. "The look on your face tells me I'm not wrong."

"Nothing I say is going to make any difference to you right now," Donovan said. "I'm sorry."

"I'm sorry too, but I can't live this way anymore. I can't be here." Lauren turned away and pushed through the door.

CHAPTER FORTY-EIGHT

Buck hugged Lauren and then gave her a quick kiss on the cheek. "I wish it didn't have to be like this."

"Me too." Lauren pulled away. "I'm really happy you've accepted a full-time job with Eco-Watch. Take care of everyone. Okay?"

"I will," Buck leaned down and gave a final wave to Abigail, who was already in her car seat.

Lauren took one last look at her house before getting into the waiting limousine. She felt so numb. As the car pulled away, she leaned back into the leather seat and tried to shut down her emotions. She'd known this moment was going to be difficult, but it was beyond what she'd feared.

"How are you holding up?" Aaron Keller asked.

"I'll be fine once I'm on the plane."

"I'm happy to hear that both your husband and Agent Montero will make full recoveries. They're very fortunate."

"Can we talk about something else?"

"Of course," Keller replied. "I have the final confirmation. You'll be met by my people in Paris at the Le Bourget executive terminal. You and Abigail will be issued your visas and other papers and taken directly to the flat. I've taken the liberty of having the cupboards stocked with a few days worth of food. It'll let you acclimate without having to run many errands."

"I can't thank you enough," Lauren said.

"My country owes you and your husband a great deal," Keller replied. "I'm truly sorry though that the circumstances dictate your sudden departure. But then again, that is life, is it not?"

Lauren nodded, hoping she wouldn't cry until she and Abigail were airborne.

"The security will be in place, but I've made it clear that you and Abigail be given as much privacy as possible."

"Do you have any clue yet why Strauss was trying to do this?"

"Not really. I think Strauss's emotional state combined with the long-term effects of his chronic drug use made him somewhat pliable to those who may have had a hidden agenda," Keller said, his voice heavy with regret. "Had he succeeded, it would have looked as if Islamic extremists had struck the United States with a biological weapon. The only real lead was the man who tried to kill you at the hospital. An Iranian national, trained in Yemen, and in your country illegally. The aftermath of such an attack with Islamic undercurrents would have probably have touched off a full-blown war in the Middle East. I think Strauss, or his handlers, were hoping that an act of this magnitude would lead to the annihilation of many of Israel's sworn enemies. The death of millions of Americans may have very well triggered the final conflict they'd hoped for."

"How did he acquire the anthrax?"

"Just days before the second Gulf War, he led the mission where it was appropriated. It was a surgical airborne strike deep into northern Iraq, very much like a kidnapping, only we raided a convoy and took Iraq's weapons of mass destruction. The mission was a success, but Strauss and his unit took heavy casualties. He was wounded and very nearly died. It was his last mission. From what we've been able to go back and piece together so far is that at some point during the original action inside Iraq, six containers of anthrax were lost. Years later, Nathan Strauss and three other men from the original unit went back into Iraq and reclaimed the canisters and transported them to Venezuela. We know the rest."

"So in his twisted way, Strauss was hoping for a lasting peace in the Middle East," Lauren said. "The end justifies the means?"

"Yes, perhaps he saw himself as some sort of catalyst from on high to bring that about, but peace won't happen through killing."

"Will there ever be peace? Can it happen?"

"I don't know, but killing hasn't solved our differences," Keller continued. "We know that Strauss and the three other men that were working with him are all dead, but we're still working on the possibility that an extremist element inside the Israeli government was helping them. Your security will continue indefinitely."

"What if the people who assisted Strauss are inside Mossad?"

"You're not being taken to a Mossad safe house. The flat is owned by an old friend of mine. He's ill and being treated at the Mayo Clinic in Minnesota. He'll be in the States for quite some time. The men and women in the security detail have no ties to Mossad and were handpicked by me. I'd trust them with the lives of my own family."

The limo turned down the access road that would take them to Signature Aviation where the chartered Gulfstream was waiting for the transatlantic trip to France. The driver smoothly swung up to the front door and stopped. Lauren was about to open the door when Keller stopped her.

"It looks like someone is waiting for you." Keller gestured to the figure standing on the sidewalk. "If you prefer, I can have my men ask him to leave."

"No, it's fine." Lauren reached out and they shook hands. "Thank you again for everything."

Lauren unfastened Abigail from her car seat, clutched her daughter tightly, and then stepped out of the car into the warm evening air. Abigail lit up at the sight of her grandpa.

"Hello, William," Lauren said.

William held out his arms and took Abigail. He pulled her close and breathed her in, as if it would be the last time he'd ever see his granddaughter. The sight nearly broke Lauren's heart, but whatever it was that William wanted to say to her, she remained resolute to get away from this place and find some perspective. Behind her, the driver unloaded the bags and set them on the ground. One of the pilots came through the door and introduced himself. He told her they were ready when she was, placed the bags on a wheeled cart, and pulled it through the door. Without fanfare, the driver slid back behind the wheel, and Keller drove off into the night.

"You realize you're doing exactly what you didn't want to do," William said. "You're fleeing your home."

"Turns out it wasn't the home I thought it was," Lauren said. As she met William's gaze, the elder statesmen nodded subtly.

"You'll be living under twenty-four-hour armed guard."

"There's still the possibility of a threat." Lauren replied. "What would you have me do?"

"Anything but this."

"I should get going, the pilots are waiting."

William handed Abigail back to her mother, then reached inside his coat and removed an envelope. "The reason I came was to give you this."

"What is it?"

"It's from Donovan."

Lauren shifted Abigail in her arms, took it from William's hand, and slid it into her purse. "How is he?"

"He'll make a complete recovery—physically. Emotionally, I don't know. He hates that you're leaving, but he also knows that he has only himself to blame. We'll all have to take this one step at a time and see where it goes." William reached in and tenderly kissed both of them. "You're very much loved here. Please take care."

Lauren watched William walk away. She went into the flight lounge and within moments the crew had escorted her out to the plane. There was no need for armed guards over the North Atlantic as she and Abigail were the only two passengers. After a short safety briefing from the flight attendant, the Gulfstream taxied out. It was well past her bedtime so the gentle motion of the airplane and the quiet drone of the engines put Abigail to sleep almost instantly. With any luck she wouldn't wake up until they arrived in Paris.

Lauren dimmed the lights and fixed her gaze out the window as the airplane rolled down the runway and lifted off for Europe. She spotted the landmarks that identified Fairfax County as home, and she finally let herself cry. Thankfully, they climbed through a thin layer of clouds and all that remained below was the orange glow of Washington, D.C. She opened her purse for a tissue and saw Donovan's letter. She set it on her lap and dabbed at her eyes until the tears stopped.

It took her a long time before she finally picked it up. She turned it over in her hands and noted the thickness, not more than a single page, she guessed. Her name had been scrawled on the face; it was Donovan's writing, but worse, messier. She debated with herself about when to read it—if at all. She finally relented and slid her finger under the flap and removed the sheet of paper.

Dear Lauren,

I of all people understand why you're compelled to leave. I've created a life you've decided is filled with too much pain, half-truths, and deception. You're wrong about you being my second choice. I married you because I couldn't imagine living without you. I didn't do a very good job at being your husband, and I won't deny that I failed us in almost every way possible, but it was never because I didn't love you. It was the exact opposite. I always felt as if I was protecting you and Abigail, but we both know I was only protecting myself from my problems, all of the emotional damage I've suffered and never effectively dealt with. I will never forgive myself for those errors in judgment. Take your time. I can assure you that many stages of both grief and elation come with making a clean break. It's an evolution, and there's much to learn but it doesn't happen all at once. I hope you find what it is you're looking for. Most of all, never forget that I'm always here for you and that I'll always love you.

Donovan

Lauren folded the note and slid it back into the envelope. She signaled the flight attendant and asked for a glass of wine. Lauren sipped sparingly and watched the eastern seaboard as it slipped away beneath the wing. She had no illusion about what she'd left in her wake. Her actions had no doubt alienated her from almost everyone in her life. Michael and Susan, William, Buck, plus everyone at Eco-Watch would no doubt condemn her for leaving Donovan. Even her mother, while ever supportive, didn't fully understand. Calvin had been sympathetic and refused her resignation, instead, he'd called it an open-ended leave of absence.

If she ever came back, she'd have to allow time for those wounds to heal. If she never returned, then it didn't really matter. She had no real idea if Donovan could, or even would, make an effort to come to terms with his issues. Maybe coming so close to death, coupled with her departure, might initiate a reassessment of his life. She knew her husband was a very complicated, conflicted man—more so than she'd ever suspected. Donovan's demons were formidable, tempered in blood and hardened by decades of pain and guilt. It might be easier for him to simply tell her goodbye and revert back to the solitary creature he was when she found him.

Climbing into the rarefied atmosphere nearly eight miles above the earth, the cloudless sky bristled with the light from countless stars. Lauren gazed out at the heavens. The light from each distant sun had traveled for millions of years to reach her at this very moment. Somehow it made her hopeful. Perhaps one day Donovan would find his peace and the resulting light would ultimately reach out across the distance and find her.

EPILOGUE

Savannah, Georgia

He rounded the wingtip and ran his hand over the smoothly painted surface. The pristine Gulfstream 500 marked an upgrade from the Gulfstream IV, a significant technological improvement over the older version, but Donovan still felt a tug of nostalgia for the original—the one that had saved his life. The brand new *Spirit of da Vinci* was still at the factory in Savannah, Georgia, but hopefully in few days he'd accept delivery. It had been five months since the accident, yet he was able to recall even the smallest detail of the events leading up to the actual crash, and he was convinced that no other airplane but a Gulfstream would have made it to the airport that night.

It was late, the large hangar was empty and quiet, but Donovan wasn't ready to go back to his hotel just yet. He continued to admire the newest addition to the Eco-Watch fleet. He'd spent a large part of his life in this setting, and the inherent structure of aviation gave him a small measure of comfort against the disarray of his life.

The sound of a door closing and the decidedly female footsteps on the concrete floor made him stop and slowly turn to look. In the back of his mind he was always hoping that somehow it was Lauren, though in his heart he knew the harsh reality. His wife was half a world away and had no intention of coming back anytime soon.

The slender figure walked beneath an overhead light and Donovan smiled. He hadn't seen Montero for months, not since she'd been released from the hospital. She'd gained some of her weight back, and Donovan thought she looked better, healthier, though she'd lost her tan.

Her injuries, coupled with her sudden thrust into the international spotlight, had been hard on her. She'd confessed to him over the phone that if it had been up to her, she would have remained in the shadows, not agreed to live the lie her superiors had concocted. She'd admitted to him that she'd had a little taste of how his life had once been and it made her miserable. She didn't want to be a symbol of patriotism, especially when the actual events were so far from the truth. She was beyond tired and more than ready for the next "it" person to come along and eclipse her.

"Hey there," Montero smiled as she drew closer. "I like the new plane. It's beautiful."

Donovan thought perhaps it was the first genuine smile he'd seen since he met her. She'd recovered physically, they both had, but he wondered how she was healing emotionally? At least on the surface she seemed more relaxed, more at peace. Donovan discovered that he was genuinely glad to see her. She'd turned down his money, and made him a promise that she'd kept even when faced with death. In his world that made her a rare creature. He had no memory of her making the phone call that night—but she'd done it, and it spoke volumes about the integrity of her character.

Donovan opened his arms and they hugged, no words were spoken. They were forever linked together by that rare combination of being the sole survivors of a crisis that took the lives of others. They held each other for what seemed like a long time.

"I've missed you. Are you okay?" Montero whispered as she pulled away, still smiling.

"I'm good. I'm done with physical therapy, all the parts seem to work the way they did before, more or less. I pulled in a favor or two and the FAA should make their final evaluation any day now and return me to flight status. I'm anxious to start working again now that the new airplane is finally here."

"Well, you look good," Montero said.

"What's the latest out of Washington?" Donovan asked. "Is

there anything new about Strauss, who may or may not have been helping him?"

"All I've heard is that a general in the Israeli Defense Force was killed in a car accident and a senior member of the Knesset was found dead in his home—apparent heart attack. The FBI isn't coming out and saying anything definitive, but the inside buzz is that the two men were being looked at as the possible puppet masters behind a very deranged Nathan Strauss. It's possible their deaths weren't as accidental as they appear."

"The less the world knows about what really happened, the better."

"I agree," Montero sighed. "I spoke with Michael a few days ago. He sounded good."

"I put him in charge of Eco-Watch while I was laid up. As I always knew he would, he did a great job. I think having something to focus on helped him recover from his injuries. We were all pretty beat up there for a while."

"I was sorry to hear about you and Lauren. I know that must be difficult."

Donovan nodded and looked away. He usually hated to talk about his private life, but with Montero the question somehow felt less intrusive, the wound less exposed. The fact that she knew his secrets made it easier.

"I'm sorry," she said. "I wasn't trying to pry."

"I know you weren't. She and I talk, it's not over. I messed up a bunch of things and they won't be fixed overnight. She's not wrong in how she feels, and I need to figure out how to make some changes. We both do. It seems we can't live together, and we can't live apart. It's complicated, so for now we've both agreed that it's an evolving situation, and neither one of us wants to do anything permanent. She and Abigail are in Europe. Abigail and I video chat all the time, but I miss her. I miss them both."

"I can't begin to tell you how much you've been on my mind the last few weeks. I finally went and saw the documentary."

"I figured you would. What did you think?"

"I know it's wildly popular, and you must hate that it's not going away anytime soon, but to be honest I thought I was going to be physically sick in the theatre. Knowing the truth, I felt so ashamed that I'd threatened to expose you, especially after you saved my life. I ended up in tears, and ultimately walked out of the theatre."

"I know the feeling," Donovan replied.

"You know," Montero looked down at the floor then back up at him. "We've talked about some of my boundary issues. How I tend to take things into my own hands to make them right."

Donovan nodded, unsure where she was going with this.

"After I'd seen the movie, I was down in Florida and I pulled the file on the theft of the Bristol Technologies Gulfstream and Michael's shooting. No big deal, the file's closed, case solved, so I took the liberty of pulling the partial fingerprints lifted from the flashlight and the flashlight itself may have been misplaced as were some irrelevant mug shots. No one will stumble onto that evidence again. Your secret is safe."

"Thank you," Donovan replied. "How about you, how are you doing?"

"Better." Montero shrugged. "I'm about finished being Washington's puppet. I'm finally changing assignments."

"Good for you. Is that what brings you here?"

"Sort of. I had a few loose ends to clean up before my resignation becomes final."

"You're quitting?" Donovan said, genuinely surprised. "I thought you loved working for the FBI. What are you going to do?"

"It's not like I can do undercover work anymore. Whatever I did, I'd be stuck behind a desk, and that's not really what I signed up for," Montero said. Then her smile turned curious.

"What's that look about?" Donovan asked. "Are you looking for a job?"

"No. Not at all. My attorney contacted me a week or so ago and it seems that an anonymous donor made a very large gift to a woman's shelter in Miami that I've been involved with for several years. It was enough of a donation that we can finally expand to other areas of Florida that need our help. The board of directors believes that I can use my newfound visibility to continue to raise funds. They've asked me to be the new executive director, and I've accepted. You don't know anything about the donation, do you? Was it you?"

"No, it wasn't me."

"Was it Mr. VanGelder?"

"I doubt it. He would have said something."

"Donovan," she whispered, "it was five million dollars."

"Good for you. I promise it wasn't me. I'm happy for you. You'll do great." Donovan knew for a fact that the money came from three private individuals. Two of the benefactors lived with their families in Washington, D.C., and had close ties with Tel Aviv. The third donor, and the person who'd orchestrated the entire bequest, had been Lauren, with the help of Aaron Keller. It was agreed that the money was a way to thank the woman whose actions helped save a great many lives.

"So, are you free for dinner?" Montero asked. "I know a great place downtown in the old historic district."

"It's getting late." Donovan said, resisting. "I'd have to stop at the hotel to clean up and change."

"I need to do the same thing," Montero replied. "Fortunately, we're booked at the same hotel."

"How did you find out where I'm staying?" Donovan realized the uselessness of the question the moment he said the words.

"I'm still a federal agent, at least for the next month." Montero smiled. "Don't underestimate me, and don't argue with me. I'm taking you to dinner and that's final. In fact, I already made us a reservation."

"You're taking me?"

"My treat. I don't know when I'll see you again." Montero slid her hand under his left wrist and brought his hand up to the light. She gently turned it over to see the wounds on either side. She cradled it, palm up, and lightly touched the skin where the screwdriver had left its permanent mark.

"The other scars are worse," Donovan said.

"Even before that night, you were the most scarred man I've ever met," Montero replied. "But this particular one has my name on it—the first of three times you saved my life."

"Three?"

"The first time was when you kept Strauss from stabbing me with the screwdriver. The second was when you carried me out of the burning plane," Montero continued quietly, almost reverentially. "The final and most important time was the fact that I would never have survived losing Alec without you. So, yes, I owe you my life three times over and this small scar is what you have to remember me by. Every time you see this, know that I'll always be there for you—no matter what."

Donovan nodded his head in a silent thank you. Her declaration of unending loyalty touched him deeply and he was at a loss for words.

Montero leaned in and kissed him gently, smiled, then slipped her hand inside his and together they walked toward the exit.